Magnates

KATHERINE GARBERA
BRENDA JACKSON
CHARLENE SANDS

MILLS &
BOON

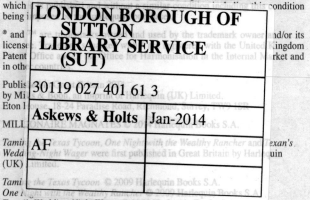
® and ~~TM are trademarks owned and used by the trademark owner and/or its~~ licensee~~. Trademarks marked with ® are registered with the United Kingdom~~ Patent ~~Office and/or the Office for Harmonisation in the Internal Market and~~ in othe~~r countries.~~

Publis~~hed in Great Britain 2014~~
by Mi~~lls & Boon, an imprint of Harlequin (UK) Limited.~~
Eton ~~House, 18-24 Paradise Road, Richmond, Surrey, TW9 1SR~~

MILL~~IONAIRE MAGNATES © 2014 Harlequin Books S.A.~~

Tami~~ng the Texas Tycoon, One Night with the Wealthy Rancher and Texan's~~
Wedd~~ing-Night Wager were first published in Great Britain by Harlequin~~
(UK) ~~Limited.~~

Tami~~ng the Texas Tycoon © 2009 Harlequin Books S.A.~~
One ~~Night with the Wealthy Rancher © 2009 Harlequin Books S.A.~~
Texan's Wedding-Night Wager © 2009 Harlequin Books S.A.

Special thanks and acknowledgement to Katherine Garbera, Brenda Jackson and Charlene Sands for their contribution to the Texas Cattleman's Club miniseries.

ISBN: 978 0 263 91172 5
eBook ISBN: 978 1 472 04467 9

05-0214

Harlequin (UK) Limited's policy is to use papers that are natural, renewable and recyclable products and made from wood grown in sustainable forests. The logging and manufacturing processes conform to the legal environmental regulations of the country of origin.

Printed and bound in Spain
by Blackprint CPI, Barcelona

TAMING THE
TEXAS TYCOON

BY
KATHERINE GARBERA

Katherine Garbera is a strong believer in happily-ever-after. She's written more than thirty-five books and has been nominated for career achievement awards in series fantasy and series adventure from *RT Book Reviews*. Her books have appeared on the Waldenbooks/Borders bestseller list for series romance and on the *USA TODAY* extended bestseller list. She loves to travel and lives in Dallas, Texas, with her two children and the man of her dreams. You can visit her on the web at www.katherinegarbera.com.

This book is dedicated to my mom and dad. I don't think I say thank you enough or let you know just how lucky I am to have you as parents. So...thank you, Mom and Dad. I love you very much.

Acknowledgements

I'd like to give a shout-out to the other authors in the TEXAS CATTLEMAN'S CLUB series—Michelle, Brenda, Charlene, Day and Jennifer. It was a lot of fun to write with you.

One

"**B**rody Oil and Gas, Kate speaking," Kate Thornton said into the phone as she did about fifty times a day.

"Hey, Katie-girl, any fires I need to put out?" Lance Brody asked.

"Hi, Lance, how was DC?" she said while she sorted through the messages on her desk. Her boss was everything she'd ever wanted in a man and, embarrassingly for her, he never saw her as anything other than his ultra-efficient administrative assistant. Which was great—really it was. That's what she was paid for.

She'd joined Brody Oil and Gas shortly after Lance and his brother, Mitch, had inherited the failing refineries. And over the last five years, Lance and Mitch had turned their fortunes around and were now members of the famed Texas Cattleman's Club.

"DC was hot and the meetings were long. Messages?" Lance asked.

"You have two that aren't urgent but that you might want to handle before you get back to the office. One is from Sebastian Huntington regarding TCC business. Do you need his number?"

"Nah, I got it. What's the other one?"

"The other one is from Lexi Cavanaugh. I didn't recognize her name but she asked for you to call her as soon as you landed."

"She's my fiancée," Lance said.

Kate felt all the blood leave her body. She knew Lance was still talking because she could hear his voice beyond the buzzing in her ears. But all she could think was after years of secretly loving this man, he'd gone away and gotten engaged to someone she'd never even heard of.

"Katie-girl? You still there?"

"Yes," she said. "Of course I am. That's it on the messages. When do you think you'll be in the office?"

"En route now. The traffic on highway 45 is heavy, though. I need one more thing from you," he said.

Please don't ask me to plan your engagement party, she thought.

"Double-check with the caterers for Thursday's Fourth of July barbecue. I want to make sure this year's party blows the top off of last year's."

"No problem," she said, hearing her own voice break. She didn't know how she was going to be able to work with Lance every day now that he was clearly another woman's man.

"The other line is ringing," she said, though it wasn't. She just needed to get off the phone.

"I'll see you soon," he said, hanging up.

Kate hung up the phone and sat there staring at her computer screen. The wallpaper on her monitor was a photo of Lance, Mitch and her taken in February when Lance and Mitch had received word they were going to be accepted into the millionaire's club. She'd bought a bottle of champagne and the three of them had toasted the brothers' success.

Back then it had seemed fine that both Lance and Mitch thought of her as nothing more than an assistant. She had believed that one day Lance would see past her horn-rimmed glasses and cardigan sweaters to the woman beneath.

Clearly, that wasn't the case.

She leaned forward, looking at the photo and realizing that part of the problem lay with her. Her thick dark hair was pulled back in a sloppy braid and her glasses were a little big for her face. She'd lost weight last year—almost eighty pounds—and hadn't bothered to get new frames for her smaller face. In fact, all of her clothes were just the old ones. They were all faded and too big for her.

She looked like someone's maiden aunt, she thought.

Having grown up in the Houston, Texas, suburb of Somerset, she was aware that taking care with her appearance was an important thing if she was going to catch a man's attention. But being overweight had made everything she wore look, well, not very nice. So she'd stopped trying.

She reached out and brushed her finger over Lance's face, trying to convince herself that she would be fine as he planned his wedding. That she could stay here in this office, working for the man she loved while he lived his life.

But she knew she couldn't. The only way she was ever going to be happy with her life would be if she took control of it, the same way she'd taken control of her body by stopping her binge eating and focusing on making herself healthier.

There was really only one way for that to happen. She was going to have to quit her job at Brody Oil and Gas.

Lance wasn't in the best of moods considering he'd just gotten engaged, a day he knew that most men considered one of the happiest of their lives. But then he wasn't marrying for love; he was marrying to ensure the future of Brody Oil and Gas. He and Mitch had grown up in the fading dreams of their father, a man who'd let the Brody name get washed up and their wells dry out.

But with Mitch's financial genius and his skills—hell make that *luck* at finding mineral deposits and oil reserves—they'd turned around Brody Oil and Gas.

He was back in Houston now, which was a relief. He hated being away from home for any length of time. He liked his life the way it was. Liked the roughness of his roughneck oil workers, liked the comfy feeling his secretary Kate gave him and liked that he had a home at the oil refinery that he'd never found anywhere else.

Few people knew that their old man had drunk away his fortune. Mitch and he had borne the brunt of the old man's anger at the loss of that fortune.

He rubbed the back of his neck as he pulled his truck into the reserved parking spot at the offices of Brody Oil and Gas.

His cell phone rang as he was getting out of the truck. He checked the ID. "Hey, Mitch. What's up?"

"I'm going to have to stay in DC a bit longer to work out the rest of the deal we put in place with your engagement."

"No problem. Do you think you'll be back for the Fourth?"

"Of course."

"I invited Lexi to join me. I want her to start getting to know everyone here," Lance said.

"That sounds good."

"You know her better than I do," Lance added,

thinking of the woman he was going to marry. "I was thinking I should get her a little gift to say thanks for agreeing to marry me. Should I ask Kate, or do you think you could suggest something?"

There was silence on the line and Lance pulled the phone away from his ear to make sure he hadn't lost the connection. "If you have any thoughts, just shoot me an e-mail."

"I'll do that. When are you going to tell Kate that you're engaged?"

"Already did. Why?" Lance walked up toward the building.

"No reason," Mitch said.

"Do you think I should have waited until I announced it to the rest of the company?"

"No," Mitch said. "She's not like the rest of the staff."

"I know that. Do you think I should call Senator Cavanaugh to follow up on anything?"

"I'm handling that. Just keep doing what you usually do," Mitch said.

"And that is?" Lance asked.

"Heavy lifting," Mitch said.

Lance smiled. From the time they were very little, Mitch had relied on him to do the heavy physical stuff. It only made sense since he was the older brother, and Lance had learned early on that their parents weren't going to watch out for either of them.

"Will do. See you on Thursday?"

"Wouldn't miss it," Mitch said.

He disconnected the call and stood there for another moment in the hot, Houston sun. It might sound like he was daft to others but he liked the burn of the summer sun on his skin.

The air-conditioning chilled him as he walked through the building. There was always a moment when he almost paused as he entered the office, unable to believe how he and Mitch had brought the empty, run-down company back to this. The lobby was filled with guests waiting to go up to different meetings. There was a full staff of security guards who protected the company.

"Good afternoon, Mr. Brody."

"Good afternoon, Stan. How's things?"

"Good, sir. Good to have you back in Houston," Stan said.

Lance nodded at the man and walked toward the executive elevators. He got on and pushed the button for the executive floor. The ride was quick and he realized he was eager to be back to work. DC was like another world, a place he didn't fit in. Here at Brody Oil and Gas, he not only fit in, he was in his kingdom.

He walked into his office and Kate glanced up at him. Her normal smile of welcome wasn't as bright as it usually was.

"Welcome back, Lance. Steve from finance needs five minutes sometime today. I told him I had to check with you first."

"No problem. I'm free this afternoon."

"Good. I'll take care of it."

"Anything else I need to know about?"

She shook her head, a strand of her thick dark hair brushing her cheek. She looked up at him and her eyes seemed wider, those dark-chocolate orbs that he'd lost himself in a time or two. He shook his head. That was folly. Kate wasn't the type of woman who'd be interested in an affair.

And despite his engagement, affairs were all he'd ever been interested in. He wasn't the kind of man who could marry a woman he felt anything for. He'd learned from his father that Brody men didn't handle lust or love well. They required devotion and dedication from their lovers or else they turned to jealousy. He had experienced it himself during his ill-fated love affair with his high school sweetheart April, when he was eighteen.

"Lance?"

"Hmm?"

"Did you hear what I said?"

He shook his head. "No, I was thinking about the trip to DC."

Kate bit her lip and looked down.

"What is it, Katie-girl? Is something on your mind?"

Kate nodded. "I need a few minutes to talk to you in your office."

"Okay," he said. "Now?"

"Yes, I think the sooner we get to this the better."

"Come on in," he said.

She stood and picked something up from her printer before leading the way into his office. Lance watched her walking in front of him, seeing the sway of her hips and the way the fabric of her long skirt brushed her calves.

Why was he just now realizing that Kate was one fine-looking woman beneath those ugly clothes of hers?

* * *

Kate had been in Lance's office many times before and today she felt a pang at the paper she held in her hand. She had made up her mind that she was going to resign. There was nothing that could change that.

Well, that wasn't true. She vacillated between being firm that she had to leave, and wanting to stay so she could see Lance on a daily basis.

But then she had to remember that part of the reason she'd lost the weight was because she was tired of sitting on the sidelines of life, and watching other people live while she just went about doing her job and going home to her empty town house in Houston.

That emptiness had started getting to her and she'd contemplated buying a cat. But she'd stopped, horrified at becoming her great-aunt Jean, the spinster and butt of most jokes by the younger generation when Kate was growing up.

"What did you want to talk about?" Lance said. He leaned one hip on the front of his desk and stretched his long legs out.

She stared at him for a minute. How was she going to get over him?

"I have been thinking about my job lately.

And I…I've decided to pursue opportunities away from Brody Oil and Gas."

"What?" Lance asked, standing up. "Why now? We need you, Katie-girl."

Katie-girl. He called her that stupid nickname that made her feel like she was five years old. And like a sister to him. She realized that she'd let the relationship develop that way, happy to have at least some sort of affection from him.

"That's the problem for me, Lance, you don't really need me. You might have back in the beginning when you hired me, but now any efficient office manager will be able to handle this. I think we both know that."

"That's been true for the last two years. Why are you leaving now?"

She shrugged. She hadn't thought that Lance would care, to be honest. "It just seems like a good time to make a move. Everything is going well here, you're engaged and Mitch is spending more time in DC. A new person will be able to transition smoothly."

He rubbed the back of his neck. "Is anything the matter, Kate? Did I do something I shouldn't have?"

"Not at all. It's me, Lance. I keep staying here

year after year because it's comfortable, and I think we both know that isn't the way to really have a successful career."

"Is that what this is about? We can promote you into a different role," he said.

She shook her head. "No. Thank you for the offer but I'm ready to try something new."

Kate was tempted to say yes to anything that Lance suggested, but she refused to let go of the fact that he was getting married, and to stay here…well, it would be the dumbest thing she could ever do.

"Will you stay until I can hire a replacement?"

She nodded. That sounded fair to her. "Of course I will."

"Thanks for that."

"I guess…here is my resignation. I'll be at my desk if you need anything else from me."

She turned to leave and felt as if she was running away. A part of her wondered if she shouldn't try to stay here and make things different between her and Lance. But how?

She'd Googled Lexi Cavanaugh as soon as Lance had told her about the engagement, and there was no way that she could compete with a woman like that.

"Kate?"

"Yes, Lance."

"I would like to have a cake at the barbecue to celebrate my engagement to Lexi. Can you order one from the bakery for me?"

"Of course," she said.

It was definitely time for her to leave Brody Oil and Gas.

She realized that she and Lance hadn't hammered out the details of her leaving the company. "I'll stay for two weeks."

"It might take longer than that to hire your replacement."

"I'd like to try to fit it into that time schedule," she said.

"Have I done something to upset you, Kate? You know I'm more of a roughneck than an executive," he said.

She steeled herself against responding to that rough aw-shucks-ma'am charm that he was able to pull off so easily. She liked that he wasn't as sophisticated and polished as Mitch was. That was why she'd fallen for him. At heart, Lance was a good old boy, a Texas man like her daddy and her brothers. The kind of guy that knew how to charm the pants off any lady.

And he hadn't had to work hard to win her affections. But she realized now that the charm was just part of his practiced act. It was as much a part of the savvy millionaire as his thousand-dollar cowboy boots and million-dollar mansion. He pulled out the charm when he needed it.

"No, Lance. You didn't do anything other than treat me like your secretary."

"Is that a problem?" he asked, his shrewd gaze on her.

"Not at all. But that's all I am to you and I decided I want more."

She walked out of his office and closed the door behind her. She knew she should stay and work the rest of the day but she needed to get away. And she didn't care if it made her seem cowardly. She went downstairs and put the top down on her Miata convertible and drove out of Houston, leaving Brody Oil and Gas behind. She only wished it were as easy to convince her heart to leave Lance Brody in the dust.

Two

Lance was speechless as Kate not only walked out of his office, but left early. He knew he'd missed something important as far as she was concerned. She said she wanted to be more than his secretary—did she mean professionally, or personally?

He started to go after her but realized he had no idea where she went when she left the offices. To be honest, she was always here when he arrived and she stayed until after he left. How was he going to operate without her? Kate *was* more than just his secretary. She was the most important piece of the office, the person who kept everything running smoothly and kept him in line.

"Damn it," he said to no one in particular. He hadn't gotten to where he was by letting things like this go. He speed-dialed her cell phone.

"I can't talk now, Lance," she said.

"Then pull over or use the headset I gave you, because you can't just walk away like that and expect me to let this go."

"Hold on," she said. He heard her fumbling around and then cursing, and a minute later she was back. "What do you want to talk about?"

"The fact that you left like you did."

"I'm sorry," she said. "That was so unprofessional, but I just didn't think I could be productive anymore today."

"I can understand that. Want to tell me why?"

"No. It'll just make you uncomfortable and make me feel like a big dummy."

Lance didn't like the sound of that. "Kate, if I've done something, just flat out tell me. I'll apologize and we can move on."

"I don't think we can," she said. Her words were sad and he wished she were still in the office so he could see her expressions. Kate had the most expressive eyes of any woman he'd ever met.

"You won't know until we talk," Lance said. He would fix this problem with Kate—he couldn't afford to lose her. "Where are you?"

"On the interstate headed toward Somerset."

"Going to your parents house?" he asked, knowing that Kate had grown up in Somerset, a wealthy suburb of Houston. He had a house there now.

"I guess so. I just got in the car and kind of drove on autopilot. I didn't realize where I was headed."

"Katie-girl—"

"Don't call me that, Lance. It makes me feel like we have a relationship beyond boss-secretary and I know that's not true."

He cursed under his breath. "We do have one. We're friends, Kate. And we have been all these long years."

"Are we really friends?"

"Of course we are. We are more than friends…you're like part of the family to Mitch and me, and to be honest, Kate, I don't think either of us will know what to do without you."

She was quiet for a few seconds.

"Kate?"

"I just can't talk about this anymore, Lance. I know to you it probably seems…how does it seem?"

"Like I've done something to upset you. Listen, whatever it is, I can fix it. You know that, right?"

"You can't."

"Kate, when have we ever encountered a problem or obstacle that I couldn't figure a way out of?"

"Lance…"

She was weakening as he'd known she would. His other line was ringing and he ignored it.

"Tell me, Kate."

"I'm not sure I can. I feel silly that you are making such a big deal out of it now," she said.

One of the first things he'd liked about Kate was her voice. It was soft and sweet and even when she got mad, which wasn't often, she kept it pleasant.

"Why don't you come back to the office and we can talk," Lance said.

"We can talk tomorrow when I come in. I think I need the night to get my mind together."

Lance knew it was important to get Kate back

and convince her to stay on before too much time had passed. He knew that she could find other jobs that would pay her as much as he did. But he needed her.

The other line started ringing again and his cell phone beeped with a text message from Frank Japlin, the head of operations at their main refinery.

"Kate, can you hold on a minute?"

"What?"

"I've got to take a call from the refinery," he said.

"Sure," she said.

He put her on hold and answered the call. "It's Brody."

"Frank here. We have a fire at the refinery. I think you need to get down here right away."

"Have you called the fire department?"

"First thing. But this blaze is burning to beat the band."

"I'm in the middle of another emergency."

"There is a lot of damage. And I heard one of the investigators say they thought the cause of the fire wasn't accidental."

Great. Just what he needed today. "See what else you can find out. I'll give you a call in fifteen minutes or so."

"Okay, boss," Frank said, hanging up.

Lance rubbed the back of his neck, thinking that damage was the last thing they needed at the refineries. The hurricane they'd had last fall had already done enough damage to them.

He needed Kate back in her chair, taking care of this mess. He'd have to call the press, the families and the insurance company. He glanced down at his phone and noticed that the line where she'd been holding was now off. She'd hung up.

Just what he needed, he thought.

Kate realized, as she was hanging on the phone waiting for Lance, that she'd spent too much of her time in that static role. Lance had gotten engaged. There was nothing he could say or do that was going to make staying on at Brody Oil and Gas okay.

She hung up the call and kept on driving. Going home to her folks' place wasn't the smartest idea. Her mom would just tell her that if she wore makeup and dressed nicer, she wouldn't still be single. And honestly, who could deal with that?

But she didn't want to go to her town house and spend the night alone. She needed some good advice. She needed to be with her best friend, Becca Huntington. Becca would commiserate with her and tell her not to go back, not to listen to Lance…wouldn't she?

She called Becca at Sweet Nothings, the lingerie shop she owned in Somerset.

"Sweet Nothings."

"Becca, it's Kate."

"Hey, there. How's things in the big city?" Becca asked.

"Horrible."

"What? Why?"

"Lance is engaged."

Becca didn't say anything for a moment and Kate realized she probably seemed like a loser to her friend. "Oh, honey, I'm sorry. I didn't realize he was dating anyone."

"He wasn't."

"Are you sure he's engaged? Lance doesn't strike me as the kind of guy who'd do something that spontaneous."

He wasn't spontaneous and he was careful not to be tied down by any of the women he got involved with. "Yes, he told me the news himself."

"Who is she?"

"Lexi Cavanaugh."

"Senator Cavanaugh's daughter?"

"Yes."

"Is it politically motivated?" Becca asked.

"I don't know. And I don't care. I quit my job."

"You did what?"

"Was that crazy? I'm so confused, I don't know what to do," Kate admitted. She'd hoped that Lance would realize she was waiting there and fall for her.

"It may have been a little crazy. I know you've had a bit of a crush on him," Becca said.

Kate took a deep breath. "It's more than a crush. I'm in love with him."

It was the first time she'd said the words out loud, and she had to admit they felt good. Or they would have if Lance wasn't engaged to another woman."

"Oh, Kate."

"He doesn't even know I'm a woman.

"Let's fix that," Becca said.

"How?"

"Come to the shop and we'll give you a makeover."

"A makeover? I don't think so. Remember the last time we tried."

Kate had felt so uncomfortable in the makeup and clothing that Becca had suggested, she'd ended up going straight home and taking it all off. She needed the comfort of her old clothing…or did she?

"I just don't know what to do," she repeated.

"Only you can figure that out. But if it were me, I'd change my hair and my clothes. Just start over and find a new love."

"I have to work for Lance for two more weeks."

"Why?"

"I couldn't just quit and walk out on him."

"All the better," Becca said. "You can go back to work looking like a million bucks and then leave. It will be a chance to get back a little of your pride."

Would her pride feel any better if she came back to Brody Oil and Gas and Lance looked at her like a woman instead of his assistant?

"I'm coming to your shop," Kate said.

"Good, we can talk once you get here. I'll have the white wine chilled."

"Thanks, Becca."

"For what?"

"Being here. Listening to me and not thinking I'm being silly."

"Why would I think you're silly? I've been in love before and I know what it can do to you."

Kate swallowed, glad she had a friend like Becca to turn to. "I've never loved anyone before Lance."

"Not even in high school?"

"I had a crush or two," Kate admitted.

They'd been friends for what seemed like forever and Becca had always been the sister she'd never had—the one person who accepted her the way she was. At home, her brothers teased her if she did anything girly and her mother was never satisfied with any of the choices that Kate made.

"That was different. And don't ask me why. I can't explain it, but Lance Brody has always been different."

"I know he has. I've never heard you talk about one person as much as you do him."

"Am I annoying?"

Becca laughed, and the familiar sound of it made Kate smile.

"No, you aren't annoying. Just in love. I'm sorry that he didn't turn out to be the guy you hoped he would be."

Kate was, too. "Maybe he is that guy, but just not the one for me."

"Probably," Becca said. "When will you be here?"

"In about twenty minutes. I just left work without asking or anything."

"I think you're ready for a change," Becca said.

"Why?"

"Because you're already acting like a rebel."

Kate thought about that. "I guess I am. Maybe Lance's engagement will turn out to be good for me."

"I bet it will. If not you'll be stronger for having loved and lost him."

Kate hung up the phone and continued driving toward Somerset. She didn't think about Lance or Brody Oil and Gas. She just concentrated on herself and the new woman she was becoming. It was way past time for her to change.

It was hot and smoky at the refinery. The fire burned for almost three hours before the firefighters got it under control. Frank was busy talking to local media and Lance was calling his brother. Mitch was in a meeting and Lance had to leave a voice mail.

"Catch me up on what's going on," Lance said to Frank.

"We have four injured."

"Have you talked to their families?"

"As soon as we identified the men who'd been injured. They're in the emergency room now. I sent JP down there to talk to the families and make certain that there were no questions as to insurance coverage, et cetera. And I asked him to keep me posted on any pressing health issues," Frank said.

"Good. Do you think we're going to have to shut down?"

Frank rubbed the top of his balding head. "I won't know more until we have a chance to talk to the fire chief."

"When will that be?"

"Soon, I hope."

"Have you stopped the flow of oil into the refinery?"

"First thing we did. We enacted our emergency protocols. And everything went exactly as it should have. I'm going to send you some suggestions for commendation for some of our guys who went beyond the call of duty."

"I'll look for that," Lance said. His cell phone rang and he glanced at it. "It's Mitch."

"I'll go see if I can talk to the fire chief," Frank said.

"We've had a fire at the main refinery," Lance told Mitch.

"Is everyone okay? How bad is the damage?" Mitch asked.

Lance caught him up. "Do you think this will impact the senator's plan to allow us more drilling?"

"Not if I have anything to say about it. I'm going to go to his office right now."

"I'll get this under control. I'm going to have a press conference later on to let everyone know we're okay and still in business."

"Sounds good. I'll get back with you after I've spoken to the senator."

Lance hung up with his brother and surveyed the mess at the refinery. Employees were clustered to one side, all of them waiting to see what the verdict would be. They were a 67,000-barrel-a-day refinery, and if they had to shut down, all of those people would be without work. And they wouldn't make their quarterly revenues.

He dialed Kate's number. She usually served as a hub during these kinds of emergencies, when he couldn't be in the office.

Her phone went to voice mail and he realized that she was serious about leaving the company. "It's Lance. I need your help. We've had a fire at our main refinery. Call me when you get this message."

The receptionist at the Brody Oil and Gas office wasn't experienced enough to handle all the calls that were coming in. But the secretaries who worked for his duty managers could. Lance usually relied on Kate to take care of liaising with them. Guess it was time to figure out how to work without Kate. He called the finance manager and asked him to send every secretary they had down to help out. He then composed a short memo on his BlackBerry and sent it to the entire company apprising them of the situation and telling them that no one was authorized to speak to the media.

Frank waved Lance over to where he was with the fire chief.

"Lance Brody, this is Chief Ingle," Frank said.

"Thanks for getting the fire under control so quickly," Lance said, shaking the fire chief's hand.

"You're welcome. It is our job."

"I know that. But I'm grateful all the same. What are we looking at here?" Lance asked him.

"We thought it was started by an explosion, but we've been talking to the men closest to the location where the fire started and none of them reported hearing one," Chief Ingle said.

"That's odd. How do you think the fire started?" Lance asked.

"I've called for our fire-scene investigators to do a thorough examination of the area. But one of my men thought he saw cans of fire accelerant."

"What kind?"

"We don't have any details but I wanted you to know what we suspected. I've called the arson investigator and he's sending his team out, as well."

"Crap. I have to notify our insurance company. They will want to work with your arson team."

Chief Ingle nodded. "They always do."

Insurance companies were very well versed in arson investigations—they didn't mess around with fires. Lance wanted someone who had Brody Oil and Gas's interests in mind. "Is it okay if I hire my own security team to be part of the investigation?"

"We'd rather not have extra people on the site," Chief Ingle said.

"Darius won't get in the way. He's the best at what he does."

"Darius who?"

"Darius Franklin. He owns his own security firm."

"Okay, but only him."

Lance understood that. The chief didn't want a bunch of men trampling over the fire scene.

"When can we go back into production?" Lance asked.

"I think we'll need at least 24 hours before I'd feel comfortable saying you can go back on line. More, if the investigation proves to be complicated."

Lance made a note of that. And when the chief moved on, he turned to Frank. "Tell all of our employees to gather in the parking lot in fifteen minutes. Then set up a number so they can call in and get a message about when to report back to work and give them that number."

"I'm on it," Frank said, walking away.

Lance dialed his best friend, Darius, and got his voice mail. Being as succinct as possible, he told Darius what had happened, that the fire chief suspected arson, and he asked Darius to come and help with the investigation. Now if he could just get Kate back, he'd have the best team any man could ask for in this situation. He reached for his phone.

Three

Kate put her phone on silence after the second call from Lance. She was tired of hurting and questioning herself and everything she'd done. She arrived at Sweet Nothings to find that Becca had made her an appointment with her hairstylist.

"I don't know that a haircut is going to change anything," Kate said.

"Don't think of it as just a haircut. You need to change," Becca said. "I've been thinking about this since you called and the only way you are going to be able to make these next few weeks bearable is to make Lance Brody realize what he's missing."

Kate took one look at herself in the mirror behind the counter and shrugged. "Not much."

"Soon, he'll see a whole new woman."

"But I'll still be me," Kate said.

"Of course you will, silly. And Lance already likes you. This will just make him lust after you."

"He's engaged to be married, Becca."

"So what? You're not going to make him do anything. Just tease him a bit and maybe get your heart back."

Kate liked the sound of that. She'd given Lance five years. And wasn't it past time to get over him?

"Okay. I'll do it."

"Good."

Becca gave her directions to the salon. As Kate drove over there, her cell phone rang again. It was Lance. She answered the call as she parked her car. "It's Kate."

"Where have you been?"

"Driving," she said.

"There's been a fire at our main refinery. I need you in the office to be my information hub."

Kate was shocked. Brody Oil and Gas was one of the safest refineries in the business. "Was there an explosion?"

"They aren't sure. I'm done looking over the fire scene at the refinery. When can you get to the office?"

She almost said tonight, but what was the point of that? This was an emergency situation but they didn't really need her. Paula and Joan, two of the other secretaries at Brody Oil and Gas, could handle the phones in this situation.

"Tomorrow morning," she said.

"Kate, I need you."

Her heart almost skipped a beat.

"The company needs you. This is one of those times when we really want to have our best players on the field."

Lance had played football and she had noticed early on that he fell back on sports analogies when he was stressed.

"You've got your best players," she said. "I'm being traded, remember?"

"Damn it. We haven't decided that yet."

"Yes, we have. Or maybe I should say I have. I will call Paula and make sure she's prepared to collect information and disseminate it. I made a procedure file for this type of emergency after the hurricane last year."

Lance didn't say anything. "I guess that'll have to do. Leave your phone on so I can get in touch with you."

"Why? I'm not—"

"Stop arguing with me, Kate. I don't like it. What's gotten into you?"

She looked at herself in the rearview mirror and realized this was the first time she'd ever said no to Lance. And he didn't like it. Maybe the way to get his attention was actually easier than changing her hair and clothes. She realized that she'd been too accommodating, and that was part of the reason he'd taken her for granted.

"I don't know, Lance. I just decided it was time for a change. Don't make this into anything other than that."

"It feels like…"

"What?"

"Nothing," he said. "Will you be in the office tomorrow?"

"Yes, I'll be there."

"Good," Lance said.

"I'm sorry about the refinery," she said, feeling bad because of the way he sounded. "Were there injuries?"

"Four men are at the hospital now."

"I'll have Paula send flowers to them and food baskets to their families."

"Thanks," he said.

"You're welcome." She felt a little guilty about not going in and taking care of the details herself, but Lance and she both needed to get used to other people working for him because Kate couldn't continue to be his Girl Friday *and* be in love with him. That was the path to pain and destruction for her. And she was tired of living for the few brief moments when she and Lance were in the office together.

"Goodbye, Lance," she said, hanging up the phone. She sat in the car for another minute but the heat was getting to her. Or at least that was what she told herself. She didn't want to think that the idea of being without Lance was causing her to feel light-headed.

Lance spent the rest of the afternoon and most of the evening at the main refinery. Darius had arrived late and had agreed to stay and work with the fire investigators. Since he wasn't an arson investigator per se, all Darius could really do was narrow down the list of suspects and conduct investigations into the backgrounds of those who might have had probable cause to start the fire.

Lance left the refinery and drove back toward Houston deciding that he was ready for a new day. This one had been too…crazy, he thought.

When he'd been a boy, he'd longed for a busy day so he wouldn't have time to go home or to think about the home he had waiting for him. But that was long ago, he thought. Now he lived alone and liked it that way.

Well, he lived alone for now. Soon he'd be bringing a bride to his mansion in Somerset and he wasn't sure he was ready to try suburban living with a wife yet. But he and Mitch had agreed he was the one who should marry Lexi.

Damn, he thought, rubbing the back of his neck. Tension seemed to take up residence there when things weren't going well.

His cell phone rang and he checked the caller ID before answering it.

"Hello, Mitch."

"Hey, big bro. How are things at the refinery?"

"A mess, but I have Darius working with the fire investigators to try to make sense of it. How's DC?"

Mitch let out a long breath. "It could be worse. I handled most of it with Senator Cavanaugh's office. Let them know the proactive things that Brody Oil and Gas are doing to minimize damage to the community and the environment. I think that helped to soothe his fears over backing expanding oil production."

"Did you tell him that with additional refineries we could rotate operations so the loss of this one for a day wouldn't impact oil prices?" Lance asked.

"Yes, I did. I'm watching the markets as they open in Japan. I think we will see US crude prices jump."

"I know we will. With the economy being what it is, that's the last thing we need right now."

"We can't control the actions of investors," Mitch said.

"I am stopping by the hospital on my way home. I think it'd be a good idea for you to call the injured workers—I'll send you a text with their names when I'm done."

"All right, that sounds good. Lexi and I are going to fly back to Houston together tomorrow."

"I haven't had a chance to talk to her. She called me earlier. Will you let her know that until the mess at the refinery settles down, I can't talk?"

"Sure thing," Mitch said.

"Did you come up with any ideas for a gift yet?" Lance asked.

"Not yet. I haven't been thinking about your love life."

Lance hadn't been, either. "This is business, Mitch. Remember, you told me that. We need the Cavanaugh connection. Today proves that."

Mitch didn't add anything to that. And Lance had to guess that being a brilliant strategist meant his brother wasn't surprised that his planning had worked to their advantage.

"I forgot to mention that Kate gave her notice today."

"She did? Why?"

"She thinks this will be a good time for her transition out of her job with us. She's not being challenged enough or something like that."

"Maybe it is time she moved on."

"I'm trying to convince her to stay," Lance said.
"Why?"

Lance didn't know, but there was no way in hell he'd admit it. "She's part of the Brody Oil and Gas family and we need her."

"Maybe she wants to be more."

"Like how?" Lance asked remembering Kate's comment earlier.

"Think about it," Mitch said. "I've got to run. Don't forget to send me the names of the injured men."

"I won't. Ally got them interviews on the morning shows for tomorrow. She's going to talk to the families and prep them on what to say."

"Good. I'll advise the senator of this so maybe he can get a sound bite in, as well."

"This could have been a lot worse," Lance said.

"Why wasn't it?" Mitch asked.

"I think because of all the preparedness we worked on after the hurricane last fall. The guys really knew what to do and how to handle things."

Lance pulled into the hospital parking lot and chatted a few more minutes with his brother before hanging up. He didn't like hospitals. Never had, to be honest. Maybe because he'd visited more than his share of emergency rooms as a child.

His father had always been blunt in the parking lot. Telling him what to say when the doctors asked about how he'd broken his arm or his leg—bicycle accident; how he'd hurt his ribs or broken his fingers—skateboard accident. Never did he tell anyone the truth. And after a while, Lance realized even he kind of believed his dad's stories.

He rubbed his hand over the scars on the back of his left knuckles. Some days he felt damned old, older than his years. He knew he had to be careful with Lexi. Had to remember to keep the engagement and their eventual marriage manageable.

Lance was always conscious that he'd inherited his father's legendary temper. And as he sat in his truck looking at the modern hospital, he couldn't help but remember the promise he'd made to himself when he was thirteen. The promise that he'd never bring a child of his to the emergency room, because he'd never have children.

He wondered if that was going to be an issue for Lexi Cavanaugh. A part of him hoped it would be so he could end the engagement and get his life back to the way it had been.

Kate was nervous as she got of out of her car the next morning. Last night the new clothes she'd purchased with Becca in Houston had seemed fun and daring but this morning when she'd put on the slim-fitting sundress and styled her new hair, she'd felt like an imposter.

It had taken her three tries to get her contacts in but at last she had her look as close as possible to the way the stylist had done it last night.

But she was nervous…and babbling, she thought. She always talked to herself but this morning her internal talk bordered on inane.

It all boiled down to one thing. What if everyone saw her and laughed?

Wasn't that silly? She was a grown woman and shouldn't care what anyone else thought but she was trying a new look—one that she was not certain of, despite Becca's reassurances that she looked *hot*. Kate still felt like fat, frumpy Kate, trying to be someone she wasn't.

She walked into the lobby, and Stan the security guard looked up. "Good morning…."

"Morning, Stan," she said, feeling awkward as the older gentleman just kept staring at her.

"You look nice today, Miss Thornton," Stan said. "Real pretty."

"Thank you, Stan," she said, the warmth of a blush on her cheeks.

She scanned her ID card and went to the executive elevator. While she waited, she stared at her reflection in the polished, mirrored wall that surrounded the elevator bank.

The hardest part about this makeover was that she simply didn't recognize herself.

"Excuse me, miss, but this elevator is for executive personnel only," Lance said, coming up behind her.

She turned around.

"Kate?"

She waited to see if he'd say anything else, but he didn't. That hurt a little bit but it was okay. Last night she'd decided to stop trying to please Lance, something that she'd done without much thought for a long time.

"I saw the workers on the *Today* show this morning. I thought they sounded good."

"Ally did a good job of prepping them. I'm glad they will all make a full recovery," Lance said.

The elevator car arrived and he waited for her to enter. She felt his eyes on her back as she moved in front of him. Was the skirt too short for the office?

But when she turned and saw him staring at

her legs, she realized that the dress was having its desired effect on him. He was finally seeing her as a woman. Kate felt…weird, actually.

Lance's attention was the one thing she'd craved and now she had it. But she wasn't sure what to do with it.

"How was your night?" she asked.

"I spent most of it on the phone…something that would have been easier if my assistant had been here."

She pursed her lips. "Maybe your assistant decided it was time to get herself a life."

"Did you, Kate? Is that what this is all about?"

She shook her head. "I've been ignoring myself for too long. I know my timing stunk last night but I had no idea there would be a fire at the main refinery."

"Who could have known? I don't mind if you take an afternoon off. In fact, if it would convince you to stay then I think we could work out more time off in your schedule," Lance said.

The elevator arrived at their floor and once again he gestured for her to go in front of him. As she walked past him, she heard him inhale sharply.

"Are you wearing perfume?" he asked.

She raised both eyebrows at him. "I am."

He shook his head. "Sorry. It's a very nice scent."

"Thank you," she said. Her new look seemed to be bothering Lance. Or maybe he just wasn't himself this morning. "I can handle the office this morning if you want to go back to the refinery."

"Thanks, Kate, but I think I am needed here. Especially if you are determined to quit."

She nodded and entered her office. The voice - mail light on her phone was flashing and she imagined she had a lot of messages waiting for her.

Lance closed the door and brushed past her to go into his office, knocking her off balance in the one-inch heels she was wearing. Lance steadied her with a hand on her waist. She turned her head and her hair brushed his shoulder.

Lance smelled good this morning but then she had always liked the scent of his aftershave. He put his other hand on her shoulder and looked down at her.

"I never realized how pretty your brown eyes are," he said.

She flushed. "I guess you couldn't really see them behind my glasses."

"Or maybe I never looked," Lance said.

"I think that there wasn't anything to look at before," Kate said. Becca had made a good point last night when she'd said that Kate hid behind her clothes and glasses.

"You are always worth a second look, Kate."

"Really?"

"Yes. I'm sorry I didn't notice before now."

"Why sorry?"

"Because you are so damned pretty."

"It's not me, it's the haircut and makeup," she said, uncomfortable with the compliment. She started pointing out all the things her mom had always told her were wrong with her. "My mouth is too big for my face."

He shook his head, rubbing his thumb over her bottom lip. "Your mouth is perfect for your face. Very lush and tempting…."

"Tempting? It's me, Lance. Kate Thornton. You've never thought I was tempting before."

"I must have been blind, Kate, because you are tempting me now," he said, lowering his mouth to hers. He kissed her.

She rose on her tiptoes and kissed him back. The moment was everything she'd imagined it would be and also completely unexpected. There was no way she could have imagined the way he tasted as his tongue slid over hers. Or the feel of his big hands in her hair. Or the way that one kiss could change her life completely.

Four

Kate tasted like heaven. She was pure temptation in his arms and he knew he'd never get enough of her. He didn't want to.

He slid his hands down the sides of her body. How had he missed this curvy body and those big, pretty eyes? Glasses and baggy clothes be damned, he'd have to have been blind to not see what a hottie his secretary was.

He turned to lean on the edge of her desk and pulled her more fully against him. Her breasts were full and felt good against his chest. He angled his head for deeper access to her mouth. He wanted more. He couldn't get enough of the taste of her. How had he missed this Kate all these years?

He lifted his head, rubbed his lips over hers and realized her eyes were closed. She looked so innocent in his arms. He remembered that he was a man who'd never learned how to handle the softer things in life. Having a lover was one thing, but this could never go beyond the physical.

As he traced the line of her face with her hair hanging free, he realized how delicate she was. "Should I apologize for that kiss?"

She opened her eyes and looked dazed for a moment but then she recovered. "Do you want to?"

"Not at all. I want to do it again but I don't think the office is the place for it."

"I agree."

His line rang, and Kate smiled at him as she reached over to answer it. "Brody Oil and Gas, Kate speaking."

Her smile faded. "Please hold."

"Who is it?"

"Your fiancée. You probably want to take that in your office."

Lance nodded. He didn't like that Lexi had interrupted his moment with Kate but he couldn't ignore her again.

"We're not done talking," Lance said.

"Of course not. We have the next two weeks to get through," Kate said, pulling out her chair and sitting down.

"When I'm done I want to see you in my office," he said. He wasn't going to pretend there wasn't a fierce attraction between them, but he didn't know how to deal with this new Kate who argued with him and didn't just do everything the way he wanted her to.

"Sure thing. You better go, you don't want to keep your fiancée waiting."

He pivoted on his heel and walked away from her. He went to his desk, sprawling in his leather chair. He reached for the phone and picked up the line where Lexi was holding.

"Hi, there, Lexi."

"Hi, Lance. I know you must be busy this morning but I wanted to thank you for the invitation to come to your Fourth of July party. I wanted to know what you need from me as your hostess."

Lance hadn't thought about Lexi acting as

hostess. "My secretary has taken care of all the details."

"I'll give her a call and see if I can help with anything. I think if we are going to make our marriage work, I should be involved with Brody Oil and Gas."

"Why?" Lance asked.

"Because that's where you spend all of your time," she said. "I know what it takes to be a good wife. You need a partner who can understand where you are coming from."

Lance knew that was the truth. But he didn't want Lexi here. He realized with a shock that when he thought of a partner—a female partner—at Brody Oil and Gas, he thought of Kate.

Why hadn't he realized that he wanted her before this? It was too late to change the past but he wanted to make things different between them going forward. But Kate didn't want any part of the company anymore and he was engaged to Lexi. He needed to sort this mess out. Was he going to try to make the match with Lexi work? And where did that leave Kate?

Mitch and Lance had determined that the connection to Cavanaugh was needed. And Lance had always put Brody Oil and Gas before everything else. He knew exactly what he needed to do, and how he needed to act. This was his chance to prove he wasn't the bastard his father had been.

He needed to be a better man. A man who wouldn't kiss Kate unless he could make a commitment to her. A man who would honor his commitment to Lexi. A man who was proud of who he was.

"You don't need to do anything for the picnic, but we can talk when you get here. Kate—my secretary—has given her two-weeks notice. If you are serious about wanting to be more involved, the picnic would be a great time for you to talk to her about the details of our events."

"I am serious, Lance. I want to make our marriage work."

There was a sincerity in Lexi's words that shamed him. He'd asked her to marry him and it was time to step up and honor that.

"I'll see you tomorrow," Lance said.

"I'm looking forward to it. Mitch has raved about the Brody Oil and Gas Fourth of July party."

"It's the one time of year when we pull out all

the stops for our workers. When we were re-building the business we decided that if we were going to be successful, we had to make everyone who worked for us feel like they were a part of the Brody Oil and Gas family."

"If your success is any indication, I'd say you've achieved that."

But at what cost? Mitch was determined and a workaholic just like Lance was. And this marriage wasn't real—it was purely business. Lexi was just another step in their plan to be successful. Was that any way to go through life, especially when he had a woman like Kate on his hands? What was he doing?

Kate couldn't believe she'd lost her head and let Lance kiss her. It was wonderful…incredible, really, but so stupid. She was here to get over him. She was supposed to be using these two weeks to put him in her past.

She wanted to go out looking her best and she supposed she could count herself successful on that item. Lance hadn't even recognized her.

The sad part about that was she hadn't done anything except wear clothes that fit her. What a difference new clothes made. She would never have believed it. Mainly because her mother had been the one to say clothes made the man, and that woman had been wrong about so many things.

She glanced down at the phone and saw that Lance was still on the line with Lexi Cavanaugh. She knew next to nothing about the woman. But at the end of the day, Kate felt she'd owe Lexi a word of thanks.

If it hadn't been for that woman's engagement to Lance, Kate might have stayed stuck in her frumpy rut until she died an old lady spinster.

A wolf-whistle brought her head up as Marcus Wall walked into the office. He was one of the petroleum geologists who worked for them, one of the men who helped decide where Brody Oil and Gas drilled and he was an expert at picking the right location for their wells. "Dang, Kate, you look good today."

She smiled at him. "Thanks."

"I never noticed how big your eyes were before," he said, coming into her office and leaning on her desk. He must have come into the office at least a hundred times before and he'd never sat close or really even talked to her.

She wanted to be flattered but instead she was

uncomfortable. She didn't want a lot of male attention. She had wanted one male's attention, and now that she had it she didn't want to let it go.

That was her problem. Lance had moved forward and she was supposed to be, too, but if her reaction to Marcus's friendly flirting was any indication, her plan was a failure. She only had eyes for Lance.

"Kate?"

"Hmm?"

He shook his head. "Is there a man behind this change?"

"How'd you guess?"

He shrugged. "I know women."

"Do you?"

"Yes, three sisters. I was raised by wolves."

"I don't think women like to be called wolves."

"True enough, but I know that when a girl—I don't mean any offense calling you a girl—gets dolled up like you are, there's a reason for it."

"Maybe I just want a change," she said, surprised that Marcus was actually helping her to understand herself. There was something hollow about the changes she'd made.

When Lance had kissed her and held her in his

arms she'd felt like a queen. But now she was back to just feeling like Old Kate, the same way she'd felt for the last few years as Lance treated her like some kind of favored pet.

"Well, this change looks very good on you. Is the big man in?"

Kate glanced down at the phone. Lance was off of his line. And it was probably way past time for Marcus to leave her office. She hoped that she didn't have guys talking to her all day. "Yes, he is."

"I'll announce myself," Marcus said.

She nodded. Marcus usually did just that. "Thanks, Marcus."

"For what?"

"For being you," she said.

"I can be so much more if you let me," Marcus said.

"For a few weeks, right?" she asked, knowing that Marcus would be the right man for a fling but nothing more. Even if she *was* leaving the company, she didn't want to have an affair with someone who worked with Lance.

This plan—which had been concocted when she'd had two glasses of wine—now seemed… silly. She needed to just keep doing her job, find a replacement for herself and get out of Brody Oil and Gas before she hurt herself any further.

"Definitely. I'm not a forever kind of man."

"Marcus, are you here to see me?"

"Sure thing, boss man. I've got good news on the new mineral rights we purchased."

"I was hoping you'd say that," Lance said. "Go on in my office. I need a word with Kate."

Marcus winked at her and then left. Lance reached over and closed the door leading to his office.

"What do you need?" she asked. She was trying to come off cool and sophisticated, but it was really hard when she felt like she was twelve. Why had she given this man so much power over her?

"I wanted to apologize for my behavior earlier."

"I think we already covered that," Kate said. The last thing she wanted to do was rehash that kiss. For her, it had been incredible and the answer to many long fantasies about this man.

She turned away from him, but he put his hand on her chair and turned her back to face him. "I don't know why this is happening to us, Kate, but I am not going to be able to ignore it. You are—"

"Don't say anything else. You have a fiancée and I'm leaving this job."

"Why are you leaving?"

Kate looked up at him and thought about blasting him with the truth. But somehow she didn't think he'd react well if she said she was leaving because she loved him and watching him get married would be about the same as ripping her heart out of her body.

"I'm leaving because I can't work for you anymore."

That was as close to the truth as she could get. Lucky for her he seemed to accept that answer.

She spent the rest of the day doing her job and realizing that all of the men in the office were starting to notice her as a woman. It should have given her hope that she'd find another man and fall in love, but instead it just made her sad because the one man she'd changed for still seemed to be oblivious—even after he'd finally kissed her.

The Fourth of July barbecue was held at Lance's home in Somerset. He lived on acreage and had set up the party out near the lake on his property. There was an area for beach volleyball, which Lance had started playing when he was in college. Later on they would play the annual management-versus-workers match.

The caterers had been cooking since before dawn and mouthwatering smells filled the air. There was a deejay playing music under a tent near the caterers and everything had been decorated in red, white and blue.

He spotted Kate first thing as he approached the party area. "Happy Fourth of July."

"You, too. Where do you need me?"

"Well, Mitch is running late, so if you want to work here with me handing out name tags and welcoming everyone, that'd be great."

The first year they'd held the barbecue they'd started the tradition of personally welcoming everyone to the event. He, Mitch and Kate. It had been the first function where they'd really needed her.

"I can't believe this is your last year doing this," he said.

He'd given up on trying to convince her not to quit. She'd made it clear that she wasn't going to change her mind, and given that he was trying to make a go at being a decent fiancé to Lexi, he thought he should probably stop trying to convince the woman who he was having nightly fantasies about to stay on.

"Me, neither. I'm going to miss it a lot. But you'll have a new hostess for this next year."

"Yes, we will. I think Lexi is anxious to talk to you about the planning of this event so she will know what's involved."

Kate bit her lower lip but nodded. "I'll invite her to the postmortem meeting with our party-planning team. It will give her a chance to get know everyone, as well."

"Thanks. Are you staying in Somerset tonight?"

"I don't know. My folks went up to Frisco to visit my brother and his family."

"You don't see your parents much, do you?"

"We're not close," she said. "I mean, they are busy with their lives and I am busy working. But if I needed more time with them, they'd be here."

Lance had learned from his own parents that the family he could count on was the one he'd made for himself. He counted his brother and Darius as his family, and the other men who were being inducted into the Texas Cattleman's Club with him.

He'd been in touch with Darius the day before to ask him about the fire, but so far there had been little news of what was going on there.

"Have you heard from Mitch? When I talked to him yesterday he said he might be running late. But we are going to need him for the annual prize announcements."

"Yes, we will," Lance said. "Feel up to playing volleyball on my team this year?"

"Oh, I don't know."

"Every year you say you will next year. But this is your last year…."

"What good will come from me playing?" she asked. "I'm not very athletic."

"It's all for fun. Come on, Kate." He wanted to spend as much of the day with her as he could. At least until Lexi got here. He realized he had to force himself to think about Lexi. All he could think about was Kate.

"Okay, I'll play, but only if Mitch gets here so one of us can man the welcome table."

"He will be here," Lance said. "What's in the goody bag this year?"

"The T-shirt and some other company goodies. We have water guns for the kids."

"Why just the kids?" Lance asked with a grin.

"Because of last year when you and Mitch didn't know when to stop."

"Are you still upset about being caught in the cross fire?"

"Of course not," she said.

He remembered how Kate had looked with her baggy T-shirt soaking wet and clinging to her breasts. To be fair, that was when he'd noticed that there was more to his secretary than met the eye, but she'd looked so distressed by the entire thing that he'd taken his shirt off and offered it to her. She'd taken it and then left a few minutes later.

"What are you thinking?" she asked.

"About the way you looked in that wet T-shirt last year."

She flushed. "Well, don't. You're not supposed to think things like that. Remember, you said you didn't want any more temptation."

"I'm thinking that wasn't my wisest decision, Kate."

"Why not?"

He glanced around the yard quickly. It was still early so there wasn't anyone here yet except for the party crew who was setting up. He touched her face and looked down into her big brown eyes.

"I can't ignore the way you make me feel."

She bit her lower lip. "Please don't."

"Don't what? Don't want you?"

She pulled back. "Don't say things like that. Because I will believe them and do something silly like kiss you. Then you will change your mind and I'll feel stupid again."

"Don't feel stupid," Lance said. He leaned down and kissed her. He'd been wanting to for the last two days since he'd seen Marcus leaning against her desk and talking to her.

He wanted to make sure she knew that he was the only man she needed to kiss.

Her lips felt so right against his and he realized he'd been more than hungry for her. Lexi or no Lexi, was tired of denying himself Kate.

Five

Mitch arrived at the picnic looking every inch the successful lobbyist. There was a part of Lance that envied his younger brother. But with Kate at his side and now his younger brother, too, Lance felt pretty good.

"You two seem happy," Mitch said. "Did Lance finally talk you into staying on as his secretary?"

Kate shook her head, and Lance realized there was still a lot of work for him to do before he had his Katie-girl back for good.

"Let's go to my office at the house and call Darius," Lance said.

"Right now?"

"Yes. I haven't had a chance to check back in with him today and the press is calling, looking for an update."

"Senator Cavanaugh is waiting for answers, as well. And until he gets them, I'm afraid that no matter what your relationship is with Lexi, he won't back the bill we need him to," Mitch said.

Lance was impressed with his younger brother. He looked nothing like their father and yet he had the old man's drive. And Mitch was savvy when it came to dealing with politicians. Lance himself was only good with gas and oil people.

"Why are you looking at me like that?" Mitch asked.

"Just wondering where you get this polish you have."

Mitch shrugged. "Mom, I guess."

"Probably. I always forget about her," Lance said. Alicia Brody had done the best she could. And when she'd walked away from their old man, Lance knew it was because she'd had enough of the roughness of her life. He'd learned a long time ago to just bury his feelings of abandonment.

"You know, I get why she left me behind," Lance said as they entered his house. "I'm the spitting image of him. But I never understood why she left you."

Mitch rubbed the back of his neck as he headed for the bar in the living room. "I think she didn't want either of us to be alone. I've always imagined she knew that if I didn't stay she'd lose you, too."

Lance didn't like the sound of that. He'd always thought of himself as the protector, the one who'd kept Mitch safe. "Really?"

"Hell, I don't know. I'm not a woman and to be fair, I don't understand them," Mitch said.

Lance laughed. His own situation with women was beyond complicated at the moment. Getting engaged hadn't made his life any easier like he'd imagined it would. Although he'd resolved to be the man Lexi deserved, he just couldn't keep his lips off Kate.

"Speaking of women, I got Lexi a necklace. Do you think she's the type of woman who'd enjoy receiving it in public?" Lance asked.

Mitch poured two fingers of whiskey into a

highball glass and downed it in one swallow. "No."

"I wasn't sure. I guess I'll give it to her when she shows up at the house later. I'm glad she's coming today."

"Her dad asked her to. I believe he wants to know what we are like beyond the glitter of DC."

"Cavanaugh knows what we are like. Texans, like him. And he shouldn't forget that."

Mitch poured some whiskey for Lance and held the glass out to him.

"To Texas boys."

Lance clinked his glass against his brother's and downed his whiskey in a quick swallow. He liked the burn as it went down.

The band started playing out back. "Let's get this business with Darius wrapped up so we can enjoy the party."

"Good idea."

Lance led the way down the hall to his den. It was decorated in dark hues of brown and leather. He'd picked out the furniture for this room himself instead of leaving it to the interior designer. He'd known exactly how he wanted the room to look.

There was a Remington black and white photograph on the wall, and a portrait painting of

Mitch and him that had been done when their first well came in. In the background was Old Tilly, as they liked to call her.

"Remember that day?" Mitch asked.

"Hell, yes. I think about it often. It was when I knew you and I were going to make it."

"I always knew we would," Mitch said. "Neither of us knows how to quit."

"True that." Lance dialed the speakerphone and Darius answered on the second ring.

"Darius here."

"It's Lance and Mitch,"

"Happy Fourth. I suppose you are calling about your arson investigation," Darius said.

Lance liked that Darius was straight to the point. He was one of Lance's best friends and the kind of guy that Lance knew he could count on.

"We are."

"I'm afraid I don't have much news. They are still saying arson and they found the source that started the fire but now they have to eliminate several possibilities as accelerants. Once they find the one used at your blaze, they will start investigating where the accelerant was sold."

"How long do you think that will take?" Lance asked.

"Who knows? But I'm in touch with them every day and you can take my word that they are working hard on your case."

Darius gave them a few more details and he and Lance made plans for drinks later in the week before hanging up.

"Are you going to be in town next week?"

"If I get Senator Cavanaugh back on our side. If not, I think I should stay in DC. This is a critical time in our dealings with him."

Lance nodded. "Thank you for doing this."

"It's my company, too, and I want it to succeed as badly as you do," Mitch said.

Lance believed that. When the old man had died, they'd both taken a vow to put the company first and make it the best damned oil and gas company in the world.

They'd had some ups and downs with hurricanes and workers' strikes, but together he and Mitch had conquered everything that came their way. This arson issue was just a complication—nothing the two of them couldn't handle.

Kate tried not to think too much about the kiss that Lance had given her at the sign-in table. She just kept her sunglasses on and her head down as she stood in the sand, playing—of all things—beach volleyball.

Lance was serving and he was very good at it. But then he was good at everything he did. And he was built for sports. Though most of the men who worked for Brody Oil and Gas were in shape, no one looked better to her than Lance Brody. She remembered last year when he'd taken his shirt off to give it to her.

He was built like an Ultimate Fighting Championship fighter and from what she had heard of his past, he'd grown up hard with a father who liked to fight.

"Kate!"

She turned around to face the net just as the ball came toward her. She lifted her hands not to hit the ball but to protect her head. She really hated playing these kind of games.

The ball bounced off her, heading toward the ground, when Marcus dove to the sand to hit it up. Joan took the ball and spiked it over the net.

Kate was shaken by her near miss and decided it was time for her to stop playing. "I'm going to sit out."

No one objected and she felt good about that. She sat on the sidelines where she watched the rest of the game and she talked to some of the families of workers who'd been with Brody Oil and Gas since Mitch and Lance had taken over after their father's death.

A lot of people commented on her new look, telling her how nice it was. She thanked them. She was starting to get used to how she looked and no longer saw a stranger in the mirror.

She grabbed a bottle of water as the game ended with Lance's team victorious. She handed the water to him and he hugged her close. "We won."

"As usual," she said, with a smile. This was one thing she'd really miss about Lance. When they were at his house, she never felt like his secretary.

"Winning is what I do best," Lance said.

"Very true," she said, thinking that was probably one of the things that drew her to him. He just had a positive attitude and kept on going until he achieved what he set out for.

"Walk with me up toward the house."

"Why?"

"Because I want to talk to you. Do you have all the fireworks set up for us?"

"Yes. Exactly as they were last year. I have the music cued and the deejay is ready to announce everything for you."

Everyone wanted to talk to Lance and though he had asked her to stay with him, she soon found herself drifting to the outside of his circle. It was then that she spotted Mitch at the welcome table with Lexi Cavanaugh.

The woman was beautiful and sophisticated and everything that Kate wasn't. She'd be the perfect match for Lance—being a senator's daughter, she knew how to socialize and work in the community. Brody Oil and Gas was always looking for ways to give back to the communities where their refineries were. And Lexi would be a conduit to that.

"Join me for a beer?"

Kate glanced over at Marcus. He had two Bud Lights and held one of them out to her. She smiled and took it. "Thanks for saving me from that ball earlier."

"No problem. You definitely looked like you were out of your league."

She shrugged. "I figured I should play at least one time before leaving."

"So the rumors are true," Marcus said. He tipped his bottle back and took a long swallow of his beer.

He was an attractive man, she realized. He

was tall, at least six foot five, and had a neatly trimmed red beard. His hair was longish on the top but cut neat in the back.

"Yes, they are true," she said, sipping her beer.

"I think it's safe to say we are all going to miss you," Marcus said.

"I doubt it. There will be someone else in Lance's office keeping you guys all organized."

"But that person won't be you," Marcus said.

"I'd take that to heart but you didn't even notice me until I had my makeover," she said, looking at him closely. As attractive as Marcus might be, he didn't hold a candle to Lance.

"True enough. But that doesn't mean I'm not telling the truth now."

"Can I ask you something?"

"Sure," Marcus said.

"Why was I invisible before?" she asked. "It was more than clothes and glasses, right?"

Marcus took another swallow of his beer. "It was more than that. I think it was your attitude. You weren't invisible exactly, I'd say you were more of the girl next door, you know? Just a comfortable woman who we didn't see as a sexual being."

"But now you do?"'

"Yes, now I do. I can't speak for anyone else."

Kate nodded looked away

"I'm not the man you wanted to notice you, right?"

She shook her head. "You're a good-looking guy but not the one for me."

He threw his head back and laughed. "Well, there is justice in the universe. I can't tell you how many times I've used almost that exact line."

That made Kate laugh. She gave Marcus a quick kiss on the cheek before turning to walk away. And she stepped right into Lance who had been standing behind her.

Lance took Kate's arm and led her away from Marcus. He'd never felt so enraged before. He wanted to be the man who made her laugh and smile—not Marcus.

"Are you okay?" Kate asked.

"I…no, I'm not okay. I don't like you flirting with Marcus."

"Why do you care who I flirt with?" Kate said, a flash of anger in her eyes.

Because she was his. But he knew that wasn't true, couldn't be true because he'd given another woman his ring.

A woman that he was quickly realizing he could never marry. Lexi was not what he needed in a woman. She didn't arouse his passion. But passion could lead to jealousy and Lance couldn't afford to be out of control, to be like his father. Maybe that was the right answer, then. Maybe Kate would be better off with a guy like Marcus, and he should marry someone who didn't get him all riled.

"Damn. I know I don't have any right to say something like that, but I want you, Kate. And I think you feel the same," he said.

She flushed but didn't try to pull away. "I do. I think you should know I've been attracted to you for the longest time."

"Good."

"Good?" she asked. "That makes you sound very arrogant."

"Yes, it is good," Lance said. He'd had a lot of time to think about Kate over the last two days. "Because anything this strong that is one-sided would be wrong."

"I guess I can see your point."

"I'm glad," he said. He leaned down and kissed her. "Come up to the house with me while I shower and change."

"Into the shower with you?" she asked.

He raised both eyebrows at her. "Would you be interested in that?"

She blushed and gave him a very shy smile. "Maybe."

He was leading her by the hand toward the house when he saw paramedics running across the lawn. He dropped Kate's hand and they both turned toward the food tent.

"I have to see who that is," he said.

"I know."

He was very aware of Kate moving behind him and he knew that she was concerned about the emergency, the same as he was.

Lexi was sitting on a bench between two paramedics. Her face was flushed.

"What happened?"

"Heat exhaustion as near as we can tell," the paramedic said.

"Are you okay?" Lance asked Lexi.

She nodded, seeming embarrassed by the entire thing. "I should have had more water."

"It's okay. Does she need to go to the emergency room?" Lance asked.

"No. She'd be fine sitting in a cool room and just letting her body recuperate from the sun exposure."

"Let's get you up to the house," Lance said.

Kate hovered nearby. The look on her face told Lance that it was past time to end things with Lexi. But not now. Not like this.

He helped Lexi to her feet. She leaned on him and he looked over her head at Kate who shook her head and walked away.

He had no choice but to let her leave and he didn't like that at all. But right now his hands were tied. He couldn't go after Kate until he took care of Lexi.

He got Lexi settled on the couch in the living room.

"Thank you, Lance."

"For what?" he asked. He hardly knew Lexi. She was a stunningly beautiful woman but other than a couple of dinners, he hadn't really even talked to her.

"For taking care of me just now. I'm sorry if that was embarrassing."

Lance shrugged. "It was nothing. I'm going to go change. Will you be okay?"

She nodded.

"I have a butler of sorts around here—Paul. He's not much company but I will ask him to check in on you."

She shook her head. "Please don't. I'll just sit here in the quiet."

"Are you sure?"

"Yes."

Lance left her and walked up the stairs to his own suite. He called Mitch on his way because he hadn't been able to find his brother in the crowded yard.

"Brody here."

"It's Lance. Can you come up to the house? Lexi had a problem with heat exhaustion. I need a shower but I don't want to leave her alone for too long."

"Is she okay?" Mitch asked.

"Pale and weak but otherwise okay," Lance said.

"Does she need to see a doctor?"

"No. The paramedics checked her out. Where were you?"

Mitch didn't answer. "I'm on my way to the house."

"Good. I'm upstairs. She didn't seem to want company but I don't like leaving her alone when she's not at her best."

"I agree. I'll take care of it."

Lance hung up and quickly showered and

changed. He thought about the two women that were a part of his life right now. It didn't matter that Lexi wasn't the woman he wanted, he still owed her respect—and the truth.

He realized this mess was of his own making. He finished getting dressed and headed downstairs, determined to talk to Lexi. He couldn't marry her—not while he felt what he did for Kate.

Kate was the woman he couldn't live without. He knew without a doubt that Kate was the one woman that he wanted. He couldn't get her out of his system.

He hurried downstairs, anxious to talk to his brother and fiancée. He had a text message from Mitch saying that he was going to take Lexi to the hotel.

Having made up his mind about Lexi and Kate, Lance felt much better. He liked the changes in his plain-Jane secretary and today he'd realized that he wasn't going to let her slip away from him—no matter what.

Six

Lexi Cavanauagh was a stunningly gorgeous woman by anyone's standards. The fact that she was his fiancée should have made him feel lucky. But she was essentially a stranger and he felt awkward around her. Not at all like he felt with Kate.

Kate. He'd already decided to end things with Lexi. But he had to be careful. He needed Lexi and her connections but he couldn't just break things off with her.

Lance came back down the stairs to the sound of raised voices. "Everything okay?"

Mitch and Lexi were standing across the room from each other. Lexi's fists were clenched at her sides and a sheen of tears glittered in her eyes.

"Lexi, what's the matter?"

"Nothing," she said.

"Mitch?"

"We were discussing an event we attended in D.C.," Mitch said.

Lance nodded. "I'm glad to see you feeling better, Lexi. I wanted to take a moment to welcome you to the family. You already know Mitch and I think you will see that we are a close group despite there being only two of us."

"I have noticed that your brother will do anything for you," Lexi said.

Mitch gave her a tense look.

"And I for him."

Lance walked across the room to the foyer where he'd left the neatly wrapped gift box. It bore the emblem of his favorite jeweler and a discreet white bow. He carried it back over and smiled at Lexi.

She didn't seem to be paying any attention to him. "Do you need to sit down?"

"No. I need to go home," she said.

"Then I will take you," Lance said.

She shook her head and noticed the box in his hands. "Is that for me?"

"Yes," he said, handing it to her.

She took it. He noticed that her nails were long and manicured. And for the first time he tried to imagine what it would be like to take Lexi to his bed. He couldn't. The only woman he pictured there was Kate.

Kate's long brown hair on his pillow. Kate's pretty brown eyes staring up at him...Kate was the woman he wanted.

Lexi sat down and opened the gift box carefully. Lance stood across the room with the first niggling of doubt since he'd asked her to marry him. Had he made a colossal mistake?

She held the box in her hands, not opening it. "Why did you get me a gift?"

"To thank you for agreeing to be my wife."

She put her head down and opened the box. He heard her breath catch and took that as a good sign.

He glanced over at his brother and Mitch stared at Lexi...the way Lance realized he stared at Kate sometimes. Damn, was his brother into Lexi?

"Will you help me put it on?" Lexi asked.

Lance started toward her and saw Mitch do the same.

His brother shrugged. "I'm just used to filling in for you."

"Thank you for that, Mitch. Without your help, I don't know what I would have done."

Lexi stood up and lifted her hair. Lance fastened the diamond necklace around her neck.

"Yes, thanks, Mitch, for filling in for your brother so well," Lexi said.

"It was no big deal. I'm used to dealing with problematic heiresses."

"Are you?" Lexi asked.

"Indeed. Our mother was one."

"She sure was. But Lexi isn't anything like Mom," Lance said, not sure what was going on between his brother and Lexi.

"No, she's not," Mitch said. Mitch's cell phone rang and he excused himself to take the call.

Lance found himself alone with his fianceé for the first time since she'd agreed to marry him. And he needed to know if there was any chance this relationship was going to work between them. He put his hands on her shoulders and turned her in his arms.

She looked up at him. Her eyes wide but not with passion, more with…he couldn't identify the emotion.

He brushed a kiss against her lips and found that her mouth was dry and the kiss was rather blah.

Lance worried that he'd be trapped in a passionless marriage. It was clear that Lexi wasn't attracted to him and he knew he wasn't to her.

"Thank you for the gift. It's very pretty."

"You're welcome," he said.

A horn honked outside and Lexi glanced at her watch. "That should be my cab."

"I would've taken you," Lance said.

"I didn't want to be a bother. Thank you for inviting me to the party today. I really enjoyed the chance to see what kind of a company Brody Oil & Gas is."

"You're welcome. Kate said she was going to invite you to attend a meeting with the party-planning staff."

"Sounds great. I'll look forward to her call," Lexi said as she left the house and walked to her cab. She kept talking brightly the entire time and Lance held the door for her as she got into the cab.

She smiled up at him as she said goodbye and he closed the door, standing there watching her be driven away.

He rubbbed the back of his neck, having a bad feeling that his marriage to Lexi was going to be a mistake. And he prided himself on not making any mistakes. He wondered if he should have ended things with her today, but he couldn't have. There was something vulnerable about Lexi. He needed to talk to Mitch about his feelings for her, as well.

There was more between the two of them than he could guess at. But that was a worry for another day. Right now he had a party to host and several staff members to take care of and that was exactly what he was going to do.

After he found Kate.

He needed to talk to her and see her. She had always been his touchstone at Brody Oil & Gas and he realized he needed her by his side now.

Kate was glad when the sun set. Soon it would be time for the Fourth of July fireworks to go off. They had always been her favourite. She'd spent most of the afternoon and evening trying to avoid Lance.

She felt…well, stupid. She was supposed to be getting over him, not falling deeper in love with him each day.

It was silly, really, but seeing the way he'd reacted to Lexi's being sick had affected her. For all his rough ways, she knew that Lance was the kind of guy who'd stand by his friends, no matter what.

And there had been a part of her that had realized that he treated Lexi like a friend and nothing more. Much the same way he'd been treating her for all these years until she'd quit.

What Kate needed was another job in another town, but she really couldn't imagine living anywhere other than south Texas. Unlike some of her friends from high school, she'd never wanted to live anywhere except here.

She liked the warmth and humidity that came with Houston. She liked the cosmopolitan city aspects of the area and the wide-open spaces that were only a few hours' drive away.

A few kids were running around with sparklers and Kate felt a lump at the back of her throat as she thought about the families.

She'd always wanted one of her own but it had never really seemed like she'd have one and now…well, now she seemed no closer to having kids and a husband than she'd been for a while.

"Hey, girl!" Becca called.

"Becca! I'm so glad you could swing by here. Thanks for coming." Kate gave her friend a hug and they walked up the tiki-light path toward the viewing area for the fireworks.

"Wouldn't have missed it for the world. Sorry it took so long to get here."

"Not a problem," Kate said. "I think Lance is going to the Texas Cattleman's Club later for an after-party and I just wanted…"

"A friend," Becca said. "I get it. So how was everything today?"

"Well, good, I think. I kissed Lance and it was…"

"What?"

"Everything I imagined it would be. But then Lexi had heat exhaustion and he had to go to her."

Becca slipped her arm through Kate's. "Was she okay?"

"Yes. But it made me realize I don't want to have an affair with Lance. I want to be able to have a relationship with him where we can be seen as a couple. Not one where I have to hide."

"Good for you. Being a mistress isn't something that would suit you," Becca said.

"Would it suit you?"

"Hell, no."

Both women laughed.

"Is there any other man you are interested in?" Becca asked.

"Not really. I think that Marcus likes me."

Becca laughed again, and Kate relaxed for the first time all day, feeling safe in the presence of her friend. Becca was the one person who she knew loved her no matter what. She didn't care if Kate was fat or wore ugly clothes—Becca liked her anyway.

"That's not surprising, you're a very attractive woman."

"Yeah, right. You're my friend, you have to say that," Kate said. "One thing that was shocking was Lance. He didn't like me flirting with Marcus."

"Too bad," Becca said. "Lance Brody had his chance with you and he let it slip by."

"Maybe I regret that, Becca."

"Good," Becca said. "It's about time you realized that, Lance."

Kate flushed with embarrassment as Lance stepped up behind them.

"Yes, it is," Lance said.

Lance joined the women and they went to the main BBQ area. They chatted while the band played, and Becca got up to dance. Kate glanced at Lance. She felt like she wanted to dance, too, but knew they couldn't—not while he was engaged to Lexi.

"I have something I want to show you," Lance said, and led her away from the crowd.

"The perfect spot to watch the fireworks."

"Where would that be?"

"In my arms."

She stopped. "Don't say anything you don't mean, Lance."

"I'm not."

"What about Lexi? How is she, by the way?" Kate asked. What she'd seen of the Senator's daughter had been brief, but she bore the woman no ill will.

"Fine. She went back to her hotel to get some rest."

"That's good," Kate said. "I can't do this— have an affair with a man who belongs to another woman."

Lance cupped her face in his hands. "Today cemented for me the fact that I need you, Kate.

I'm sorry I didn't wake up earlier to the fact that you are an incredible woman."

Kate steeled her heart against just believing his words. "What changed your mind?"

"Seeing your hot body," he said.

"That's not flattering," she said.

"Yes, it is. And it's the truth. I'm not going to lie to you and try to make you believe that I had some kind of emotional realization when you said you were going to quit. It was really when I got a look at you…I realized that you had everything I wanted."

"Lance—"

"What? Would you prefer I made up lies and told you stories? You know I'm not that kind of guy. I'm also not the kind of man who lets something he wants slip through his fingers. And I want you, Kate."

His raw language got to her as little else could. She'd long wanted Lance and hearing him tell her that he felt the same…it was a powerful aphrodisiac.

He pulled her into his arms and kissed her. There was a lot of passion in his kiss and she stopped trying to think this through, stopped trying to make her attraction to Lance go away.

The thought that maybe this was the only way to free herself entered her mind.

But she knew she was only placating herself. She wanted Lance Brody and now that he had his arms around her, she wasn't going to walk away. Not until she had the chance to experience what it was really like to be his woman.

That was the one thing she'd wanted since her very first day at Brody Oil and Gas. She wrapped her arms around his shoulders and went up on tiptoe to bring her body more fully into contact with his.

He slid his tongue over hers and she tangled her fingers in the silky hair at the back of his neck. As she ran her fingers through it, she felt everything inside of her clench.

She was in Lance's arms!

Lance had no real plan of seduction. He just wanted to kiss Kate because it seemed a sacrilege not to. This was the Fourth of July and he was a red-blooded male, a Texan who'd learned the hard way that you had to fight for what you wanted.

And he wanted Kate Thornton. He lifted her into his arms and stepped off the lighted path. He walked up to his house with patriotic music blaring in the background and fireworks going off all around them.

Kate rested her head on his shoulder and held on to him with a strong grip. He knew that the attraction between them was mutual but until this moment hadn't realized just how much that would mean to him.

He just wanted to know what she'd be like in his bed. To know if the woman he couldn't live without in his work life would also be as important to his personal life. His gut said yes.

"You look fierce," she said.

"Do I?"

She nodded. "Are you sure about this?"

"Hell yes," he said, reaching down to open the door to the living room. He walked up the stairs to his bedroom without pausing to turn on a light.

"I'm not," she said.

The shyness in her voice stopped him. He couldn't force himself on her. He never wanted passion between them to be all about him. He knew Kate well enough, had observed the changes in her and knew she had doubts about herself.

And he wanted to show her that he loved her as she was…well, loved her body, he corrected.

"I'm not rushing you, Kate," Lance said. He set her on her feet and led her out onto his private balcony, gesturing to one of the lounge chairs that faced the east and the fireworks.

"How about a red-hot and boom?"

She shook her head. "I had one last year and think I still might be a little drunk from it."

He laughed. It was then that he realized he was nervous. He knew his way around an oil field and a boardroom but a woman—one who mattered to him—that was an entirely different subject. And Kate had somehow become this woman who mattered to him.

"Champagne?" he asked.

"I'm good," she said.

"Still nervous?"

"A little. You know, I've been wanting to be here with you…like this…for longer than I can remember," she said.

"Is it what you imagined?"

She shook her head, those long silky curls of hers brushing against her collar.

"What can I do to make it better?" he asked. He sat down next to her and put his arm around her shoulder. She was practically a little bird now with tiny arms and shoulders. He hugged her close. "Why'd you lose weight?"

She shrugged and looked away.

"Sorry, was that too personal?"

She started to nod and then turned to pin him with her dark-chocolate stare. "I had to. It wasn't healthy for me and I was tired of being invisible."

"You weren't completely," he said.

"Yes, I was. Or you would have invited me up here a lot sooner," she said, standing up.

She paced over to the railing and leaned back against it, facing him.

"Does it bother you that I didn't?"

"Of course. But not for the reasons you think. It bothers me because I have wasted so many years of my life."

"You're not old, Kate," he said.

"I'm old enough. And it took your engagement to another woman to snap me out of the trance I've been in."

"My engagement?"

"I told you, I've wanted you for a long time," Kate said.

"I'm sorry, Katie-girl. My engagement…it was done for political purposes."

"Really? What about Lexi? Does she know that? Don't you care for her at all?"

Lance stood up, as well. "She knows that we are engaged for our families' sakes. And to be honest, tonight I realized that I can't go through with the fake engagement."

"Why not?"

Lance wasn't the kind of man who liked to talk about his feelings but he knew better than to keep quiet this time. "It just didn't seem right to marry her."

He walked slowly over to Kate, stopping when barely an inch of space separated them. "Don't you want to know why?"

Kate stared up at him. How could he have ever missed how beautiful her eyes were?

"Why?" she asked in a breathy voice.

"I can't marry her when you are the one woman I can't get out of my mind."

"You can't… Are you serious?"

"Serious as a heart attack, baby. And I'm not about to let you go until we've figured this out."

Seven

Kate felt overwhelmed by Lance. She put her hands on his chest and leaned forward to kiss him, licking her lips the second before her mouth touched his. She kept her mouth open, feeling the exhalation of his breath against her. She closed her eyes and rubbed her lips over his.

She let herself make this moment into a memory that she'd remember for the rest of her life. If the last week had taught her anything it was that Lance was important to her. And that forever… well, forever might not be in the cards for them.

But now was. Right now. She curled her fingers around his arms and touched his tongue lightly with hers, stroking it into his open mouth. She tasted the beer he'd drunk earlier and something that was starting to be familiar to her. A taste that was just Lance.

She started to withdraw from his mouth and felt his teeth close lightly around her tongue. He angled his head and she felt his hand on her ribs right below her breasts. His other hand tangled in the hair at the back of her head.

He held her so strongly as his mouth moved over hers, as he took complete control of the embrace and of her body. Shivers spread down her body from her lips past her neck. Her breasts felt fuller as she continued kissing him. She leaned forward and felt the tips of her breasts brush his chest.

She moaned, and then was embarrassed and broke away.

He stopped her. "What is it, honey?"

She shook her head. How had she thought that she could be with this sophisticated man? Had she forgotten that the hair and clothes were just window dressing? Inside she was still Kate Thornton.

But this was Lance Brody and he didn't take

no for an answer. He pulled her back into his arms, his hands falling to the small of her back, holding her against his rock-hard body. His erection nudged the bottom of her stomach.

She glanced up and saw that he was watching her. And she realized she wanted to see more of him. All of him. How often did dreams come true?

If she walked away now, the makeover would be just what she'd called it—window dressing. Nothing more than a facade on her dusty old life. But she had changed.

She put her hands on Lance's face, drew his head down to hers. "You are the best kisser."

He smiled at her, just a little half smile that made her pulse race. "I'm just getting started."

Kate let herself relax and stop worrying about the future, about everything other than this moment. She wanted Lance. He wanted her. Together, they were going to make this moment one of the most memorable.

Lance kissed her again and then lifted her in his arms. She realized she liked the way he carried her around. She loved the feeling that came with being in his arms. Since Kate was big for most of her life, Lance was the first man to carry her as an adult. And it made her feel beautiful, like the sexy girls that men always carried in the movies.

Lance carried her over the threshold, back into his bedroom. He kissed her so tenderly before slowly undressing her.

She crossed her arms over her breasts, knowing despite the weight loss that she still wasn't perfect. This body…she glanced down at it. Her breasts had fine white stretch marks. And her stomach wasn't flat. She wondered sometimes if it would ever be.

"What are you doing?"

"I'm not very good-looking naked," she said.

He shook his head and drew her hands away from her body, holding her arms open so she felt so damned exposed. Too exposed. She couldn't do this.

Just when she was about to turn away, he pulled her into his arms, hugging her close to his clothed body. "Kate, can't you feel what you do to me?"

He took her hand and drew it down his body to his erection. It was hard and proud, pressing against his jeans. She stroked him through his clothes.

He traced his finger over her breasts, circling around the white fleshy globe before coming closer to her nipple. It beaded up and she bit her lower lip, waiting in anticipation of his touch.

"Katie?"

"Hmm?"

"You have one hot, sexy body," he said. His finger rubbed over her nipple, making it impossible for her to remember her own arguments.

A moment later, his head dipped down and he suckled her, drawing her nipple into his mouth. She rubbed her hands over his short hair.

"Lance, take your shirt off," she said. She surprised herself with her demand. But she wanted to enjoy every second she had with Lance, and she *needed* to see his chest.

He lifted his head and stood there in front of her. "You take it off for me."

She reached for his shirt and drew it up and over his head. He tossed it aside and she couldn't help but reach for his chest. She touched his muscles over his breastbone and then followed the line of hair that tapered down, disappearing into his waistband.

"I like you without your shirt on," she said.

"Do you?"

"Yes."

She felt more vulnerable now than she had just a second before. She hadn't meant to leave herself so open to him. Yet, at the same time, she knew there was no other way for her to react to him.

He didn't say anything else, just bent to trace the line of her neck to the base. He licked her there and then dropped the softest kiss on her.

She couldn't think as he stood back up and lifted her onto the bed. He bent down to capture the tip of her breast in his mouth. He sucked her deep in his mouth, his teeth lightly scraping against her sensitive flesh. His other hand played at her other breast, arousing her, making her arch against him in need.

She fumbled with his trousers. He should be naked. She pulled back. Again the brazen woman she hadn't realized she was came to the scene. "Take your pants off."

He stood up and unfastened them, kicking off his pants and underwear in one smooth move. He came back down on top of her. She reached between them and took his erection in her hand, bringing him closer to her, spreading her legs wider so that she was totally open to him. "I need you now."

He lifted his head; the tips of her breasts were damp from his mouth and very tight. He rubbed his chest over them. Then he donned a condom.

She slid her hands down his back, cupping his butt as he thrust into her loosely. Their eyes met. Staring deep into his eyes made her feel like their souls were meeting. She felt her body start to tighten around him, catching her by surprise. She climaxed before him. He gripped her hips, holding her down and thrusting into her two more times before he came with a loud grunt of her name.

After disposing of the condom, he held her, pulling her into his arms and tucking her up against his side.

She wrapped her arm around him and listened to the solid beating of his heart. She closed her eyes and let out her breath, snuggling closer to this man that she'd wanted and loved for so long. She felt his arms wrap around her and she realized that in this moment, she had everything she'd ever wanted. Her dreams were coming true.

Lance woke up with a hard-on and his hands on Kate's breasts. She felt so incredibly good. He rubbed his erection against her buttocks and lowered his head to her neck. She shifted in his arms, rubbing against him.

He nibbled on the skin exposed by the morning sunlight. She was beautiful. He knew she didn't think so but as he looked down her body, wrapped in his arms, he'd never seen a more beautiful woman.

He rubbed his palm over her breast until her eyes opened halfway and she moaned softly. The same noise she'd made last night when he'd made love to her.

He shifted on the bed, so that he was lying next to her, his morning hard-on pressing against her hip. It had been a long time since he'd had a woman sleep over and it felt right to Lance that Kate was there.

"Morning." He took her mouth with his, letting his hands wander over her body. That she was here in his bedroom was just as it should be.

"Good morning," she said, putting her hand in front of her mouth.

He pulled her hand away from her face and kissed her. "You taste good this morning, honey." He swept his hand down her body. "Look good, too."

She flushed and buried her red face against his chest. He put his arms around her and held her. He didn't understand it but Kate was more beautiful this morning than she had been last night. Her dark hair was thick and curled in disarray around her shoulders. The makeup she'd had on yesterday had worn off and her eyes were clear.

"You slept with your contacts in. Do you need to take them out?"

She shook her head. "I got the kind you can wear for a month. I had a really hard time getting them in initially."

"Then why wear them?"

"Glasses were part of the old me."

"So was I, but not anymore."

Kate laughed. "Glasses have always been a mask for me to hide behind and I don't want to do that anymore."

He traced his hand over her shoulder and down her back. She shivered with awareness and her nipples beaded. She was so wonderfully responsive. He pushed her back down on the bed and then bent to lick each nipple. He blew gently on the tips. She raked her nails down his back.

"What are you doing?" she asked.

"Making love to you this morning," he answered, kissing his way to her stomach and tasting her flesh there.

"Why?"

"Because I can," he said.

He kissed her soundly, thrusting his tongue deep into her mouth until she was writhing on the bed and moaning his name.

He continued to kiss and nibble his way down her body, taking time to draw her nipples out by suckling them. When she arched off the bed and clutched his head to her breasts, he decided to move lower, to nibble at her stomach and trace the faint scars left from her weight loss. He hadn't realized how proud he was of Kate until now. She'd really taken charge of her life.

He moved lower until he knelt between her thighs and looked down at her. "May I kiss you there?"

She swallowed, her hands shifting on the bed next to her hips.

"No one has ever done that," she said.

"If you don't like it, I'll stop," he said.

Her legs moved and he took that as a yes.

He leaned down, blowing lightly on her before tonguing her soft flesh. She lifted her hips toward his mouth.

He wrapped his hands around her hips and drew her up to him, holding her to his mouth as he tasted her. He pushed her legs farther apart until he could reach her dewy core. He pushed his finger into her body and drew out some of her moisture; he lifted his head and looked up her body.

Her eyes were closed, her head tipped back, her shoulders arched, throwing her breasts forward with their berry-hard tips, begging for more attention. Her entire body was erotically beautiful in the morning sunlight.

He lowered his head again, hungry for more of her. He feasted on her body, carefully tasting the moist flesh between her legs. He used his teeth, tongue and fingers to bring her to the brink of climax but held her there, wanting to draw out the moment of completion until she was begging him for it.

Her hands grasped his head as she thrust her hips up toward his face. But he pulled back so that she didn't get the contact she craved.

"Lance, please."

He scraped his teeth over her clitoris and she screamed as her orgasm rocked through her body. He kept his mouth on her until her body stopped shuddering and then slid up her, holding her tightly in his arms.

He rolled over, keeping her with him until she straddled him. "Sit up, honey."

She did as he asked, bracing herself on his shoulders. He shifted his hips until the tip of his cock found the portal of her body. The warmth of her against him made him realize he wasn't wearing a condom. He reached for the one he'd left on the nightstand last night.

He quickly opened it. "Sit up."

"Let me do it," she said.

He handed the condom to her and with a little help from him, he was sheathed. He shifted his hips again and slipped the tip of his erection into her.

"Take as much of me as you want," he said.

"I want it all," Kate said. "But I'm not sure…"

He put his hands on her hips and guided her down on him. But the feel of her around him quickly eroded his self-control and he found himself holding her hips tightly while he thrust up inside of her, trying to get deeper. He pulled her legs forward, forcing them farther apart until she settled even closer to him.

He slid deeper still into her. She arched her back, reaching up to entwine her arms around his shoulders. He thrust harder and felt every nerve in his body tensing. Reaching between their bodies, he touched her between her legs until he felt her body start to tighten around him.

He came in a rush, continuing to thrust into her until his body was drained. He then collapsed on top of her, lying his head between her breasts.

A week later, Lance still hadn't had the chance to talk to Lexi, who had gone back to DC. But he had managed to keep Kate on as his assistant. And he'd taken her to dinner every night—and made love to her most of those nights, as well.

The investigation into the fire was going painfully slowly. Mitch was back in DC and Lance hadn't spoken to him since the Fourth. They were ready to get back to work at the main refinery. They needed to be producing barrels of oil each day, not sitting idle.

He picked up the phone and dialed Darius's number.

"This is Darius."

"Darius, my man, what news do you have from the refinery?"

"Not much. The arson investigator is still tracking the accelerant to try to find the source."

"Do you trust the man?" Lance asked. "Is he competent?"

"Yes, I think he is. I'm going to call his office later. I'll follow up with you when I have news."

"Thanks, Darius. I appreciate you taking this case."

"That's what friends are for, right?"

"Indeed."

"Speaking of friends…what's this I hear about your engagement?"

Lance looked at the open door leading to Kate's desk. He could hear her hands moving over the keyboard of her computer.

"It's complicated."

"With women, that's the only way a situation can be."

Lance laughed. "More so than usual. I can't say any more until I talk to the lady involved."

"Gotcha. I can appreciate that."

"Thanks, Darius."

He hung up the phone as Kate entered his office. "Marcus needs five minutes to talk to you later."

"Anything else?" Lance asked. Marcus was hanging around the office too much lately and Lance knew it was because of Kate.

"This came for you via courier. Said it was

urgent," she said, handing him a letter-sized envelope.

He stopped her with a hand on her wrist. He suspected the envelope held the bracelet he'd ordered for her last night. He wanted Kate to have something, and until he could talk to Lexi, a ring was out of the question.

Was he really thinking of marrying Kate Thornton?

"Close the door for me."

"No. People will talk if we close the door. It's never closed when I'm in here."

"Katie-girl…what are you thinking?"

She blushed and gave him a hard stare. "Nothing."

She turned on her heel to leave. He stopped her, reaching over her head to close the door, trapping her.

"Turn around."

She did, slowly.

"Was that so hard?"

She shook her head. "You are way too bossy for your own good."

"You like it," he said, thinking of last night when he'd ordered her to come while they were making love, and she had.

She blushed.

"What did you want from me?"

Everything, he thought. He wanted every secret in her dark brown stare to be revealed to him.

"I think this package is actually for you. Have a seat in my chair."

"Lance…"

He gestured to his chair and then followed her back across his office. She wore a short skirt and a sleeveless sweater today. Her hair had been left loose and hung down her back in silky waves.

Each day, instead of growing used to her look he found something new about her that attracted him.

He wondered if that would stop or go away with familiarity. But somehow he doubted that it would. There was something about Kate that just kept deepening for him each day.

"Why are you staring at me like that?" she asked.

He shrugged. "Just thinking about how pretty you are."

"I'm not," she said.

"That's not the way to take a compliment."

She swallowed. "But I look in the mirror every day, Lance."

He walked over to her, leaning one hip on the side of the desk. He turned her toward him and looked down into her face.

"You are beautiful, Kate. I'm not sure why I never noticed it before but you get prettier each and every day."

"Thank you, Lance. When I'm with you I feel…like the woman I always dreamed of being."

"I'm glad," he said. He reached for the envelope and checked the return address. It was the bracelet he'd ordered. He opened the envelope and a small black jewelry bag fell out.

"I'm not much of a gift wrapper, but I wanted you to have this," Lance said.

Kate reached for it and he opened the bag. He took her hand in his and turned it palm up.

He shook the jewelry bag until the bracelet dropped out into her hand. The jewel-encrusted charms glittered. She bit her lower lip and closed her fist over the bracelet.

"Thank you. It's so beautiful. But why are you giving me this?."

"I wanted you to have a piece of jewelry that

you didn't buy for yourself, something that would remind you of me each time you put it on."

The look on her face told him everything he needed to know.

Eight

Kate spent the rest of the day admiring her bracelet and romanticizing her relationship with Lance. It had developed into something altogether different than she'd expected, something more than she'd ever expected from any relationship.

She found herself cautioning her heart not to believe that Lance was the man of her dreams. She felt like there was still something that had to be worked out between them. She hadn't asked about his engagement to Lexi and if he'd broken it off. But Lance had said he would do it and she trusted him.

And the bracelet. She stopped working at her computer and touched it. It was a beautiful piece of jewelry. The only other man to ever give her any jewelry had been her dad, who had gifted her with one-karat diamond stud earrings when she'd graduated from high school.

This was different. Although her head was telling her to be cautious, her heart was going full throttle, and she couldn't seem to stop it. Everything was out of control—and she liked it.

"Kate, can I see you in my office?"

She picked up her notepad and stepped into Lance's office. It was after hours and much of the staff had gone home.

"Yes, Lance?" she asked. She stopped when she noticed that there was a picnic basket on his desk and a bottle of wine opened and chilling in a wine bucket.

"Join me for dinner?" he asked.

"I guess the boss won't notice if I'm away from desk for a few minutes."

"I already cleared this with the boss."

She closed the door behind her. She didn't want any of their co-workers to see this. Her relationship with Lance was too personal to let the world know about it.

"Then I'd love to join you," she said. "How did you plan all this without me?"

Lance poured her a glass of white wine and handed it to her. "I am capable of doing things on my own."

"I know that. It's just…"

"What?"

"It must have taken some effort for you to surprise me like this…and I didn't think you would do that."

"Why not? I like surprising you," he said.

She wasn't used to this, to this being in a relationship, and she hardly knew what to expect. She'd gone from invisible to this…and it was overwhelming.

"Thank you."

"You're welcome," he said. "I want this to be a special night for you."

Lance was everything she wanted in a man, she thought. She couldn't deny that, no matter how cautious she was trying to be.

Spontaneously, she went up on tiptoe and kissed him. She'd been wanting to all day long.

He caught her close and kissed her back. "Working together is a kind of torture."

"How?" she asked. One hand was roaming up and down her back, the other at the hem of her skirt.

"Seeing you all day, wanting to lift this little skirt of yours and bend you over my desk…" He trailed off as he dropped kisses all along her neck and throat.

"What else do you want to do?" she asked, turned on by the image he'd put in her mind.

"Lots of things, Katie-girl. But I really want to know what you want to do. What is your fantasy?"

"In the office?" she asked.

"We can start there," he said.

"Take your shirt off," she said. Since they'd started sleeping together, she fantasized many times about coming into his office and seeing him sitting there with his shirt off.

"Take my shirt off?"

She nodded.

He reached between them, the backs of his fingers brushing her breasts as he unbuttoned his shirt. She shook from the brief contact and bit her lip to keep from asking for more.

"Now you take yours off," he said.

"Um…I thought I was in charge."

"You are, but I need some incentive to keep on going."

"And if I take my blouse off…"

"I'll be like putty in your hands."

She reached between the two of them and took the hem of her sleeveless sweater in her hands and drew it up over her body. She was wearing a very sexy bra that she'd bought at Becca's store. The cups were all lace and it fastened in the front.

"Very nice," Lance said, running his finger down the center of her body, over her sternum and between her ribs, lingering on her belly button and then stopping at the waistband of her skirt.

He took the front clasp of her bra between his fingers and snapped it open. She stood there on the precipice of something that she couldn't explain. He rubbed his finger over the spot where the clasp had been. The cups were still covering her breasts but she felt…wanton and wicked.

He slowly traced the same path upward again. This time, his fingers feathered under her lacy bra, barely touching her nipples. Both beaded, and a shaft of desire pierced Kate, shaking her.

She needed more. She wanted more. Her heart

beat so swiftly and loudly she was sure he could hear it. She scraped her fingernails lightly down his chest, tangling them in the hair that was there. The dark stuff was tingling against her fingers. He moaned, the sound rumbling up from his chest. He leaned back against his desk, bracing himself on his elbows.

"I'm all yours, Kate," he said.

His muscles jumped under the touch of her fingers as she traced the line down the center of his body. She circled his nipple but didn't touch it, following the fine dusting of hair that narrowed and disappeared into the waistband of his pants.

He pushed the cups of her bra off her breasts. It hung open around them. He pulled her closer until the tips of her breasts brushed his chest.

"Kate." He said her name and she quivered. This was what she'd always wanted from Lance. And now it was hers. He was hers.

His erection nudged her center and she clenched her vagina, wishing he was inside her. She shifted around, trying to feel the tip of his penis against her mound, but it was impossible with her skirt on. Her skirt was hiked up but it wasn't enough.

He kissed his way down her neck and bit lightly at her nape. She shuddered, clutching at his shoulders, grinding her body harder against him.

He found the zipper on the side of her skirt. It loosened as he pushed his hands under the fabric. His big hands slipped into her panties, cupping her butt and urging her to ride him, guiding her motions against his hard-on. He bent his head and his tongue stroked her nipple, and then he suckled her.

Everything in her body tightened. She grabbed Lance's shoulders, rubbing harder and faster against his erection as her climax washed over her. She collapsed against his chest. He held her close. Having Lance act out her fantasy, having him be the man who fulfilled her sexually was more than she'd expected. She wrapped her arms around him, resting her head on his chest and listening to the beat of his heart.

This was more than just a fantasy. This was love—real love—and she didn't know what she'd do if this didn't last.

Lance had never seen anything more beautiful than the passion in Kate. She was more than he'd ever imagined she could be. Her makeover had shown him the woman she was, but the last week he'd helped her realize the woman she could be.

She was exquisitely built. He knew she had body issues, but he loved the imperfection of her. It was what made her a real woman and not some airbrushed ideal that he'd never be able to touch. She was so soft and feminine that she brought out all of his protective instincts, making him want to shield her from the world.

He pushed the straps of her open bra down her arms. Her breasts were full and her skin flushed from her orgasm. Slowly, he caressed her torso, almost afraid to believe that Kate was his.

Her nipples were tight little buds beckoning his mouth. He loved her breasts and couldn't get enough of them.

"I'm sorry," she said, her voice pitched low and a slight blush covering her cheeks and neck.

"For what?"

"Coming without you," she said.

There was something very fragile about Kate and no matter how much headway he made with helping her to realize how much he wanted her, she still was unsure of herself. He pulled her more fully into his arms, cradling her to his chest. She closed her eyes and buried her face in his neck. Each exhalation went through him. He wanted her.

He was so hard and hot for her that he might come in his pants. But he was going to wait for her signal. That was the point of this entire dinner that he'd planned. He wanted some time alone, away from his place, where he could let her have the lead in their relationship.

He felt the minute touches of her tongue against his neck, and his cock hardened. Her hand slid down his chest, opening his belt, unfastening the button at his waistband and then lowering his zipper.

Her hand slid inside his boxers, up and down his length. He tightened his hands on her back. He glanced down his body and saw her small hand burrowed into his pants, saw her working him with such tender care he had to grit his teeth not to end it all right then. But he wanted to be inside her the next time one of them climaxed.

Glancing down, he saw her smiling up at him. He stepped away and laid down the cashmere blanket he'd brought in earlier, urging her over to it. She took a step and her loosened skirt fell off, pooling at her feet. She was left in just her skimpy lace panties and a pair of heels.

"Woman, I wish you could see yourself right now. You'd never doubt your sex appeal again."

She smiled up at him. "It's you," she said.

He leaned down, capturing her mouth with his as he shoved his pants further down his legs and then brought them both down on the blanket, settling down on top of her. She opened her legs and he positioned himself between her thighs.

The humid warmth of her center scorched his already aroused flesh. He thrust against her without thought. Damn, she felt good.

He wanted to enter her totally naked. But they'd had a birth control discussion and she didn't take the pill so that meant he had to keep wearing condoms.

"Can you reach my pants, honey?"

She stretched her arm to grab them. She fished the condom out of his pocket and handed it to him.

He pushed away from her for a minute, rising up on his knees. He glanced over at her and saw she was watching him. Her eyes were on his erection and that made him swell even more. He put the condom on one-handed and turned back to her.

"Hurry, Lance. I need you."

It was the first time she'd asked him to come

to her and he couldn't resist. She opened her
arms and her legs, inviting him into her body and
he went. He lowered himself over her and rubbed
his erection against her mound. He shifted his
entire body against hers, caressing her.

She reached between his legs and fondled his
sac, cupping him in her hands, and he shuddered.
"Don't do that, honey, or I won't last."

She smiled up at him. "Really?"

He wanted to hug her close at the look of wonder on her face. Kate was a joy as a lover because
she enjoyed the hell out of him and his body and
their lovemaking. "Hell, yes."

He shifted and lifted her thighs, wrapping her
legs around his waist. Her hands fluttered between them and their eyes met.

He held her hips steady and entered her
slowly. He thrust deeply until he was fully
seated. Her eyes widened with each inch he gave
her. She clutched at his hips, holding him to her,
eyes half-closed and head tipped back.

He leaned down and caught one of her nipples
in his teeth, scraping very gently. She started to
tighten around him, her hips moving faster, demanding more. But he kept the pace slow, steady,
wanting her to come again before he did.

He suckled her nipple and rotated his hips to catch her pleasure point with each thrust, and he felt her hands in his hair as she threw her head back and her climax ripped through her.

He started to thrust faster. He leaned back on his haunches and tipped her hips up to give him deeper access to her body. Her hips were still clenching around his when he felt that tightening at the base of his spine seconds before his body erupted into hers. He pounded into her two, three more times, then collapsed against her. Careful to keep his weight from crushing her, he rolled to his side, taking her with him.

He kept his head at her breast and smoothed his hands down her back. He wanted to just lie here with her in his arms for the rest of the night, but a knock on his office door had them scrambling to their feet.

Kate was horrified that someone was at the door and she and Lance were naked.

"Shh. I've got this. Go stand in the corner and get dressed."

"I can't believe I did this and now we got caught! My mom always said that if I behaved poorly, God would catch me out."

Lance wanted to laugh but knew better. It was just that his mom had said the same thing once. It seemed something all mothers said. And he'd done enough "naughty" things in the course of his life to know that this wasn't God's hand.

"Lance, you in there?" Stan asked.

"Be right there," he said. He pulled his pants up and fastened them.

He found his shirt and put it on. He wasn't about to embarrass Kate by answering the door half-dressed. She was fumbling with her clothes and he wanted—no needed—to get her back into his arms.

"What do you need, Stan?"

"Sorry, sir, but there is a Mr. Martin from the arson investigation here to see you. He's not on the list for the building so we couldn't let him in, and you weren't answering your phone, but you were still in the building according to your logs—"

"Not a problem, Stan. Tell Mr. Martin to have a seat and I'll be down to get him in a few minutes."

"Yes, sir."

He closed the door on Stan and turned back

to find Kate completely dressed. Her arms were wrapped around her waist and she watched him with those wide eyes of hers. Only right now they seemed wounded and scared.

"Can we postpone our dinner?"

"Yes," she said. "I need to clean up in the washroom and then—"

He stopped her with a finger over her lips. "Why don't you go home, honey? I'll stop by when this is over."

She shook her head. "I think I need to be alone tonight."

"Why?"

"Because I need to reflect on this. That sounds silly, doesn't it?"

"Not really."

"Good. Because I want to make sense of this. Changing my image is one thing, but changing my core values…that's something different."

"Making love with the man you are dating isn't a change in your values."

"Yes, it is, Lance. I wouldn't be in this situation with any other man."

"Why not?"

"Because you're the one I love," she said, and turned on her heel to walk away.

"Wait a minute, Kate."

She stopped, but didn't turn back. He wanted to say the hell with Martin and just keep her here until they finished this discussion.

But the refinery was his top priority right now. He was torn. For the first time since he'd taken over Brody Oil and Gas, a woman was coming between him and his responsibilities.

"Not now, Lance."

"You love me?"

"Yes," she said. "And I have to decide if I still want to have an affair with my boss. Because when Stan knocked on that door, all the love I felt for you was embarrassing and I don't want that."

"You shouldn't be embarrassed. Stan doesn't know you were in here or what we were doing," Lance said.

"But I do. And I'm the one who will bare the shame of it. I don't want to feel ashamed of anything between us. I hadn't before but then all of a sudden…"

Lance understood. He realized that he needed to make this relationship between them more permanent. But he couldn't until he broke things off with Lexi. He'd hoped to do that face to face, but a phone call might have to do it.

He pulled her back into his arms and refused to let her go. "Kate, I'm not hiding you or ashamed of you."

"I know that, Lance. But I have been hiding. I know half the office has always guessed that I was in love with you and now…well, now it seems like you just noticed me since I'm…sexy."

He was proud of her for thinking she was sexy. It was a complete turn around for her.

"Well, you are sexy. But that's not what this is about. Listen, I have to wrap things up with Lexi. Then you and I can—"

"What do you mean you have to wrap things up with her?" Kate asked.

"I haven't had a chance to talk to her yet. It's not a big deal."

"Are you still engaged?" Kate asked.

"Not to my way of thinking," Lance said.

Kate pulled away and put her hands on her hips. "To anyone's way of thinking…are you engaged?"

Lance looked down at her. This night was certainly not going his way. But he hadn't lied to Kate from the beginning and he wasn't about to start now.

"Yes, I am still engaged."

Her lip quivered and her face lost all color. "I can't believe this. I'm an idiot."

She turned on her heel and he stopped her once again. "You aren't. I meant everything I said to you."

"Really? Because the only way for that to be true is for me to be your mistress. Is that what you had in mind for us?"

"No," he said.

Lance's phone started ringing and he knew he had to answer it. Damn it. "This is not over, Kate."

"Yes, Lance, it is."

Nine

Kate looked down at the speedometer and realized she was driving way too fast. Anger had gotten the better of her, and she could still feel the flush of shame on her cheeks. She forced herself to slow down.

A part of her sort of understood where Lance was coming from. She got that he might be waiting to talk to Lexi in person to break their engagement. And if he felt for her even a tenth of what she did for him, then the emotions and the attraction would have been hard to resist, engaged or not.

But the main thing that was bothering her was her own reactions. She'd forgotten who she was. Her new clothes and hair and make-up had made her feel like she was a different person.

And it was only as she'd been standing in the corner of Lance's office, trying to quickly get back into her clothes, that she'd realized she was making a mistake.

Love shouldn't feel like this, she thought as she turned into the garage of her town house. She parked her car and went inside.

Love should be something to be celebrated and shared. And for so long she was used to her love for Lance being her dirty little secret. It hadn't occurred to her that she'd allowed that to become the rule for their relationship. She'd been used to hiding it and had allowed herself to be hidden.

The last week had been wonderful but she realized tonight that she wanted more.

She looked at the bracelet he'd given her. She knew that he didn't think less of her than he did before. But she had no idea what he really wanted from her. Did he just want to continue their affair until it ran its course?

And was she willing to keep working for him—and sleeping with him?

That was the problem with being a modern woman, she thought. The lines in these situations were blurred. And she didn't know which way to turn.

She turned the air-conditioner down and walked through the house to the shower. She washed, wishing she could wipe away the memories of Lance's body inside of hers, of that closeness that they'd had together for too short a time.

She put on a sundress and walked through her home. She'd decorated it with antiques that she and her mom had found in Canton up near Dallas, and with photos of her family. But there was nothing that was really hers in it, much like the new clothing had been window dressing for a person she wanted to be. This house was what she'd always imagined a city girl would have.

But she'd never made that city girl's life her own. Now she wanted to. No, she needed to if she had even the slightest hope of surviving this love she had for Lance.

She didn't know the depth of her love for him before this month. Now she loved the way he smiled at her when no one else could see them. She loved the way he went out of his way to surprise her and she loved the way he made her feel like she was it—the only woman in the world that he wanted to see and spend time with.

And that kind of love…well, it wasn't going to go away. So she had to figure this out. Could she continue her affair with him while he was still engaged?

There was a knock on her door an hour later and she knew who it was without even looking through the peephole.

She unlocked the door and opened it, but stood in the doorway. "Lance."

"Can I come in?"

She tipped her head to the side, considering it. He'd been to her place once before but never as her lover. All of their trysts—what an old-fashioned word, she thought—had taken place at Lance's.

She decided to let him in. Obviously they needed to talk. "Sure. Is everything okay with the investigation?"

"Yes. Mr. Martin was getting some restless employees at the fire scene one he needed me to keep them clear."

She led the way into her living room and heard him close the front door behind him. She sat down in the Kennedy rocker that had been her grandmother's and took a sip of lemonade.

"Can I get you a drink?"

"A beer would be great," Lance said. She noticed he had the picnic basket in his hands. "Have you eaten?"

"No, I haven't," she said.

"I'll set this up while you go get my beer. I am starved. It has been a really long day."

"Yes, it has," Kate said. Sleeping with the boss took a lot out of her. She didn't like the way that sounded—even to herself. She found a Coors Light in the fridge and brought it out to Lance. He smiled at her as he took it.

He took a long draw from the bottle, then set it on the coaster on the coffee table.

The food he'd put out was a cold pasta and chicken salad. It was exactly the kind of dinner she liked on a hot July night and she didn't kid herself that Lance hadn't planned it that way.

He was a man who noticed things.

"Thanks for dinner," she said, as she sat down beside him on the couch and picked up her fork.

Kate steered the conversation to work and to

Mitch, who was due back from DC by the end of the week. She did her level best to make sure that they didn't have a chance to talk about her confession of love.

But then they finished their meal and Lance leaned back against the couch, stretching his long arms along the back of it. "So you love me?"

Lance had thought of nothing else during his drive over to her place. No woman had ever told him she loved him. And that included his fiancée and his mother. He wasn't a man who went out searching for the softer things in life. He took what he wanted and let the devil take the rest.

But he wanted Kate's love.

Now that she'd said she loved him, he wanted to hear her say it again. And he wanted to take her and have her say it while he was buried hilt deep in her sexy little body.

"I…yes, I do love you, but that doesn't mean that I'm going to just let you walk all over me."

"I didn't think for a moment that it did. Actually I have no idea what it means."

"What are you saying?"

"Just that love isn't something I've had a lot of experience with."

"Well, you're the only guy I've ever loved so I guess neither of us knows much about this," she said.

But Kate knew love better than Lance did. He knew she'd come from the kind of family that people liked to complain about but was filled with love.

"And I'm not sure that's a good thing," Kate said.

"Why not?"

"Because love shouldn't be one-sided. It's not healthy."

"Listen, Kate, I'm not about to promise you something I can't deliver." Losing Kate wasn't something he was prepared to do. Having had her, he didn't know if he'd ever be ready to let her walk out the door.

"I appreciate that, Lance. But I have to do what's healthy for me, too. I just can't keep loving a man who never puts me first."

"That's not fair. I've put you first."

"Yes, but in the privacy of your office or your home," Kate said quietly.

She was tired of being hidden from the world, which suited him fine—he got that. But he didn't want Kate to think she could manipulate him into doing whatever she wanted. It was important to him that she let him take the lead in their relationship.

"What can I say?"

She bit her lip and then leaned forward so that her face was turned away from him and her arms rested on her knees.

"If I have to tell you, then I guess that means there isn't anything to say."

Lance wasn't sure what she wanted. Hell, that was a lie, he knew exactly what she wanted. "I'm not going to say I love you, Kate. I just told you I have no experience with that emotion."

"I don't understand how you can say that. You have dated a lot of women."

"None of them have loved me."

"Well, your mother did and your father, too, right? And Mitch loves you."

Lance shrugged. The devotion his brother and he had didn't fit into the mold of what he'd call love. It was just a bond that had been forged in the fire of their upbringing. And there was little in the world that would change that. "I don't know. What's between Mitch and me isn't like you saying you love me."

"Why not?" she asked.

"Because I want you to love me. That feels right to me, Kate. A part of me thinks you belong to me. Right or wrong, that's the way I feel."

"Belong to you?" she asked.

He nodded. What would he do if she said to get out? Not just out of her house but out of her life? He'd just told her that she was his. And she was. That was as much as he could feel for a woman.

"I like the thought of being yours, Lance. But I'm confused."

"I can appreciate that. What would it take to clear things up for you?"

"You are still engaged to Lexi," Kate said.

"I'm ending that, Kate. I can't marry another woman when I'm involved with you."

Lance realized in that moment that he'd do whatever she asked if it was in his power. He needed everything in his relationship with Kate to be resolved. It was past time for him to figure out what he wanted as a man.

And everything kept pointing to Kate.

"I guess I need some time to think about that," she said. "I feel like I've been loving you forever and maybe it's time to figure out what that really means to me—and to you."

Lance didn't like the sound of that. But he wasn't about to beg for her affection. He'd heard too many fights between his parents that had gone the same way.

"I'm not going to play games with you, Kate. If you want to be with me—if you love me—then I think you can put a little effort into being with me."

Kate crossed her arms over her chest. She looked at him and he knew he'd said the wrong thing. "I've been loving you for a long time, Lance Brody, and you never even knew I was alive. So you do what you have to. I'm not playing games with you. I'm just standing up for myself. And I don't like you trying to push me around."

"I'm not pushing you around," Lance said.

He should have guessed that her love wasn't real. It was probably tied to the sexuality of their relationship and the fact that he was the first man to make her feel like a woman.

Kate shook her head. "I didn't say you were doing anything wrong. I just need to think. And you need to end things with Lexi. I'm not going to stop loving you overnight, Lance."

"Well, I'm not too sure about that. It seems

like you have a checklist of things I need to do to win your love and once we check them all off you'll be mine." Lance stood up and walked to the front door. "I guess you haven't changed as much as you'd like to think you have because you are still standing on the sidelines of life, waiting for it to happen to you."

Kate watched Lance walk away and fought not to call him back. But he'd lied to her. He was still engaged to another woman and worst of all, he didn't love her.

She closed the door and went back inside. She walked through the quietness of the living room, seeing the remains of their dinner.

She didn't understand how a man could be so perfect that she'd fall in love with him, and yet so disappointing.

She didn't know if it was just a sop for her heart or not, but she couldn't force herself to believe that Lance didn't care for her at least a little bit. Even if he didn't call it love.

Her house phone rang and she checked the caller ID.

"Hello, Lance."

"Listen, Kate. I'm not sure what I said back

there that made things get out of control the way they did. But I don't want to end this relationship."

Kate didn't, either. But as she looked around her lonely little town house she knew they couldn't continue the way they had been. There was a reason why Lance's engagement had spurred her into action. A reason why she'd been motivated to change things that she'd been content to leave before. And that reason was that she'd finally figured out that no man—especially not Lance—was going to fall in love with her if she just kept being there.

"I can't do this right now. I really need to think."

"Can't do what?"

"Talk to you. Because I'll agree to whatever you say and that's not healthy. Not for either one of us. You said you didn't know what love was, hadn't experienced it like this, and I know what you meant."

"What did I mean?"

He'd meant that he'd never had anyone like her in his life, someone who'd been so in love with him that they'd take whatever scraps of affection he threw their way. But she was done with that. She had more pride than that…she deserved better.

"You meant that it was okay for me to keep loving you," she said.

"More than okay," Lance said.

"Why? Do you love me?" Kate asked.

He hesitated and she had her answer.

"Damn it, Kate. I don't know what to say. I want you like I've never wanted any other woman," Lance said.

That didn't matter. Her physical appearance could change. Would that mean he wouldn't want her anymore?

"That's not enough."

"It's a start," Lance said.

"Yes, I guess it is. But I want the man I love to love me back. I want you to need to be with me the way I need to be with you."

"Katie-girl, you are making this more difficult than it has to be. Let me come back to your place and I'll prove to you that I need you just as much as you need me."

Kate was tempted to say yes. She almost did, but then she thought about the fact that sex wasn't love. It didn't mean that it couldn't be but with Lance, right now sex was just sex, no matter how good it was.

"I don't mean making love, Lance."

"Making love—you just said it yourself. It's an expression of our emotions."

"Ours? Do you love me?"

"Hell, girl, I just said I don't know."

"I know. I was pushing and I'm sorry. But I just don't know what else to do. You broke my heart when you got engaged. And tonight I found out you are still engaged."

She was rambling, so she just stopped talking. But she knew that some element of truth had been revealed there. She couldn't just keep loving him. Not now that she'd realized that he didn't really love her. And not now that she knew he was still engaged to Lexi.

"I'm not going to marry Lexi Cavanaugh, Kate. I can't marry another woman if I'm involved with you."

"Good. That makes me feel better. But until things are resolved between the two of you, I have to keep my distance."

"Why?"

Kate thought about it. She'd left the office feeling ashamed and didn't like that. And she knew it stemmed from the fact that she wasn't sure that Lance was her man.

She needed that certainty. If she had that then

everything they did together would be motivated by love. And that would be enough for her.

"I just have to. I'm sorry."

Silence buzzed over the open line and she wondered what Lance was thinking. No matter how well she'd come to know him over the last week, he was still an enigma to her.

And she realized that he probably always would be. That was part of what had made her fall in love with him to begin with. There were secrets and pain in Lance Brody's eyes and those very things had drawn her to him.

No matter what she did she had a feeling she was always going to love him.

"Goodbye, Lance."

He cursed under his breath. "Are you quitting Brody Oil and Gas, as well as quitting me?"

"Yes. I am. I won't be coming back to the office at all. In fact, I need to get away from Houston."

"You do that," he said. "Run away if you think that will help. But to be honest, I don't believe it will."

"How would you know?"

Lance didn't strike her as a man who'd run away from anything.

"My mother did it and I don't think she was any happier after she left us."

Lance hung up before she could say anything else. Kate was faced with the fact that she'd hurt Lance more deeply than she'd imagined she could. But she couldn't keep putting him first. She needed to take care of her heart, which felt as if it had been broken in two.

Ten

Figuring that this evening wasn't going to get any better, Lance put a call in to Lexi. He got her voice mail and even he knew better than to break an engagement via a message, so he simply asked her to call him back.

He didn't want to go home or to the office. Those two places were haunted by Kate even in his mind. Instead he drove to the Texas Cattleman's Club. Drinking with his buddies was exactly what he needed.

He tossed his keys to the valet and went

straight inside to the game room. He needed a drink and a game to set his mind straight.

His cell phone rang as he went to the self-service wet bar and poured himself a whiskey.

The area code was Virginia. That could only mean Lexi.

"Brody here," he said, answering the phone.

"It's Lexi. I got your message. What did you need to talk to me about?"

Lance took a swallow of his drink and sank down onto one of the large leather chairs.

"I wanted to have a word with you about our engagement," he said.

"Good. Father was asking me about it earlier today and I told him we hadn't talked about the arrangements. I know we didn't talk about dates but I was thinking the sooner the better."

Lance felt like an ass. There was no other way to put it. But he couldn't make the same mistake his father had. That marriage to his mother had ruined the old man. And may have been the trigger to all that anger in him.

"Lexi...I don't know how to say this."

"Say what?" she asked. "I was at Papyrus earlier today and found some beautiful invitations.

I am having them send you a sample so you can let me know if you approve or not."

This was getting worse by the second. He took a deep breath.

"Lexi, I can't marry you."

"What?"

"I'm sorry. But I am involved with another woman and I…" Lance choked on the words he had to say. *He loved Kate.* Hell. He loved her. Suddenly all of his doubts were gone and he knew why he couldn't let Kate go.

Love.

The one emotion he'd never let himself experience until Kate. That was why nothing had seemed right earlier when he was walking away. But Kate was the first person who should hear those words.

"I just can't marry you feeling the way I do about someone else."

"Who is it?"

"Kate Thornton."

"Your secretary. Lance, please, men of your station don't marry secretaries."

"I don't care. Kate's the woman I can't get out of my mind and I would make all of us miserable if I went through with a marriage to you."

Lexi was silent, and Lance knew that this wasn't the best way to deliver this kind of news. He should call Mitch and ask him to go to her and make this right.

"I'm very sorry."

"I am, too. My father really wanted this marriage."

"I know. And if it means he can't back the bill we asked him to then we will have to find another way to expand our operation. I just know that I don't want to consign either of us to a miserable life."

He took another swallow of his drink and then realized the truth he'd just spoken. Happiness was very important to him. He'd been searching for the happiness that had eluded him his entire life, and he wasn't going to find it unless Kate was by his side.

"I guess there's nothing more to say to you," Lexi said.

"I am sorry. But I think that you'll thank me for this one day."

"Please don't say that. This isn't something that I'm going to recover from easily."

"I didn't realize that you cared for me," Lance said.

"Well, I wouldn't have agreed to marry you if I didn't."

"Lexi—"

"I'm being cruel. You are a stranger to me as I am to you. I don't blame you for breaking this off."

She hung up and he sat there, feeling as if his life was like this empty room. And it had been for a while now. But he knew how to fill it.

The answer was Kate. But before he could go to her he had to take care of Lexi, had to make sure that Mitch ran interference with the senator.

He dialed his brother's cell phone. Mitch had just gotten back from DC. And he knew his brother wasn't going to be pleased.

"Its Mitch."

"I broke off my engagement with Lexi Cavanaugh," Lance said.

"What?! Why?"

"I couldn't marry her feeling the way I do about Kate."

"Kate? Since when do you care about her?" Mitch asked. "Does Lexi know this?"

"I just called her and she sounded upset. Listen, I know it may have complicated things with the senator but I think I love Kate and I can't let her slip through my fingers."

"This does more than complicate things, Lance. Damn it. I wish you'd spoken to me before you called Lexi."

"I'm sorry."

"You should be. I have no idea how I'm going to fix this. We need the senator on our side," Mitch said.

"If anyone can figure out how to make this work, it's you."

"I will figure it out. So you love Kate?" Mitch asked.

"Yes, I do. Damn it. I wanted her to be the first one I told."

"Well, what are you waiting for? Go tell her."

Lance was nervous as he drove to Kate's town house. He had no idea what to say. For once he had no idea how to handle a situation. This wasn't at all what he was used to. But then neither was Kate. And he was damned sure whatever happened he was going to make her listen to him.

When he got to her town house it was empty and her car was long gone. Where was she?

Lance searched for Kate for as long as he could but then realized he needed a professional.

He called Darius the next morning around ten. He stood in his office, unable to sit at his desk without seeing Kate as she'd been last night when she'd taken control of their lovemaking. He'd never realized that a woman could complete him on so many levels.

"It's Lance."

"Hey. I don't have any news on your fire," Darius said. Lance heard the sounds of a radio in the background.

"I'm not calling about that. I need a favor."

"Another one? They are stacking up. You are going to owe me."

"Yes, I am. But this is important."

"What do you need?"

Lance took a deep breath. "Kate Thornton is missing and I need you to find her."

"Okay, did you call the cops?" Darius asked.

"No. I don't think there has been foul play. I just need to find her and she's not taking my calls."

Darius started laughing. "You've got woman troubles."

"Yes, Darius, I do. And this woman—I need to find her. She's not like anyone else."

"Seriously?"

"Yes."

"Okay, I will help you. Give me her cell number."

Lance rattled off the number.

"Did you try her friends and family?"

"I called Becca Huntington, her best friend, but only got voice mail. And her parents haven't heard from her."

Lance looked out of the skyscraper window, wondering where the hell she was. He needed her and she wasn't here. He was going to tell her about this moment when he had her back in his arms.

Love should mean that they could count on each other. He knew she was hurting and that was why she'd left, but he needed her back.

"Give me a chance to work on this and I'll get back to you."

"Thanks, Darius."

"You're welcome, man."

Darius hung up and Lance paced around his office. He should be working. Work had always been his refuge when life got complicated but he just couldn't make himself do it this time. The only thing he could think about was Kate.

He saw her as she'd been when he'd first come back from DC, with her horn-rimmed glasses and baggy clothes. He pictured her in that short skirt and sleeveless sweater of yesterday and he realized that he'd cared about Kate for a long time. He just hadn't been paying attention.

His phone rang in the midafternoon. It was Darius.

"I've found her."

"Great. Tell me where she is."

"I think you need a plan. What are you going to do when you see her?" Darius asked.

"Tell her that she can't leave again and that she's mine."

"That's a horrible plan. Women need finesse," Darius said. "Stay in your office. I'm on my way over there."

Darius hung up before Lance could argue. Mitch walked into his office ten minutes later.

"What are you doing?" Mitch asked.

Lance had been pacing since Darius's call. "Waiting for Darius. He found Kate but he thinks... He's right I need a plan."

"What are you going to do?" Mitch asked.

Lance knew there was only one thing he could do at this point. He loved Kate and he wanted her to be his wife. "I'm going to tell her we are getting married."

Mitch nodded. "It makes sense. But I think you need to do it right this time. Kate's loved you forever."

"How do you know that?" Lance asked.

"Everyone knows that. I think you're the reason she stayed with us in the lean years. You've always been the man for her."

"I have?" Lance felt like he should have noticed this. No wonder Kate had reacted the way she had to his engagement to another woman. "I want to make this engagement the stuff of her dreams."

"Do you know what her dreams are?" Mitch asked.

He didn't. But he did know that Kate appreciated romantic gestures. The idea came to him then. He'd ask her to marry him in the formal dining room of the Texas Cattleman's Club. He would fill the space with candles and flowers and make it as romantic as he could.

He wanted Kate to know from the moment she stepped inside that he loved her. He wanted her to feel like the years she'd spent waiting for him to find her were worth it.

Because they were to him.

"Will you do me a favor?" he asked Mitch.

"Another favor," Darius said from the door. "You better hope we don't all call them in on the same day."

"Good, you're here. Mitch?"

"Sure, I'll help you out," Mitch said.

"Great. This is what I need you to do."

He told his brother and his best friend his plan, knowing that this was the way a man should get engaged. He should have his friends and family by his side, not be alone in a hotel room in a strange city.

Mitch agreed to go get Kate and bring her to the Cattleman's Club. Darius agreed to go get the ring that Lance had ordered from a downtown jeweler. And Lance went to the club to make sure every detail was perfect when Kate arrived.

Kate worked out in the Ritz's exercise room and then grabbed a bottle of water before heading for the elevator. She'd needed to get away, but going home to her parents hadn't seemed right. She really didn't want to travel anywhere so she'd packed a bag and come here.

She could be pampered, and order room service and forget about Lance Brody—except it wasn't working. Not at all. She'd woken from her sleep missing his arms around her.

She couldn't sleep without his chest under her cheek and the soothing beating of his heart in her ear. She wondered if she'd made the biggest mistake of her life in letting him go.

But at the same time, she knew there was no future for them unless she'd stood her ground.

And so here she was, on her ground and alone.

Being by herself wasn't a big deal, but being lonely was. She felt bereft, like she didn't know who she was or what she wanted.

Kate waited for the elevator feeling more out of place than she ever had before. And it wasn't the opulent surroundings that made her feel that way. It was her own emotions.

Lance had been her constant for so long, and a big part of her had believed that he always would be. She didn't know who she was if she didn't love Lance. And that was a big part of her problem. Getting over him was going to take longer than a week and she wondered if, having loved him and been his lover, she ever could.

The elevator arrived and she got in, pushing the number for her floor. When she arrived there, she got off and saw a man standing in the hallway near her room.

From the back he was almost as tall as Lance and for a minute her heart stopped beating, thinking it might be him. But then she realized how silly that was. Lance didn't know where she was.

As she got closer, she recognized the man as Mitch. He was on the phone but looked up as she approached.

He disconnected his call and put his phone in his pocket.

"I bet you are wondering why I am here."

"Yes, I am."

"Can we talk in your room?"

She nodded and moved past him to her door. She put her keycard in and then led the way into the bedroom. Mitch sat down in one of the guest chairs and she sat on the bed.

"Lance asked me to come."

"Why?"

"He needs to see you."

"And he couldn't come himself," Kate said. "You are your brother's emissary a lot." But she was elated. Lance had taken the only step he could to make their relationship work.

"I know, and I think its time I stopped speaking for him," Mitch said. "I've got a lot of work to do back in DC to fix the mess his broken engagement caused."

Kate nibbled her lower lip. "I'm sorry, Mitch."

He shook his head. "Don't be. Lance was always the man for you."

She shrugged. "I don't know about that any longer. I'm not sure where we stand."

"That's why he sent me here. He needs to talk to you face to face and since you weren't answering his calls, he figured an invitation from me would serve him better than another voice mail."

"I didn't mean to be childish," Kate said. "I just needed time to think. I don't know if you can understand this, Mitch, but when you love someone the way I do Lance, it makes you weak."

"Give Lance a chance to make it up to you," Mitch said. "Whatever he did to cause a rift between you, I know he's committed to making it right."

"I'm not sure he can. I want things from him... I guess you don't need to know this."

"I don't suppose I do," Mitch said. "But if you need to talk then don't stop."

She shook her head. She didn't need to talk to anyone except for Lance. "Where is he?"

"At the Texas Cattleman's Club in Somerset. You are invited to join him for dinner in the main dining room."

"Okay, I don't know where the club is."

Mitch laughed. "I'm going to escort you there."

"That's okay, Mitch. I can find my own way. Just leave the address for me."

"Are you sure?"

She nodded. "What time do I need to be there?"

"At six."

Mitch left and Kate took a shower. She got dressed, taking her time with her hair and make-up. She hadn't brought a formal dress with her but a quick call to the boutique downstairs fixed that. Soon she was dressed in a stunningly gorgeous cocktail dress and sexy heels.

And as she caught a glimpse of herself in the mirror, she realized that for the first time the outer woman matched the inner one. Regardless of what Lance said to her tonight, she was finally at peace with who she was.

Eleven

Kate gave her keys to the valet at the club and followed his directions to take the stairs to the entryway. She held her evening bag in one hand and fiddled nervously with the bracelet on her wrist.

She walked slowly up the steps in the heat of the Texas summer evening, feeling the weight of her hair against her bare back as she moved. A doorman opened the door for her as she approached and she smiled her thanks.

"Good evening, ma'am. May I help you?"

"I'm here for dinner with Lance Brody."

The man smiled at her. "Of course, right this way."

He led her to the left of the anteroom and then stopped at the bottom of the stairs. The club was a converted mansion and though Kate had heard about it before, this was the first time she'd been inside.

She noticed red rose petals on the stairs in a path.

"Follow the petals, ma'am."

She did, holding on to the banister for support as she climbed the stairs. She was speechless at the amount of planning Lance had done for this night. And she had a feeling that no matter what he said, she wasn't going to be able to walk away from him.

She got to the top of the stairs and saw Darius waiting for her.

"Hello, Kate. You look very nice tonight."

"Hi, Darius. What are you doing here?"

"Another favor for Lance. That boy is going to owe me big-time."

Darius offered her his arm and escorted her to

the main dining room. The room was lit only by candles, and fresh flowers had been placed on every table.

Darius led her to the table in the center of the room that had been set for dinner. He seated her.

"Lance will be here in a few moments. He wanted you to have this."

Darius handed her a white envelope. Her name was scrawled across the outside in Lance's spidery writing.

Darius walked away as she slid her finger under the flap of the envelope to open it. She pulled out a card which had a picture of the two of them from the Fourth.

Inside was a simple message.

I'm sorry. Your love is a precious gift and I'm blessed to have it.

She put the card down and turned to see Lance approaching. He wore a suit and looked so good in it. He was so handsome and sexy that she felt tears burn the back of her eyes because she knew that Lance Brody was her man, that he belonged to her.

"Hello, Kate."

"Thank you for the card," she said.

"You're welcome. I'm sorry things got out of hand the way they did."

She shook her head. "It's okay. I think I expected you to catch up to all the feelings I'd had for you for so long. But that was expecting too much."

Lance reached down and pulled her to her feet. He kissed her softly on her lips. "No, it wasn't."

He hugged her close in his arms and whispered in her ear. "I love you, Kate Thornton. I don't know how I didn't recognize it before this. But I can't live without you by my side."

She pulled back to look into his eyes. She needed to make sure that he believed what he was telling her, and she saw his love reflected there. She hugged him even closer and closed her eyes, afraid that she was dreaming this entire thing.

But Lance's arms around her were solid and real, and his scent filled every breath she took.

"Have a seat, Kate," he said.

She sat down and Lance got on his knee next to her. He took her hands in his and lifted them to his mouth to kiss them.

"Will you marry me, Kate?"

She stared down at him for a nanosecond before she said, "Yes!"

She stood up and Lance did, too. Kate threw herself in his arms and hugged him close to her, knowing that she'd found the man of her dreams.

Mitch and Darius congratulated them both, and Lance decided that they shouldn't wait to get married. He wanted to go by private jet to Vegas that very night.

"I can't get married without my best friend," Kate said.

"That's why I called her. Becca?"

Becca stepped into the room, smiling at her. "I've even invited your parents."

Since Lance had thought of everything, there was nothing else to do but say yes.

Lance stood in the wedding chapel at the Bellagio Hotel, waiting for his bride. His brother was standing next to him, and his best friend was seated next to Kate's parents.

He was filled with such joy and love for Kate that he knew this was the right thing to do. This was the way a man should feel when he thinks of his fiancée. And he knew that he'd asked the right woman to marry him this time.

The minister that they'd hired for the event smiled at him, and Lance felt a sense of rightness in his world that had long been missing. He and Mitch had been lucky in business and had the devil's own luck when it came to finding new wells, but this was the first time he'd felt lucky in love.

The music started, and Darius and Kate's parents stood up. Becca Huntington walked down the aisle first but then Kate stepped out and he stopped breathing. She was exquisite, this woman who was going to be his wife.

She walked slowly toward him and Lance couldn't see anyone but her. The minister went through the ceremony but Lance was just waiting for the end, waiting to kiss her and claim her as his for now and forever.

They exchanged I do's.

"I now pronounce you man and wife," the minister said. "You may kiss your bride."

Lance looked down into Kate's face and saw the love shining there in her eyes. He took her mouth with his and kissed her, showing her how happy she'd made him and what this evening meant to him.

Darius and Mitch clapped as they made their union official.

"I love you, Mrs. Lance Brody," Lance said.

Kate beamed at him. "Well, it's about time," she said, pulling him into another kiss.

* * * * *

ONE NIGHT WITH THE WEALTHY RANCHER

BY
BRENDA JACKSON

Brenda Jackson is a die "heart" romantic who married her childhood sweetheart and still proudly wears the "going steady" ring he gave her when she was fifteen. Because she's always believed in the power of love, Brenda's stories all have happy endings. In her real-life love story, Brenda and her husband of thirty-six years live in Jacksonville, Florida, and have two sons.

A *New York Times* bestselling author of more than fifty romance titles, Brenda is a recent retiree who worked thirty-seven years in management at a major insurance company. She divides her time between family, writing and traveling with Gerald. You may write Brenda at PO Box 28267, Jacksonville, Florida 32226, USA, by e-mail at WriterBJackson@aol.com, or visit her website at www.brendajackson.net.

To the love of my life, Gerald Jackson, Sr.

To everyone who joined me on the Madaris/
Westmoreland Family Reunion 2009 Cruise to Canada.
This one is for you!

"Provide things honest in the sight of all men."
—*Romans* 12:17

One

"What are you doing here, Summer?"

Summer Martindale's eyes froze on the document in front of her at the sound of the husky voice. It was a voice she hadn't heard in almost seven years, yet she distinctively remembered the sensuous timbre and how every audible vibration could stir her senses in a way that even today she could not explain.

In a way she wished she could forget.

She inhaled deeply and after a moment, she lifted her eyes and stared into Darius Franklin's dark and intense gaze. It was a gaze that was emitting a chilling glare.

Summer could just as easily glare back but refused to let him know how disturbing it was to see him again. What had once been between them was over and done with. He had made sure of that in the worst possible way, which she could never forgive him for. His actions had caused her pain—a degree of pain she vowed never to experience again.

"I could ask you the same thing, Darius," she finally responded. Her tone was just as sharp as his had been.

He stood tall, all six foot one inches of him, as he leaned in the doorway with his arms crossed over his chest and his gaze fixed directly on her. She thought at that moment the very same thing she'd thought when she'd first laid eyes on him. Darius Franklin, with his pecan tan complexion, close-cut black hair, charcoal gray eyes and neat pencil-thin mustache, was an extremely handsome man. But there were other noticeable changes. His cheekbones appeared more pronounced and his lips seemed firmer.

His dark stare, as well as the way a muscle seemed to twitch in his jaw, were all the evidence she needed that he wasn't happy to see her and if truth be told, she wasn't happy to see him, either. It would be a lie to claim she hadn't thought about him over the years, because she had. Yet at the same time, the memory of what he'd put her through—the humiliation, heartbreak and pain—made her regret ever lowering her guard and letting him into her life.

He stepped away from the door and she watched his every move, wishing she weren't drawn to how fit his body was, and wishing a tug of desire had not invaded her stomach. Although he wasn't as lean as he used to be, he wore his masculinity well. Well-toned muscles outlined his chest and shoulders—muscles she could easily see through the material of his chambray shirt. And then there were jeans that hugged his firm hips and strong thighs. They were thighs that could keep a tight hold on hers as he thrust deeper and deeper inside of her.

She forced the turbulent memories away. Her gaze moved back up to his eyes and she tried not to flinch at the cold look in them. Something inside her shivered and she wondered how a man she had once fallen in love with so deeply could end up treating her so shabbily.

"I live here in Somerset."

His voice cut through Summer's thoughts. *He lived here in Somerset? Maverick County?* That information immediately filled her with apprehension and dread, as well as curiosity. *When had he left the Houston Police Department and why?*

"I live in Somerset, as well," she heard herself say. "I moved to town last month to work here at Helping Hands as a social worker."

Surprise lit his eyes. "A social worker?"

"Yes."

She understood his surprise. When he'd last seen her seven years ago, he'd been twenty-four years old and a detective with the Houston Police Department. And she'd been a nineteen-year-old trying to escape the clutches of an abusive fiancé by the name of Tyrone Whitman. After she had broken off their engagement, Tyrone had refused to get out of her life, to leave her alone. He had stalked her for months before he'd finally caught her alone in her apartment, and for three hours he had held a gun to her head, threatening to blow her brains out.

While the SWAT team had been trying to talk Tyrone into surrendering, Darius had broken into the apartment by coming through a bathroom window. He'd apprehended Tyrone and saved her. That night, Darius Franklin had become her knight in shining armor.

He was the same man who had stopped by her apartment the next day to repair the window, and the same man who, after learning that a not-too-smart judge had posted bail for Tyrone, made it his business to become her protector until the trial. After that, he was the same man who she began seeing on a daily basis, who would drop by when his shift changed to spend time with her, to show her how special he thought she was.

The same man who during that time, for one night, had been her lover.

"So, you went to college and got your degree?" he asked, and for a split second she could have sworn she detected a degree of admiration in his voice, but the look in his hard gaze told her she'd been wrong.

"Yes, I got my degree," she responded, proud of her accomplishment and quickly remembering he was one of the few people who'd encouraged her to do so, and convinced her that she could. He had made her believe in herself. And a part of her had believed in them, in a future together. He had proven her wrong.

"Congratulations."

"Thank you," she said briskly, putting aside the document she had been reading. "So, why are you here, Darius? Although we've established the fact that we're both living in Somerset, I'm sure this town is big enough for the both of us. What brings you to Helping Hands?"

"I'm here to install the security system as well as the billing account for the shelter," he said, as if that explained everything.

She nodded. "I was told the Texas Cattleman's Club would be sending someone over to do those things," she said, finding it hard to concentrate.

She had heard a lot about the Texas Cattleman's Club, a group of men who considered themselves the protectors of Texas and whose members consisted of the wealthiest men in Texas, mostly from old money. The TCC was known to help a number of worthy causes in the community and Helping Hands, a newly opened women's shelter located in the small, impoverished section of wealthy Maverick County, was one of them. They provided all the shelter's funding.

Summer had interviewed for the position at the shelter and once she had been offered the job, had decided it would be a good way to have a fresh start. She had made the move from Austin, where she had been living for the past six years.

"How did you get the job?" She couldn't help but ask.

He shrugged. "I own a security company."

She raised a brow, surprised he had gotten out of law enforcement. He'd made a good police detective and she'd figured it would be his career. "How long have you been living in Somerset?" she asked.

"Around six years."

It was the same amount of time she had lived in Austin. He had moved here a year after they had broken up. She quickly recalled that they really hadn't broken up since they had never truly been together…at least not like she'd assumed they had.

"If you're through with your interrogation, I'd like to get to work," he said.

"Fine. I'll get out of your way if you need to work in here for a while," she said, getting up from her desk. Seeing him again after all this time was just a bit too much. Bittersweet memories were trying to invade her brain and she was determined to fight them back.

"If you need anything, just let the shelter's secretary, Marcy Dillard, know. I'll use this time to go to lunch."

She grabbed her purse out of her desk drawer and quickly moved past him toward the door.

"Summer?"

She paused just before reaching the door and turned around. "Yes?"

He still had a hard look in his eyes. "I would say welcome to town, but I wouldn't mean it."

She narrowed her gaze. "Then I guess that means we'll have to learn to tolerate each other, doesn't it?"

Without waiting for him to respond, she turned and continued walking out the door.

* * *

Darius leaned back against the desk and watched Summer until she was no longer in sight. It was only then that he made an attempt to begin breathing normally again. But it was hard because although he couldn't see her, he still managed to feel her presence.

Seven years was a long time, yet today when a startled Summer had looked up at him and met his gaze, he'd felt a sensation that was like a swift kick in the gut. Potent memories had flooded his mind, forcing him to recall what she had come to mean to him in such a short period of time, and just how deep her betrayal had cut.

He hit his fist on the desk, angry and frustrated. How could he still find her so desirable after all this time? After all she'd done? Why had seeing her sent sensuous shivers down his spine? She was seven years older, no longer a mere nineteen-year-old who hadn't decided what she wanted out of life other than to be free of an obsessive ex-fiancé. She was just as stunning as he remembered. Even more so.

She had matured beautifully. She was about five-eight, tall and slim with shoulder-length straight brown hair and hazel eyes he could always drown in. Her skin tone, the color of café au lait, had always tempted him to lick her all over.

Darius bowed his head momentarily as even more memories he had tried so hard to forget resurfaced.

After college, he'd gotten a job with the Houston Police Department as a detective with aspirations of moving up the ranks. Authorities had been called to the scene regarding a domestic dispute, and Darius and his partner, Walt Stewart, had been the first to arrive.

A young woman who had obtained a restraining order against her ex-fiancé was in danger. The man, named Tyrone Whitman, had broken into her apartment and was holding a gun to her head, threatening to kill her unless she took him back.

While Walt tried talking him into surrendering, Darius was able to get into the apartment through a rear bathroom window, overtake Whitman and free Summer.

Concern for her safety when Whitman was released on bond allowed Darius to convince himself that it was important to keep checking on her. But then it became obvious it was a lot more than that. Point-blank, he had been attracted to her and thought she was a special woman who'd gotten mixed up with the wrong guy, and was trying to get her life together. Against his better judgment, although he'd been warned by Walt that Summer wasn't really what she seemed, he had fallen for her, and fallen hard.

He'd assumed he had gotten to know her, and thought she felt the same way after a night they had spent together filled with so much sexual chemistry that it could only end one way: they had made love. Deep, passionate love. Shudders passed through him just remembering that night and the effect it had on him. It was a night he could never forget, although over the past seven years he had tried like hell to do so.

And it was a night that apparently had meant more to him than it had to her.

The following day he had left town when he received word of his brother Ethan's near-fatal car accident. He'd had to leave immediately for Charleston and when he couldn't reach Summer, and had been unable to leave her a message because her voice-mail box was full, he'd left word with his partner to let her know what happened. When he had returned to Houston a week later, he discovered that Summer had packed up and left town without leaving word as to where she'd gone. She'd told Walt to tell him that she wanted to build a new life for herself and was leaving town with an older man. A very wealthy one—something Darius was not.

After nearly losing his brother, it had almost destroyed him to find out that he had lost her, that she had turned her back on what could have been between them to take up with a man with money.

A hard smile formed on his lips and he wondered what she would think to discover that he was now a wealthy man, thanks to smart investments and the success of his security firm. She thought he'd been hired as a laborer for the TCC—he could just imagine her reaction when she discovered he was a member of the Texas Cattleman's Club. The same club that was funding the shelter, including her salary.

Another thought crept into his mind, one that made his skin crawl. What if she knew already? What if the reason she was in Somerset was because she'd heard about his success and assumed after all this time she could ease her way back in his good graces? A woman looking for a wealthy husband would do just about anything. He'd been gullible before and wondered if she thought he would be gullible again. Considering her actions seven years ago, he wouldn't put anything past her.

He leaned against her desk as those thoughts filled his mind. She wasn't wearing a ring on her finger, which was a good indication that she wasn't married. And she *had* acted surprised to see him. But then it could have very well been an act. He had found out the hard way just what a good actress she was. One thing was for certain: he wouldn't be letting his guard down. She had taken advantage of his heart before but she wouldn't be doing so again.

He was about to begin the work he'd come to do when his cell phone went off. Recognizing the special ringtone, he pulled it off his belt and clicked it on. "Yes, Lance?"

"Hey, man, sorry I missed your call earlier."

"No problem. I just wanted you to know that I heard from Fire Chief Ingle. I'm meeting with him tomorrow evening to go over some things. He indicated that he'll have the official report ready in a week and that it contains proof that the fire was deliberately set."

Lance Brody was Darius's best friend from college at the University of Texas, where the two of them, along with another good friend, Kevin Novak, had been roommates. The three had forged a bond that would last a lifetime. There was nothing one wouldn't do for the other and Darius could rightly say that he could give his two friends credit for his financial success.

Lance, along with his younger brother Mitch, had come from old money and together they owned Brody Oil and Gas Company. The two had included Darius in a number of successful investment opportunities. So had Kevin, who'd made his fortune in real estate development.

Lance and Kevin had grown up in Somerset and had tried convincing Darius to move there after college but he had opted for the job in Houston instead. Then, shortly after that incident with Summer, he'd decided he would move to Somerset to start a new career and a new life.

He worked closely with his friends, and Lance had hired him to investigate a fire at the Brody Oil and Gas refinery a few weeks ago. Although there was significant damage, no one had gotten seriously hurt. Darius had no doubt the fire had been the work of an arsonist, and now Chief Ingle had confirmed his suspicions.

"I can't wait until we nail Alex. I intend to make sure that he rots in jail," Lance was saying.

Lance and Mitch were certain they knew the identity of the arsonist. He was the long-time hated rival of the Brodys, a man by the name of Alejandro "Alex" Montoya.

"Calm down, Lance. The man is innocent until proven guilty," Darius said.

"Wait until the report comes out. Mark my word, Alex Montoya is the person behind that fire."

"That may very well be the case," Darius said, knowing just how convinced Lance was of Alex's guilt. "But it has to be proven. How's Kate?" Darius asked, trying to change the subject. Lance and Kate had eloped to Vegas a few weeks ago.

"Kate's fine and I know what you're trying to do, Darius."

Darius couldn't help but chuckle. "If you know, then humor me. I need like hell to laugh about now."

"Sounds like it's been one of those days for you," Lance said.

"You don't know the half of it. Summer is here."

There was a pause. "Summer? *Your* Summer?"

Darius could have really laughed out loud at that one, since Summer had never truly been his. But at one time he'd thought she was, and he had told Lance all about her. "Yes, Summer Martindale."

"What's she doing in Somerset?"

Darius sighed deeply. "She's a social worker at Helping Hands. I showed up to set up security and work on the billing system for the place, and walked right into her office."

"Must have been one hell of a reunion."

"Hey, what can I say?"

Lance chuckled. "You can say you need a drink. Sounds like it, anyway. Meet me at the TCC Café when you're ready to take a break for lunch."

Moments later, Darius hung up the phone thinking Lance was right. He needed a drink.

Summer settled into the booth at the Red Sky Café three blocks from the shelter. It was the first week of

August and such a beautiful day that she had enjoyed the walk. It had given her a chance to compose herself after seeing Darius again.

She glanced around the café. The Red Sky was a place she had been frequenting for lunch since working at Helping Hands and she had become friendly with the owners. The Timmons had grown up in this section of Maverick County and had been instrumental in approaching members of the TCC about the need for a shelter in the community.

The shelter was a full-service center that provided a safe place for women who'd experienced all types of violence to heal and plan for their future. Helping Hands had opened their doors a few months ago and she'd been hired as part of its counseling team. Summer couldn't help but appreciate the members of the Texas Cattleman's Club for funding the shelter. She of all people knew how important such a facility was.

She had dated Tyrone for a few months, but it was only after they'd gotten engaged that she'd discovered his mean-spirited, possessive nature that on occasion would become abusive, both mentally and physically. She had sought the help of a shelter in Houston and there had found the strength to break things off with him. The social worker at the shelter had helped her to see that although she couldn't control Tyrone's behavior toward her, she could control how she responded to it and remove herself from the situation.

Her choice to end things was something Tyrone couldn't accept and he had begun stalking her, which was the reason she'd put the restraining order in place. Months had gone by when he'd appeared at her apartment one night, and forced his way inside, threatening her life. Chills went up her spine as she remembered that time.

After her own horrible experience with Tyrone, not to mention her heartbreak with Darius, she didn't trust her instincts where men were concerned so she just left them alone. Over the years she had buried herself in her books, getting her degree. After college she had concentrated on her work as an advocate for battered women.

"What are you going to have today, Miss Martindale?"

Summer smiled as she glanced up into the face of Tina Kay, one of the waitresses. Tina had been one of her first clients at Helping Hands and at seventeen, one of her youngest. A runaway after being shifted from foster home to foster home, Tina had become the victim of physical abuse at the hands of her boyfriend, a guy who had convinced her she deserved the beatings he'd been giving her.

Summer couldn't help but recall her own story. After high school, she had wanted to see the world. Aunt Joanne, who had raised her after her parents had been killed in a car accident when she was thirteen, tried to get her to remain in Birmingham. But she'd left Alabama to work her way to California. Along the way, she ended up in Houston where she found a job as a waitress at a chain restaurant. That's where she'd met Tyrone. The company he worked for frequently made deliveries to the restaurant. Something told her he was bad news, but she had wanted to believe there was some good in him. Boy, had she been wrong.

"Just the usual," Summer finally said, relaxing in her seat, looking forward to her grilled chicken salad.

She took a moment to study Tina, who looked so different than the young woman who'd come to the shelter with a swollen eye, cuts around her mouth and bruises on various parts of her body. "And how have you been doing, Tina?" she asked.

Tina's smile widened. "I've been doing fine. The Timmons are letting me use the apartment above their garage. I've enrolled to take classes at the local community college next month and thought I'd brush up on my math. That's always been my weakest subject. I ordered one of those do-it-yourself math books online."

"And how are those self-defense classes going?" The shelter offered the classes weekly and attendance was always at capacity.

"They've been great. The instructor is just awesome. I've learned a number of techniques to protect myself."

She could hear the excitement in Tina's voice and felt good about it. The man who had roughed Tina up had left town but there was a warrant out for his arrest. Summer's thoughts shifted to Tyrone, who'd gotten a twenty-year sentence. It would have been less if he hadn't told the judge just where he could shove it. She shook her head, wondering how she could have ever thought that she loved the man. She could now admit that at eighteen she had been young and rather foolish.

"I'll be back with your order in a second," Tina said.

When Tina walked off, Summer settled back in her seat, allowing herself to think about the man she'd left at the shelter. The one man she had tried so hard to forget. She'd thought moving to Somerset would be a fresh start. A new town. New people. A new job. She hadn't figured on being confronted with a blast from her past.

One thing she told the women she counseled at the shelter was that they could confront and conquer any challenge they were presented with, and she knew she needed to take that same advice. Fate was playing a cruel trick by putting her and Darius in the same town. But she would handle it. And she would handle him.

An irritated and frustrated Darius walked into the TCC Café and glanced around at his surroundings. What used to be a twenty-six-room mansion had been converted into a place where the TCC members could unwind and relax, which was just what he needed.

In addition to the café, the TCC also included a golf course, a state-of-the-art spa, riding stables and an air-conditioned pool house with a retractable roof as well as numerous meeting rooms, game rooms, a well-stocked library and a formal dining room.

Darius, Lance and Kevin, along with Mitch and

another friend of the Brodys named Justin Dupree, spent a lot of time shooting pool in the game room. Last fall they were practically glued to the club's projection television screen during football season.

He saw Lance sitting at a table in the back. The café served both lunch and dinner and it wasn't uncommon for Lance to meet him here for lunch. However, nowadays Lance was quick to rush back to the office since his new wife Kate had decided to remain at Brody Oil and Gas as Lance's administrative assistant.

Darius shook his head. Knowing Lance the way he did, he doubted his best friend let Kate get much work done. Hell, he wouldn't either if he had the woman he loved pretty much underfoot all day.

The woman he loved.

Something twisted in his gut at the thought. Thanks to Summer, he doubted he would ever be able to love another woman again.

"I need a beer," he said, frowning, sliding into the booth across from Lance.

"I've already ordered you one. I was looking out the window when you drove up," Lance said, studying Darius carefully.

"Thanks. I had hoped to at least get the security analysis completed on most of the computers today so I can decide what software will work best," Darius said, smiling a thanks to the waitress who placed a mug of beer in front of him.

"So, you're going to do it instead of one of your men?"

Darius nodded. "Heath left yesterday for Los

Angeles to guard some actress who's been getting death threats, and Milt is still in Dallas," he said of two of the six men who worked for him. "The others have been assigned to various other projects around town. That means I'll have to go back over to the shelter when I leave here."

Lance nodded as he took a plug from his own beer. "It also means you'll be seeing Summer again."

Darius didn't say anything. Yes, that meant he would probably see Summer again today. No telling how many more times he'd see her before he finished up what needed to be done at the shelter.

Because of the nature of what went on at women's shelters, Helping Hands needed top security twenty-four hours a day, seven days a week. The TCC had decided to upgrade all the computers to eliminate the risk of getting hacked. The majority of the women seeking refuge at the shelter were the victims of domestic violence, women whose lives could be placed in danger if their batterers discovered their where-abouts.

"Tell me about her, Darius."

Darius met Lance's gaze. "I've practically told you everything about how we met and how things ended. She went to college and got a degree, and now works for the shelter."

"Did you mention anything to her about being a member of TCC?"

"No. She thinks my company was hired to handle security at the shelter."

Lance smiled. "In a way, that's true."

"Yes, which is why she doesn't need to know any different." Darius felt his face harden when he said, "There can never be anything between me and Summer again."

Yet he knew making sure of that wouldn't be easy. Summer was the type of woman who easily got under a man's skin. Just the memory of walking into that office and finding her sitting behind the desk had the power to make him feel weak and vulnerable.

And that was the one thing he could not let happen. He did not have a special woman in his life and preferred keeping it that way. Desire for anything more had died seven years ago with Summer's betrayal.

Two

"Mr. Franklin wanted me to let you know he left for lunch but will be coming back, Ms. Martindale."

"Oh. Thanks, Marcy," Summer said, trying to keep her voice as normal as she could. After taking a file off Marcy's top tray, she went into her office and closed the door behind her.

Today she had taken an extra-long lunch, hoping by the time she returned Darius would have finished what he'd come to do. But it seemed that would not be the case. Summer bit her lip, deciding she would be professional as well as mature about the matter. He had a job to do and so did she, and as long as they each knew where the other stood, there was no reason they couldn't at least be decent to each other. But then what right did he have to be upset with her since she was the injured party? He was the one who'd left town after discussing their night together with his partner. He probably didn't know Walt had told her the truth, and he was upset because she had left town when he'd returned. It was crazy how men thought sometimes, but it didn't matter now. He had made it quite clear what he thought of her and she hoped she'd left no doubt in his mind just what she thought of him. So there. That was that.

She dropped down in her chair thinking, no, that wasn't that at all. Not as long as the sight of him could send sensations oozing up her spine. Whenever he looked at her, even with anger flaring in the dark depths of his eyes, she felt stirrings in places she didn't want to think about. He'd always had that effect on her. In the past she'd welcomed it, but now she despised it.

She drew in a deep breath and for the first time in years, she felt like the world was closing in on her. It had taken her a while after leaving Houston to pull herself together and decide that no man—Tyrone or Darius—was worth that much pain. But she had moved on with her life. She was proud of her accomplishment and intended to obtain her doctorate after working in her field a few years.

"Don't you have anything to do?"

Summer blinked and saw Darius standing in her doorway. She glared at him—so much for thinking they could be decent to each other. "You should have knocked before entering my office."

He shrugged. "The door was open."

"And that gives you the right to just walk in? I could have been with a client."

"In that case, I would hope you'd be professional enough to shut the door for privacy. But you aren't with a client *and* you knew I was coming back, so stop making a big deal out of it," he said, stepping into her office and closing the door behind him.

Summer just stared at him for a moment, wondering how on earth the two of them were supposed to get along. Of course, whoever hired him had no idea they knew each other, and there was no way she could go to anyone at the TCC and request that they swap security companies without a valid reason.

"Look, Darius. You have a job to do and so do I. Evidently, I'm the last person you expected to see today. However, we're professionals and are mature enough to make the best of it. It shouldn't take you more than a day at the most to finish up here and—"

"Wrong."

She lifted her brow. "Excuse me?"

He crossed his arms over his chest. "I said you're wrong. Finishing up things here will take me every bit of a week. Possibly two."

His words hit her like a ton of bricks. "You've got to be kidding."

"I don't kid."

She pressed her lips together to keep from saying, *No, but you do kiss and tell.* Instead, she asked, "Why will it take *that* long to install a security system?"

There was a pause. A long pause. And for a moment, she wasn't sure he was going to answer her.

"The reason it will take so long is because in addition to installing a new security system on all the computers in this building, I'll be setting up a billing system for the Texas Cattleman's Club. I'm getting paid well to do a good job and I don't intend to do otherwise by rushing through things just to make your life less miserable."

"My life isn't miserable," she all but snapped.

"Sorry. It was foolish of me to assume that it was. And I see you're not wearing a ring so I guess you didn't get a rich husband after all."

Summer wondered what he was talking about and decided she really didn't want to know. "Look, Darius—"

He moved to her desk so quickly she jerked back in her chair. He placed his palms down on her desk and leaned over, his face within inches of hers. "No, you look, Summer. You're right, we are two professionals. Two adults who just happened to have had an affair that led to nowhere. I'm over it and so are you. So let's move on."

"Fine," she snapped.

"Great." He straightened his tall form, moved away from her desk and looked at a closet door across the room. "Unfortunately, the mainframe is in this office so I'll be spending more time in here than any other place. You might be inconvenienced a few times."

"If I'm scheduled to meet with clients, I'll use one

of the vacant conference rooms," she said, trying to keep her voice civil.

He nodded. "And if you're not scheduled to meet with a client?"

"I have the ability to work through distractions."

He lifted a brow and held her gaze for a moment. "Do you?"

"Yes."

"Then we don't have anything to worry about," he said, looking at his watch. "Are you meeting with a client sometime today?"

"No, I just have paperwork to do. Will you be shutting down my computer?" She could tell they were both trying to be courteous and hold a decent conversation in less-than-biting tones. But in spite of everything, she couldn't stop the sensations that stirred inside of her every time she looked into his eyes.

"No, but if that changes I'll give you advanced warning."

"Thank you."

He moved to the other side of the room. "Right now I need to get into this closet."

She swallowed as she stared at him under her lashes. His hands were on his hips, unconsciously drawing emphasis to his jean-clad hips and thighs. Tapered. Perfectly honed.

Deciding she had seen enough—probably too much—she picked up a file off her desk, leaned back in her chair and began reading. She tried like heck to concentrate on the document in front of her, but every so often she would look up and glance over at Darius. He was standing in front of a huge unit that had a bunch of wires running from it. He was concentrating on the computer's mainframe but her eyes were concentrated on him, drinking him in with feminine appreciation. He might be an arrogant ass but he was a good-looking one.

And as if he could feel her eyes on him, he looked up and met her gaze. Their eyes held for a moment longer than necessary before she dropped hers back to the document in front of her, thinking, *so much for working through distractions.*

Darius stared at Summer. Although he wished he were anyplace else other than here, he couldn't stop looking at her and remembering. She had gone back to reading, so he let his gaze travel over her, noticing the way her shoulder-length hair had fallen in her face. She absently brushed it back, giving him a view of her face once again. It was a face that had been his downfall the first time he'd seen it.

He could vividly recall just when that had been. After crawling through her bathroom window, she had seen him before Whitman had known he was in the house. With eye contact, Darius had encouraged her to stay calm and not give him away. Using the training he'd acquired, it had taken only a couple of quick kicks to bring Whitman down. He hit the ground before he'd realized what had happened to him.

It was then that a nearly traumatized Summer had

rushed into his arms, holding on to him as if her life depended on it. Even after the police officers had rushed in and handcuffed Whitman, she had still held on to him, like she was too shaken to let him out of her sight. Since it had been almost quitting time, he had followed the squad car that had taken her to the hospital to get checked out. He'd also dropped by her place the next day to repair her broken window.

During the weeks that followed, he would find some excuse or other to see her, and when he'd learned that her ex had been let out on bail, he had made it a point to drive by her house a couple of times a night just to make sure she was okay. Most of the time they would sit in her living room and talk.

During that time Summer had shared a lot about her life. He knew she had been raised by an aunt and that she had left her hometown of Birmingham, Alabama, for California with dreams of becoming an actress or, better yet, to find a rich older man to marry. At the time he'd thought she was teasing, but he'd discovered a few months later she'd been dead serious.

He'd found out the hard way that while he had been falling in love with her, she had been looking for a man with a lot more money than he'd had.

He fought back the anger that tried consuming him all over again, anger that seven years hadn't erased. He must have muttered something under his breath because she looked up and again their eyes met.

He tried looking away but couldn't. And when he moved to close the closet he told himself to head straight for the door and walk out. However, he couldn't do that, either.

Instead, he found himself crossing the room to where she was sitting. Although he had tried to forget it, he was still bothered by the fact that she had left him for another man. A man who had been old enough to be her father from what he'd heard.

By the time he reached her, she was standing. "What is wrong with you?" she asked, backing away from him until her back hit a solid wall and she couldn't go any farther.

His lips curved into a forced smile. "There's nothing wrong with me, Summer."

"Then what do you think you're doing?" she asked in a whisper.

"You still ask too many questions," he murmured, just seconds before leaning in and capturing her mouth with his.

The instant their mouths touched it registered in Summer's brain that she didn't have to accept his kiss. She could outright refuse it. However, any thoughts of doing so tumbled from her mind as he expertly took control of her mouth in a way she remembered so well.

His tongue surged between her parted lips and the moment it tangled with hers, she was a goner. Instead of being swamped with memories of the past, she was overtaken by sensations from the present, where he was causing a stir within her so effortlessly.

And it wasn't just about tongue play; it was a lot more than that. It was about body heat and the way she felt pressed against him, with his arms wrapped firmly around her waist and hers finding their way around his neck.

And then it was about a need. She could not characterize his, but she could certainly define her own. It had been seven years since she had been kissed by a man. Seven years of denying herself this one particular pleasure as well as numerous others. Those denials, especially the primal ones, were coming back to haunt her in the worst kind of way, thanks to him.

And then, she thought, when he pulled her body closer to his, closer to his heat, there was the idea, the very fact, that after all this time she was still attracted to him and he to her. Some things couldn't change. There was the chemistry, physical attraction, sexual tension. Lust was a strong benefactor, especially when motivated and fueled by sexual need.

He changed the angle of his mouth to deepen the kiss and tightened his hold around her waist. And then he used his tongue to taste her in a way he'd never done before. It was as if he were trying to get reacquainted with her flavor, sliding his tongue from one side of her mouth to the other.

Then, in a move she could only deem as sensuously strategic, he captured her tongue with his and began mating with it in a way that nearly brought her to her knees. He was building desire within her, slowly escalating their fiery exchange. Her hands moved from his neck to his shoulders, and then she spread her palms over his back as he elicited a response from her that she felt in every pore of her body.

Despite the greedy protest of her lips, he finally pulled his mouth away from hers. She drew in a much-needed breath. The kiss had been totally unexpected—completely without warning—and had managed to leave her breathless, speechless, with her senses heightened to their full capacity.

And then reality returned. She stiffened, determined that he would not assume the kiss would be the first of many, or that he was on the verge of finding his way back into her heart with the sole purpose of finding his way back into her bed.

Too late she began berating herself for letting the kiss last as long as it had. He was staring at her and she wondered if the kiss—especially the intensity of it—had been some kind of point he'd wanted to make. Probably, but she had news for him.

"If you want to keep your job, Darius, I would advise you to never do that again," she said in a cutting tone. "If you do, I will report your actions to the Texas Cattleman's Club. I'm sure there are other security companies they could use to do what you were hired to do."

She thought she saw a smile touch his lips before his gaze narrowed slightly. "Does it matter that you kissed me back? Moaned in my ear? Rubbed your body against mine?" he asked with a hint of scorn in his voice.

Summer felt heat flush her cheeks. Had she actually done all those things while they'd been kissing? Okay, she had returned his kiss, possibly even moaned a few times in his ear, but had she really rubbed her body against his? Due to the intensity of the exchange, that may very well have been a possibility. But that didn't mean she'd given him free rein to enjoy her mouth anytime the mood suited him. She needed to make sure he understood that.

"Fair warning, Darius. Kevin Novak of the TCC will be meeting with me this week to see how things are going at the shelter, and we'll be discussing ways that things around here can be improved. I'm sure getting this job was a feather in your cap and I'd hate to ask that you be replaced, but I will if you don't keep your hands to yourself."

His gaze locked on to hers for longer than necessary, and then he stepped back. Evidently, he realized she hadn't just made an idle threat. There was a long silence as they stood there staring at each other and then to her surprise, he smiled and said, "You enjoyed that kiss just as much as I did and I will bring up that fact to Mr. Novak if he questions me about anything. If you're thinking about putting me on the hot seat, then be ready to join me there. The TCC hired you to do a job, just like they hired me."

His dark eyes hardened. "And need I remind you that I've been living in Somerset a lot longer than you have? People around here know I'm a professional who's selective when it comes to friends. I have a tarnish-free reputation. This is a nice town, close-knit. You're the stranger here, Summer, not me. But I will heed your wishes. The next kiss, you'll initiate. Until then, you're safe with me."

She lifted her chin, wondering when he had become so arrogant, so sure of himself. For him to assume she would make a move on him was outright preposterous. "That won't happen."

He smiled. "Then I guess that means you're safe with me."

She was about to give him a blistering retort when his cell phone rang. "Excuse me," he said, and Summer watched as he quickly pulled it from his belt clip. She figured it was probably some woman calling him.

He muttered a few words to the caller and then glanced back at her and said, "I need to take this call. Remember what I said." And then he turned and walked out of her office.

Darius strolled into the lobby of the shelter, a safe distance from Summer's office, yet close enough so he could see if she left. He pulled in a deep breath and then remembered he had Kevin holding on the phone.

"Okay, Kev, I can talk now. What's up?"

"Just a reminder we're meeting at the TCC's game room Thursday night to shoot pool."

Darius couldn't help but grin. If Kev was calling to remind everyone, that meant he was feeling lucky. "I won't forget."

"Where are you?" Kevin asked.

"At Helping Hands. I decided to install the security system myself since I'm the one who's going to set up TCC's billing account for the shelter. Besides, all my men are handling other projects."

Darius then remembered something. "Your name came up in a conversation I had with the social worker here, Summer Martindale. You're supposed to meet with her sometime this week."

"Yeah, don't remind me. That was something Huntington was supposed to do and he delegated it to me like he's the king and I'm one of his lowly subjects. That man really grates on my last nerve."

Darius understood just how Kevin felt. He, Lance, Mitch and Justin all felt the same way. The five of them, along with Alex Montoya, were the most recent inductees into the Texas Cattleman's Club. This didn't sit well with some of the club's old guards—namely Sebastian Huntington and his stuffy cohorts—who for some reason felt the younger men really weren't deserving of membership in what was known as the most exclusive social club in the state of Texas.

"Hey, man, I thought all of us agreed to just overlook Huntington and his band of fools," Darius reminded his friend.

"Yeah, but he just rubs me the wrong way at times. He doesn't want to put his full support behind the shelter since the funding of it was our idea and not his."

"But he was outvoted, so eventually he'll get over it," Darius said. "And if he doesn't, then that's too bad. Maybe it's a good thing that he's having you do it instead of him. He wouldn't do anything but find fault with everything anyway."

"You're probably right. So, you've met Ms. Martindale?"

"Yes. She's the Summer I was involved with before moving here to Somerset."

"Damn, man, she's *that* Summer?"

"Yes, she is *that* Summer." Kevin didn't know as much about what had happened as Lance, but both of his best friends knew Summer had screwed him over in a bad way, which was the reason he'd wanted to leave Houston and start a new life here in Somerset.

"I need you to do me a favor," he said to Kevin.

"Sure. What do you need?"

It had always been this way between him, Lance and Kevin since their college days. Kevin had agreed to the favor without even knowing what would be required of him. The three trusted each other implicitly. "I'll go into full details when I see you Thursday night, but when you meet with Summer Martindale, if my name comes up, I don't want it mentioned that I'm affiliated with the TCC."

"No problem."

Darius had made the decision to tell Summer the truth when he was good and ready. He couldn't wait to see her face when she realized he was probably just as wealthy as the old man she had left him for.

He and Kevin began talking about the update he'd gotten on the fire at the Brody refinery. Darius was listening to Kevin's take on why he thought Alex Montoya was responsible when he heard footsteps on the tile floor. He glanced up to see Summer walking out of her office. He was standing behind a pillar, so she didn't have a full view of him, which to his way of thinking was a good thing. That way he could check her out at his leisure.

She walked over to a row of file cabinets and he quickly recalled that he'd always thought her walk was a turn-on. There was a sexy sway to her hips with every step she took. She was wearing a pair of brown slacks and a light blue blouse. The lush curves of her hips and the firm swell of her breasts were outlined to perfection by her outfit. He couldn't help standing there staring, taking in everything about her. He easily picked up on the differences in her, differences that, considering everything, he still couldn't help but appreciate.

She seemed a lot more self-assured, had taken ownership of her life and didn't easily back down from a fight. She certainly didn't have any problems trying to put him in his place earlier. The key word was *trying*. As far as he was concerned, when it came to her, he didn't have a place, especially not one she could put him in.

He should not have kissed her. But in all honesty, he could not have *not* kissed her. And now that he had, he wanted to kiss her again. Hold her in his arms. Take her to bed.

Darius tightened his hand in a fist at his side, not liking the way his thoughts were going and liking even less that he wanted to do those things with the same woman who had crushed his heart. But her response to the kiss had caught him off guard—her complete surrender had made him hard in a way he hadn't been in years.

He had forced himself to end the kiss before he'd taken a mind to do something stupid like take her on her desk. He had been that far gone and she had been right there with him, although she'd gotten a little hot behind the collar later.

"Darius? You still there?"

His concentration was pulled back into the phone conversation, and he was trying like heck to recall what Kevin had just said. "Look, Kev, I'll get back with you later. There's something I need to do before it gets too late."

"Sure, man."

After snapping the phone shut, Darius walked toward Summer. She glanced in his direction with a surprised look on her face. "I thought you had left."

He forced a smile. "I'm sure you were hoping so, but I'm not the type who takes off without letting a person know why, unless there is reason outside of my control. Not like some people."

She glared at him. "And just what is that supposed to mean?"

"Think about it. When you do, it won't take you long to figure things out. I'll be back tomorrow."

Without giving her a chance to say anything else, he walked away.

* * *

Darius tried to keep his composure as he eased his long legs into his car. Moments later, after he'd driven away from the shelter and was headed toward home, he let out the expletive that he'd been holding back. Summer was certainly playing the innocent act well, having the gall to pretend she hadn't a clue what he was talking about when he'd thrown out his dig. He couldn't help but wonder what else she was concealing. For all he knew she could very well know about his vast wealth or his membership in the TCC.

He tightened his grip on the steering wheel. Despite the deep animosity he was feeling toward her, his body refused to deny that it wanted her. She could stir embers of passion within him without saying a word. All it took was a look, her presence or her scent to bring his libido to full awareness. He had to do something about her. She had invaded his comfort zone. His space.

For six years he'd been living in Somerset, enjoying peace and harmony. Of all the cities for her to relocate to, why Somerset? Avoiding her wasn't an option, although it would make his life a whole heck of a lot easier. Her very presence unsettled him in the worst way.

He breathed in deeply and fought back the anger that was getting him riled all over again. If she wanted to pretend, then two could play that game. He was in a position to teach her the very lesson she deserved to learn. She'd wanted a rich husband and in his own way, he would let her know just how she'd lost out on one. He would bide his time, get on her good side and then, when she assumed things were going great between them, after he'd gotten her back in his bed, he would do the very same thing to her that she had done to him.

Walk away without looking back.

Three

The following morning, with butterflies floating around in her stomach, Summer swiped her security card through the scanner before stepping into the shelter, hoping she was early enough to have arrived before Darius. He was the last person she wanted to see. She hadn't gotten much sleep last night and he was the reason. She'd been unable to get the kiss they'd shared yesterday out of her head.

As she made her way toward her office, she refused to even consider the reason why she'd taken more time getting dressed this morning than she usually did. Why she had spent a good ten minutes more putting on her makeup and why had she pulled out the curling iron for the first time in weeks.

When she stopped at Marcy's desk, she checked her watch. Marcy wasn't due in for another hour or so. Summer unlocked Marcy's desk to retrieve a clipboard that listed all her appointments and meetings for that day. Perusing the clipboard, she began to see what her day was going to be like.

"You look nice today."

Summer didn't bother to turn around. She didn't have to. She had left home with a made-up mind that no matter what, she was not going to let Darius rattle her. She was not going to allow him to make her come unglued and she would not look for condescension in his every word. So with that resolve, she would take his compliment in stride and assume he meant no more by it than what was said.

She turned around and her hands automatically tightened on the clipboard the moment she did so. She then swallowed deeply as the nervous sensations stirring in her stomach escalated. How was it possible that he looked even better today than yesterday? He was casually but impeccably dressed. A different pair of jeans and a different shirt, but the utterly breathtaking look was still there. All lean. Well-defined muscles. Perfect abs. And with the tan-colored Stetson sitting on his head, tilted at an angle that shadowed his dark brows, she couldn't help but admit he was truly a fine, handsome specimen of a man.

"Thank you for the compliment. You look nice, also," she heard herself say, determined not to get in a sparring match with him. "Will you need to be in my office today?"

"No, I'll be working in the other offices the majority of the day, other than when I start setting up the accounting for the TCC. It will be a while before I start on that."

She nodded, not wanting to prolong her time with him. "Then I guess I need to let you get started."

"How about lunch?"

She stared up at him, certain she had misunderstood. "Excuse me?"

He smiled and she felt a semblance of heat stirring in her blood, through her veins, in a number of other places she didn't want to think about. "I asked if you wanted to do lunch with me."

"Why?" She couldn't help but ask.

"Why not? You gotta eat and so do I."

"But that doesn't mean we have to share a meal," she pointed out.

His smile widened and the heat stirring in her blood intensified. "No, but it would mean that we're trying to put the past behind us and move on," he said. "It's not like we're going to become bosom buddies, because we aren't. But I'll be hanging around here for the next couple of weeks, so we might as well learn how to get along. I'm not going anywhere and I doubt you are, either. So, what about lunch?"

"I'm not sure that would be a good idea, Darius."

"What was it that you said yesterday? Oh, yes, your very words were, 'We're professionals and are mature enough to make the best of it.'"

Summer breathed in deeply. Yes, those had been her very words.

"I promise not to bite."

She opened her mouth to say something and changed her mind, quickly shutting it. A twist of emotions rumbled in her chest and she knew why. Darius was offering the olive branch, the chance to move on and put what they'd once shared behind them since there was no way it could ever happen again. And deep down she knew she needed that.

She couldn't continue carrying the bitterness of the last seven years. If they were doomed to live in the same town and would be running into each other on occasion, at least they could be civil to each other. But there was no chance of them ever getting back together. For her, the pain had gone too deep.

"Lunch will be fine," she heard herself say, hoping she didn't live to regret it.

"Great. You pick the place, just as long as they sell good hamburgers."

She couldn't help the smile that touched her lips. Some things evidently never changed and his love for hamburgers was one of them. "Too much ground beef isn't good for you," she said, quoting what she'd told him over a hundred times in the past.

And as expected, he rolled his eyes. "Yeah, yeah, I know, and the key words are *too much*. I've become a physical fitness addict, so I don't indulge in too many things that aren't good for me, but there's nothing wrong with enjoying a big, juicy hamburger every once in a while."

Summer decided not to say anything more on the matter. It was evident by his perfect body that he was into physical fitness. "I guess not. I'll be in the lobby at noon."

Darius stretched his neck to work out the kinks as he leaned back in the chair, away from the computer. He glanced up at the clock. It was almost noon.

He stood and stretched his entire body, refusing to acknowledge the anticipation he felt over joining Summer for lunch. Instead, he tried convincing himself that his nerves were the result of knowing he was slowly but surely breaking down her defenses and in good time, he would have the upper hand.

He was leaving the small office when his ears picked up the sound of commotion coming from the front of the building, near the lobby. He quickened his stride and when he rounded the corner, he saw a man standing outside the building with a baseball bat in his hand, threatening to break the glass door if he wasn't allowed to come in to get his wife and children. Summer, Darius saw, was talking to the man on the intercom, trying to reason with him.

He watched her, amazed at how calmly she was speaking to the man, clearly determined not to get ruffled by the vulgar language he was using and the threats he was making.

He glanced over at Marcy, who was sitting at her

desk. "Have the police been called?" he asked, shifting his attention back to the scene being played out a few feet away. "And where the hell is security?" he continued, keeping his gaze fixed on Summer. She continued to appear composed as she tried to settle the man down and convince him to go away.

"The police are on their way. Our security guard called in sick this morning."

Darius looked at Marcy. "They didn't send a replacement?"

"Not yet."

Darius frowned. Huntington and his group had voted against the idea of Darius's firm being in charge of all the security for the shelter. Instead, Huntington had recommended a security company the TCC had used in the past, claiming it was top-notch. The majority of the members had gone along with him except for Lance, Kevin, Mitch and Justin. When they had been outvoted, as a compromise, they had pushed for the club to consider Darius to handle the security for all the computers and to set up the billing system.

Huntington had fought hard against it, saying Darius was too new to the club to take on such tasks, but he had lost the fight when Alex Montoya had sided with them instead of Huntington's group. Darius got the feeling that in addition to the bad blood between Alex and the Brodys, there was bad blood between Alex and Huntington. But then it seemed Huntington had a beef against anyone under the age of forty who joined the club.

The sound of breaking glass recaptured Darius's attention and in a flash he raced forward and placed himself in front of Summer just as the man who was wielding the bat forced his way through the broken glass toward her.

"Be a man and hit me instead of a woman. I dare you," Darius snarled through gritted teeth, not trying to hide the searing rage coursing through him.

The man evidently thought twice about following through on Darius's offer and dropped the bat, taking a step back. Within seconds, the shelter was swarming with police officers. Two of them quickly came through the broken glass door to apprehend the man, who didn't put up a fight.

Darius turned to Summer. "Are you all right?" he asked in a low voice. He hadn't realized just how angry he was until now. If that man had harmed a single strand of hair on her head, Darius would have gone ballistic.

In a way, Darius wished the man had taken him up on his offer. That would have given him the excuse he needed to flatten him. The man had just proven what a coward he was. He was willing to take a bat to a woman, but had wasted no time backing away instead of squaring off with a man equal to his size and weight.

He watched Summer breathe in deeply. "Yes, I'm fine. It's not unusual for a husband to show up wanting to see his wife and children, and when we tell them they can't, most move on. Once in a while, we get someone like Mr. Green who refuses to abide by our rules and causes problems. Usually when that happens, security handles it."

Darius nodded. He would be calling a special meeting of the TCC to make sure something like this didn't happen again. He didn't want to think what could have happened had he not been there. There was no doubt in his mind that the man intended to use that bat on someone.

Before he could say anything, a police officer approached them to obtain their statements. After recording all the facts, the officer advised Summer that she would need to go down to police headquarters so formal charges against the man could be filed.

No sooner had the officer walked away than a woman Darius recognized as a staff member walked up. "Excuse me, Ms. Martindale, but some of the women are upset. They heard a man was trying to force his way inside."

Summer nodded. "Okay, I'm on my way to meet with them."

She then turned back to Darius. "Thanks for your help. I really didn't think he would go so far as to break down the glass. I was hoping that I'd be able to talk some sense into him."

She glanced at her watch. "I need to calm down the women and then go to the police station. I guess lunch is off now."

He shook his head. "No, it's not. Go meet with the women and then I'll drive you to headquarters. Afterward, on the way back, we'll grab something to eat."

"Okay. Thanks." She started to walk away and then glanced at all the glass around the door.

"Go on. I'll make sure this mess is cleaned up and get the glass replaced," he said.

She gave him an appreciative smile before hurrying off with the staff member.

When she'd rounded the corner, Darius released a curse and pulled the cell phone from his belt, hitting the speed dial for Lance's number. His best friend answered on the first ring. "Hey, what's up, Darius?"

"There was an incident here at the shelter and security was not in place. We need to call a TCC meeting."

"I thought we were never going to get out of there," Summer said as they left police headquarters. Darius led her over to his car.

After calming down the women and children, she'd had to meet personally with Gail Green to let her know what her husband had done. Then Summer had to assure Gail that the shelter wouldn't be putting her and her two children out because of the incident.

Gail and her two little boys had arrived at the shelter three days ago after fleeing from their home in the middle of the night. The bruises on her body were evidence enough that she'd been in an abusive situation, but like a number of other women who sought refuge at the shelter, she had refused to press charges.

"I thought they handled everything in a timely manner," Darius said, smiling faintly as he opened the car door for her.

She rolled her eyes. "Spoken like a true ex-cop."

He chuckled before closing her door and moving around the car to the other side. The clock on his console indicated it was after three and they still hadn't eaten lunch.

"Where to?" he asked when he got settled behind the wheel with his seat belt in place. "And don't say back to the shelter because it won't happen. I'm taking you somewhere so we can grab something to eat. I'm hungry even if you're not."

As if on cue, her stomach growled and Summer couldn't help but grin. "Sorry. I guess that means I'm hungry, too. Have you tried that café around the corner from the shelter? The Red Sky."

"No. I've passed by it a few times but have never eaten there."

"Then I guess this is your lucky day because that's where I want to go."

"All I want to know is do they make good hamburgers?" he asked, easing his car into traffic.

"I've never eaten one of their burgers. I'm a salad girl."

He glanced over at her and grinned. "So, you haven't kicked that habit?"

"You want to consult Dr. Oz to determine which of us is eating healthier?"

"No."

She couldn't help but laugh. "I figured as much."

It felt good to laugh. She would never admit it to anyone, especially to Darius, but Samuel Green had truly frightened her and she was glad Darius had been there. When Mr. Green had burst through that door after breaking the glass, she'd had flashbacks to that time with Tyrone when she'd been exposed to his true colors. She had seen his anger out of control, and that anger had been directed at her. A backhand blow had sent her sprawling across the room but she had been quick enough to make it to the door before he could do anything else.

That had been the one and only time Tyrone had raised a hand to her, and she made sure it was the last. A courier had returned her engagement ring to him in the same box it had come in and later that same day, he'd been notified of the restraining order she'd filed. Thinking about it now, she appreciated the fact that she'd gotten out of an abusive situation. She had known when it was time to part ways even if Tyrone hadn't.

She glanced over at Darius. "Did you get much work done today?"

He shrugged. "Not as much as I would have liked, but that's okay. Typically, a job of this sort wouldn't take a whole lot of time, but security is a concern at the shelter, as it should be."

There was no way she would argue with that.

"And as far as the billing system goes," he continued, "I understand the TCC has money, but they want a firm accounting of how their money is being spent."

"Yes, and rightly so," she said, wondering if he thought she felt otherwise. "This shelter is fortunate to be funded by such a distinguished group of men. Do you know any of them?"

He lifted a brow. "Any of whom?"

"Members of the TCC?"

"Why would I know any of them?"

She noted that he sounded offended by her question. "I didn't mean if you knew them personally. I was just wondering if you've ever met any of them. After all, you were hired by them."

He didn't say anything for a moment. "Yes, I've met some of them. They're okay for a bunch of rich guys, and I respect the club for all the things they do in the community. It's my understanding that some of the members prefer not having their identities known. They like doing things behind the scenes without any recognition."

Summer nodded. She could respect that, knowing there were a number of wealthy people who preferred being anonymous donors. She appreciated everything the TCC had done so far and all the things they planned to do. She was definitely looking forward to her meeting with Mr. Novak on Friday. Presently, Helping Hands could accommodate up to fifteen women and children that needed shelter care. Already the TCC had plans in the works to expand the shelter's facilities to triple that amount.

"You've gotten quiet," he said.

She glanced over at Darius and couldn't help but feel a rush of gratitude. He had stood back and let her handle things until the situation had gotten out of control. She appreciated his intervening when he did, playing the role of knight in shining armor once again.

She continued looking at him. His eyes were on the road and her mind couldn't help but shift to another time when he'd been driving her someplace. It had been their first official date. They had gone out for pizza and afterward he had taken her home. She had invited him inside and later, sitting beside him on the sofa, the kissing had begun. A short while later she had been lying beneath him in her bed as he made love to her in a way she hadn't known was possible. The intensity of the memories of that night was almost enough to push everything that had happened over the past seven years into the background.

Almost, but not quite.

"Summer?"

She blinked when she realized they had come to a traffic light and he had glanced over at her, catching her staring. "Yes?"

"Are you sure you're okay? I guess incidents such as what happened earlier are expected to some degree, which is the reason I'm installing state-of-the-art security software on all the computers—to reduce the risk that the location of the women seeking refuge is discovered. But still, it has to be unnerving when one of the husbands or boyfriends shows up."

If you only knew. "Yes, and what's really sad is the fact that the women have to go into hiding at all. The Greens have two beautiful little boys and today their father showed up demanding them back with, of all things, one of their baseball bats. The person we saw today was not a loving father or husband but a violent and dangerous man."

Summer frowned and then she sighed deeply. Tonight she would get a good night's sleep and try to forget the incident ever happened. Fat chance. She would remember it and she would imagine what could have happened had Darius not been there.

"Here we are."

She looked around. Darius had pulled into the café's parking lot and brought the car to a stop. She glanced over at him. He was staring at her with an intensity that sent shivers of awareness through her body.

Sexual chemistry was brewing between them again. She could feel his body heat emanating from across the car. Summer forced the thought to the back of her mind.

"Umm, I guess we should go on inside," she forced her mouth to say. The way he was looking at her made her want to suggest that they go somewhere else, but she fought the temptation and held tight to her common sense.

She decided now was as good a time as any to thank him. "I really do appreciate what you did today, Darius, and I want to—"

"No, don't thank me."

His words stopped her short. "Why?"

"Because I didn't do any more than what was needed. No more than any other man would have done."

She contemplated his words. He was a man of action. Twice she had seen him in full swing and neither time had he accepted her words of gratitude. "I *will* thank you, Darius Franklin, because you deserve to be thanked."

And before he could respond, she got out of the car.

"Hey, Ms. Martindale, do you want your usual spot?" Tina asked when Summer walked in.

"Whatever is available," Summer answered, feeling the heat of Darius's chest close to her back. His nearness was almost unsettling.

"You must come here often," he said, moving to stand at her side.

She glanced over at him and smiled. "Practically every day. It's not far from the shelter and I enjoy the walk. And I like their grilled chicken salads."

Moments later they were being escorted to a table in the rear. Darius shifted his full attention to the people whose tables they passed. They either greeted her by name or smiled a hello. "You're pretty popular, I see," he said when they had taken their seats.

She shrugged. "Most are regulars who know that I work at the shelter. They believe it benefits the community and appreciate our presence."

They halted conversation for a while to scan the menu. Darius was the one deciding what he wanted since Summer was getting her usual. However, she was inclined to check out the soup of the day, or at least pretend that she was doing so. It was hard concentrating on anything, even food, while sitting across from Darius. As he studied his menu, she studied him over the top of hers.

She almost laughed out loud at the intense expression on his face. Deciding what hamburger he wanted couldn't be all that serious. But then Darius had always been a very serious man. Especially when it came to making love.

For a heart-flipping moment she wondered why a memory like that had crossed her mind, but she knew. Darius was the kind of man that oozed sexuality as potent as it could get, making those incredible urges consume the lower part of her body. They'd only had one night together, but it had been incredible. No matter what had happened after that, she could not discount how he'd made her feel.

He was the most gifted of lovers. Pleasing her had seemed to be the most natural thing in the world to Darius. She hadn't realized just how selfish Tyrone had been in the bedroom until after she'd made love to Darius. How could she have realized when Tyrone had been her first? No matter what her sexual experience had been with Tyrone, one time with Darius had made everything just fine.

Darius glanced up and she took in a lungful of air. The intensity of his gaze—she wanted to look away, but she couldn't. It was as if she were held captive by his deep, dark eyes.

"Here are your waters."

Summer almost jumped when Tina appeared with

two glasses of water. "Thanks." Barely giving her a chance to set the glass down in front of her, Summer picked it up and took a long gulp, feeling the need for the ice-cold water to cool her down.

Tina hung around long enough to take their food and drink order before moving on again.

"So, what do you like about your job?"

She glanced over at him to answer his question, making an attempt to keep her gaze trained on his nose instead of his eyes. "Everything, but mostly the satisfaction I get from helping women in distress, those who might feel broken up because of what has happened. I like letting them know they aren't alone and somebody cares."

What she didn't add was that she enjoyed giving them the same support he had given her during those first crucial days, when she had begun doubting herself, second-guessing the situation and believing that maybe she had been the cause of Tyrone's problems instead of the other way around.

"I notice there's not a director at the shelter," he said.

Her gaze drifted down from his nose to his lips. Focusing on his mouth was just as bad as looking into his eyes. He had a sexy mouth. It was a mouth that could move with agonizing slowness when talking… or when being used for other things. She swallowed before responding.

"When I was hired by the TCC it was decided that I could handle it all for now. When they complete the proposed expansions and decide to fill the position, I'm hoping I'll be considered for the job."

Darius nodded. He had not been a part of the TCC committee that had done the hiring for Helping Hands, which was one of the reasons he'd been surprised to discover her working there. He would have recognized her name the second it came across his desk.

"The shelter is pretty full now. How do you manage it all?" he asked.

She shrugged. "It's not so bad. I think the most challenging times are when I'm called in the middle of the night to a police station or hospital to comfort a woman who's been beaten or raped."

Darius's jaw twitched at the thought of anyone treating a woman so cruelly. Mistreatment of a woman was one thing he could not tolerate.

"It's also difficult at times when manning the abuse hotline. Someone is there to take calls twenty-four hours a day—usually a volunteer trained to do so. Every once in a while, a call will come through that I need to handle. Those are the ones that can get pretty emotional, depending on the circumstances."

Darius could tell from her voice that she was dedicated to what she did every day. To stay on safe ground and not stray on to a topic neither of them wanted to deal with, he decided to keep her talking about her work at the shelter.

For the first time since seeing her again, he was lowering his guard a little.

When the waitress finally delivered their order, he

had to admit the food looked good. And after a bite into his hamburger, he had to own up that it tasted good, too. One of his uncles in Charleston once owned a sandwich shop that used to make the best burgers around. As a kid, he enjoyed the summers he spent there and the older he got, he found himself comparing every hamburger he ate to his uncle Donald's. None could compare, but he had to admit this one came pretty close.

"How does it taste?"

He glanced over at Summer and could only smile and nod, since he couldn't talk with a mouth full of hamburger.

A half hour later, on the drive back to the shelter, he reflected on a number of things he hadn't expected. Mainly, he hadn't figured on sitting across from her for almost an hour and enjoying her company without animosity or anger seeping in. However, what couldn't be helped was the sexual tension. Although they had tried to downplay it with a lot of conversation, it was there nonetheless.

There was a lot about her he could barely resist. Her scent topped the list. Whatever perfume she was wearing filled his nostrils with a luscious fragrance that seemed to get absorbed right into his skin. And then there were her eyes. He was fully aware that she'd tried to avoid looking at him, which had been hard to do since they were sitting directly across from each other. Each time he would catch her staring at him, he would feel a pull in his stomach.

Thankfully, his hands were gripping the steering wheel because at that moment, it wouldn't take much for him to reach over and touch her, stroke that part of her thigh exposed beneath her skirt. Seeing her flesh peeking at him was making his mind spin, so he tried focusing on the road and decided to get her talking again. Anything to keep his mind off taking her.

"So, where do you live?" he asked.

He kept his gaze glued to the road. She didn't need to see the heat in his eyes, a telltale sign that although he wished otherwise, she was getting to him.

"I bought a house a block from the post office," she said.

He noted she didn't provide him with the name of her street. There were a couple of new communities sprouting up near the post office, as well as a number of newly renovated older homes that had been for sale. "Nice area," he heard himself say.

"I like it. My neighborhood's pretty quiet. Most of the people on my street are a lot older and are in bed before eight at night."

He nodded. From the information she had just shared he could safely assume that she had purchased one of the renovated homes in the older, established communities. Doing so had been a smart move on her part; they were a good investment.

She then opened up and began telling him about it, saying she was having a lot of fun decorating the house. He didn't find that hard to believe. When she'd lived in Houston, her apartment had been small but nice and he'd been surprised to learn she had done most of the decorating herself.

All too soon he was pulling into the parking lot of the shelter. "Thanks for taking me to lunch," she said, reaching to unsnap her seat belt even before he could bring the car to a complete stop. "Although I have to admit, riding in the car instead of walking only means I have to get my daily physical activity some other way," she added.

He came close to saying that he knew another way she could get her physical activity, and it would be something she would enjoy—he would make sure of it. Instead, he decided it would be best to keep his mouth shut.

"But since it will probably be dark when I leave today, I'll take the day off from exercise," she tacked on, getting out of the car.

He glanced over at her. "Why are you staying late?"

"Because I have a lot of work and can't leave until I'm finished. I'm meeting with Mr. Novak on Friday and there are a number of reports I have to run. More than likely, the TCC will have heard about the incident today and will want a full report on what happened."

He tightened his mouth after almost telling her that he'd already given them one. While at police headquarters, he had gotten a call from Mitch, Justin and Kevin. Lance had told them what had happened. Minor details had been given on television—since it was a women's shelter, no television crews or reporters were allowed to show up in order to protect the women staying there.

He knew if Summer stayed beyond five o'clock, she'd be pulling a long day. But for some reason, he had a feeling that was probably the norm for her. "Isn't there someone who can help you with those reports?"

"Afraid not. Besides, I'd rather run them myself, especially since I plan on pleading my case to Mr. Novak for an expansion of the shelter sooner rather than later."

Darius didn't say anything, but considering what had happened earlier that day, he wasn't crazy about her walking out to her car alone. Although the parking lot was well lit, he still didn't like it. Two security guards had shown up after the incident. He decided that before he left for the day, he would talk to the guards and make sure one of them walked Summer to her car.

When they reached the door he decided that unlike her, he intended to leave at a decent time. He had a meeting with the fire chief later, and it was a meeting he didn't want to miss. And besides, the last thing he needed was to end up in the office late at night with Summer—alone.

Four

Darius grabbed a beer out of the refrigerator and popped the top before tilting the can to his mouth, appreciating the cool brew that flowed down his throat. When the can was empty, he scowled before crushing the aluminum and tossing it into the recycling bin.

His frown deepened as he sat down at the kitchen table, thinking that today had certainly not gone like he'd planned. He was convinced that the incident at the shelter was the prime reason his protective instincts toward Summer had kicked in. He had been ready to do bodily harm to anyone who even thought of hurting her. And he could admit that the reason he had driven her to police headquarters and then later to lunch was because he hadn't wanted her out of his sight. He was becoming attached again, and that wasn't good.

He rubbed a hand down his face. Maybe he needed to rethink the notion of exacting some sort of revenge on her and instead, just put distance between them and let it go at that, treating her the way he would other groupies or gold diggers whenever they crossed his path.

But he wasn't able to do that. If anything, today proved that when it came to Summer, he didn't think straight or logically. Right now, the only thing he should be thinking about was hurting her the way she had hurt him. Therefore, regardless of any protective instincts he might have, he would continue with his plan to make her think something special was going on between them. Then, at the right time, he'd drop the bomb that she meant nothing to him, and she'd discover she had gotten played, just like he had.

When his cell phone went off, he stood and pulled it off his belt. "What's up, Lance?" After his meeting with Chief Ingle, he had stopped by the TCC Café and had dinner with Kevin and Justin. Lance and his wife had driven to Houston to attend some sort of function there.

"I got your message. So Ingle thinks the fire was started with some sort of petroleum-based product?" Lance asked.

"He's pretty sure of it. But it wasn't one that could easily be detected, which is the reason the investigation took so long. They're trying to narrow the components down. However, he believes it's the same kind found in lubricating oils used for ranch equipment," Darius responded.

"Something that Montoya could easily get his hands on, since he owns that cattle ranch," Lance was quick to point out.

Darius shook his head. "His men are the ones working his ranch the majority of the time, Lance. Montoya's heavily involved in his import/export business."

"For crying out loud, Darius, you just don't want to believe he's responsible for that fire, do you?" Lance asked with frustration in his voice.

"What I don't want is for you to be so convinced Montoya is behind the fire that you start overlooking any other possible suspects."

"There aren't any other possible suspects, Darius. Montoya is the only one who hates me and Mitch bad enough to do such a thing. At the end of your investigation, you'll see that all the evidence points in Montoya's direction."

A few hours later, the fire investigation was the last thing on Darius's mind when he finally eased into bed, determined to get a good night's sleep. Moments later, after a number of tosses and turns, he discovered doing so wouldn't be easy when thoughts of Summer filled his mind. When he thought of what could have possibly happened had he not been there today. Even now he was worried that she was still at the center working, and he was tempted to go check for himself to make sure she was all right. But then he quickly recalled he had spoken with security to make sure someone escorted her to her car whenever she did work late.

He breathed in deeply, getting angry with himself that his concern for her, this feeling stirring deep within him, was making him weak. He refused to let that happen. But each time he closed his eyes, he saw her, remembered a better time between them, a time when she had been his whole world.

He stared up at the ceiling, determined to remember that she was not his whole world any longer, would never be it again. It was something he couldn't lose sight of. He would keep up his guard with her, no matter what.

"Thank you for walking me to my car, Barney, but it really wasn't necessary."

"No problem, ma'am. Besides, it was Mr. Franklin's orders."

Summer raised a brow at the uniformed guard. "Was it?"

"Yes."

Summer pondered that. How could Darius give an order to a guard who didn't work for him? Evidently, Barney had no problem following an order from someone who wasn't his boss.

"Well, good night," she said, opening her car door and getting inside.

"Just a minute, Ms. Martindale. This was pinned to your windshield beneath the wipers," he said, handing the piece of paper to her.

Summer tossed the flyer onto the seat beside her. "Good night."

"Good night."

Summer drove off, noticing Barney was still standing there, watching her pull out of the parking lot. No doubt he was still following Darius's orders. After what happened today, she could understand his concern and appreciated him wanting to make sure she was all right. Just like she had appreciated him taking her to lunch.

There had been something strange about sitting across from a man who had once undressed her, rubbed his hands all over her naked body and made love to her in a way that thinking about it took her breath away. A man who'd shown her that foreplay was an art form that could be taken to many levels, and that a person's mouth was just as lethal as his hands when making love.

When her car came to a stop at a traffic light, she turned on the radio, hoping the sound of music would drown out her thoughts of Darius. That wasn't going to happen, she thought, when she recalled how long after she'd left Houston she would lie in bed and think of him.

Her stomach growled and she remembered she'd missed dinner. When she got home she would make a sandwich and a glass of iced tea. It was one of those hot August nights.

As she waited for the light to change, she glanced over at the flyer she'd thrown on the seat and picked it up. Her breath caught in her throat and chills ran up her spine when she read the words, "I take care of my own."

The light turned green but she didn't realize it until the driver behind her blasted his horn. She accelerated, wondering which husband or boyfriend had placed the note on her car. It wouldn't be the first time one of the abusers of the women at the shelter blamed the staff for keeping his family from him. Mr. Green had taken the same position earlier that day. She wouldn't be surprised if it had been Mr. Green who had placed the note there, since her car had been parked in one of the spaces reserved for shelter personnel.

Summer tossed the paper aside, thinking of Mr. Green and the baseball bat, and his terrified wife. She sighed. She had long ago stopped trying to figure out why some men could treat a woman they claimed to love so shabbily.

The next day, Darius studied the computer screen in front of him and tried not to think about the woman a few doors down. She had been holed up in her office all morning and it was almost noon. He would bet any amount of money she would not be stopping for lunch.

A part of him knew it was really none of his business whether she ate or not, but another part decided to make it his business. Just as well, since he hadn't been able to concentrate worth a damn anyway.

Before arriving at the shelter, he had dropped by the refinery to take a look around the area damaged by the fire, hoping he would find something that had been overlooked previously. He hated admitting it, but Lance was right. All the evidence accumulated so far was pointing at Montoya, especially since the man didn't have an alibi for that night and he'd been seen in the vicinity of the refinery. However, the evidence was too cut-and-dried to suit Darius—way too pat. As far as he was concerned, if Montoya wasn't guilty, then someone who knew about the feud between Montoya and the Brodys was certainly making it look that way.

Darius stood as he checked his watch, deciding it was time to feed his stomach and satisfy his desire to see Summer again. He had fought the impulse to drop by her office and say hello when he had arrived at the shelter. But he couldn't fight it anymore.

Her office door had been closed, which meant she was either counseling someone or buried knee-deep in work. She had mentioned getting ready for that meeting tomorrow with Kev. But still, she had to eat, and he kind of enjoyed that café where they had eaten yesterday. The hamburger had been delicious.

Walking down the corridor, he went to the secretary's desk. "Is Ms. Martindale in a meeting with someone?" he asked Marcy.

Marcy stopped thumbing through a bunch of folders on her desk long enough to look up and smile at him. "No, she's going over some papers. If you need to talk with her about something, just knock on her door."

He returned her smile. "I think I will. Thanks."

Strolling back the way he'd come, he came to a stop in front of her door, hesitating a moment before knocking, convincing himself he was only pretending to be a nice guy when in fact, she really didn't deserve his kindness.

"Come in."

He opened the door and walked into her office, closing it behind him. She didn't look up. "Ready for lunch?" he asked.

She lifted her gaze from the document she'd been reading to fix it on him. The moment their eyes met, a slight tremor touched him. And if that weren't bad enough, he could feel a deep stirring in his gut. He stood there, fully conscious of the effect she was having on him and not liking it, but unable to do anything but stand there and take it like a man who wanted a woman, a woman he should have gotten from under his skin long ago. She broke eye contact with him and looked back down at the document she'd been reading. "I can't today."

You can't or you won't? Instead of asking, he said, "Yes, you can. You'll think better on a full stomach."

When she looked back up at him without saying anything, as if giving his words some serious thought, he decided to add, "Besides, that hamburger I ate yesterday was pretty good and—"

"And you probably don't need another one today. Too much beef," she finished for him, pushing her papers aside. "Why don't you try a salad?"

He chuckled. "That's rabbit food."

She rolled her eyes. "That's healthy." And then she said. "Okay, I'll have lunch with you, but only if we walk to the café."

He felt the amusement leave his face. "Walk?"

"Yes. Walk."

He noticed she was watching him intently, probably expecting him to back down. He couldn't help the smile that touched the corners of his lips when he said, "Fine. We'll walk."

"You really didn't expect me to do it, did you?"

Summer glanced over at Darius. They had been walking for the past few minutes in silence, which gave her the chance to wonder how, for the third day in a row, she'd been in his presence. He was right. She hadn't expected him to agree to walk to the café with her. Not that she thought he wasn't in any kind of shape to do so, but mainly because he didn't have a pair of walking shoes tucked away in a desk like she had. He was wearing cowboy boots, and they comple-mented his jeans and chambray shirt. And he had grabbed his Stetson off the rack to put on his head, which, considering the heat of the sun, had been a good idea. He looked good in his Western attire, too good to be walking with her on the dusty sidewalk. Every so often when someone needed to squeeze by them, Darius's denim-clad thigh would brush up against hers, making her very aware of the strength of his masculinity.

"No, I really didn't," she said finally. "But you have to admit it's a beautiful day outside. A perfect day to walk."

She couldn't help remembering the last time they had taken a walk together, late one afternoon when he'd shown up at her place after getting off work. They had strolled to the neighborhood park and on the way back had stopped at a corner store for ice-cream cones. That had been a perfect day to walk, too.

She breathed in deeply in an attempt to erase the memory from her mind. For three days, she had allowed him to invade her personal space and she wasn't exactly happy with the fact that he'd done so. She had appreciated his help yesterday, but somehow she needed to get him to understand that being cordial to each other didn't mean they had to share lunch every day.

"How is Aunt Joanne?"

She nearly missed a step and felt his hand on her elbow, reaching out to steady her, keeping her from falling. She stopped walking and glanced up at him. He was standing a scarce few inches in front of her and met her gaze. Darius had met Aunt Joanne when she had come to Houston to give Summer much-needed support during Tyrone's trial. Her aunt had liked Darius, and Summer wanted to believe that Darius had liked her aunt, as well, that his feelings toward Aunt Jo had been genuine and not fake—like the ones he'd displayed toward her.

"Summer, what's wrong?"

She swallowed and fought back the tears that threatened every time she thought of losing her aunt. "Aunt Jo died two years ago."

She saw surprise and then sorrow in his eyes. "I'm sorry. What happened? Was she ill?" he asked. He moved his hands from her elbow to her hand, and she could feel him wrapping his fingers around hers.

She shook her head. "No, in fact she'd had a physical the day before and had called to tell me how well it went, and that the doctor had even joked about her being fifty-five and would probably live well past ninety-five because she was in such good shape."

Summer paused a moment and then continued. "On her way home from work one night, she stopped at an ATM. A guy came up, demanding her money. She emptied her account and gave him all she had, but he shot and killed her anyway."

"Oh, Summer, I'm sorry to hear that," he said, pulling her into his arms. And she went without hesitation, ignoring the fact they were standing in the middle of the sidewalk. She was being given the shoulder to cry on that she had needed so badly two years ago. Burying her aunt had been the hardest thing she'd ever had to do. Less than a year after graduating from college, she'd lost the only person who'd been there for her consistently.

"That's it, Summer, get it all out," Darius urged gently in her ear. "Let it go." She felt the strength of his arms wrap around her shoulders, drawing her close.

Summer wasn't sure just how long she stood there, on a public street, being comforted by the only man she had ever loved—and who had done her wrong. She wasn't sure if she could ever forgive him for breaking her heart.

Pulling herself together, she eased back out of his arms, breaking all physical contact with him. "Sorry about that," she said softly.

"Don't apologize. Are you okay?"

"Yes, I'm fine." She nudged her hands into the pockets of her slacks and glanced down at the pavement. "It's still hard for me sometimes."

"I imagine that it would be, and I really meant it when I said that I'm sorry, Summer."

The sincerity in his voice as well as the warmth of his tone touched her in a way that it should not have. She lifted her head to glance back up at him. "Thank you."

"You're welcome."

As they continued their walk toward the café, Summer's head was spinning with confusion over whether she could trust this man who had crushed her heart once before but seemed filled with pure compassion for her. Should she listen to her head, her heart...her body? She suddenly felt like she was nineteen again, and she didn't like it at all. Not at all.

Five

"You haven't been listening to a thing I've said," Justin Dupree complained while eyeing Darius curiously. The two men were enjoying a meal at one of the exclusive restaurants in town with plans to drop by the TCC later and play pool with Lance, Mitch and Kevin.

Darius took another sip of his beer and gave his friend an apologetic smile. "Sorry, what did you say?"

A smile touched the corners of Justin's lips. "I said Monica Cooper has been giving you the eye all night."

Darius raised a brow. "Who?"

Justin rolled his eyes. "Monica. You know. Sultry lips Monica."

Darius couldn't help but grin as he leaned back in

his chair and took another sip of his beer. "No, I don't know her, but I'm sure you do."

There weren't too many single women with sultry lips that Justin didn't know. He had a reputation of being Somerset's number one jet-setting playboy. Heir to his family's multimillion-dollar shipping company, Justin could probably talk a nun out of her clothes. He could also close any business deal he wanted—he had a reputation of being a tough-as-nails, ruthless businessman. Darius was proud to consider him a friend.

Justin smiled. "Yes, I know her. Her dad owns a nice spread outside of Austin. She comes to Somerset every summer to visit her aunt. She seems taken with you."

Darius didn't even bother looking over his shoulder at the woman. Instead, he said, "That's nice." He knew Justin had to be wondering why he wasn't showing Monica, or any woman for that matter, any interest tonight. Even their waitress had given him a flirty smile. But the only woman he could think about at the moment was the one he'd had lunch with today. The one he couldn't get out of his mind.

The one he had held in his arms while she'd cried.

"Okay, Darius, what's going on in that brain of yours? Lance said you still don't want to believe that Montoya was behind that fire."

Darius studied the contents of his beer bottle before glancing over at Justin. The two of them were best friends to the Brodys. Justin was Mitch's best friend like he was Lance's.

In a way, Darius felt guilty. He hadn't been thinking about Montoya and the fire, and he really should be. He had been thinking about Summer. But now that Justin had brought it up…

"I'm just not as convinced as everyone seems to be. Like you, Montoya is a shrewd businessman. Always on top of his game. Smart as a whip. I can't see him being stupid enough to set fire to his enemy's refinery, not when all fingers would point his way. He has no motive."

Justin shook his head. "Sure he does. You just said it. He and Lance are enemies."

"But that's just it, Justin. They have been enemies for years. That's nothing new. According to Lance, that goes as far back as high school. Competing against each other every chance they got."

"Yes," Justin said, "and they are still competing against each other today, in practically everything. The only reason Montoya decided to join the TCC was to be a deliberate thorn in Lance's side. On top of that, Montoya is friends with Paulo Ruiz, and everyone knows that guy has underworld connections and is as shady as they come. For all we know, Ruiz may have been the one to arrange the fire for Montoya."

Darius nodded, but he still wasn't convinced. "Well, all we got now is circumstantial evidence that wouldn't hold up in court. Unless there is valid proof, then—"

"I'll get it," Justin said, interrupting Darius.

Darius raised a dark brow. "And just how do you plan to do that?"

Justin smiled. "You'll find out when I lay all the evidence you need at your feet."

Hours later on the drive away from the TCC, Darius couldn't help but reflect on what Justin had said over dinner. Granted, he didn't know Montoya as well as the others since he hadn't lived in Somerset all his life, but he couldn't help but admire someone who had worked hard to propel himself from rags to riches. He'd heard that Montoya had once been a groundskeeper at the club.

And Darius had a hard time believing that someone that driven to succeed would risk losing it all in a situation where he would automatically be labeled the guilty party. Darius was convinced that if Montoya had been involved in the fire, he would have done a better job of covering his tracks. The man didn't even have a valid alibi, for crying out loud. Definitely not the stance of a guilty arsonist.

Darius decided that before going to bed he would go back over the information he had collected so far, especially his interviews with a number of employees who had left the company within the past couple of years on bad terms. He then cursed under his breath when he realized he'd left the file with his notes back at the shelter.

Darius turned on the radio, deciding he needed to hear some music. He let out a deep breath as he recognized the song as one that had been playing earlier today at the café while he and Summer had shared lunch.

The image of Summer sitting across from him as she tried to put the pain of losing her aunt behind her flooded his mind. He'd liked her aunt and thought it was tragic how the woman had lost her life. He could just imagine what Summer had gone through during that time. But he really didn't want to think about that. Then why was he? Why did he have to constantly remind himself that he couldn't—and shouldn't—care?

He glanced at the clock on his car's console. It was close to ten. Tomorrow he would spend the day at the refinery, checking out a few things and questioning a number of the employees, including one who claimed he saw someone fitting Montoya's description in the refinery's parking lot the night of the fire.

The moment he stopped at a traffic light, his cell phone went off. He quickly slid it open. "Yes?"

"Darius, this is Walt. I got a message that you called."

Darius smiled. Hearing his old partner's voice reminded him of working as a detective in Houston. They'd had some good times together, despite Walt's miserable attitude. "Yes, Walt, how are things going?"

"Pretty much the same. I'm sure you heard that Smothers finally retired. We were all glad about that."

"Yes, I heard." John Smothers was a tough detective who should have retired ages ago.

"So, what's up? You said you needed my help with something," Walt said.

"I'm investigating a case of arson here in Somerset

and need you to do a background check on one of the company's employees. I heard from another employee that the man used to work for a company that burned to the ground a few years ago in Houston."

"Sure, what's the employee's name?"

"Quincy Cummings," Darius said, hoping Walt would be able to obtain information about the guy.

"I'll let you know something in a day or so," Walt said.

"Thanks, I appreciate it."

"So, what's been going on with you, Darius? The last time we talked was over a year ago. I thought you were calling to let me know you had gotten married or something," Walt said in a joking tone. But for some reason Darius was annoyed by Walt's words—they had definitely hit a nerve. It could be because Walt had been the one to tell him about Summer and the things she had said about him.

"Not hardly. I plan to stay single for the rest of my days," Darius said, wondering why each and every time he talked to Walt, his marital status came up.

"Same here, man. Women are nothing but liars. None of them can be trusted. Hey, remember that good-looking broad you had the hots for when we were partners? The one who dumped you for some rich old man when you were out of town? I don't recall her name but I—"

"Summer," Darius cut in, trying to keep his tone from showing the irritation he felt.

"What?"

"I said her name was Summer. Summer Martindale," Darius said, ready to end the call.

"Oh, yeah, that's right. I wonder what happened to her after she left Houston. If she and that old man she ran off with are still together."

"I wouldn't know," Darius said shortly, deciding not to mention that Summer was now living in Somerset and he had not only run into her but had kissed her again. "Look, Walt. I appreciate you calling me back. Let me know if you find something out on that employee."

"Sure thing, pal."

Darius hung up the phone. Walt was the kind of man who believed misery loved company and had always seemed miserable, mainly because he'd had a tough time when it came to women.

Deciding he needed that file he'd left back at the shelter, he made a turn at the next traffic light. A few moments later, he was pulling into the parking lot and was surprised to see Summer's car in the usual spot. Why was she still here?

It didn't take him long to get out of his car and walk toward the shelter's entrance. The security guy named Barney recognized him but followed security procedures before allowing him entry.

"Is Ms. Martindale in her office?" he asked the man as he stuffed his ID back into his wallet.

"Yes, sir, and I did as you asked and walked her to her car last night."

"Thanks. I appreciate it."

Walking toward Summer's office, he stopped at the night-duty secretary's station. He had met the older woman, Raycine Bradley, the evening before. "Good evening, Ms. Bradley, is Ms. Martindale meeting with someone?" he asked.

The woman smiled at him. "No. I think she's packing up to call it a night. Finally."

Darius nodded, thinking Summer should have done that long ago. "I think I'll go hurry her along," he said, heading to the corridor that led to Summer's office.

Moments later he knocked on her door.

"Come in."

He stepped into her office and closed the door behind him. She was standing at a table with her back to him sorting out papers. Without looking his way, she said, "I promise I'll be leaving in a few minutes, Raycine."

Darius crossed his arms over his chest and leaned against the closed door. "That's good to hear. I intend to do everything in my power to make sure that you do."

Summer swirled around and stared at Darius in surprise. From the look on his face, he wasn't a happy camper. "What are you doing here?" she asked.

"I need to ask you that same thing," he said in a curt tone, moving away from the door to stand in the middle of her office with his hands braced on his hips.

Now she knew what had him upset. He didn't like the fact she was still there. She couldn't help wondering why he was making it his business. "I had a lot to do for tomorrow's meeting with Mr. Novak. In addition to that, a new woman checked into our facilities today."

She saw the look of concern that immediately showed on his face. "How is she?"

"She was a lot better once we got her settled in and assured her that if her husband showed up here, we wouldn't let him near her."

Darius shook his head. "It's sad that any woman has to worry about something like that."

Summer sighed deeply. "Yes. Been there. Done that."

But she didn't have to remind him of that since he'd been a part of that particular drama in her past. She had truly believed a restraining order would keep Tyrone away from her. He had proven her wrong. She didn't want to think about what might have happened if Darius hadn't shown up when he did, putting his life on the line for her.

Not wanting to think about Tyrone any longer, she asked, "So, are you going to tell me why you're here?" His gaze stroked her like a physical caress she couldn't ignore.

"I left something I need for tomorrow. I forgot to mention that I won't be back here until next week, when I start setting up the billing account."

"Oh." She should have been thrilled that she wouldn't be seeing him for the fourth day in a row but a barrage of emotions she couldn't explain tried to engulf her. She fought them back.

"I'm working on a case that requires my attention elsewhere," he added.

She wanted to tell him that he owed her no explanation. Instead, she said, "Sounds real serious."

"It's a case involving arson. You probably read about it in the papers a few weeks back. A fire at the Brody Oil and Gas refinery."

"Yes, I do recall reading about it," she said, leaning against the table. "And you think it was deliberately set?"

"It looks that way. I've been asked by the Brody brothers to find out who did it."

Summer eyed Darius. She recalled how much he'd enjoyed his job as a detective. Once in a while he would tell her about a particular case he was trying to solve. "Got any leads?" she asked.

"Not enough to suit me, which is the reason I need to spend a day at the refinery." He moved over toward her. "So, what do you need me to do?"

She straightened her stance. "About what?"

"About helping you pack up and get out of here, like you should have done hours ago."

"I told you why I'm still here."

"But your reason isn't good enough. I can see you staying over for an hour or so, but damn it Summer, it's going on eleven o'clock and knowing you, you'll be back here first thing in the morning."

"Of course. My meeting is at eight."

Darius wondered how she would feel knowing he had just finished playing a game of pool with the man she would be meeting with. And now Kev knew she was someone from his past, someone who had once meant a lot to him. His friend knew how much she had hurt him, as well. "So, what can I do to help?" he asked.

When Darius came to a stop in front of her, Summer released a resigned sigh. It wouldn't do any good to argue with him. Besides, she was too tired. "I guess you can help by stapling these papers that I've already sorted."

"Okay."

She tried to scoot over when he joined her at the table but their arms touched nonetheless, and she felt it—a spark of sensations that swept through her. She inhaled a sharp breath.

He glanced over at her. "You're all right?"

She breathed in deeply before saying, "Yes, I'm fine. Why wouldn't I be?"

"No reason."

There was a reason and they both knew it. Memories filtered through her mind of a night she just couldn't forget. There was no way she could deny that over the years she had lain in bed missing a warm, hard body beside her, and being awakened by the taste of a desire so potent it could blind you.

"If you're meeting just with Kevin Novak, why are you making all of these handouts?"

His question cut into her thoughts and she glanced over at him. "For the other members of the TCC, for him to share with them. I want everyone to know what's going on here at the shelter, that we're benefiting the community and that I'm competent enough to handle things."

Darius reached out and touched her arm. "You're worried for nothing. If they thought you weren't competent enough to handle things, you wouldn't be here."

"But what if—"

He reached for her. "For crying out loud, woman, you worry too much."

She should have seen it coming and backed away from him. But the moment his mouth touched hers she knew she could not have moved an inch. And now that her stomach was contracting with desire, there was no way she wasn't going to enjoy it while it lasted.

That was one thing she was truthful about, the fact that Darius knew how to kiss, even during those times when he should be doing something else. Like now. He had offered to help her, not seduce her. Awareness, bold and daring, raced through her, made her acknowledge that Darius was the only man who could ever make her purr in his arms. The only man who'd made her feel she'd been cheated out of many more nights with him.

If only…

She didn't want to think about if only. She only wanted to think about now, not what did or didn't happen seven years ago and during the years in between. She didn't even want to think about why being in his arms felt natural, like a place she should be. A place she belonged. His mouth felt in sync with hers, also totally natural, connected to hers while kissing her so perfectly.

When he finally ended the kiss, she couldn't do anything but pull in a deep breath, still tasting him on her lips. She didn't bother giving herself a mental shake and questioning why she had let him kiss her. She knew very well why. She wouldn't do as she'd done the last time, pretending she hadn't wanted any part of it since, like before, she hadn't resisted. She doubted that she could have even if she'd wanted to.

But she didn't want to talk about it. Without saying anything, she turned back to the table and gathered up what was left of the papers she had sorted. She was fully aware that he was watching her, but following her lead, he didn't say anything, either. Out of the corner of her eye, she could see him neatly stacking the handouts she'd made. They turned at the same time and their gazes locked for a mere second before simultaneously, they stepped into each other's arms again.

It seemed what was happening at the moment was Summer's mind was refusing to remember the bad times, only the good. And there had been good times, as good as good could get. They had only shared a bed once but before then, they had shared companionship, although she'd found out later he'd had an ulterior motive for doing so. But she wouldn't dwell on that now. The only thing she wanted to dwell on was the way his mouth was taking hers, with a hunger she could feel all the way to her toes, with an intensity that had her stomach churning as they were enjoying this kiss to the fullest.

It didn't even bother her that he was holding her

in a possessive and intimate way, with his hands cradling her backside to fit her pelvis snugly against the front of him. She could feel the muscled tone of his body and his erection, hard and strong, pressed against her.

Taking his cue, she wrapped her arms around his neck as he sank deeper into her mouth, sending points of pleasure all through her. She felt sensations in her fingers as she caressed the back part of his neck, and through the material of her skirt where she was making contact with his denim-clad thigh. And she was very well aware of when he changed the angle of his mouth to position hers more to his advantage.

His efforts had her mind reeling, filling her with an urgent need to recognize and accept what was taking place, giving her the resolve to simply stand there, indulge and take it like a woman. And she was. She was taking it like a woman who needed every stroke of his tongue, every bit of his taste and every mind-blowing, tantalizing sensation his mouth was making her feel.

When the kiss ended moments later, she couldn't resist placing a lingering heated kiss on his jawline. Nor could she resist taking the tip of her tongue and tracing along his upper lip before finally taking a step back.

Darius drew in a deep breath and fought the urge to pull her back into his arms again, ask if he could follow her home and make love to her with the same intensity that he had made love to her that night. But this time, his heart wouldn't come into play, only his lust.

He wished the kiss could have wiped away all the wrongs of the past and he could move on without feeling animosity in his heart. Unfortunately, it hadn't. What it had done was make him fully aware of how vulnerable his heart still was when it came to Summer, and just how hot and strong his desire for her still burned within every part of his body.

"Finish up in here so I can walk you to your car," he heard himself say in a deep, throaty voice. A yearning for her was stirring his insides, thundering all the way through his veins, making him want to say the hell with it and take her on that very table.

But he couldn't. He wouldn't.

"I'll be fine, Darius. I don't need you to walk me to my car."

As he studied her, he saw the way her eyes glowed in a seductive lure. He doubted she even realized it. He needed to act accordingly and not give in to what she was asking for without even knowing she was doing so.

"I'm walking you out anyway, Summer."

He saw the lure in her eyes quicken to a sharp edge and he wouldn't be surprised if she stood her ground. Then it would become a standoff, since he had every intention of walking her out. In fact, he intended to follow her home to make sure she got inside her house safely.

"Fine. Suit yourself, Darius."

Her words ripped through the air. He could tell by her tone that she wasn't happy, but that didn't bother him. When it came to her safety there was no compromising. He moved from the table to stand in front of her desk, convincing himself that it was his protective instincts kicking in where she was concerned, and nothing more.

Darius watched as Summer grabbed her purse and then he followed her out the door, pausing in the hall while she locked up her office. The shelter was quiet since most of the people in residence were probably in bed, asleep. "What did you have for dinner?" he asked when they began walking down the corridor toward the lobby.

"I worked through dinner."

Darius pressed his lips together to keep from saying a word that might have burned her ears. Knowing she had missed a meal bothered him a lot more than he cared to admit.

"And please, Darius, no sermons. I'm too beat to listen."

He glanced over at her. "I don't do sermons."

"Could have fooled me."

He halted his steps and brought her to a stop before rounding the corner that led to the lobby. She might be too beat to listen to what he had to say, but there was no doubt in his mind that she had plenty of energy for an argument and was gearing up for one. However, he had no intention of obliging her.

He leaned forward and placed a light kiss on her

lips. "You're much prettier when you're not trying to be difficult."

She frowned up at him, clearly caught off guard. "I'm not trying to be difficult."

He couldn't help but smile. "Could have fooled me."

He didn't even try to hold back a chuckle when she narrowed her gaze at him. Ignoring the look, his hand took hold of her elbow. "Come on, Summer, let me grab that file off my desk and then get you home before you fall flat on your face from exhaustion."

Summer glanced over her shoulder before opening the door to her house. She had been fully aware that Darius had followed her home. She could have been nice and invited him in, but she'd decided not to. There was only so much Darius Franklin she could take, and after the kisses they'd shared in her office tonight, she had reached her limit for today.

She didn't have to wonder what there was about him that made her feel so raw and exposed yet at the same time so well protected. Whenever they kissed, she couldn't help but recall the passion. And then there were the memories of the hopes and dreams that had blossomed in her heart of what she'd assumed was a promising future between them. She had even allowed her dreams to include marriage and babies.

She headed for the bathroom to take her shower, wondering if at any time during the past seven years Darius had regretted bragging about their night

together in such a degrading manner to his partner,
Walt Stewart. She appreciated the fact that Walt felt
she needed to know just what Darius had said.

Pain tore into her heart every time she realized just
how wrong she had been about him, and that made her
determined not to make another mistake by giving
him her heart a second time. But she *had* enjoyed their
kiss. In her mind, one didn't have to do with the other,
just as long as she knew where she stood with him and
where he stood with her.

He was now a dedicated businessman who seemed
to enjoy what he did for a living and she had a new life,
a new career and was no longer looking over her
shoulder, fearful of seeing Tyrone. The past seven
years had been good for her, although lonely. When it
came to men she had learned the hard way to play it
safe, and she would continue to do so.

And one sure way to do that was to make sure she
didn't assume anything where Darius was concerned.

Darius needed a shower to relax. After making sure
Summer had gotten home okay, he had driven straight
home with memories of their kisses running all through
his mind. Having her in his arms had felt natural, like
that was where she belonged. Considering what she'd
done to him seven years ago, was that weird or what?

When he had reluctantly ended their kiss, she had
taken her tongue and swept it across his lips. He still
felt a stirring deep in his gut just thinking about it. It
had been unexpected. It had felt good.

And now he knew where she lived and would make it his business to get her to invite him over to her place one night. It might take a while to work up to that, but he would get there. He wouldn't see her again until Monday, which was just as well since he of all people knew Summer was the type of woman who could grow on a man.

She was the type of woman who could easily get under a man's skin. And he had to admit that she had gotten under his tonight. She had made sensations he hadn't felt in years rush through him, reminding him what it was like to lose control with a woman.

Darius headed toward the shower with a deep frown on his face. No matter what Summer evoked within him, he was determined to remain immune to her charms. He had no intentions of making the same mistake twice.

Six

"How did your meeting go on Friday?"

Summer glanced up and met Darius's gaze. She had wondered if he would be dropping by the shelter today. She hadn't expected to see him Friday, but she hadn't known for sure when he would be back to complete the project he'd been hired by the TCC to do.

"I think the meeting went great. Mr. Novak appreciated the handouts and was very attentive to what I had to say. He agreed that based on our occupancy log, it would be a good idea to consider expanding the facilities sooner than later. He said he'd take his recommendations back to the other members of the TCC."

Darius nodded. "And how was your weekend?"

"Busy as usual. And yours?" she asked, watching

him carefully. She used to have the ability to read his thoughts, but now his expressions were unrevealing and she didn't have a clue as to what he was thinking.

"It was okay. After spending Friday at the refinery, I had to follow up several leads," he said, stepping into the room.

She immediately felt his heat, breathed in his scent and admitted to herself that she had missed seeing him around. "And you're still certain the fire was intentionally set?"

She tried not to notice how good he looked standing in front of her desk with a cup of coffee in his hand. All it took was a glance at his mouth to remember their kisses right here in this office last week.

She refused to admit she had purposely left her office door open on the off chance he dropped by Helping Hands today. On a number of occasions he had caught her unaware and she didn't want that to happen this time. She also refused to admit that she had thought about him a lot over the weekend, wondering how he was spending his time—and with whom. The latter was something she had no right to concern herself with, but she couldn't help it.

"I'll pick up the official report from the fire marshal this week, but so far, all evidence still points to arson," he said.

"Then I'm sure you'll be the one to solve this case."

Darius didn't want to think about what effect her confidence had on him at that very moment. She'd always had a way of making him feel that he could leap tall buildings with a single bound if he had to. He used to tell himself the reason she felt that way was because he had been the one to save her from a dangerous situation, and he shouldn't put much stock into it. But he had anyway.

"So, what's next?"

That was another thing that had drawn him to Summer, her interest in his job. She would ask questions and seemed to understand his excitement about it as well as his frustrations. He would enjoy getting off work at the end of his shift and dropping by her place to tell her how his day had gone.

"I'll continue to conduct an investigation over at the refinery while working on the security and the accounting systems here. Since the TCC wants me to personally handle both, I've delegated my other projects."

There, he'd just told her his plans which meant, whether she liked it or not, he would be hanging around for a while. He wondered if she had assumed he would be moving on and assigning the shelter job to someone else, but he couldn't read her expression.

"Well, I'll let you get back to work. I'll see you at noon."

He watched as her brow lifted. "Noon?"

He smiled. "Yes. We're doing lunch."

She stared at him. "Are we?"

"Sure we are, and I'll even let you twist my arm into getting one of those salads you seem to like so much."

There was a pause, and Darius sensed she was trying to determine whether it was worth the effort to start an argument with him. When she began speaking, she spoke her words slowly as if to make sure they were understood. "I don't want you to assume we're going to lunch together every day, Darius."

"Don't you like my company?"

She hesitated, and he watched her nervously lick her top lip with her tongue before she answered. "Whether I like your company or not has nothing to do with it. We have issues we haven't yet resolved."

They had issues yet to be resolved? She made it sound like she had been the injured party and not the other way around. He hadn't been the one to skip town with a man old enough to be her father who could buy her all the things Darius couldn't afford on his detective salary. They would resolve things all right, but his way. Pretty soon she would see how it felt to have someone you assumed loved you turn around and leave you high and dry with a broken heart.

"Some things can't be resolved and are better left alone," he said. "And in our case, maybe that's the way things should be, Summer. What happened between us was seven years ago. People change and they grow to regret things they did when they were young and foolish."

Darius maintained eye contact with her, assuming she was thinking about what he'd said. He made it sound as if he was giving her a chance to redeem herself, and that he was willing to forgive her for what she had done. Little did she know how far from the truth that was.

"Maybe you have the right idea," she finally said. "It *was* seven years ago and we've grown a lot since then."

"I'd like to believe we have." Deciding he didn't want to discuss it any further, he asked, "So, do we have another date for lunch?"

She hesitated and then said, "Yes, we do."

After Darius walked out of her office, Summer couldn't help wondering if she was making a mistake by agreeing to put the past behind them. He evidently found it easy to do so, but he hadn't been the one to get his heart broken. But then, on the other hand, she couldn't discount the fact that Darius had saved her life. And then another part of her wondered if perhaps she had put more stock in their affair, and had expected more from the relationship than he had.

She had gone a long time without getting involved with a man and she wasn't so sure if she could handle Darius—she wasn't even sure if she wanted to. She had gotten used to being by herself. Why was he determined to invade her space?

The only thing she was certain about was the way he made her feel whenever he touched her. To be honest, he didn't even have to touch her to make her hormones react. He could stand five feet away and she had the ability to feel how the tension in the air surrounding them seemed to vibrate, emitting all sorts of sensuous stirrings and longings. He had been in her office less than fifteen minutes and already her vital signs were at their highest peak.

But she was no longer concerned by the staggering degree of physical chemistry flowing between them. It had always been there, from the first. What she was concerned about was how easily she wanted to forgive him and believe that what Darius had said was true. Seven years ago, they had been different people with different values, at a different place in their lives. People change. And they come to regret decisions and actions of their past. Decisions and actions that they can't change.

She knew some men didn't like confrontation and Darius was probably of the mind that even if they hashed the issues out, it would not change anything. But still, was it too much to expect an apology for sharing something private and personal with his partner? Couldn't he see that doing so had degraded what they'd shared?

Even now she could vividly recall that day, after she and Darius had spent the night together. He had left her bed that morning seemingly in a good mood, making plans for them to spend the day together. But first he had to go home to get a change of clothes and stop by police headquarters to complete some paperwork, and she had to work a few hours at the restaurant where she was a part-time waitress.

When she'd returned home, she had waited for Darius. When hours passed, she had gotten worried. That evening, Walt had appeared on her doorstep with a message from Darius saying he'd had to leave town unexpectedly on police business. After delivering that message, Walt had asked if he could talk to her privately. That is when he'd told her how Darius had come to the station that day and bragged about finally sleeping with her. He had made a bet with Walt that it would take less than a month to share her bed. Discovering their one night together hadn't been anything more than a chance for him to win a bet had hurt her deeply. And then to know he'd gone back and told his friend had been another crushing blow.

While listening to Walt level with her about what Darius had done, she had barely been able to maintain her composure. Only after Walt had left did she break down and let it all out. She knew she had to leave Houston immediately and did not want to see Darius again, ever. It had been bad enough with Tyrone, but the hurt Darius had inflicted was even worse because in just a short time, she had fallen in love with him.

She had been too ashamed to call her aunt to tell her what had happened, so in the days that followed, she'd made some quick decisions. One of her regular customers at the restaurant, an author of academic books named Jack Lindsey, would be spending a year in Florida with his wife while he penned his next book. Jack had offered her the chance to accompany them as his assistant, to organize and edit all of his notes. He had made the offer before, but she had turned him down because of Tyrone's threats regarding what he would do if she ever left town. But with no future for her in Houston, she had quickly packed up and left town with the Lindseys.

The Lindseys had been wonderful and she had enjoyed the year she had spent with them on their beach property in Miami. She had buried herself in her work, determined to put Darius out of her mind and go about healing her heart. When she hadn't heard from him in over two weeks, that had only verified everything Walt had said. Their night together had been a conquest for him and nothing more.

Since both Mr. and Mrs. Lindsey were former teachers, they had encouraged Summer to pursue a college degree, and Mrs. Lindsey had even tutored her on those subjects Summer had felt would hold her back from getting accepted to any college. Using the money she'd made working for the Lindseys, along with a very nice bonus they had given her at the end of the year, she had remained in Miami to attend college there. She had poured all her time and energy into her classes, determined to reach every goal she had established for herself and refusing to wallow in the hurt and pain Darius had caused her.

Summer got up from her desk and looked out the window, not sure how she would handle the one man she thought she would never see again.

What she was up against now was how he could make her feel. Whenever she was around him, he was capable of bringing out feelings and desires that she wished would stay buried. In seven years, no man had made her remember how it felt to be a woman. A desired woman. It was something Darius could do so effortlessly.

When he met her gaze, she could see the desire in his eyes, and on most occasions he wasn't trying to mask it. It was as if he knew exactly what he was doing to her, what buttons to push, what words to say.

She had thought about him a lot over the weekend, wondering how and what he was doing. And, she thought as she bit her lower lip, with whom. She wished she could claim she didn't care, but she did. She couldn't help but notice how ladies would glance their way whenever they walked into the café together. There was feminine interest in their eyes and she couldn't very well blame them for it. After all, she was a woman, too.

She sighed deeply before checking her watch. It was time to make her rounds and greet everyone. She would keep herself busy until lunchtime.

Darius stared long and hard at the computer screen, thinking he must have missed something while setting up the billing system. He needed to go back and recheck. Or better yet, he thought, leaning back in the chair and rubbing the bridge of his nose, it would probably be a good idea if he kept his mind on what he was doing and stopped thinking about Summer. Having her on his mind was probably the reason he'd thought he'd found a number of irregularities in the TCC's accounting.

Deciding to give both his eyes and his mind a break, he pushed away from the desk and stood, needing to stretch his body. He had been sitting at the computer practically all morning and the limited space under the desk had been murder on his long legs.

He glanced at his watch. He had another hour to go before lunch and he couldn't deny he was looking forward to dining with Summer again. He tried convincing himself that spending time with her meant absolutely nothing, and was just a part of his plan for revenge. There was no reason to think it was anything more than that.

He breathed in deeply, truly wishing he believed that. But he knew if he wasn't careful, he would be succumbing to Summer's charms all over again. And he didn't want that. He had given his heart to her once and what she'd done had almost destroyed him, made him unable to put his complete trust in another woman.

He had asked her how her meeting with Kev had gone, but he'd already been privy to that information. To say she had impressed Kev was an understatement. Besides stating the obvious about what a good-looking woman she was, Kev had been taken with her keen sense of intelligence as well as her concern for the women who sought refuge at the shelter. Kev also felt she had a lot of good ideas that the TCC should definitely take under consideration.

Sitting back down at the computer, he resumed setting up the Helping Hands account, trying to push thoughts of Summer to the back of his mind. However, once again a few discrepancies within TCC's accounting system popped up.

He pulled back when his cell phone went off. It was Lance. "Yeah, Lance, what's up?"

"Kate's fixing dinner tonight and wants you to come eat with us."

Darius smiled. He liked Kate and would be the first to say she was just what Lance needed. "I'd love to."

"Great. I'll let her know."

"Lance?"

"Yeah?"

Darius paused, not sure if he should mention anything about the discrepancies he'd found in TCC's accounting. Huntington and his band of tight-wads managed the accounting for the club—namely the money they got from fundraisers and endowments. And everybody knew his group kept a tight squeeze on TCC's money supply. If there was anything wrong with the club's funds, they would know it. But still…

"Darius? What is it?"

Darius breathed in deeply. "Nothing," he finally said, deciding not to jump to any conclusions about the discrepancies until he'd had a chance to look at them more carefully.

"How are things going with you and Summer Martindale?"

Darius frowned. "You talk as if we're a couple."

"Aren't you?" Lance countered.

"Not yet."

There must have been something in his voice that gave him away.

"I don't know what your plans are regarding her, Darius, but be careful. They can backfire on you. If you're going to pursue her, then you need to forget about what happened seven years ago and move on."

Darius didn't say anything for a moment and then admitted, "I can't."

"You should try, man. When the shit blows up in your face, don't say I didn't warn you."

"Today I came prepared," Darius said, glancing down at his feet.

Summer followed his gaze and noted he had removed his boots and was now wearing a pair of leather loafers. That meant he had come to the shelter today prepared to walk over to the café, and *had* assumed she would have lunch with him. She wasn't sure whether she liked the fact that he'd known she would give in.

She returned her gaze to his face. "So I see. You're ready?"

"I'm always ready, Summer."

She had absolute confidence in the truth of that statement. "Excuse me for a second. I need to let Marcy know I'm leaving."

She walked over to Marcy's desk. Marcy was in her late fifties and was someone Summer had become close to since working at the shelter. "I'm going to lunch now, Marcy."

Marcy smiled. "Okay. Did you ever get that dripping faucet at your house fixed?"

Summer shook her head. "Not yet, but I better do so soon, since it's keeping me from getting a good night's sleep." She then turned to rejoin Darius and together they left the building to walk over to the café for lunch. Her morning had been busy and she needed time away from the shelter. She always enjoyed her lunch, at least whenever she could make time for it.

It was a beautiful day and for some reason, Summer couldn't push aside the pleasurable sensations she was feeling with Darius beside her. She felt lucky today. She had counseled two women that morning and after listening to their stories, a part of her felt blessed that she had cut her ties with Tyrone when she had, otherwise she could have been one of them. And although Tyrone had caused unnecessary drama that had landed him behind bars for twenty years, she was free to make choices about her life. Now it was her job to convince those two women they could make choices about their lives, as well.

"So, how has your day been so far?" Darius asked.

She began sharing bits and pieces of how busy she'd been as they continued their walk to the café. Although his legs were a lot longer than hers, he adjusted his steps to keep in line with hers. More than once, while sharing her ideas about a number of things she would like to see happen at the shelter, she would glance up and see how absorbed he was in what she was saying. They were ideas she hadn't shared with Kevin Novak for not wanting to overwhelm the man since everything she had in mind included a hefty price tag. But they were expenditures she felt would greatly benefit the women who sought refuge at the shelter.

Then, while it was on her mind, she asked about his brother, something she should have done long before now since she knew how close the two of them were. Like her, he had lost his parents at an early age, and he and his brother had been raised by their grand-mother.

"Ethan is doing fine now."

She opened her mouth to ask what he meant by that when suddenly a warm, masculine arm snaked around her waist to stop her from stepping in a rut in the cement sidewalk. "Thank you."

"Don't mention it," he said, releasing her.

Summer tried to ignore the sensations that raced through her veins at his touch. When they reached the café and he opened the door, she quickly moved past him, wondering how she was going to get through her meal.

Kate Thornton Brody smiled up at Darius. "You need a woman in your life," she said.

Darius lifted a brow, wondering where that had come from. He glanced across the living room and shot Lance a questioning look, but all his friend did was smile and shrug his shoulders. Damn, he hadn't been in the house five minutes and already Kate was on him about being single.

Seeing that Lance wouldn't be giving him much help, Darius reached out and placed a friendly arm around Kate's shoulder. "Sweetheart, you know I prefer being single."

She gave him one of her sidelong looks that said

she'd taken what he'd said with a grain of salt. "So did Lance at one time."

"But now he has you and he's a lucky man," Darius said truthfully. He had known Kate ever since she began working for Lance as his very competent administrative assistant when he took over Brody Oil and Gas a few years back, and had always liked her.

"What's for dinner? I'm starving," he quickly said, before Kate could make another comment about the state of his affairs or lack of them.

"Didn't you eat lunch?" Lance asked, finally moving off the sofa.

Lance's question reminded him of Summer...not that he could forget. He hated admitting that whenever he had lunch with her, it was a pleasant experience. She was a great conversationalist. Always had been. And today she'd seemed more relaxed with him, more at ease. And as usual, she had looked beautiful sitting across from him.

"Yes, I had lunch," he finally said. "A salad."

Humor lit Lance's eyes. "A salad? What kind of foolishness is that?"

"Don't let Lance tease you, Darius. There's nothing wrong with eating a salad," Kate said, walking back toward the kitchen.

When she was gone, Lance looked at him and chuckled. "I take it you had lunch with Summer."

Darius met Lance's amused look. "What makes you think that?"

"She's the salad girl."

Darius couldn't help but smile. When he'd left Houston because of Ethan's accident, Lance had shown up in Charleston to give him the support he needed. It was during that time that he had told Lance all about Summer, even how much she liked eating salads.

"I'd like to meet her. Invite her over one—"

"It's not that kind of relationship, Lance, and you know it," he said quickly, deciding to squash any foolish ideas that might be floating around in his best friend's head.

"Whatever you say," Lance said, smiling.

"I'm serious, Lance."

"Of course you are. I believe you."

Darius frowned. He could tell his friend really didn't believe him. "It's hard to love someone who has hurt you deeply," he said.

The amusement disappeared from Lance's face. "I'm glad everyone doesn't feel that way, Darius, or I wouldn't have Kate as my wife. If you recall, I almost lost her when I announced my engagement to another woman. But she still found it in her heart to give me another chance."

Darius's frown deepened. "So, what are you trying to say?"

Lance held his friend's gaze. "What I'm trying to say is that if you love someone, there can always be forgiveness."

"I really appreciate you walking me out to my car again, Barney, but it's really not necessary," Summer said to the security guard at her side.

"No problem, Ms. Martindale. Besides, it's Mr. Franklin's orders."

Summer shook her head, still not sure how Darius could give orders when he wasn't paying the man's salary. She was just about to ask Barney how that was possible when he suddenly said, "Someone has slashed your tires."

"What?"

"Your tires," he said, pointing his flashlight on her car. "They've been slashed."

Summer followed the beam of light and saw what he was talking about. She hauled in a deep breath, recalling the last time her tires had been slashed and who had been responsible. She forced herself to calm down as old fears tried to resurface.

That was all seven years ago. Tyrone was locked up and couldn't touch her. More than likely, the husband or significant other of one of the women at the shelter was venting his anger on her since the shelter was standing in the way of the person he really wanted to take it out on. But it couldn't be Samuel Green, since he was still locked up, held without bond.

"I need to follow procedures and report this to the police, Ms. Martindale," Barney was saying, interrupting her thoughts. "Please come back inside while I contact the authorities and complete an incident report."

Summer turned her attention away from her tires. "Yes, of course."

She moved to follow him back inside. She'd heard

reports of acts of revenge being directed at staff members who work with victims of violence. Incidents of rock throwing, drive-by shootings and even bomb threats had been reported. As far as she was concerned, the person who damaged her tires was nothing but a bully.

"Are you all right, Ms. Martindale?" Barney asked with concern when they had reached the door to go back inside.

She forced a smile on her lips. "Yes, I'm fine." She heard the words she'd just spoken, but wasn't sure she believed them herself.

Seven

"What's this about your tires getting slashed last night?"

Summer glanced up and saw Darius leaning in her office doorway. News had spread quickly. The evening crew from last night had a lot to share with the staffers that had arrived that morning. She'd figured he would hear about the incident sooner or later. She wished it had been later, since she really didn't want to talk about it right now.

"I'm sure you've heard the story, Darius, and I'm not in the mood to rehash it."

"Humor me," he said, crossing the threshold and closing the door behind him. She couldn't help but study his features. There was something different about his eyes. Their darkness was still striking, but now they contained an element of hardness she hadn't seen since that first day he had discovered her working at the shelter. And his lips were pressed together in a tight line. On most days, it wouldn't take much to look at his lips and remember how they had introduced her to pleasures of the most decadent kind in a single night.

"I'm listening."

Summer blinked. While she had been staring at him, probably like a lust-crazed woman, he had taken a seat in the chair in front of her desk. She leaned back, trying to relax under the intensity of his direct gaze, but found it difficult to do so.

"What you've already heard is probably correct," she started. "Barney walked me out to the car like he's been doing since that incident with Samuel Green and noticed my tires had been slashed. We came back inside, called the police to report it and he filled out an incident report. End of story."

"I don't think so."

She heard the near growl in his voice. He was angry, she could tell. And she knew his anger was not directed at her but at whomever had slashed her tires. Given his mood, that was a comforting thought.

"I want to find out who did it," he said in the same tone of voice. "What did the police say?"

She shrugged. "Not much. They would have liked a list of the women residing here to check out the names of husbands and boyfriends, but because of our confidentiality policy, we couldn't provide it for them. I contacted the TCC earlier today to see if we could have two guards here at night instead of one."

"I thought there were two guards here since the night of that incident with Green."

"That lasted all but two days before one of them was pulled. Evidently, the TCC rehashed the idea and felt only one was needed. That's why I called them— to see if they would reconsider since the staff members around here were beginning to get nervous. However, the man I spoke with at the TCC said adding an additional guard wasn't going to happen."

"Who did you talk to?"

"I asked for Kevin Novak but the person I talked to was an older gentleman by the name of Sebastian Huntington." She saw his jaw twitch. "You know him."

"Yes, I know him."

Summer noticed that he'd said the words in a tight voice with more than a little distaste. "He wasn't very friendly," she added. "Nothing at all like Mr. Novak."

He didn't say anything but from the way he was looking at her, she knew he was taking it all in. And then he asked, "Is there anything else?"

She shook her head. "No, nothing other than the piece of paper that had been placed on my car, which I also mentioned to the police last night."

He lifted a brow, his posture on full alert. "What paper?"

"One night last week someone placed a note under the wiper blade. Barney had walked me to my car, and he pulled it off and gave it to me, thinking it was some kind of sales flyer. It wasn't until I stopped at a traffic light and glanced at it did I notice what it said."

"And what did it say?" he asked, leaning closer and moving toward the edge of his seat.

She swallowed, remembering precisely what was written in bold letters on the paper. "It said, 'I take care of my own.'"

The moment Darius left Summer's office he darted into an empty conference room and called Kevin. He picked up on the second ring. "This is Kevin."

"Kev, were you informed that Huntington had reduced the number of security guards at Helping Hands?"

"No."

An angry Darius went on to tell Kevin about the incident that had occurred last night.

"Huntington has no right to make those kinds of decisions without discussing it with the committee first, and I am part of that committee," Kevin said, almost livid.

"The man's been a part of the TCC for so long I believe he thinks he owns it, which is why he constantly overlooks anything the younger members have to say," Darius said.

"And how is Summer Martindale?"

"She's a little shaken up, although she was trying not to show it. The staff here is nervous—first Green breaking doors down and now this tire-slashing incident.

It doesn't bode well. There have been revenge-type incidents reported in various cities around the country, and they are aware of it. We need to make sure they feel protected."

Darius tried to convince himself that his concern for Summer was no different than his concern for any other woman he'd once been involved with, but deep down a part of him knew that wasn't true. He would even go so far as to admit missing her whenever he spent time away from Helping Hands.

They were feelings that he didn't want to feel. One way to remedy that was to start keeping his distance, but then he wouldn't be able to make her feel the way he had felt when she'd left. He just needed to make sure he kept things in perspective.

"I totally agree," Kevin said, bringing Darius's attention back to the matter at hand. "I'll confront Huntington myself, and if I have to, I'll call a special meeting of the board."

Moments later, Darius hung up the phone feeling a lot better than he had before making the call to Kev. He knew his friend wouldn't like the "executive" decision Huntington had made regarding the security at the shelter any more than he did. As usual, the man was trying to throw his weight around, fighting for power he really didn't have. But Darius relaxed a bit, knowing Kev was on it.

He glanced at his watch. He needed to leave for a while to attend to business concerning the fire at the refinery—he had to talk to several guys who had been off work the day he'd met with the employees the last time. But he intended to return to the shelter before Summer left for lunch. The thought of her walking anywhere alone troubled his mind.

From now on, he would make sure that she was well protected. At all costs.

Three days later, Summer glanced over at Darius before looking down at her watch. It was a little past eight in the evening. She had volunteered to stay for a few hours to help man the abuse hotline, and he had surprised her when he volunteered to assist her.

At first, she hadn't been sure whether women on the other line would want to unload their pain and anguish to a man, but from overhearing bits and pieces of his conversations, she could tell he was handling things quite nicely. She would be the first to admit that he had a good demeanor for assisting those who called in, male or female.

"What time are you leaving?" she asked him. Since the night her tires had gotten slashed, he had made it his business to return to the shelter every day after being at the refinery in the mornings, to walk her to the café for lunch. And if she remained late in the evenings, he did so, as well. Then he would not only walk her to her car, but would follow her home to make sure she got in safely.

"I'll leave when you leave," he said, glancing over at her.

In a way, his protectiveness irked her. She didn't

want him to feel like she needed him in any way. "There are two security guards now, so I'll be all right." She really hadn't been surprised when, the day after the tire-slashing incident, two guards were on duty. There was no doubt in her mind that Darius had had something to do with it, although what exactly, she wasn't sure.

"I plan to leave in a few minutes," she said.

He smiled over at her. "Then so will I."

And he did. After she had handled the last call she would take, she gathered up her belongings and headed for the door with him by her side. He nodded to the guards on duty as they passed.

"Nice night," he said.

She looked up at the sky and saw the full moon and the stars, and how they illuminated the otherwise dark sky. He was right. It was a nice night.

"I'll be following you home again."

She glanced over at him. "It's your gas."

She said nothing as they continued walking. When he opened the car door for her, she slid inside, noticing how his gaze shifted to her legs when her skirt accidentally showed a little bit of flesh. She started to say something about his wandering eyes and decided not to. It probably wouldn't do any good anyway.

The drive to her place was uneventful and whenever she glanced in her rearview mirror, he was there. She would admit that, considering the incidents of the past two weeks, she felt a semblance of security knowing he was near, just like the days and nights following that episode with Tyrone.

She parked her car in the driveway and was surprised when he parked behind her and got out of his vehicle. The other times he had followed her home, he had stayed in the car while she went inside and then left. She wondered why he had changed the routine, and she didn't like the way her skin seemed to feel warm all over as he came closer.

"You have a two-car garage. Any reason you aren't parking in it?" he asked, coming to a stop in front of her.

"It's full of boxes. I haven't unpacked everything yet." She paused. "Why did you get out of the car?"

She appreciated him seeing her home, but she had no intentions of asking him inside. Her house was her place. Her own private space. When she had moved to Somerset and found what she thought was the perfect neighborhood along with the perfect house, she had moved in, determined to keep bad memories from past experiences outside. Darius was a reminder of a bad past experience.

"I overheard you mention to Marcy that you had a dripping bathroom faucet that was keeping you awake at night. I thought I'd take care of it for you."

"Now?"

"I don't have anything else I have to do."

Summer sighed. She did. She wanted to take a shower and go to bed. "Thanks for the offer, but I'll get around to calling a plumber later this week."

"No need. It will only take a minute. Then I'll be out of here."

Standing in the shadows, she could barely see the features of his face in the moonlight. But what she did see was a man who had first been her friend and then her lover. She didn't know what he was now, aside from very determined to look out for her.

From the look of things, his mind was made up. She really wanted the faucet fixed. Since he *had* volunteered, she might as well take him up on his offer. "All right, then. Thanks."

"I've told you more than once that you don't ever have to thank me for doing what I do when it involves you, Summer."

She swallowed. Yes, he had said that more than once. Most times had been when they were sitting on a sofa, hugged up while watching television. She'd enjoyed those nights when they would sit curled up with a movie, sharing a bowl of popcorn in her living room, talking.

Another thing she had appreciated about him was that he had never tried pressuring her into sex. That night when they had finally made love, it was because it was something they both wanted, not something he had pushed her into doing.

"Yes, I know you don't need my thanks, but I don't want you to think I don't appreciate it," she finally said.

"Fine. Let me grab my toolbox out the car."

She waited while he went back to his car. Moments

later, she grabbed her mail out of the box and opened the door, hoping she wasn't making a mistake letting him inside.

He followed her and closed the door behind them. The click of the lock made her fully aware that they were alone, totally and completely. Trying to ignore her nerves, she threw the mail on the table. Since she paid most of her bills online, she knew the majority of it was nothing but junk mail anyway.

"Nice place," he complimented, glancing around. She knew he was taking stock of her place.

She tried to ignore how at home he looked in her living room. Like he belonged there. "Thanks."

This house was a lot more spacious than her apartment had been, and since she had a job that paid well, she could afford nice furniture.

"Which bathroom has the dripping faucet?"

"The one in my bedroom." Too late she realized that he was going to go into her most private room.

"Which way?"

"Down the hall to your right."

When he disappeared around the corner, she inhaled deeply, deciding she needed to do something other than just stand there while he repaired the faucet. She needed to at least appear busy. Unfortunately, there weren't any plants she had to water, nor were there dishes in her sink that she needed to wash. Her gaze lit on the junk mail that she had placed on the table and she decided now was as good a time as any to go through it.

* * *

Darius moved down the hall toward Summer's bedroom, thinking she had a lovely home. It was an old house, but very well cared for and maintained. He also liked the vibrant colors that suited her decor and the furnishings that blended in so well. And she was still neat as a pin, he thought, entering her bedroom and glancing around. His gaze came to a stop on the queen-size bed and he couldn't help but wonder what man had probably shared it with her. A rich, older man, no doubt.

Overhearing the conversation about her dripping faucet had given him the perfect excuse to invite himself in. For some reason, he had wanted to see the house that she was living in without him. Although they'd never actually discussed marriage seven years ago, as far as he was concerned, it had been the next thing on the agenda for them. He'd known that after what Whitman had put her through, it would be hard for her to put her trust in any man, but he had been willing to be patient and give her whatever amount of time she needed to learn to trust a man again. She'd needed to know that he was someone she could depend on. Someone who would always be there for her. Too bad she hadn't given them a chance.

Forcing those thoughts from his mind, he headed toward her bathroom. He had just stepped over the threshold and placed the toolbox on the floor when she frantically called out his name.

He rushed to the living room and saw total shock on her face. "Summer? What's wrong?"

She stared up at him, barely able to force words past her lips. But he did hear the one single name she said. "Tyrone."

He looked at her, confused, not sure why she was bringing up the man who'd caused her nothing but grief. "What about Whitman, Summer?"

She glanced down and he followed her gaze to the mail sprawled at her feet. He quickly figured that something in one of the letters must have upset her.

He bent down, picked up the envelopes and flipped through them. Then he saw a letter from the Texas Parole Board. From the look of the envelope—specifically, all the stamp marks all over it—the post office had made several attempts to deliver it to her.

He pulled out the letter and read it, and then took a deep breath. As a former police officer, he was familiar with Texas law regarding those who'd been victims of violent crimes. A standard letter was issued to notify victims of the parole board's decision to release an inmate.

Darius glanced up at the date of the letter. It had been sent over a month ago. Tyrone Whitman was now a free man.

"I want you to drink this and please don't tell me that you don't need it because you do," Darius said, walking over to where Summer sat on the sofa with a cup of coffee laced with brandy in his hand.

Something had had him on edge all day, and he hadn't been able to figure out what. But now he knew.

The thought that the man who had caused Summer so much grief had only served seven years of a twenty-year sentence made him very angry. But right now, Summer didn't need his anger. More than anything, she needed his support.

Surprisingly, she took the cup without giving him a hard time and took a sip. A frown appeared on her face and he knew why—he had made it a little too strong but if anything, it would help her sleep.

"I can't believe it," she said, breaking the quiet stillness of the room and leaning forward to place the cup on the coffee table. "How can Tyrone be out of prison? That makes no sense."

Darius had to agree with her. It definitely made no sense given the man's crime. They should have put him in jail and thrown away the key. There was no way Whitman should be free to walk around. At least not on this planet. How could they have done such a thing?

He cringed whenever he thought about the final days of the trial and the threats Whitman had shouted out to Summer, saying what he would do to her if he ever got out. He wondered if Summer was remembering those days. He doubted she could forget. She stood and began pacing the floor. He watched her. He of all people knew how she felt, how upset she had to be.

"Tomorrow I'll make a few calls and try to pinpoint his whereabouts," he said, trying to make her feel secure. "Usually when someone who has committed a serious crime is paroled, they're released with a number of restrictions. I bet Whitman can't leave Houston."

She stopped pacing and glanced over at him with blatant hope in her gaze. "You think so?"

"I'll find out tomorrow."

Seeing the panic she was fighting to control gave him pause. At that moment she was no longer the confident, self-assured woman he had watched over the past two weeks. Now there was real fear in her eyes and a sign of helplessness in her voice, and he didn't like it.

Crossing the room he pulled her into his arms. And when she began to tremble while he held her close, whatever hard casting surrounding his heart began to crumble. She needed him and there was no way he could not be there for her.

As if she was relieved to be able to hold on to something solid, she wrapped her arms around him. He was unprepared for the slew of emotions that rushed through him. He would protect her with his life if he had to, and would never let Whitman get close to her again.

He pulled back slightly, wanting to look at her, to make sure she was okay, and when his gaze settled on her lips, he was drawn to them like a magnet. Without any control, he lowered his mouth to hers.

The moment he drew her tongue into his mouth and began feasting on it, he felt sensations all the way to his toes and couldn't do anything but shiver with the pleasure of their intimacy. He drew his arms around her, tightening his hold to bring her body flush with his.

Summer felt his hardness, firm and rigid, pressing

against her and marveled that his body was letting her know how much he wanted her. The only times she'd ever been kissed with such heat and passion was when he did the kissing.

He shifted the angle of his head, which caused her to follow as she tilted the curve of her mouth to his and nearly moaned out loud when his tongue took hold of hers with an intensity that made her weak in the knees.

When he finally released her lips, she leaned into him and sighed deeply. She had needed that kiss. She had needed the connection.

He felt firm, warm and solid—everything she needed at that moment. And in his arms she felt safe and secure. Protected. The thought that Tyrone was no longer locked up behind bars sent real fear through her, fear she was trying hard not to show. But every time she remembered those threats he'd yelled out in the courtroom while being taken away, she couldn't ignore the real panic that wanted to overtake her entire being.

"I don't want you to stay here tonight. You should come home with me, Summer."

She leaned back in his arms and met his gaze. "I can't do that, Darius. I'll be okay and—"

"No, Summer, think about it. I don't want to scare you, but until we know for sure that Whitman is in Houston, I don't want you here alone. What if those two incidents at the shelter had nothing to do with a disgruntled husband or boyfriend? What if Whitman is in violation of his parole and is not in Houston but here in Somerset and responsible for leaving that note on your windshield as well as slashing your tires?"

Darius saw the glint of real fear in her eyes when she considered those possibilities. What he'd said was true. He was not deliberately trying to scare her but she had to face the facts. And until he checked to see just where Whitman was and what he was doing, he would not let her feel safe. Hell, as far as he was concerned, as long as Whitman walked the streets he wouldn't advise Summer to feel safe. She had become an obsession to the man. In Whitman's eyes, she had betrayed him and he intended to teach her a lesson for doing so. He had made that threat in the courtroom with a crazed look in his eyes. Darius would never forget it.

"I'll go back to the shelter and sleep on the sofa in my office, and—"

"And what if word gets around to the women at Helping Hands that you, the woman who counsels them, is in the same predicament they are? Will that offer them any real hope for a brighter future when the man who disrupted your life seven years ago is still doing so?"

Summer's throat tightened as she stared up at him. She wished she could go anywhere but home with him. Being in such close quarters when she was feeling so vulnerable would be temptation she wasn't sure she could handle.

"Go on and pack an overnight bag for now, at least until I find out a few things tomorrow. If I get information indicating Whitman is in Houston behaving himself under the watchful eye of a parole officer, then I'll bring you back here tomorrow. Until then, you're going to be with me, Summer."

Summer breathed in deeply. A part of her wanted to scream out that this had all been a mistake, a nasty nightmare, and she would wake up any minute snuggled in Darius's arms for another reason, one that didn't have anything to do with Tyrone.

Darius released her, dropping his arms. "Get your bag so we can go. I'll wait here."

Summer looked at Darius, knowing his mind was set about her going home with him. There was nothing she could say to make him consider leaving her here tonight. But a part of her didn't want to be here tonight, the part that vividly recalled Tyrone's threats. She was well aware of what the man was capable of.

Because she hadn't lived in town for long, she hadn't gotten to know her neighbors. There were elderly couples that lived on either side of her that she would see on occasion. But other than the staff at the shelter, Darius was the only person she knew in Somerset. She had planned to join some community organizations but hadn't gotten around to doing so.

Making a decision, she said, "All right. It won't take me long to get my things."

A faint smile touched his eyes. "Take your time. I'm not going anywhere."

Her heart felt full. Some things had changed, but Darius was Darius, the man who'd always been and forever would be her knight in shining armor. The one person she could always depend on to be there for her.

Without saying anything else, she rushed off to her bedroom to pack.

Eight

Summer fell in love with Darius's home the moment she walked through the door. Although it was too dark outside for her to see everything, she knew he had taken her to a sprawling two-story ranch house. When she stepped into his living room, she felt a sense of comfort. She knew it was strange for her to feel that way, but she couldn't help it. During the short drive he had made her feel safe, assuring her that he would find out everything he could about Tyrone's whereabouts and that until he did, she would stay with him.

She glanced around and wondered if he'd hired an interior designer to decorate his home. Everything was color coordinated perfectly, and the furniture complemented the decor. A huge brick fireplace took up one entire wall and a bevy of windows guaranteed sun-shine deep in the house during the daylight hours.

To shield the foyer from the interior rooms, a glass-blocked wall was erected between the main living area and the front door. The furniture in the living room was dark, rich leather and looked com-fortable as well as sturdy.

"You have a beautiful home, Darius," she said when he followed her inside, carrying her overnight case.

"Thanks. Come on and let me get you settled in the guest room. It's past midnight and you have to be tired."

She was, and couldn't wait to get a good night's sleep, or at least try, she thought. But then she figured that he had to be tired, as well. He had spent the day at both the shelter and the refinery.

Moments later, after following him up a flight of stairs, she stepped into the guest bedroom. She glanced around in total awe. The spacious room had a high roof beam with Old Hickory decor. The king-size bed appeared massive, and the bedspread was a colorful patchwork that matched the country curtains.

"Evidently, your security company is doing well," she said.

When he didn't respond, she glanced over at him and saw a hardness that had formed around his mouth. What had she said to irritate him?

"Darius?"

"Yes, it's doing well," he finally replied in a somewhat biting tone. "There's a guest bath over there with a Jacuzzi tub," he said, pointing across the room. "My bedroom is at the end of the hall if you need anything. Good night."

Summer held her composure as she watched him quickly leave, closing the door behind him. Again she wondered what she had said that had hit a nerve with him. Why had commenting on his success bothered him?

She moved toward the bed and decided that when she saw him in the morning, she would find out.

Darius lay in bed wide awake, staring up at the ceiling. After he'd left Summer, he had made his rounds, making sure everything was locked and secured before going to his bedroom. There he had continued to stew over her comment, which had reminded him that a man's wealth was all she cared about.

He rubbed a hand down his face, not wanting to think that, but what else was he supposed to think? Now that she knew he had a little money, would her attitude toward him change?

He had brought her to his home to protect her, but that didn't mean he had to forgive her for all her past deeds. He wasn't sure that he could. His hands tightened into fists. He heard a sound and glanced over at the illuminated clock on the nightstand. It was almost two in the morning. Since his state-of-the-art security system hadn't sounded to alert him of an intruder, he guessed that Summer was up and moving around in his home. Evidently, she couldn't sleep, either.

Easing out of the bed, he slipped on a pair of jeans. He walked out of his bedroom and immediately saw a light shining downstairs.

When he reached the living room, he didn't see her anywhere. He gently pushed open the kitchen door. She was sitting at the kitchen table drinking what appeared to be a cup of tea, wearing a silk bathrobe belted around the waist. And although he had a feeling she was fighting hard not to do so, he could tell by the trembling of her shoulders that she was crying. Tears from any woman were his downfall—and when they came from Summer, doubly so.

Crossing the room, he fought the tightening of his heart. Hearing his movement, she whipped her head around and met his gaze. But she hadn't been quick enough to wipe away her tears. Without asking what the tears were for, he reached out his arms. "Come here, Summer."

She stared at him for a moment and he wasn't sure exactly what she would do. Then she rose to her feet and crossed the distance separating them. He pulled her into his arms and when he did so, she buried her face in his chest.

"Shh. It's okay, sweetheart. Things are going to be okay."

She shook her head and wiped her eyes, pulling back slightly to look up at him. "No, they're not. I've gotten you upset with me and I don't know why."

At that moment, he felt like a total ass and wished there was a way he could take back his earlier behavior, but he couldn't. So he stood there and held her in his arms, remembering times past when he would hold her the same way just moments before he would claim her mouth with his.

He knew at that moment that his desire for her was just as keen as it had ever been and, unable to fight what he was feeling, he gazed into her face just seconds before using the tip of his tongue to trace a line across her lips.

He heard the catch in her breath and tried to ignore it. He eased closer, unable to stop his body from responding to it. His hard erection pressed against her, warming him in a way he hadn't been warmed in a long time. His tongue left the corners of her mouth to glide over her bottom lip before pulling it into his mouth to suck on it a little. And then there was the feel of her nipples pressing into his bare chest like hardened tips.

He released her bottom lip, but only long enough to press his mouth fully onto hers, needing this taste of her, liking how she trembled in his arms not from fear but from his safekeeping. He had thought about this part of their relationship many times, the moments when he would capture her mouth and take them both to another level. Then one night their kissing had driven them to lose control and they had made love. He continued to kiss her deeply, wanting to lose himself in the kiss again like he had that night. And wanting to lose himself inside of her. He couldn't for the life of him remember connecting to any woman and feeling this way.

"Darius."

The sound of his name sent shudders of arousal through him. It was spoken in a breathless tone, a voice barely able to do anything but purr out a sexy timbre. It made the heat within him rise to a temperature that could easily cause him to boil over.

He shifted his hips and thighs to plaster them closer to the juncture of hers. Every cell within his body felt vibrantly alive, sensitized to her. His mind was finally in sync with what the rest of his body already knew. He wanted her.

He had to have her.

There was no question about his wants and his needs, only about how long he could last without having them satisfied. He pulled back, separating their mouths, but his gaze held hers and he knew she saw in his features the desire he could not hide. His entire being was ruled by an urge to mate with her, to share a physical intimacy to a degree he hadn't had since the last time they'd been together.

While her eyes continued to hold his, she brushed the back of her hand across his cheek and the caress sent shivers through him. He let out the breath he'd been holding, and his hands dropped from her waist to cup her backside, bringing her snug against him.

He could feel the fluttering in her stomach stirring against his erection, making it throb. His nostrils picked up her scent and blood pounded through his veins. He felt himself losing what little control he had and fought to rein it back in. Then she did something he hadn't expected. She made a move he couldn't combat.

She reached out and eased down his zipper before inserting her hands through the opening to cup him, as if she needed to touch, stroke and massage his aroused body part, getting reacquainted with its size and thickness. She didn't break eye contact with him, and he grew even more aroused with her bold ministrations. The more she stroked, the more his body vibrated, making blood rush through his veins, all going directly to that throbbing part of his body.

Minutes ticked by as he continued to stand there and stare at her while she literally drove him over the edge with her hand. He studied her face, saw the intent look in her eyes, the need to touch him this way. There was a feminine glow in her gaze that stirred everything male within him, and then once again, catching him off guard, she leaned in closer, stood on tiptoes and slid her tongue all around his lips, leaving a wet path in its wake. She caressed his mouth with the tip of her tongue the same way her fingertips were now stroking his aroused shaft.

He heard himself groan at the pleasure easing up his spine and he knew if he didn't stop her now, he would embarrass himself in her hands when he preferred being inside of her body.

Now it was his turn to catch her off guard. He gently pushed her hand away seconds before sweeping her into his arms. He leaned down and kissed her with a voraciousness that had her moaning in his mouth.

When he finally pulled away, he took in a deep breath and knew he had to get completely submerged inside her body before he lost it. He stared down at her kiss-swollen lips as he held her in his arms.

"Do you know what you've asked for?" He wanted to make sure they were on the same page.

She held his gaze. "Yes. I know."

"You sure it's what you want?" He had to make doubly sure.

She shifted in his arms and ran her wet, warm tongue across his bare chest. The muscles in his stomach tightened and he knew, without her uttering a single word, he had gotten his answer.

Without saying anything else, he carried her upstairs to his bedroom.

Summer felt hot.

And when Darius placed her on his bed and joined her there, she felt passion that had been bottled up inside of her, ready to boldly claim its freedom. Every bone in her body seemed to vibrate, needing a release.

Her head began spinning when Darius removed her clothes with a swiftness that sent pieces flying everywhere. Then he stood and in record time, dropped his jeans and put on a condom he'd taken out of the nightstand drawer. Moments later, when she lay flat on her back, naked, he towered over her and she felt her thighs quiver with a yearning she hadn't felt in years.

He leaned back to slowly peruse her body and she felt heat every place his eyes touched, especially around her feminine core where his gaze seemed to linger, making sensations stir deep within her. The look in his eyes gave her more than an inkling of what he was thinking, and when he reached out and lifted her hips, placing her legs across his shoulders, she literally cried out before his mouth had a chance to touch her.

She cried out again when his mouth did touch her. He pushed his tongue inside, working it around in her with a greed that sent sparks shooting off in her, scorching everywhere it touched and weakening every bone in her body, turning her muscles to mush.

He spread her legs wider as his mouth continued to inflict upon her torment that was unyielding. What he was doing had captured her senses, totally wrecked her brain cells and fractured all rational thought. Physically, she was beginning to feel herself break into pieces and she grasped the strong arms on each side of her, trying to let him know there was no way she could take any more.

As if determined to prove to her that she could, he continued his torment on her body, tightening his grip on her thighs as his tongue dived deeper inside of her. When he flicked across a sensitive part of her, she shattered, and helplessly screamed his name as an onslaught of sensations ripped into her.

It was only then that he pulled back and straddled her, and before her lungs could fill with more air, he entered her in one deep thrust as he captured one of her breasts into his mouth, sucking deeply on a nipple.

The joining had been so perfect it nearly brought tears to her eyes. She grabbed hold of his head to hold him to her breast and wrapped her legs around him to keep him inside of her. But the movement of his body told her he wasn't going anywhere.

He began moving, retreating and then pushing back in. Over and over again. Harder. Deeper. Faster. She felt every hard inch of him, felt the strong veins of his erection throb deep inside of her and push her over an edge that had her moaning yet again.

And when he shifted his mouth to her other breast and began the same mind-wrecking torment, her moan turned into another scream. She felt every nerve in her body explode, and she began riding a wave that took her across the top of anything and everything. When his body stiffened and bucked mercilessly while he tightly gripped her hips, she knew this was the fusing of not only their bodies, but their minds and souls.

And at that moment, nothing else existed in her world but the man who continued to push in and out of her while screaming her name. This was the same man who'd first shown her how beautiful the joining of a man and woman could be. The same man who moments later slumped down on the bed beside her and pulled her into his arms, holding her as if he never, ever wanted to let her go.

Summer awoke with the sunlight shining on her face and a strong, hard body plastered to her own. She shifted slightly and looked over at the man sleeping beside her, the man whose strong masculine leg was thrown over hers and whose arms, even in sleep, were wrapped around her.

Memories of last night flowed through her mind. It was the first time she had made love in seven years and it had been everything that she had remembered and more. Same man. Same passion. Same love.

She closed her eyes thinking that by rights, she should be upset with herself for still loving him and for the weakness that allowed her to tumble back into bed with him, especially after the way he had cheapened their first night together. But then she couldn't feel remorse when every part of her body was rejuvenated, like it had been awakened from a long sleep by pure pleasure. It had been making love with Darius the last time that had made her appreciate the fact she'd been born a woman, and it was his lovemaking now that was deepening that appreciation.

But still…memories of her pain, her humiliation wouldn't completely go away. How could a man who was so caring when it came to her so easily dishonor her the way he had? She had fallen in love with him completely and when he had made love to her that night, that love had intensified to a point that totally overwhelmed her.

He hadn't said the word *love* to her, but she had been certain of his feelings and had felt he'd displayed with his actions what he hadn't spoken. But she'd discovered her assumptions had been wrong. She did not intend to make the same mistake twice. All she and Darius had just shared was a sexual release. For her, it was a long time coming. She would not assume anything about their relationship ever again. She would accept it for what it was.

He shifted in bed and she tilted her head to look over at him. Before she could say a word, he leaned over and kissed her with a tenderness that made her groan. She didn't have to mull over what they were about to do again, this time in the brightness of the sunlight. And when he eased his body over hers, she wrapped her arms around his neck and eagerly gave him the mouth he seemed so intent to claim.

Summer stood at the window in her office. She kept replaying in her mind what had transpired last night and this morning. Although Darius had made love to her with an intensity and passion that nearly brought tears to her eyes, on the drive back over to her place this morning, she could sense him withdrawing. Why? Was she afraid she might assume just because they had slept together that she would think he wanted her back in his life? If that was the case, then he didn't know how wrong he was about it. She knew better than to think that way. She had learned her lesson well.

He had insisted on driving her to the office after he'd taken her home to dress, and he hadn't had a lot to say about what they had shared last night. Instead, he'd kept the conversation centered on Tyrone and all the things he would be checking on, saying he would take a trip to Houston if he had to.

He was still displaying those protective tendencies,

but she could feel him putting up his guard, shielding emotions from her, keeping them out of her reach. More than once while in his arms last night and this morning, she had been tempted to ask him why he had done what he did seven years ago. But then she would decide to leave well enough alone. What happened was no longer a threat as long as she kept her heart out of the mix. Besides, she had bigger fish to fry. Tyrone Whitman and his whereabouts were what she needed to stay focused on. It was the only thing she should care about, the only thing that mattered.

The thought of Tyrone being free made her skin crawl, but she refused to allow him to make her live in total fear. More than ever she was convinced he was the one who'd left that note on her windshield and slashed her tires, mainly because those were things Tyrone would do. Saying he took care of his own was something he'd said to her more than once. The reason she hadn't made the connection before was because she had assumed he was still locked up in prison. But now she knew that was not the case.

She glanced up at the clock on the wall. Darius said he would be coming back to walk her over to the café for lunch, and not to leave without him. This would be one time she did what he asked without any hesitation.

The phone on her desk rang and she immediately went to pick it up, hoping it was Darius with good news. "Hello?"

The person on the other end didn't say anything. "Hello?" she repeated. Chills ran down her spine when the person finally hung up. She tried to convince herself it was probably just a misdialed number. But deep down she had a feeling that wasn't true.

Darius's hands tightened on the steering wheel as he turned down the street that would take him to Helping Hands. Already he was regretting the news he was about to deliver to Summer.

He had made a call to the Houston Police Department as soon as he'd dropped Summer off at work. He'd been told Walt was out of town on an investigation, so he had spoken with Manny, another detective he knew. It had taken Manny less than an hour to find out what he wanted to know.

Manny had verified Whitman was out on parole with an order not to leave Houston. However, according to Manny, Whitman could not be found at what should have been his current address, and his landlord hadn't seen him in weeks. Since Whitman had a week or so left before they could haul him in for violating parole, so far he hadn't broken any laws…unless it could be proven he had left Houston.

There was no doubt in Darius's mind that Whitman had been in Somerset and was possibly still around. Since Somerset was such a small town, it would be easy for Whitman to find out where Summer worked—as well as where she lived. The thought of her being at Whitman's mercy again was enough to make every fiber of his being roar in anger.

He shifted his thoughts to last night and this morning.

While making love to her, he had tried holding himself back but he hadn't been able to control his emotions. Never had he been so affected by making love to a woman. It was as if the last seven years hadn't existed and there had never been a wedge between them. Last night and this morning fit perfectly into his plans. After this morning, he was supposed to take her back home, tell her about all the wealth he had accumulated over the years, that he was a member of the TCC and that not only did he know Kevin Novak but that Kevin was one of his closest friends. He had wanted to see the hurt in her eyes.

But Whitman's parole made that impossible—at least that's what he told himself. If it was determined the man was a threat to Summer, that would mean she'd stay with him for a while. She wouldn't like the idea, but he was determined to protect her at all costs.

Summer had been hoping, praying that the last seven years in jail would have changed Tyrone and she would no longer matter to him. It was disheartening to know she had been wrong and there was a strong chance he was stalking her again.

She told Darius about the strange phone call she had gotten that morning, and he, too, was convinced it had been Tyrone.

"Come on, let's go to lunch."

During lunch at the café Darius received a call. After the conversation ended, Summer knew from the look on his face that she was not going to like what he had to say.

He proved her right. "Before coming to the shelter I stopped at police headquarters to alert them that Whitman might be in the area. I provided them with a description of how he looked the last time I saw him, figuring his looks hadn't changed much over the years. But even if they had, Somerset is a small enough town that a stranger would stick out like a sore thumb."

He stopped talking, but she could tell there was more. "And?" she prompted.

"And they think he's been seen. A couple of the police officers who were cruising the area a few blocks from the shelter got suspicious of a guy who met Whitman's description. When they tried to approach him to question him, he ran."

Summer didn't say anything for a moment. "I refuse to let Tyrone scare me again, Darius. Although it didn't work the last time, I'm going to get another restraining order."

"That's a good idea. If he is taken into custody here in Somerset for any reason, his parole will automatically be revoked."

Darius hesitated a moment and then said, "Although you're refusing to let Tyrone scare you, I'm hoping you'll continue to stay with me until this issue with him is resolved. It will only be a matter of time before he finds out where you live, if he doesn't know already. Alarm or no alarm, if he ever breaks inside your home again, depending on his frame of mind, there's no telling what he will do. If knowing he will go back to jail and serve out the rest of his sentence hasn't deterred him, that can only mean he doesn't care. And people who don't care will do just about anything to get back at the person they think has betrayed them."

Summer knew what Darius said was true. Tyrone had held a gun to her head, willing and ready to end her life as well as his own. She really didn't want to go home with Darius again, but she didn't have a choice. Even after what they had shared last night and this morning, she could still feel tension between them. She could tell he still had his guard up.

"Summer?"

She met his gaze, felt the heat in the dark depths of his eyes. He wanted to keep her safe. And he wanted her. Summer knew that no matter how guarded he was being, he couldn't deny he enjoyed having her back in his bed, and she would admit she enjoyed being there. Intimacy between them wasn't just good, it was off the charts. Sexual tension was always oozing between them, even when she didn't want it to, like now.

Knowing he was waiting on an answer, she said, "Okay, I'll move in with you for the time being if you think it will be for the best."

Nine

A week later, as Darius sat in the TCC café waiting to meet with Lance, he was convinced that Summer moving in with him had been the best thing to keep her safe. Although he wasn't sure just what her being underfoot was doing to his peace of mind.

At first, he had put up his guard, finding excuses to work outdoors in the evenings to stay away from the house. But living under the same roof made it difficult to deny his desire for her when she was near.

Evidently, she hadn't been sure just where she should sleep the night she had returned to his place. They had stopped by her house to get more of her things, and after she had gotten settled at his place and taken a shower, she had gone to sleep in the guest bedroom.

He had stayed outside deliberately talking to his ranch foreman, and when he had come inside and found her asleep in the guest bedroom, he tried to convince himself that her sleeping arrangements were fine with him.

He'd taken a shower and crawled into his own bed. But knowing that she was asleep in another bedroom didn't suit him. However, his stubbornness, the cold hard casting around his heart, just wouldn't thaw any.

After the third night, he realized that he had finally reached his limit. He got out of bed and went into the guest bedroom to discover her wide awake. She had been unable to sleep those nights, too.

He could vividly recall that particular night, and how he had stood in the doorway and stared at her across the room, wanting so much to despise her, and also his weakness for her. Without saying a word, he had reached out his hand to her and she had eased out of bed, crossing the room to place her hand in his.

Darius sighed deeply thinking it had been at that particular moment that he could no longer deny that she was and would always be a part of him. He had faced the truth that the reason he was so determined to protect her was because he still cared for her. Deeply.

Since then she had shared his bed every night and he'd enjoyed waking up with her beside him each morning. And he was getting used to her being in his home, in his space. Being under the same roof with her gave him a chance to get to know the new Summer, the one that had grown up without him. And he couldn't help but admire the woman she had become, the dedicated social worker who understood what it was like to be a woman in jeopardy. A woman who had been abused.

In the evenings he no longer found reasons to stay away from his home. Together they would prepare meals, clean up the kitchen and talk about the day's events, only bringing up Whitman when they needed to. He had been sighted several more times in Somerset. Darius had even approached the Texas Rangers about Whitman informing them that he had violated parole. Although he had yet to be apprehended, Darius was convinced that eventually he would be, and was glad, in the meantime, that he was keeping Summer safe.

"Sorry I'm late. I sort of got detained," Lance said, breaking into his thoughts and sliding into the chair across from him.

Darius couldn't help but laugh. Based on the satisfied smile on his best friend's face, he could only assume Kate was the reason he was late, and now he understood what it was like to have a woman under your skin and close at hand.

"No problem. I just wanted to give you a copy of the official fire department report and provide an update on my investigation. I checked out all your employees who were questionable and was able to rule out each and every one of them."

Lance nodded. "I figured you would. I told you who I suspect."

Yes, Lance had told him, Darius thought, several times. But Darius still wasn't convinced. Something didn't sit right with him.

Darius checked his watch. It had become a routine for him to drive Summer to work every morning and pick her up in the afternoon, and he did not want to be late. It was a routine he was beginning to get accustomed to. And it was one he liked, whether he wanted to admit it or not. Business would have to wait.

Summer came down the stairs and looked around, not seeing Darius anywhere. She went into the kitchen, deciding to make a cup of tea. It wasn't unusual for him to go outside and spend time with the men who ran his ranch in the afternoons, and she had been fully aware that when she'd first come to stay with him he had used that as an excuse to put distance between them.

Now that had changed. He no longer avoided her in his home and she spent every night in his bed. She still wasn't assuming anything and knew once Tyrone had been captured, Darius would expect her to leave and return to her home. She wouldn't be doing herself any favors if she became attached to his beautiful home, which she already loved. It was far enough from town to offer peace and quiet that anyone would cherish, yet at the same time it was a place where a family could be raised.

She shook her head, determined to get such foolish thoughts out of it. What she and Darius were sharing was physical and nothing more. She turned at the sound of footsteps and knew it was him.

He walked through the back door, saw her and smiled. He might not love her but there was no doubt in her mind that he enjoyed having her around. He closed the door behind him, locked it and just stood there, staring at her. When he had brought her home from work she had gone upstairs to take a shower. Now she felt refreshed but at the same time, hot. And the way he was looking at her was making her feel even hotter.

Without a word, she crossed the kitchen floor and wrapped her arms around his neck. Then, leaning upward she captured his mouth with hers. His response was immediate and he didn't waste any time letting her know it, or letting her feel it. His thick erection was throbbing against her, making her senses come unglued and sending sensations rushing through her veins and all over her skin.

Moments later she pulled back and met his gaze. "We need to prepare dinner," she said in a ragged voice, barely able to breathe.

"Later." And then he swept her off her feet and headed upstairs to his bedroom.

Bodies joined. Summer moved with Darius as his lips brushed a kiss beneath her ear and whispered just how much he enjoyed being inside of her, making love to her, being one with her.

The rhythm he had established was perfect, and floated them toward fulfillment. The air surrounding them was charged and the more he thrust into her body, the more her senses seemed whipped with a pleasure so profound it took her breath away.

"Now!"

As if on cue, her body began convulsing right along with his, endlessly, as shivers tore through them, pulling them down yet at the same time building them up. And when she cried out in pleasure, every pull of her feminine muscles was regulated by his steady yet rapid strokes into her body, making her lift her hips and use her thighs to squeeze him tight, clench him for all she was worth.

She tossed her head back when he surged even deeper inside of her, gripping her thighs and taking her all over again, pushing her toward another orgasm and doing everything in his power to make sure they both got there.

They did.

Instead of letting up, the heat was on yet again, and the workings of her inner muscles signified that such a notion made perfect sense, given the depth of their desire, their passion and their sexual hunger. It was as if they were making up for lost time and then some, filling a drought, satisfying a yearning, soothing an ache.

And when he began moving inside of her in quick, rapid successions, she cried out his name as shivers of pleasure tore through her once again.

"Do you know how beautiful you are? And you're even more beautiful after making love."

Summer glanced over and saw Darius had awakened. He was smiling, and the look in his eyes was filled with the same heat she still felt on some parts of her body. "Thank you."

She knew at that moment she would have to broach the subject she had tried putting behind her since seeing him again.

His betrayal.

"And you are a very handsome man, making love or not," she said softly. Truthfully. She paused a moment and then asked the one question she needed answered. One she could not put off asking any longer. "Why did you make that bet?"

A confused look appeared on his face. "What bet?"

Summer was certain there was no way he could not know what bet she was referring to. But if he wanted to pretend to have a loss of memory, she could remedy that. "I'm talking about the bet you made with Walt about how quick you could take me to bed."

In an instant, he was up, leaning over her. The look on his face was one of incredulous fury. "What the hell are you talking about? I never made a bet like that."

She wondered why he was not going to own up to it now. "That's all right, Darius. It doesn't matter."

"Yes, it does matter," he said in a hard voice. "Especially if you believed it."

She frowned. "Why are you denying it?"

"Because I never did such a thing. How could you have believed something like that?"

She drew in a deep breath and held his gaze. "Because Walt told me what you did. He felt that I had a right to know."

His face hardened. "Walt!" he all but roared.

"Yes," she countered in a voice filled with just as much conviction. "Yes, Walt Stewart. He was your partner at the time. Or have you forgotten about him, as well?"

"No, I haven't forgotten about Walt. In fact, I spoke with him just last week about that arson case I'm investigating. What you're saying doesn't make sense, Summer, because Walt knew how I felt about you. There's no way he could have told you something like that."

Summer's head began spinning and it took her a second to find steady ground. *Walt knew how I felt about you...*

Could he be saying that he had cared as deeply about her as she had about him? She continued to stare at Darius and noted the way he was looking back at her. Then he asked slowly, with disbelief, "And Walt actually told you that?"

"Yes."

Darius released her and eased out of bed, seemingly barely able to keep the lid on raging anger. She swallowed, slowly realizing the impact of what now appeared to be a blatant lie. But why?

"Put on some clothes. We need to talk, and this is not the place for us to do it," he said, interrupting her thoughts. He picked up his jeans and eased into them. "Please meet me in the living room."

Summer stared at his back as he walked out the room.

* * *

Darius paced his living room with his hands in tight fists. Why in the hell had Walt told Summer something like that? How could he have told her?

He could vividly remember sharing a beer with Walt one night after their shift had ended and telling him just how much Summer had come to mean to him. Walt had sat there listening, not saying anything, mainly because Darius hadn't given him a chance to say anything. His heart had been filled with love, and he had wanted to share those emotions with someone he had considered a friend.

He and Walt had gotten hired around the same time and had easily become friends. He was well aware of Walt's issues with the opposite sex because of his ex-wife's betrayal, but Darius had overlooked them because it hadn't been his issue or concern.

Now he had to wonder just how deep Walt's deception went. He knew what Summer had been told, but what about what Walt had told him about Summer, and the message she had supposedly left for him? According to Walt, Summer had left town with an older man. A rich man.

"I'm here now."

Darius stopped his pacing and turned around. She stood there, not in the shorts and blouse he had taken off her earlier that night, but in one of his T-shirts that had been thrown across a chair in his room. Whether it was her intent or not, her wearing his shirt meant something to him. It was as if she was giving him an unspoken acknowledgment of their connection, a connection that had started seven years ago and by some work of miracle was back in full force.

Making love to her over the past weeks had closed old wounds. But now he was discovering that those wounds were self-inflicted due to his belief of Walt's lies. "Let's sit and discuss this, please. I'm beginning to think we've been played."

He watched as she took a seat on the sofa, trying not to notice that his shirt hit her mid-thigh, and how sexy she looked in it. More than anything, he had to keep his mind on the issues at hand, issues they needed to dissect and resolve. After she was seated, instead of sitting beside her on the sofa, he took the leather wing chair that sat not far away.

"To take up the conversation we started in bed, I want you to know, I want you to believe, that at no time did I discuss sleeping with you with Walt. There was no bet."

He watched her features. She held his gaze as intensely as he was holding hers. He saw in her eyes a desire to believe what he said. But...

"Then how did he know about that night?" she asked. "He knew that you had spent the night over at my place."

Darius thought about her words. "He must have driven by your apartment and seen my car parked out front."

He could tell from her expression that she was taking his explanation into consideration, agreeing that it was possible. However, there was still lingering doubt in her eyes.

"Why didn't you contact me?" she then asked him. "He told me you left town and would be gone for a few days, but I never heard from you again. It was like you *had* scored and put me out of your life."

Darius leaned back in his chair. "Did he not tell you why I had to leave immediately or where I had gone?"

"He didn't go into any details. He just said you'd been called away on police business and would be gone a few days."

Darius jaw tightened. "The reason I had to leave when I did was because I got a call that Ethan had been critically injured in a car accident and was being wheeled into surgery. Since I'm his only family, I had to get to Charleston. For a while, I wasn't sure Ethan was going to make it. I was by his bedside day and night and did not have use of my cell phone. And when I did call, I got a message that you had gotten your cell number changed."

He saw the shock in Summer's gaze and before she could say anything, he knew she hadn't known. "Walt didn't tell me that," she said angrily, getting to her feet. "I didn't know."

Connecting his fingers in a steeple, he placed them under his chin. "When I returned to town almost two weeks later, after Ethan's condition had stabilized, I went straight to your place from the airport, only to be told by your landlord that you had moved out a few days earlier, and that an older man in a Mercedes had picked you up and that you had left with him."

She nodded. "Yes, that was Karl Lindsey."

He paused for a second and then said, "Walt is the one who told me why you had left."

She shifted in her seat and his gaze was drawn to a flash of her thigh. His attention went back to her face when she said, "Yes, Walt just happened to drop by that day Karl was there, and just on the off chance you cared enough to ask, I told him that I had taken a job with Karl and would be moving to Florida for a year."

Darius raised a brow. "A job?"

"Yes, Karl had been one of my regulars at the restaurant. He's a writer. He offered me a job as his assistant, editing and organizing his notes. He had offered me the same job before but Tyrone had forced me to turn it down. When I hadn't heard anything from you, and after Walt told me what you did, I decided to take Mr. Lindsey's offer and moved to Florida with him and his wife and—"

"His wife?"

Summer didn't say anything for a moment as she studied his expression. Then she said, "Yes, Lola, his wife. You sound surprised."

Darius stared at her as a deep sharp pain ripped through him. For the first time he was seeing that trust on both sides had been shattered because he and Summer had been quick to believe the lies of others. He had been so quick to believe the worst of her and she of him. Not because they thought of each other as devious people, but because their relationship had been in the early stages, at a very delicate period when trust, faith and love was building. He didn't want to think of how strong their relationship would be if it had been given a chance to grow.

"Darius?"

He hated telling her what he'd thought, what he'd assumed, but knew that he had to do so. "The message Walt gave me, the one he claimed you left, was that you had met this old, rich man and that you couldn't waste your time with someone who was nothing but a college-educated cop with no aspirations of being anything else."

She stared at him. He saw the hurt and pain in her eyes and knew why. Just like she had believed Walt's lies about him, he had believed the man's lies about her.

"Why were we so quick to believe the worst of each other?" she asked in a whisper that he could barely hear. "We played right into Walt's hands," she added. "That's sad."

As far as he was concerned, it was worse than sad. It was pathetic. Seven years wasted. He then said the only thing that he could say at that moment. "I'm sorry."

She breathed in deeply. "And I'm sorry, as well."

Darius could only sit there silently for a moment, wondering how one went about repairing a love that had been destroyed by lies. Lies that had been so easy to accept. Inside of him, a voice said, *One day at a time.*

"Summer, I—"

"No, Darius, I think we both need time to come to terms with what happened, the lies that were told and why we were so quick to believe them. I haven't been in a relationship with anyone since you, serious or otherwise. I've grown accustomed to being by myself, not wanting a man to share my life. I don't trust easily anymore. I'm more cautious. I really don't know if that can change."

He could read between the lines. She was letting him know when it was all said and done, regardless of the fact that they had lived together for the last few weeks or so, getting along marvelously, complementing each other's personalities, she was not all that certain that she wanted to give them another chance because of their lack of faith and trust in each other. From what she was saying, she still didn't want a man in her life. Things had changed. She had changed. In a way, he understood.

Over the years he had kept most women at bay, being selective about who he wanted to spend his time with and not allowing himself to get serious about anyone. But he could see all that changing and wondered if she could. Their relationship—and he considered them to be in a relationship—had to undergo some serious repairs. Major repairs. But he thought they could do it.

They had uncovered a lot tonight. But he still had something else to come clean about—his association with the TCC.

"Summer. I—"

"Will you contact the authorities to see if anyone has seen Tyrone again?" she cut in to ask.

He knew she was trying to get off the subject. He would let her do so for now since tonight had been overwhelming, to say the least, and he wasn't sure how she would handle the unveiling of another lie. One that had been his own, as a way to hurt her. He would tell her another time. Soon. Tomorrow.

"Yes, I'll do that."

There was no need to tell her that he planned on killing two birds with one stone by driving to Houston tomorrow to meet with Tyrone's parole officer and that he would also be paying a visit to Walt.

He studied her, wondering if she knew the significance of what she had admitted moments ago. He was the last man she had made love with. She hadn't wanted a man in her life in seven years, yet she had shared herself with him.

At that moment, all he could think about was what they had shared. The heat. The passion.

"I guess we could sit here and stare at each other all night," she finally said, "but I prefer going back to bed."

He rose to his feet, accepting the gravity of the mistakes they'd both made. But he also accepted that she needed him now like he needed her. "Then I don't plan to keep you up any longer."

He crossed the room to her. They had a lot left to talk about, still more truths to tell. But at that moment, they needed to be together and they both knew it.

Darius held his hand out to her and she took it. Together, they returned to his bedroom.

* * *

While en route to the shelter the next morning, Darius received a call. "This is Darius."

He listened attentively to what the caller was saying and then he said, "That's good news and I appreciate you calling to let me know. I'll pass the information on to Ms. Martindale."

He clicked off the phone and glanced over at Summer. "That was a Texas Ranger friend of mine. He was calling to let me know that they picked up Whitman this morning."

Darius saw a wave of relief pass through her. "Where?" she asked.

They had come to a stop at the traffic light and Darius glanced over at her. "Less than a block from your house."

He hated telling her the next part but knew that he had to. "He had a gun and a rope in his possession."

Summer stiffened and Darius understood why. Chances were Whitman had discovered where she lived, and a good possibility existed that he had planned on using that information for no good. Since he had violated parole in more ways than one, Darius knew he would return to prison and serve his entire sentence.

She didn't say anything, staring straight ahead, out the windshield.

"You okay?" he asked.

She turned to him. "Yes, I'm okay."

She might be okay, but he wasn't. How could he

have been so wrong about her? He couldn't wait to confront Walt about the lies he'd told. "I have something to take care of this morning and won't be back in time to join you for lunch."

"All right."

She didn't seem to be in a talkative mood and he figured she needed time to digest everything he had told her about Whitman.

"Since Tyrone is in police custody, there's no reason I can't return home now, is there?"

None other than I don't want you to go. I've gotten used to having you around. I've fallen in love with you all over again. "No, there's no reason you can't," he said.

He breathed in deeply and at that moment, he knew there was no use denying what he'd known all along. He loved her. He had not stopped loving her.

And all this time he had tried convincing himself that he would seek revenge for what she had done, when he knew he couldn't have gone through with that plan no matter how much he'd thought he wanted to hurt her.

From the first moment she had turned her eyes on him he had been a goner, and although he'd convinced himself over the years that he had gotten over her, the simple truth was, he hadn't. Coming to terms with his love for her was a monumental release of the hold he'd placed on his emotions. All the built-up tension and anger he'd felt since seeing her again left his body, flowed out of his muscles. It strengthened his heart, propelling him to do whatever he had to do to make her his again.

Ten

A few hours later, Summer slipped into her walking shoes to go to the café for lunch, reflecting that this was the first time in quite a while that she would be doing so without Darius by her side.

She drew in a huge breath of profound relief, knowing what could have been another nightmare with Tyrone was now over. She shivered when she thought of the items that had been in his possession. There was no doubt in her mind he intended to do her harm, and she was grateful yet again to Darius for keeping her out of harm's way.

Darius. The man she still loved.

She wondered if she'd sounded convincing when she told him that she didn't want a man in her life. A part of her did want to belong to him, totally and completely, but was afraid to get her hopes up again. Even though she knew the truth now, it couldn't erase the pain she had felt for seven years.

Besides, there was nothing Darius had said to make her think that he wanted to renew what they'd once shared. When she'd mentioned returning to her place now that the threat with Tyrone was over, he hadn't said anything to talk her out of it, he hadn't said that he didn't want her to leave.

He had apologized for believing the lies Walt had told him. And she had apologized to him, as well. Later, they had made love but no promises had been made. There had been no discussion of a future together. Although he hadn't said as much, she had a feeling that he didn't want a woman in his life.

That left her with the same life she'd been living since leaving Houston. The kind of life she had gotten used to. It was somewhat lonely but safe. She would continue to live it without the man she loved.

The anger within Darius told him to strike out the moment he saw Walt walking toward him. But he fought to hold his rage in check. There was only one thing he wanted from the man and that was for him to explain why he'd done what he did.

Without telling Walt why, he had called and requested to meet with him in Laverne Square, a newly developed area of Houston near the Madaris Office

Park. He rose from the bench when he saw the curious look in Walt's eyes.

"Darius, didn't you get my message that the guy you wanted me to check out was clean? I left it on your voice mail last week."

"That's not why I asked you to meet with me," Darius answered, trying to keep the bitterness out of his voice.

Walt lifted a brow. "Oh. Then what's up?"

Darius looked directly into his eyes. "I'm here about the lie you told me about Summer Martindale."

Walt held his gaze for an instant before shifting his eyes to look out over the pond in the square. Time stretched on and for a moment, Darius wondered if he was going to say anything. Then Walt turned his gaze to Darius.

"She came with a lot of baggage and was trouble with that crazy boyfriend of hers. You didn't need her."

His words, spoken as if he'd had a right to make that decision, slithered down Darius's spine. "You were wrong, Walt. She wasn't trouble and you knew how I felt about her. I not only needed her but I loved her."

"You have a lot to learn about women, Darius. You can never let one get under your skin, and you can never admit to loving one."

Darius stared at him for a moment. "Actually," he said in a deep, cutting tone, "there's a lot that *you* need to learn about them, and recognizing a good one when you meet her is at the top of the list."

A deep frown settled on Walt's face. "There aren't any good ones."

Walt had extreme issues, but Darius couldn't concern himself with that right now. As far as he was concerned, what Walt had done was unforgivable. When he thought about all those wasted years when he and Summer could have been together, years when he had loathed her very name, he practically wanted to kill the man. It was all for nothing. All for lies.

Filled with total disgust and having nothing else to say, Darius started to leave.

"Hey, wait, man, we're okay, aren't we? We're still friends?" Walt asked in a lighthearted tone.

Darius stopped walking and looked over his shoulder. Their gazes locked. The message he was certain Walt saw in his eyes was blatantly clear.

"No. Our friendship died the day you lied to me. I loved her, but because I thought you were my friend, I believed you. A true friend would not have done what you did."

Without saying anything else, he walked off, leaving Walt standing there.

Summer was just about to go to the café when one of the security guards escorted a very well dressed, distinguished-looking older man through the entrance. It didn't take a rocket scientist to figure out from the way the man was carrying himself that he was someone of authority, someone of importance, which could only mean he was a member of the TCC. Kevin Novak had given her a heads-up that over the next few months, members of the TCC would probably be dropping by to check out the shelter since he had asked them for more money.

Putting on her brightest smile, Summer crossed the lobby to greet the man. "Welcome to Helping Hands," she said, extending her hand to him. "I'm Summer Martindale, a social worker here."

The man took her hand and looked at her. "So, you're the young woman who's been causing so much excitement."

Summer forced her smile to remain intact when she recognized his voice. He was the person she had talked to on the phone when she'd called requesting additional security guards. "Am I?" she couldn't help but ask, not liking the way the man seemed to be staring down his nose at her.

"Yes. I'm Sebastian Huntington, a member of the Texas Cattleman's Club."

"Nice to meet you, Mr. Huntington."

He didn't say anything to indicate that the feelings were mutual. Instead, he glanced around. "Things seem calm enough around here. I really don't see why two guards are needed. But then, you've managed to convince Kevin Novak differently."

She was about to say the reason things appeared calm was because everyone felt safer with two guards when he once again looked down his nose at her and arrogantly said, "And then there's Darius Franklin, who's evidently quite taken with you. He's also been singing your praises at the TCC meetings." A sneer touched his lips as he studied her features. "Now I see why."

Surprise flickered in her eyes. "Darius?"

"Yes. He's one of our newest members."

Now she was confused. *Darius was a member of TCC?*

"How long has he been a member?"

The man frowned down at her like she'd asked a stupid question. "Not long enough for him and his friends to be throwing their weight around. He's only been a member for over a year."

Summer nodded. "Oh, I see." And the sad part of it was that she really did see. Darius had lied to her.

"Ready to go?"

Summer slowly lifted her gaze from the document at the sound of the deep, husky voice. Had it been nearly three weeks ago when here in this office she had heard that voice again for the first time in seven years?

After Mr. Huntington left, instead of walking to the café, she had gone to the library. There she had researched information on the Texas Cattleman's Club branch that was located in Somerset. Darius was listed as a member, having joined the same day as Kevin Novak and several other men, and from the photographs she had seen, it was apparent that he and Mr. Novak knew each other very well. Why had he pretended otherwise when she'd told him of her meeting with Mr. Novak? Why had he deliberately kept his membership in the TCC from her?

Instead of answering his question, she asked one of her own.

"Why didn't you tell me you were a member of the Texas Cattleman's Club?"

She saw surprise light his eyes and knew he was probably wondering how she'd found out. "Mr. Huntington dropped by to check out the place and mentioned you're a member," she said, leaning back in her chair.

"So, my question is, why didn't you tell me, Darius? You had several chances to do so when I was preparing for my meeting with Mr. Novak, and many after that. Why didn't you tell me?"

A part of Darius wished he'd have told Summer everything last night. How would she react to finding out he had withheld the information because of his plan to hurt her?

Any chance of rebuilding a relationship with her would probably be destroyed now. But still, he had to be upfront and honest with her. Lies were the reason they were in the situation they were in now.

Sighing deeply, he entered her office and closed the door behind him, leaning against it. "The reason I didn't want to tell you is because I was still operating under the belief that you had left Houston with a rich man. A man you had chosen over me because of his wealth. With that belief festering in my mind as well as my heart over the years, I had grown to resent you for choosing wealth over love."

When she didn't say anything, he continued. "I figured that if that was true, once you found out about my wealth, the fact that I had become successful, I could get my revenge by seducing you, taking you to bed and then walking away from you the same way I thought you had walked away from me. I wanted to hurt you the way you had hurt me."

Summer still didn't say anything for a moment, and then in a low voice, she asked, "You hated me that much?"

Darius breathed in again, hearing the deep hurt in her voice. "I thought I did, but once I got to know what I thought was the new Summer Martindale, the one who's dedicated to the women at the shelter, the one who works tirelessly after hours when her shift is over, I realized that no matter how much I wanted revenge, I couldn't have gone through with it. And do you know why, Summer?"

"I have no idea," she said in a sharp tone.

He held her gaze. "Because I realized that although I'd tried over the years, I couldn't replace love with hate. Although I wanted to hurt you, I couldn't because I still love you."

Their gazes held and for a moment, he wondered if she believed him. He hoped and prayed for some sort of sign that she did. He had been wrong for wanting to get even with her, but at the time he'd felt it was something he had needed to do because of his pain.

"So many years have passed, Summer. We owe it to ourselves to try and rebuild the relationship that was destroyed because of our lack of faith and trust in each other. In Houston today, I made a point to see

Walt. I had to know why he'd done what he did. His reason was he saw me falling for you and figured I'd get hurt. But the truth of the matter is that I was hurt in the end anyway. Not by you, but because I'd believed the worst about you."

He moved away from the door to stand in front of her desk. "I'm asking that you give me a chance to do what I wanted to do seven years ago and that is, love you the way a man is supposed to love a woman. Please allow me into your heart, Summer. Give me a chance to prove that I am the right man for you."

He took another step closer. "Will you put behind you all the hurt and lies of before and move forward in the way we should have years ago? Can you find it in your heart to love me as much as I love you? To work on rebuilding a relationship of love, trust and faith?"

He saw the single tear that fell from her eye and literally held his breath before she began speaking.

"Yes," she said slowly. "I can work on rebuilding our relationship because I love you, too, and I want you in my life. I want a future with you, not because of your wealth but because you are a man who's proven more than once that he can be there when I need someone, that he has my best interests at heart, and protects me when I need protecting."

She pushed her chair back and walked around her desk to him. "We have a lot of years to make up for, but I knew that night we made love again it was something I wanted. I was just afraid to hope for it."

Darius pulled her into his arms and held her tight, close to his heart. And then he lowered his mouth to hers. He wanted her with him always and from the intensity of their kiss, it seemed she wanted the very same thing.

Moments later, he pulled his mouth away from hers. "Ready to go home, sweetheart?" And to make sure she understood, he added, "Not to your place, but to mine. A place that you will one day consider ours, I hope."

She smiled up at him. "Yes, I'm ready."

He took her hand in his and they walked out of her office together. He knew there was a lot of work ahead, rebuilding their relationship into the kind they both wanted, the kind they deserved. Lies had destroyed their relationship, but love had restored it. Their love would make it all happen for them.

They would make sure of it. Together.

Epilogue

Three weeks later

Summer stepped outside on the porch and glanced around. It was a beautiful day and the smell of flowers was everywhere.

She felt butterflies move around in her stomach at the same time she saw the car pull into the yard. She smiled. Darius was home.

She glanced around again, thinking how easy it was to think of his ranch as home. She never returned to her place, and every week more and more of her things would show up here.

And then one night while they were busy unpacking some more of her boxes, he had got down on his knee and proposed to her. He asked her to be his wife, the mother of his babies and his best friend for life. Somehow through her tears she had accepted. The moment he had slipped the ring on her finger, more love and happiness than she'd ever thought possible filled her heart. They hadn't set a date yet, and had decided to take things one day at a time.

She had met his friends and could see the special friendship they shared. She liked them a lot. Tonight they would be joining Lance and Kate at the TCC for dinner.

As soon as the car came to a stop, she moved down the steps, and when Darius opened the door and got out, she was there waiting.

He pulled her into his arms and kissed her, making her feel wanted and loved. Things were so good between them that she would occasionally pinch herself to make sure it was real. And over and over he would prove to her that it was.

He pulled back and studied her face with concern. "Are you okay? I stopped by the shelter and Marcy said you had left early."

She smiled up at him. "Yes, I'm fine. I just wanted to be here when you got home. I thought that I would pamper you a little before we left for dinner."

A grin curved his lips and she could tell he liked the idea. "Pamper me?"

"Yes. Are you interested?"

Instead of answering, he swept her off her feet into his arms and carried her up the steps. *Yes,* she thought, *he was interested.*

She laughed, knowing once he got her inside the house he intended to show her just how interested he was.

* * * * *

TEXAN'S WEDDING-NIGHT WAGER

BY
CHARLENE SANDS

Charlene Sands resides in Southern California with her husband, high-school sweetheart and best friend, Don. Proudly, they boast that their children, Jason and Nikki, have earned their college degrees. The "empty nesters" now enjoy spending time together on Pacific beaches, playing tennis and going to movies, when they are not busy at work, of course!

A proud member of Romance Writers of America, Charlene has written twenty-five romance novels and is the recipient of the 2006 National Readers' Choice Award, the 2007 Cataromance Reviewer's Choice Award and the 2008 Booksellers Best Award.

Charlene invites you to visit her websites www.charlenesands.com, www.petticoatsandpistols.com and www.myspace.com/charlenesands, to enter her contests, check out her new releases and see what's up.

This book is dedicated to all of my friends and fellow authors on Petticoats and Pistols. I've never met a smarter, more wonderful, more gregarious group of authors. Thanks to Pam Crooks, Stacey Kayne, Cheryl St.John, Kate Bridges, Linda Broday, Mary Connealy, Pat Potter, Karen Kay and Elizabeth Lane for being great Western blog pardners.

Y'all make it fun!

One

Cara shut down the ballroom lights and stood in the middle of the floor of Dancing Lights, flanked by a wall of mirrors and elegant surroundings that she'd insisted upon when designing her studios. A smile emerged just as Elton John's voice carried over the speakers. The song stirred up vivid memories and Cara slowly closed her eyes. She moved her hips, swaying to the rhythm and the poetic lyrics.

There's a calm surrender to the rush of day
When the heat of the rolling world can be turned away

An enchanted moment, and it sees me through
It's enough for this restless warrior just to be
with you

And can you feel the love tonight
It is where we are
It's enough for this wide-eyed wanderer
That we got this far
And can you feel the love tonight

"Can you feel the love, Cara?" Kevin had said to her the day they'd married.

Kevin had brought her hand to his mouth and nibbled, his dark blue eyes piercing hers. She'd tingled with excitement from that single gesture. Cara *had* felt his love, with every heart-stopping glance, every tender touch and each tantalizing kiss.

"Yes, I feel it, honey," she'd replied.

He'd kissed her lips, whispering, "This is our song, babe."

They'd hung on to each other and sung the lyrics along with Elton's smooth tones, moving to the music as their family and friends looked on. She thought she'd married her Prince Charming, her college sweetheart who could make her laugh one moment and sizzle the next.

Cara's heart swelled thinking back on her wedding day, thinking of being in Kevin's arms, of loving him for all she was worth and hoping for the same kind of happy life she'd wished for so many of her dance students through the years.

She'd had such big dreams.

"Why, Kevin?" she whispered in the silence of the Dallas ballroom.

Gorgeous Kevin Novak, with the penetrating blue eyes and short blond hair, had often been mistaken for David Beckham. She and Kevin had their own private joke about it since, with her curly blond hair and sky-blue eyes, she hardly looked like Posh Spice. Cara smiled briefly at the memory.

They'd had such good times in the beginning, until Kevin had decided building his real estate empire was more important than building their marriage. He'd become a die-hard workaholic, neglecting her needs in favor of the next big deal. He'd broken her heart—hearing their song again brought it all back. The happiness she'd hoped for with Kevin had eluded them. Cara still felt the ache in the pit of her stomach.

She'd moved on with her life, leaving Somerset to start a new life in Dallas, but she hadn't escaped the deep hurt and anguish Kevin had caused.

Cara snapped her eyes open and stared at the fading shadows in the mirror. Her silhouette reflected back the new, confident woman she'd become. She was a businesswoman now, owner of a chain of dance studios, and a choreographer and dance instructor as well.

No longer that optimistic, hope-filled girl who'd wanted a life and children with Kevin, it was long past time for Cara to rectify her situation.

She punched off the CD player and headed to the

phone to call the man she hadn't spoken with in over four years. She'd waltzed around this issue long enough.

It was time to divorce her husband.

Kevin Novak chalked the cue stick with slow, deliberate twists, contemplating his next shot. He was one of the best pool players at the Texas Cattleman's Club, but his pal Darius Franklin was making him sweat for the win. "You know darn well Montoya is responsible for setting the fire."

Kevin bent over the carved-oak vintage pool table and took his shot, the solid orange cue ball angling into the corner pocket. He knew darn well Darius didn't believe Alejandro Montoya was responsible for the damaging blaze set at Brody Oil and Gas. But he wasn't above using distraction to earn a win.

"I don't know that for a fact, Kev. The fire was definitely an act of arson, but I'm not pointing fingers yet."

"Montoya has always been a pain in the ass."

Kevin missed his next shot and Darius lifted his cue stick, eyeing the pool table. "True, but arson? That's an accusation I'm not ready to make. It looks like a professional job and if that's the case, I'd have to rule him out."

"I say he's guilty." Lance Brody, another of Kevin's old frat brothers from the University of Texas, chimed in. Kevin's four best friends were all members of Texas Cattleman's Club in Maverick

County. They watched the game, sipping drinks and cajoling from the sidelines of the club's game room.

"I'm with Lance," Mitch Brody said, agreeing with his brother. "Montoya's got an ax to grind."

Justin Dupree nodded, taking a swig of beer. "I think Montoya is guilty, too. He's got issues with Lance. Always has."

Lance scoffed. "*I* have issues with him." Their rivalry went back to high-school days.

Darius eyed the striped blue ball and took his shot. The ball rolled into the side pocket and Kevin winced.

"Nice shot."

Darius laughed. "It hurt you to say that, didn't it?"

"Like a knife in my heart."

Darius shook his head. "You're a sore loser, Kev."

"I haven't lost yet."

And when Darius missed his next shot, Kevin went full throttle, unwilling to give an inch. His competitive nature wouldn't allow a loss. He sank the next four solid-color balls, then the eight ball, winning the game.

Satisfied, Kevin shook his friend's hand. "You gave me a run for my money."

Darius slapped a twenty in his palm. "I'll get you next time." He lowered his voice, setting his cue stick into its case. "So you really think Montoya set the fire?"

"I'm thinking he did. I also think he's behind blocking my project in downtown Somerset. He's got it in for the Brody brothers and their friends. Wasn't a coincidence to find the area I'd designated for a major development is being declared an historic district. He's got to be behind the rezoning. It's all a little too suspicious."

Lance walked up and put his arms around their shoulders. "Come on, you two. Let's forget about Montoya for a minute. We need to set a date for my wedding reception. Kate deserves more than the Las Vegas elopement she got."

Kevin grinned. "Yeah, you really know how to impress a girl."

Justin added, "Lance really pulled out all the stops on that one."

"Funny, guys." Lance pulled a frown, but Kevin knew he didn't mind their teasing. He'd found his soul mate in Kate and wanted to provide her a beautiful reception.

When the game-room phone rang, Lance walked over to pick it up. "Cara? Is it really you? It's good to hear your voice."

Kevin froze. All heads turned his way and he met with four pairs of curious eyes. Emotions washed through his system. A tic worked his jaw while he stood rigid and waited.

"Okay, I'll get him. He's right here." Lance nodded his way, holding the phone up. "It's…Cara. She wants to speak with you."

Kevin strode across the room to take the phone. Before speaking, he turned to look at his friends, and with a quick gesture signaled them to continue playing and butt out.

The guys turned around and Kevin spoke into the receiver. "Cara?"

"Hello, Kevin."

So formal.

God, he hadn't heard her voice in four years. Not once. Not since she'd left him high and dry and made a new life for herself in Dallas. He'd kept up on her through friends and what little he'd read in the newspapers about her successful dance studios.

She sounded the same—sassy if not a little stiff. There was an awkward moment of silence.

"I guess it's time for us to end it," she said.

Images of Cara getting remarried immediately entered his mind. After four years, why else would she call? Had she fallen in love with another man?

Kevin didn't know how he'd feel about that. She'd walked out on him and their marriage. She'd tried to file for divorce but Kevin had sent the papers back to her. He'd given her an ultimatum— if she wanted out, she would have to come back and face him.

"I'm coming to Somerset. I'd like to make an appointment with you to discuss the…divorce."

"Fine." Kevin's lips tightened.

"It's business, Kevin. You should understand that. I need an expansion loan for my studios. The bank recommends… Well, let's face it. We both need to get on with our lives."

It's business.

How many times had he said that to her when he couldn't make it home for dinner? When he'd come in so late that he'd plopped into bed beside her and held her tight until they'd fallen asleep? She'd wanted children and Kevin had asked for her patience. His business had come first, but only because he'd wanted to provide a good life for her. He'd made his millions, but she never understood that he'd done it all for her. And how had she showed him her undying love? She'd packed up in the middle of the night and left him. Just like that. After five years of marriage.

Damn her.

"I'm good with that," he said. "When are you coming in?"

"Tomorrow?"

Kevin turned to find all four of his friends silently watching him. "Tomorrow is good. Meet me at the office at five."

Kevin hung up the phone and contemplated his next move. Cara wasn't going to get away with breezing into his life for a day to get her divorce. No, he wouldn't make it so easy for her.

A plan began to formulate in his head and his lips lifted. "Cara's coming to town tomorrow," he said needlessly. "She wants to finalize the divorce."

"I've seen that expression on your face before," Darius said. "What's got you looking so damn smug?"

"Nothing," he replied innocently.

"Like the nothing that nearly got us expelled from UT? Remember when we stole Professor Turner's prized Shakespeare bust from his classroom?" Lance asked, narrowing his eyes. "That kind of nothing?"

Kevin shrugged.

"I don't like it," Lance said. "You looked fit to be tied when she called, and now you're looking like a fat cat who just lapped up a pint of milk."

Kevin only smiled and finished his beer. "I'd better get going."

"I feel for Cara already. That girl won't know what hit her," Darius added.

Kevin walked to the door of the game room, shaking his head. "That *girl* is my *wife*. And she deserves everything she gets."

Darius shot him a warning look. "I always liked Cara."

"Yeah," Kevin said on a deep breath, before exiting the room. "So did I."

As the elevator closed to take Cara up to Kevin's office, she caught sight of herself in the doors' reflective surface. She must have glanced in the mirror a dozen times before leaving her Houston hotel room, making sure she looked just right for her meeting with Kevin. On any given day she wore her curly blond hair pulled back in a clip, but today she let the curls fall to her shoulders freely, glossed her lips with a light berry shade and made sure she wore a soft sapphire dress that accented her figure and her blue eyes.

Because it wasn't any given day.

Today, she'd see her husband for the first time in four years.

And a small part of her wanted him to see what he'd thrown away. She hadn't wilted like a delicate flower when they'd separated. She'd been broken but not beaten by his betrayal of trust. He hadn't cheated on her in the classic way, but he had shattered his vows by abandoning their love.

Cara had grown from that experience. Through her pain, she'd managed to create a successful business in a field she loved. She'd come here for Dancing Lights and that expansion loan she needed from the bank, but she'd also come for her own personal reasons.

She drew oxygen in as she exited the elevator and glanced around Kevin's new office space. He'd certainly come up in the world, from his smaller office on the outskirts of Houston to this impressive space on the tenth floor of a downtown high-rise building.

She walked to the reception desk and waited for the receptionist to finish her phone call.

"May I help you?" she asked.

"Yes, I'm Mrs. Novak. I have an appointment… with my husband."

The young woman's eyebrows shot up, surprise evident on her face. Kevin had replaced a great many things since she'd left and apparently sweet, aging Margie Windmeyer, his loyal secretary, hadn't fit in with the new decor.

Looking baffled, the receptionist paged through her appointment book.

"He's expecting me." Cara's nerves jumped at the edginess in her tone. She wanted to get this over with.

"Yes, Mrs. Novak." The receptionist gave up looking for her name on the books and pointed toward a set of double doors. "Right through there."

Cara nodded and stared at the doors for a second. Then, with her slim briefcase tucked under her arm, she entered the office.

Kevin stood with his back to her, staring out the arched window behind his desk. Both hands tucked into his suit pants, she was treated to a captivating view of his tight backside. His physique hadn't suffered through the years—that much she could determine right away.

As he angled toward her, his profile and the sharp, handsome lines of his face struck her with force. He turned fully around and stared at her, his gorgeous, piercing-blue eyes not giving anything away.

He cast her a half smile. "Cara."

She stood in the middle of the large office, re-fusing to let her nerves go raw. It was a shock to see him. She couldn't possibly have anticipated this moment—how she'd react to seeing him again. She'd imagined it a hundred times, but nothing compared to the reality. Seeing him brought back bitter-sweet memories of all they'd had and all they'd lost, which swept through her in a matter of seconds.

She got hold of her bearings and smiled a little. "Hello, Kevin."

Kevin eyed her up and down, the way he used to when he wanted to make love to her. Heat swelled and coursed through her body, a remnant of what they'd once shared coming to light. Suddenly, the enormity of her mission here struck her. She would put an ending note on the last chapter of their marriage.

"You look…well."

Kevin taunted her. "You look *beautiful*."

"Thank you." Cara held on to her defenses, despite the bitter way he offered up the compliment.

"Have a seat, Cara." He gestured and she sat in a brown leather chair facing him.

Cara fidgeted with her briefcase, finally setting it on Kevin's desk. She crossed her legs and tapped her fingers on the arms of the chair.

Kevin's gaze fell to her thighs, where the material of her dress gathered. She refused to squirm under his direct scrutiny. But she wished he'd sit down.

"Are you getting remarried?"

His blunt question surprised her. She shook her head. "No."

He nodded, folding his arms across his rigid body.

"It's just time, Kevin. We need to move on. I'm planning to expand my business and I need to get a large bank loan."

"You don't want my name on anything legal, right?" His eyes narrowed on her.

"You're a businessman," she responded with patience, wondering what happened to the Kevin Novak she'd married. This man seemed so different, so dark and contemptuous. She'd never seen this side of Kevin before. "You know how it works."

"Yeah, I know how it works." His cutting, derisive tone sobered the moment even more.

Kevin finally took a seat behind his desk. He braced his elbows on the chair arms and steepled his fingers. "Don't you find it strange that we're sitting here in my office, speaking formalities?"

"Strange?"

The corner of Kevin's mouth lifted in a wry smile. "Yeah, strange. Considering how we started out. Hot and heavy from the moment we laid eyes on each other."

Cara recalled her college sorority sister's birthday bash, with balloons and loud music and alcohol flowing. She'd taken one look at Kevin and fallen in love instantly. They'd spent the entire night flirting shamelessly. Cara had never been so aware of her own sensuality until that day. She and Kevin had blown off the party. They'd had a party of their own that night.

Heat crawled up her neck at the erotic memory. "That's the past, Kevin."

Kevin let her comment drop. He leaned back in his seat and stared into her eyes. "I understand your dance studios are doing very well."

Cara's heart sped up at his implication. She straightened in her seat and leaned forward a bit. "I'm not here for your money, Kevin." She glanced around the elaborate surroundings. Exquisite Southwest artwork adorned the walls of his very tastefully decorated office. "Though I see you've become a huge success. That was always most important to you."

Cara made her point and leaned back in her seat, content to put a name on the mistress who'd stolen her marriage from her. "I'm only here for your signature."

"And you'll get it," Kevin said.

Oh, boy. That was easy, Cara thought, sighing silently with relief.

"Under one condition. I want something from you, Cara."

So Kevin had terms. She'd be willing to hear him out. She wanted nothing more than to get this whole ordeal over and done with. "I'm willing to do anything, within reason."

Kevin grinned a little too widely. "Considering you abandoned me and our marriage, I think my request is quite reasonable."

Cara went numb. She didn't like the look on her husband's face. "You forced my hand, Kevin. I hung on to our marriage for years, hoping. But you gave me no option—"

"And I'm giving you no option now. If you want your precious divorce," he said, "you'll have to agree to my terms."

Two

Kevin watched Cara's sudden panic when his request finally sank in. Momentarily silenced, Cara blinked rapidly, giving him a chance to really look his wife over.

He hadn't realized what four years of separation had done to him. He'd never met a woman he admired more than Cara, or thought more beautiful or talented. Cara had it all. He'd always thought so, and everything he'd done, he'd done for her. He'd wanted to prove to her and her wealthy family that she'd married well. That he could give her all the things she deserved.

God, how he'd loved her.

Kevin inhaled sharply and Cara's head snapped up. "You can't be serious, Kevin."

"I'm not joking."

Cara stood abruptly and stared straight into his eyes. "No, I don't suppose you have a sense of humor anymore."

He caught a slight whiff of her exotic scent, the same fragrance she'd worn when they'd been truly man and wife. Memories of hot, erotic nights flooded his senses. Of her silky smooth skin against his flesh, her breath against his cheek, her soft, sensual body tucked under his.

He wanted her again. He'd given her no other choice but to accept his demand. He wouldn't let Cara have the last laugh. "On the contrary, babe. I have a great sense of humor, when something is funny. This, however, isn't funny."

"It's ridiculous! You want me to live with you for a week? Why, Kevin?"

Kevin arched his brows, but remained silent.

Her blue eyes sparked like raging fire when she caught on. She shook slightly and pointed her finger. "This is blackmail."

"You owe me for walking out."

Indignant, Cara raised her voice. "You walked out on *us!*"

Kevin's gut tightened. "No, Cara," he said with quiet calm. "I worked hard to give us a good start."

Cara shook her head so hard her blond curls whipped across her face. "No, no, no. I won't let you get away with that. I wanted *you*. I wanted a *family. Children.* You only wanted to amass a fortune. You were never there for me, Kevin."

He shrugged. He'd heard this all before and he'd never agreed with her take on their marriage. He'd asked for one thing from Cara—patience. He'd wanted to give her the world. "So your solution was to run away?"

Cara backed up a step and lowered her voice. "I couldn't do it anymore. I needed more from you."

"And leaving Somerset solved the problem for you." Kevin snapped his fingers. "Just like that, you were gone."

A sharp, stinging pain sliced through his gut. Kevin didn't think Cara had the power to hurt him anymore, but seeing her again brought back all the bitter memories. They'd argued the night before Cara had left and had gone to bed angry with each other, but that was nothing compared to the memory of finding that Cara had slipped out of the house before dawn, leaving only a note in her wake.

"It wasn't as easy as you make it seem." Cara's pretty mouth turned down. She filled her lungs with a fortifying breath and opened her slim attaché case, pulling out the divorce papers. "If you'll forget this nonsense and just sign the papers, you and I…"

"Will be done?"

Cara closed her eyes. "Yes. Please, Kevin. This is difficult enough."

She got that right. It was difficult seeing her again. All the old, hurtful feelings came tumbling back. Her leaving had cut him deep and left him bleeding. He'd hidden his injury from those around him until he'd become numb inside, then bitterness had emerged. He'd spent the next few years resenting Cara Pettigrew and trying to wash away her memory with an occasional one-night stand, women who would never measure up. He'd refused relationships and poured all his energy back into his business.

Kevin shrugged off his pain the way he'd learned to, from years of experience. He stood his ground. "I told you, I want one week with you, Cara. One week at my penthouse. And then I'll sign the divorce papers."

Cara's shoulders slumped. She shoved the papers back into the attaché case and snapped it shut. "I can't do that."

Kevin walked around his desk and approached her. Her eyes gleamed like diamonds and her skin appeared soft as a baby's, but it was her very kissable mouth, tight as it was at the moment, that had him moving in even closer. He'd never gotten over his anger with her, but he'd also never gotten over wanting her. And now that she was here, he wanted one last fling with his wife.

Before he ended their marriage for good.

He touched her wrist and slid his finger tenderly up her arm. Goose bumps broke out on her skin and Kevin felt a moment of satisfaction. "If you want the divorce, you're going to have to pay for it."

Breathless, Cara looked deep into his eyes. "You've changed, Kevin."

"I won't deny it."

Cara moved back a step and Kevin dropped his hand from her arm. She worked the inside of her lower lip in that adorable way that always made him hot for her.

"I'll make you a counteroffer."

Kevin smiled inside. He should have known his feisty wife wouldn't give in without a fight. It was a trait he'd always admired about her. "I'm listening."

"One night. You get one night and that's all."

Initially Kevin balked. One night wasn't nearly enough to exact his payback. He wanted more time with her. His plan was to romance her into falling in love with him again. The ultimate revenge for dumping him would be in his rejection of her. Then he'd sign her divorce papers.

A thought struck and Kevin acted swiftly. "You've got a deal. If and only if you agree that our one night will be two weeks from tonight."

"Two weeks? I can't possibly—"

"That's my offer. You stay in town for two weeks, and in exactly fourteen days you'll have your divorce. Take it or walk away now with those unsigned papers, babe."

Cara narrowed her eyes and crinkled her nose. She mulled it over for a few seconds, then finally gave him her uplifted chin. "Fine. But only because I need that bank loan. You've got me up against a wall."

Her scent drew him closer. She looked so darn beautiful when she was indignant. He arched a brow. "Baby, I've *had* you up against a wall. Remember?"

Recollection replaced the surprise on her face and her features softened with the memory. Kevin wrapped his hands around her slender waist and tugged her against him, his fingers splayed across her backside.

"Kevin," she whispered, before his mouth claimed hers.

Kevin could kiss and Cara fell into him for all she was worth. His expert lips teased and tempted her with little nibbles until sizzling heat built up. She tried a vain attempt to pull away, but Kevin only brought her up tighter, pressing her hips to his with a subtle grind that swept through her system. Her knees buckled, her heart slammed as the frenzied kiss overwhelmed her. She found it hard to breathe. And when she opened her mouth to take in oxygen, Kevin mated their tongues and the tantalizing thrill escalated.

He cupped her head in both hands and kissed her again and again, their breathing labored and intense. In the past, this kind of kiss had meant only one thing—a steamy night under the sheets. Kevin could always turn her inside out…

The sobering thought of his blackmail returned full force.

Damn him. Damn him. Damn him.

She didn't want this. She didn't want to be swayed by memories of hot, mind-blowing sex with her husband. She'd put those thoughts out of her mind, for the most part. She'd come here for a signature and instead got a near-orgasmic experience just from one kiss.

She pushed at his chest and broke off the kiss.

Kevin glanced at her lips, which she was sure were red and swollen, and smiled. "Two weeks is gonna be a long time."

"We could finish it here and now." Cara nearly died of mortification when Kevin noticed her glancing at the top of his uncluttered desk.

"Tempting," Kevin said, his gaze raking her over. "But we made a deal."

"Couldn't we undo that deal, Kevin?" She prayed her plea came through sure and steady, instead of desperate.

Kevin stepped away from her and shook his head. "The way you undid our marriage? No, Cara. This time you're not running away from me. In fact, I want you to have dinner with me tomorrow night. I'll pick you up at seven."

Cara jammed her hands on her hips. Who was this man? Certainly, he wasn't the man she'd fallen in love with and married nine years ago. "You can't issue orders like that to me, Kevin. I'm not at your beck and call."

Chagrined, Kevin scratched his head, acknowledging his mistake. "Sorry," he said. "Guess I'm out of practice wining and dining a lady."

His confession touched something deep in her heart. Furious with him as she was, it was nice to know that behind all his anger there was a glimmer of the man she'd once known. And to know that Kevin was out of practice with women instilled great comfort within her.

Kevin made a point of clearing his throat and beginning anew. "Cara, I'd like for you to join me for dinner tomorrow night. We have a lot to catch up on. And I could use your advice about something."

Curious, Cara raised her brows. "My advice?"

"Yes, you always had a level head and you know the parties involved. I want to run something by you. Will you join me for dinner?"

After raising her curiosity level a notch, Cara could hardly refuse. "Yes, okay. I'll have dinner with you. I'm staying at the Four Seasons."

Kevin nodded. "I'll pick you up at seven." He moved to his desk to retrieve her attaché, and without pause laid a hand to her back and walked her to the door. Handing her the briefcase, he looked into her eyes. "I'm looking forward to seeing you tomorrow night, Cara."

Cara nodded, biting her lip to keep from making a snarky retort like, *You're blackmailing me into this. What choice do I have?*

But in fact she did have a choice. She could've made up an excuse not to have dinner with him. Maybe that would have been the wiser move. Yet Cara had been curious, not only about the advice Kevin wanted, but to learn what had become of her friends in Somerset.

After leaving him, she'd lost touch with so many

people and she'd always regretted that. Maybe it was time to renew those friendships while she was here.

Cara bounded out of Kevin's office with a bounce in her step. This wasn't how she'd envisioned her encounter going—especially succumbing to Kevin's kiss the way that she had—but her goals were in sight.

And that was all that mattered to her.

Cara walked the distance to her hotel, willing to trudge the ten blocks in high heels rather than hailing a cab. It was a good way to cool off from Kevin's melt-your-heart kiss and his blatant blackmail. She didn't know which of the two disturbed her more.

She'd had little power over Kevin's kiss. From day one, she'd never been able to resist him. That's why she'd stolen off in the middle of the night four years ago, fearing that if she'd told him her plans he'd convince her to stay. He'd make his argument, as he had so many other times, and kiss her into oblivion.

But she'd thwarted his blackmail attempt. Somewhat. She could take some satisfaction in that. He'd wanted a week with her when it was clear their marriage was over, and she'd offered him *one* night. Some might not think it a victory, but Cara knew how determined Kevin was and his compromise certainly meant a win, small as it might be.

Cara clutched her briefcase and thought of the divorce papers inside. Soon, she'd have the independence she needed to expand her business without relying on her mother's money, which she'd managed to do so far. Since leaving Kevin, she'd looked forward to being her own woman and was proud of her accomplishments. Everything she'd achieved, she'd done on her own. Though her mother had offered to fund her dance studios, Cara wanted to make it on her own. So Cara viewed negotiating with Kevin to get him to sign the divorce papers as a business proposition—a means to achieving her goal.

"Soon, Cara-Bella," she whispered, smiling at the nickname her dance instructors had bestowed upon her, claiming she danced like a princess.

Soon, you'll have what you came here for.

As she moved along the sidewalk, taking in the sights and sounds of downtown Houston, gradually her steps slowed to a stroll. She calmed herself by window-shopping, glancing at the familiar storefronts, noting which had revamped their exteriors and which had gone out of business, replaced by newer, more upbeat trendy shops.

People moved along the sidewalks at a quick pace, but that didn't stop her from spotting Alicia Montoya across the street, bogged down with several shopping bags. She waved, trying to get her attention. "Alicia!"

Alicia swiveled her head and saw her. Surprised, she smiled and waved back, then gestured toward the street corner. Cara met her there after crossing the street.

"Cara, it's so good to see you!" She gave her a double-armed, shopping-bag hug.

Cara chuckled and knew the first moment of actual joy since coming to Houston. She hugged her back. "Alicia, I'm happy to see you, too. It's been years."

She and Alicia had become friends in her first years of marriage with Kevin, despite her brother's objections. Alex Montoya didn't want his family involved with any friends of either Lance or Mitch Brody. Both those men had been close to Kevin since their college days, along with Justin Dupree and Darius Franklin. Alex's extreme hatred carried over to anyone involved with the five men of the Texas Cattleman's Club.

"Yes, it has been. I wish we had stayed in touch," Alicia said quietly.

"I'm really sorry about that, Alicia. I went through a hard time. Leaving my home and everything I knew…wasn't easy. I needed to make a clean break."

Alicia's chocolate-brown eyes softened. "I understand. But you're here now."

"Yes, I'm here for two weeks. I'd actually planned on calling you, so I'm doubly glad I spotted you. Looks like you bought out the store."

Alicia glanced down at the shopping bags she held. "I know, I went a little crazy. I don't shop much, so I had some making up to do. Where are you staying?"

"In a hotel just down the street. Do you think we can get together while I'm here?"

"I was just going to suggest that. We can meet in Somerset for lunch."

"Sounds great." Cara handed Alicia her business card. "Here's my cell number. I'm looking forward to it."

Alicia smiled when she read the card designed with two dancing figures silhouetted by twinkling lights. "Dancing Lights. I like it, Cara. I'd heard you opened a dance studio."

Cara shrugged. "All my gymnastics and cheer-leading really paid off, I guess. We teach all kinds of dance at the studio. It keeps me out of trouble."

Thoughtful, Alicia glanced at the card again. "I'll call you at the end of the week. I have to meet Alejandro now. He's expecting me."

Cara nodded. She couldn't send a greeting to Alicia's brother. Not when he'd tried to break up her friendship with Alicia, simply because she'd married Kevin. Guilt by association didn't sit well with her.

"Okay, I'll see you soon. I'm really looking forward to it." The sentiment held true—Cara wanted to renew friendships she'd allowed to dissolve when she'd left town. Alicia was a sweetheart and had lent a compassionate ear to Cara when her marriage had fallen apart. She'd love to get acquainted with her again.

Cara stopped in the food court of the Galleria and picked up an Asian salad for dinner before heading to her hotel. When she entered her room, she kicked off her shoes and sat down on the bed, exhausted from the turmoil of the day.

Not two minutes later, a knock came at her door.

She groaned and lifted herself off the bed. "Yes," she said, opening the door to a hotel employee.

"Mrs. Novak? This came for you. Special delivery."

An "ohh" escaped from Cara before she realized it. The young man handed her a dozen black calla lilies and lavender orchids, beautifully arranged in a vase.

"Thank you," she said and gave him a tip before closing the door. Admiring the lilies, she set them down on the dresser and plucked the card out.

She read the note. "I didn't forget your favorite." Tears stung her eyes for a second. She knew the exotic flowers were from Kevin. Cara had a thing for the unique-colored lilies and it had been the one extravagance she'd requested for their wedding.

Emotion stirred in her stomach and she flopped onto the bed. Staring at the ceiling, her throat constricted and she whispered in the silence of the room, "You didn't forget, did you, Kevin."

Kevin sank the putt and eagled the eighteenth hole, then pumped his fist once, twice, in a fair imitation of Tiger Woods. The TCC's golf course wasn't exactly a tournament course but Kevin was too happy with the turn of events lately to give a damn. He liked winning.

"Lucky shot," Lance muttered with mocking disgust.

"Lucky, my ass. That's pure skill, Brody. That makes five wins to your two, this month."

"I had you beat until those last three holes," Lance

grumbled. "It's as if you can't wait to get off the course today."

At the reminder of time, Kevin glanced at his watch. He had to stop by his office, change and get ready to pick up Cara.

"Got a hot date or something, Kev?" Lance's mouth curled into a smirk.

Kevin set his putter into his golf bag. "I'm seeing Cara tonight."

Lance whistled low and long. "Is there an inkling of hope for you two?"

Kevin glanced at Lance. "Not even a chance."

Lance blinked. "You're saying that you're over her?"

Kevin gritted his teeth. Damn right, he was over her. No matter that seeing her yesterday had reminded him of good times they'd shared or that he looked forward to seeing her again tonight. "Yeah, I'm over her."

"But you're taking her out tonight, right?"

"Yeah, I'm taking her out."

"Hey, just tell me to butt out, buddy. But I saw the look on your face yesterday when she called. You were hopping mad. And anger means you still care. And it also means that you're up to something. I know you, Kevin."

"I'm having one last fling with my wife before I sign the divorce papers," Kevin said in his own defense. "There's no crime in that."

"Unless you have an ulterior motive."

Kevin shrugged. "She'll be here for a couple of weeks." Thanks to his blackmail.

After stowing their bags on the back end of the golf cart, he and Lance settled in the seats, Kevin taking the driver's side.

"So you plan on dating her, and then what?" Lance wouldn't give up.

Kevin stared at him thoughtfully and exhaled. Every one of his friends knew how much Cara had hurt him when she'd left. Though Kevin wouldn't openly admit his plan to anyone, it wouldn't be hard for any one of his friends to put two and two together.

"You're going to win her back and dump her, aren't you?" Lance said, his face twisting in disbelief. When Kevin didn't deny it, Lance shook his head. "Oh, man. Kev, if you have a second chance with someone special, take it. Don't blow it, the way I almost did with Kate."

Kevin tossed Lance's words back at him. "This is the part where I say, butt out, buddy."

He didn't need a lecture. Ever since Lance had married Kate, he seemed to want everyone else to follow suit. Only Kevin wasn't shopping for happily-ever-after anymore. He just wanted a little payback for all the heartache and humiliation Cara had caused him.

"Okay, fine," Lance said. "But don't say I didn't warn you."

Later that day, Kevin went to the office to look over some contracts before sending them to his legal department. He wanted a clear head when he picked up Cara. One of the things he'd learned over the past four years was to surround himself with employees he trusted, and delegate the work. He found that freed up more of his time for pleasurable endeavors, which lately amounted to a round of golf or a game of pool with his buddies.

Anticipation stirred his blood. Cara posed a greater challenge than beating Darius in pool or Lance at golf. And, hell, he had to face facts—he was looking forward to spending his nights with her again.

Just like old times, a voice in his head said.

Kevin left the office at five, drove to his apartment, showered, shaved and checked on the arrangements he'd made for his first date with Cara.

He arrived at her hotel room a little early and knocked on the door.

"Just a minute," she called from inside.

Kevin smiled just hearing the lilt of her sassy voice.

She opened the door wide and whispered, out of breath, "You're early."

She fixed a silver hoop earring to her lobe, looking a little flustered but beautiful all the same in a black silky dress that showed off her long, shapely dancer's legs. Her hair curled past her shoulders and was held up on one side by a crystal clip.

"You look gorgeous, Cara." He stepped into the room.

Cara looked him up and down, surprise registering on her face. And before she could comment on *his* attire, he shook his head and added, "It's a shame you're going to have to take off all your clothes."

Three

Dressed in jeans and wearing leather boots Kevin had provided, Cara sat upon Dream Catcher, the five-year-old mare who had been born at TCC's stables when Cara had been living with Kevin. Though she had grown up with horses on her parents' estate, Cara had forgotten how much she loved riding. She and Kevin had taken an occasional ride in their early years of marriage, before he'd been too obsessed with work to take the time.

The day Dream Catcher was born, Cara had rushed to the stables and the moment she'd seen the feisty little filly, she'd fallen a little bit in love. To sit upon the sweet mare and ride off into the hills of Maverick County with Kevin seemed almost like a dream.

The Texas sun lowered on the horizon and cast hues of orange-gold over the valley as they rode in silence. There was a quiet settle to the land, a peace like nothing Cara had experienced for a long time. She'd been so caught up in the fast pace of Dallas that she'd forgotten what it was like to be with nature. Kevin seemed to understand that, setting the slow pace and enjoying the scenery. There was an odd sense of comfort being here with him. She could almost forget his blackmail and his manipulation.

Almost.

She slid a glance his way and let go a little sigh. Looking just as comfortable atop a horse as he was cutting a deal in his downtown office, Kevin acclimated well. Dressed in solid Wranglers, a blue plaid shirt and black Stetson, her husband dressed down *very* nicely.

"You're staring at me," he said with a grin.

"Oh, you'd like to think so." Caught, Cara averted her gaze, hiding her own grin.

"I know so. See anything you like?"

Cara sobered at his question. "I don't know, Kevin. Do I?"

Kevin clucked his jaw a few times. "You need to lighten up, Cara. Enjoy the scenery."

"And you think you're part of that scenery?"

"Me?" he said, lowering the brim of his hat. "No, ma'am. I wouldn't presume."

Cara chuckled. Okay, maybe she should just lighten up. She didn't like Kevin's blackmail, but she could enjoy the ride. If for no other reason than that she was atop Dream Catcher on a glorious, late-summer evening.

"I see a whole lot I like," Kevin said quietly, after a minute.

Cara sensed his gaze on her, and a burning heat crawled up her neck. She didn't dare look at him. A lump formed in her throat. She didn't trust herself to respond.

They rode in silence until the dirt path led them to a rise. "Wait here," Kevin said mysteriously, and clicked his mare into a trot. He rode on about ten yards to the peak of the rise, then turned toward her. "Okay, come on up." He gestured with a wave.

Dream Catcher followed the path in a trot, until Cara met Kevin at the top of the rise. Looking into his eyes first, then following the direction of his gaze, Cara gasped at the view below. "Oh, Kevin. This is amazing."

A small, well-kept cottage on the TCC property was lit outside by at least a hundred pillar candles. A table, dressed in white linen, was set with fine china, crystal wineglasses and lilies of every variety.

"It's beautiful." Tears stung her eyes. Why couldn't he have done something like this years ago when their marriage was shaky, when she needed attention, when she needed to know she was more important than his business? *Oh, Kevin,* she thought, *why are you doing this now, when it's too late?* The question plagued her, but she pushed it out of her mind.

Lighten up, Cara. This is temporary.

"I'm glad you like it." Kevin pushed his horse on, and Dream Catcher followed him down the other side of the rise. When they reached the cottage, Kevin dismounted. He walked over to Cara and reached for her. She slid down the left side of the horse into Kevin's arms. He held her, their gazes entwined, as luminous candles lit the background.

"You were always gorgeous in candlelight, babe."

Cara smiled, the compliment warming her heart.

Kevin tilted his head, the brim of his Stetson grazing her forehead. She braced herself for the kiss, tightening up inside in anticipation.

Kevin brushed his lips over hers in the lightest feather-touch of a kiss, then backed away. Cara blinked, a little surprised.

He took her hand. "Have a seat." He guided her to the table and pulled out a chair for her. "I'll see to the horses."

She watched him take the reins of both horses and go behind the cottage. When he returned and sat down, a chef appeared at the table wearing a white coat and tall hat, a waiter standing just behind him. "I hope you enjoy the meal Mr. and Mrs. Novak," the chef said.

"I'm sure we will," Kevin returned, with a nod.

Cara sat quietly while the waiter served their first course, a little pastry puff filled with light cheese and raspberries. She took her first bite and closed her eyes. "Oh…this is heaven."

When she opened her eyes, Kevin's gaze was on her, watching her enjoy the pastry with a gleam in his eyes. "The chef came highly recommended."

Cara was again tempted to ask, why was he going to so much trouble? But she'd already decided that she would just go with the flow and see where that would take her, so she remained silent on the subject. "I can see why. He's already got my vote for Chef of the Year."

Kevin poured them each a glass of wine.

"You said something about needing my advice?" Cara sipped her wine and the smooth liquid warmed her inside. "But you haven't said a word about it yet."

Kevin lifted his glass to his lips and sipped. "It's not a pleasant subject, Cara. I hate to spoil the night, but yes, I do have something I'd like to tell you. It's regarding Alex Montoya and the recent fire at Brody Oil and Gas. I think it was set deliberately."

"You think Alex did it?" Cara's voice elevated with disbelief. Sure, the Brody brothers had issues with Alex, and vice versa, from their teen years, but Cara never thought Alejandro Montoya capable of something as criminal as arson.

"I do, Cara. I'd like your opinion about this. Hear me out."

Kevin gave a detailed description of what had transpired between Lance, Mitch and Alex through the years, and then added a final note about how Alex had managed to hamper his newest revitalization development. He explained how Alex had helped back a faction that had that particular area in Somerset declared historic, thus killing the project. "I have no proof regarding the fire, but you know everyone involved. What do you think?"

Cara shook her head. She thought about the accidental meeting she'd had with Alicia just yesterday. Alicia would be devastated if her brother was involved with the fire in any way. "My gut instincts tell me Alex wouldn't do anything so drastic. It's not his style, Kevin. Yes, I can see him behind the scenes, working to preserve the Somerset area. He may have even done that to spite you, but that's not a criminal act."

"No, it just caused me a major headache and financial losses."

"You may not agree with me," she said with a shake of her head, "but I don't think Alex had anything to do with the refinery fire."

"Okay, noted. You and Darius are the only ones. Lance, Mitch, Justin and I all think he's behind it."

Cara sipped her wine. "Maybe you're not being objective. Maybe you want to blame Alex. Maybe you're so pissed at him, you want him to be guilty." Kevin winced and Cara continued. "Revenge can be sweet, isn't that what you always said?"

"No, I never said that."

Cara blinked and leaned forward. "Oh, sorry, that must have been the *other* husband I married nine years ago."

"Must have been." With a smug look, Kevin lifted his glass and finished off his wine. He poured himself another glass as the waiter cleared their dishes and brought the next course.

"So, is that all you wanted to ask me?" Cara dived into her asparagus salad, her appetite flaring to life.

"Yes."

"Are you sorry you asked for my opinion?"

"No." Kevin spoke with an earnest tone. "I always valued your opinion. That hasn't changed."

Cara sat back in her seat and stared into Kevin's eyes. "You can be so charming—when you want to be."

"I want to be. Right now. With you."

Why? Cara didn't understand it, but the voice in her head told her to go with it and enjoy these last few days with Kevin. Soon enough, their marriage would be over.

When they finished all four courses of the main meal, Kevin suggested they go inside the cottage for coffee and dessert. "The chef made us something special."

"I should be full, but I can always fit in dessert," Cara said, feeling the zipper of her jeans expanding a bit. She was slender and, at five foot eight, she could afford to eat a decadent dessert once in a while.

Kevin stood and reached for her hand. With fingers entwined, they entered the cottage, climbing the steps, their boots scraping the wooden floors. Cara made a quick tour of the quaint cottage, noting the rustic stone fireplace, cozy chintz sofa and several swag-draped pane windows. "It's lovely here."

"It was the groundskeeper's home at one time. TCC let it go to ruin, practically. I renovated it and now it's available—"

"For impressing your dates?" she blurted, in a teasing tone.

Kevin whipped around and grabbed her by the waist, bringing her flush up against him. "You have a mouth on you, don't you?"

Cara pulled her head back to look at him fully. "You always liked my sassy mouth."

Kevin's gaze devoured her mouth. He cupped her head with one hand and pulled her close, his lips so near. "I still do."

Cara's heart pumped double time when he kissed her. He tasted of robust wine and warmth. He tasted familiar and fine. He tasted of all the sweet things in her life she missed. "Kevin."

"I love it when you whimper my name," he said between kisses.

"I didn't whimper," Cara protested mildly. Kevin cupped her derriere and tugged her in. Hip jamming hip, she felt his desire, rough against rough as their jeans brushed.

Kevin nibbled on her throat. "Really? Guess I'm gonna have to do something about that."

There were times when Kevin hated his methodical mind and this was one of them. Every instinct he possessed told him to seduce Cara, here and now, and take advantage of the remote, romantic cottage setting. But Kevin had a plan in mind, and the culmination of that plan had to happen later rather than sooner.

He'd kick himself tomorrow for his damnable obstinate nature and pay the price of losing out on a wild night of sex with his wife. Yet all wasn't lost. He needed more from Cara tonight and he'd take what little his plan allowed.

He nipped at Cara's lips over and over, sweeping his tongue through her mouth with frenzied heat. A little tiny moan escaped her throat that sent Kevin's straining erection into overdrive.

With an effort that took all of his will, he pulled away from her to look deep into her eyes. Her hazy-blue surrender unnerved him.

He needed to touch her and feel the softness of her skin, caress the firm mounds of her perfect breasts. Nothing was going to stop him, his plan be damned.

"Baby," he murmured, licking the soft center of her throat. "Let me touch you."

She trembled and whimpered helplessly.

Kevin kissed his way down to the first button of her blouse. With nimble fingers, he undid that button, then the next and the next. Her breasts, cupped in white cotton, spilled out, an invitation he couldn't ignore.

He palmed her breasts and closed his eyes, relishing the remembered feel of her, the way she fit so completely in his hand. His thumbs simultaneously caressed both erect tips, her nipples straining against her bra, until Kevin freed them from the torture.

"Ohh," she moaned, leaning closer to him with a need he knew he couldn't satisfy tonight.

"You feel as good as you look, baby. As good as I remember," he murmured.

Kevin bent his head and kissed the tips of her breasts, first one, then the other. Always responsive to his touch, she arched back and Kevin drew her deep into his mouth, suckling and teasing the rosy buds with his tongue.

He wanted to take her here and now, to ease the desire straining against his jeans, to begin to rectify four years of wanting her, despite his anger. It was hard to back off, to pull away from what she offered and what he wanted, but Kevin was determined to see his plan through.

"Did you hear that?" he asked quietly.

Breathlessly, she replied, "You mean the pounding of my heart?"

Kevin smiled and kissed her lips. "No, outside. Something spooked the horses. I'll go check."

Cara appeared a little surprised by his quick dismissal. He turned and walked out the front door. Behind the house, the horses calmly waited. Kevin leaned against the cottage wall, beside a hibiscus vine in full yellow bloom, and shut his eyes. "Harder than I thought," he whispered.

He waited just a few moments, until his breathing slowed and his internal thermostat cooled down. Then he untied the reins of both horses and guided them toward the front of the cottage. Cara waited on the porch steps. "False alarm," he said. "Must have just been a coyote howl off in the distance."

Thankfully, Cara had buttoned her blouse and straightened her unruly, honey-blond hair. He only had so much willpower where his wife was concerned. He tilted his head and sighed, without falsity. "We should go. It's getting late."

Cara blinked a few times, then nodded. "Of course."

Kevin helped Cara onto Dream Catcher and then bounded up onto his horse. They headed to the TCC stables in silence. Once they were safely back at the entrance, Kevin glanced at Cara. "We never had dessert."

Cara broke her silence with an acknowledging light in her eyes. "We'll have to lie to the chef and tell him it was fabulous."

He dismounted, then reached for her and, once again, she slid down the horse and into his arms. Kevin stared deep into her eyes, holding her loosely around the waist. "It *was* fabulous."

Cara searched his eyes. She had questions, but Kevin had only one answer. He kissed her soundly on the lips, tasting her once again. "Have dinner with me tomorrow night. I'll make up for the dessert we missed."

"How can you do that? I'm sure the chef is on to bigger and better things."

He chuckled, knowing Cara was messing with him. "Easy. I know what you crave."

Cara jammed her hands to her hips and shook her head in denial. "I bet you don't."

"Oh, no? Hot fudge over chocolate cake with vanilla ice cream and a dozen cherries."

"Tasty's?" Cara's smug expression changed to one of longing. "I haven't had Tasty's for—"

"Four and a half years? I took you there for your birthday, remember?"

A thoughtful look crossed her expression and she smiled sadly. "Yeah, I do remember."

"So, how about it? Burgers and dessert at Tasty's tomorrow night?"

Cara opened her mouth, then clamped it closed with a quick snap. He could always tell when she waged a war of decision in her mind.

"Don't overthink it, babe. Just go with it."

The comment opened her eyes wide and she made a quick decision. "Okay. But, Kevin," she began in a solemn tone, "maybe we shouldn't get in over our heads. We both know why I came to Somerset."

"Oh, don't worry. I haven't forgotten."

"G-good."

"But I'm not making any promises."

Cara's mouth tightened into a frown.

Kevin planted a brief kiss over her down-turned lips. "Come on, I'll drive you back to the hotel. You can think about Tasty's all the way home."

* * *

Cara didn't think about Tasty's all the way back to her hotel. She thought about Kevin. He'd touched her in ways she hadn't allowed another man since they'd split up. Sensual images flashed vividly in her head. Her body still prickled. Nope, no man since had even made her feel like trying. Oh, she'd dated at times, but nothing had ever come of it.

Kevin had been sweet and attentive all night and just minutes ago he'd nearly made her forget her own name.

It's Cara Pettigrew, she thought sourly. Not Cara Pettigrew-Novak.

She was still his wife, but in name only. She had stopped being a Novak four years ago.

Cara slipped out of her riding clothes, tugging off the new leather boots Kevin had given her. He'd remembered her shoe size, she realized. How many men would even know their wife's shoe size?

"Remember why you left him," Cara whispered in the quiet of her room. He'd been fun and loving for the first few months of their marriage and then he'd become obsessive and driven. For success? For money? For power? Cara wasn't sure of his motivation, since he'd made a decent living and she'd never complained. She hadn't asked for riches. She'd grown up wealthy. She'd seen how her own father had been driven and how much his obsession had hurt his marriage—and her. She'd been the daughter her father never had time for.

"Money doesn't guarantee happiness," she'd tell

Kevin. But her husband hadn't listened. His competitive nature made him want to prove his worth to Cara and her family. He wanted to measure up, she presumed, though she'd never once implied that he wasn't enough for her.

When the hotel phone rang, Cara was grateful for the interruption of her thoughts.

"Oh, hi, Mom."

Perhaps *grateful* was too strong a word. Her mom had been like a watchdog lately and she was the last person Cara wanted to speak with about Kevin. Especially after what had happened between them tonight. Ever since Cara had made her decision to divorce Kevin, her mother had been *overly* supportive.

"Did he sign the papers yet?"

Cara flinched. Her mother got right to the point. She couldn't possibly tell her mother the truth, that she'd been blackmailed into sleeping with her estranged husband before he'd sign on the dotted line. "No, Mom. Not yet. But we had a…meeting tonight. Kevin is cooperating."

"But, dear, I don't see why there's a problem. You're not asking for much. Actually, you're being quite fair with the settlement. What's the holdup?"

What was the holdup? She didn't know what purpose it served to hang around Somerset for two weeks, but she had to tell her mother something. "Well, Kevin is really busy."

"He hasn't changed," her mother chimed in bitterly. "Just like your father."

Cara swallowed that and continued, "Mom, you know I liked living in Somerset. I'm catching up with friends while I'm here. Taking a little vacation."

"Dear, a vacation is relaxing in a villa in Siena, not begging for signed divorce papers from your husband. I'm worried about you, Cara. You've done so well for yourself in Dallas."

"I was happy here, too, once upon a time."

Her mother's silence was quite telling. She couldn't blame her for being protective. Cara had been hurt by the separation. She'd really loved Kevin, and no mother wants to see her child in pain. Cara understood all that.

"I know, dear, that's why ending it quickly is better for you. It's been dragged out long enough."

"I agree with you, Mom. And I'll get back to Dallas as soon as I can."

"Well, all right. I hope to see you home soon. I love you, dear."

"Love you, too."

Cara hung up the phone and took a long pull of oxygen, thankful the conversation hadn't lasted too long.

When the phone rang again, Cara let it ring four times. She was through talking for the day. All she wanted to do was climb into bed and get to sleep.

But her curiosity got the better of her. She picked

up the receiver, hoping it wasn't her mother on the other end with more pearls of wisdom.

"Hello?"

"Hi, baby." The deep timbre of Kevin's voice oozed through the phone line. "What are you doing?"

"I'm getting out of my…uh, getting ready for bed."

"Yeah? Me, too. I just got out of the shower."

The visual image of Kevin's hard-ripped body wet from head to toe and wrapped in a skimpy towel swept through her mind. She mouthed a silent *oh,* thankful that the word didn't slip out accidentally.

She cleared her throat.

"What do you wear to bed these days?" Kevin asked.

The question was so audacious, Cara laughed. "Wouldn't you like to know?"

"I would, Cara," he said with quiet sincerity.

"Nothing."

Kevin let go a sexy groan.

"Much. Nothing much. I mean, just an old Dancing Lights T-shirt."

"I can picture you wearing that."

"Kevin, why are you calling so late?"

"Had a good time tonight, Cara. Just wanted you to know."

Cara nibbled on her lower lip. She squeezed her eyes shut, yet couldn't shake off images from tonight of Kevin's lips on hers, his mouth making love to her breasts, the tantalizing look of pure lust in his deep-blue eyes when he'd taken off her blouse. "Thank you." She paused, then added, "It was a good night. I enjoyed riding Dream Catcher."

"I thought you might."

"Why are you being so sweet to me?" Cara blurted. She couldn't figure out his motivation. "Our marriage is ending."

Kevin didn't miss a beat. "Yes, but there's no reason we can't be friends, Cara. No reason we can't end this on a happy note."

"Marriages usually don't end on happy notes, sweetheart."

He paused, and she realized she'd used his favorite endearment. "Ours could. We can be different from everyone else. So, are you picturing me dripping wet in my towel or what?"

Cara gasped and then laughed aloud. He'd caught her, but she'd rather die than admit it. "I see you haven't lost your sense of humor after all, Kevin."

"I've lost a lot of things, Cara." His playful mood suddenly changed. "But not my sense of humor."

Cara didn't want to deal with the serious tone of his voice now. Sudden panic developed and she searched for an escape. "Kevin, I'd better get to bed."

"Yeah, me, too. Sleep tight, babe. Dream good dreams."

Cara nearly choked out a quick good-night. She knew what would fill her dreams tonight.

Good or bad, they'd be of Kevin.

Wearing nothing but a small towel.

* * *

The next day the image of Kevin stayed with her all morning long. Restless from those thoughts, Cara left the Four Seasons and walked the Houston streets, stopping in at boutiques along the way— she was bored with the few changes of clothes she'd brought for a trip she had thought would only take two days.

She'd told her mother she'd be taking a little vacation and, though she'd had to rearrange her entire schedule to stay on in Houston, Cara decided, a shopping spree would do her good. Why not enjoy the city while she was here?

By the end of the day, she'd filled two shopping bags with gifts for her dance instructors, a Gucci French flap wallet for her mother and several new outfits for herself, including a scarlet dress to match the new Valentino slingbacks she'd purchased.

The time had flown by. She had just enough time to rush back to the hotel and shower before Kevin came knocking.

It bothered her that she'd changed her clothes three times before her date with him for burgers at Tasty's. Why was she trying to look pretty for Kevin?

But the minute she opened the door and saw the glint of appreciation in his eyes, she thought it was all worth it.

"Wow, you look great. Too good for Tasty's." Kevin toured her body up and down leisurely, and Cara knew a moment of satisfaction.

She'd tried on the dresses she'd picked up today, but decided instead on a pair of formfitting, black pants, very high black heels and a white, flowing, off-the-shoulder blouse belted at the waist with a gold-and-black twist rope. "Stop right there if you think you're gonna weasel your way out of taking me to Tasty's."

"Okay," Kevin said with a teasing twist of his lips. "If I have to. Are you ready to go or do you want to invite me in?"

He peeked over her shoulder and into her hotel room. His gaze focused on her king-size bed. Cara wasn't about to let him in. Her husband was a dangerous man and she'd never been able to resist him when he smiled and spoke with charm.

Kevin still had a perfect body, broad of shoulder and slightly muscular, enough to show his strength without overkill. Four years hadn't changed that. His grooming was impeccable, and darn if he didn't look like he belonged on the cover of *GQ*.

Right now, his blue eyes gleamed with the kind of mischief that could get them both into deep trouble. She shoved at his chest lightly and pushed him out the door. "I'm ready for a burger."

Kevin took her hand from his chest and entwined their fingers. He leaned over to whisper in her ear. "And I'm ready for dessert. It's been a long time, Cara. I need to satisfy my craving."

Four

Kevin helped Cara into his jet-black Jaguar, and then got in and started the engine. His Jag roared to life. All that power at his fingertips at one time had been a big turn-on. But now, Kevin looked across the seat to find his wife sitting beside him and he couldn't think of a bigger turn-on. Cara, dressed for a casual date with him in her classy style, took his breath away.

He gritted his teeth with determination. He wasn't going to make it easy for her to walk away from their marriage. Damn her, anyway. She'd been the primary reason he'd worked sixteen hours a day. She'd come from wealth, and his pride wouldn't allow her to climb down that ladder to marry someone who couldn't provide her the same sort of elevated life-style.

The success he'd achieved had been for her and for their marriage. But her patience had run out and she'd followed suit. He'd never forgive her for leaving him high and dry. The humiliation he'd suffered alone was reason enough for this retaliation. But it was more than that. He'd loved Cara. Really loved her. And she'd destroyed that love.

Cara glanced his way with a quizzical look. "You're quiet."

"It's been a long day."

Kevin snapped on the CD player and smiled. "Oldies, to get us in the mood."

Elvis came on and Cara turned up the volume to "All Shook Up." She knew all the words and sang along with the music. Her toes tapped in rhythm and she swayed her body back and forth. Graceful and elegant, Cara knew how to move.

He'd been resentful when he'd learned about her success with Dancing Lights, somehow seeing the studio as his competition. She'd moved from him to bigger things. Yet, from a purely professional stand-point, he secretly admired her acumen. She hadn't used her family's money for the start-up of her en-terprise, but instead had taken out small-business bank loans to fund the studios. Now she was willing to end their marriage to expand her business.

Kevin pushed those bitter thoughts out of his mind. He was on a mission and couldn't forget his game plan.

By the time they reached Tasty's, his spirits had lifted and he grabbed Cara's hand as they bounded up the steps to the fifties diner. They sat in a red-vinyl corner booth and ordered cherry Cokes and Tasty Burgers.

The dated chrome jukebox stood in the opposite corner next to the long Formica lunch counter, and mini-jukeboxes anchored each booth. "Pick some songs," Kevin said as he put two quarters in.

They both leaned in close to view the playlist. "Oh, look. They have one-hit wonders! 'Pretty Little Angel Eyes' was one of my favorites." Cara punched in its number, along with a few other obscure songs from the past.

"What do you suppose happened to these artists?" she asked, her expression thoughtful.

He shrugged. "They tried and failed. They probably went on to lead productive lives in some other field."

Cara nodded. "One would hope. It'd be a shame not to do what you love to do, though."

"Most people don't, Cara. Most don't enjoy the work they do. They simply have to do it to survive."

Cara's sky-blue eyes softened. "I feel extremely lucky that I found something I love to do."

Kevin searched her expression for any sign of regret and found none. It irked him that she could dismiss their marriage so easily. "You were always good at everything you attempted."

"Thank you," she said. She sent him a smile that flattened quickly.

"What's wrong?" Kevin asked, curious about her change of expression.

She shook her head and looked down at the tabletop. "Nothing."

"Something," he prodded.

She lifted her shoulders. "It's just that, at times, I think I failed as…a wife."

Floored by her admission, Kevin furrowed his brow. "Why?"

Emotions surfaced on her face and her eyes narrowed with pain. "I don't know. Maybe because nothing I said or did kept you at home."

Kevin leaned way back in his seat and studied her.

She continued. "My mother had the same issue with my dad. He was never home. Always working, until the day he died. You know he died of a heart attack. Fell facedown on his desk at the office." Cara looked up for a second, holding back tears. "My mother said he died doing what he loved best."

Anger bubbled in his gut. Cara had it all wrong if she was comparing her father to him. Their situations were entirely different. Cara's father had had more wealth than he knew what to do with, while Kevin had had nothing and worked hard to bring their life up to a certain standard of living. He'd been determined to make his first million by age twenty-five.

For Cara.

Always for Cara.

"You think I didn't love you enough?" Kevin asked. "That I wasn't home because I wasn't…

what? Happy with you? Or because I found you lacking in some way?"

Cara shrugged. "It doesn't matter now, Kevin."

They'd had this argument before, but never with so much raw honesty. "I say it does—"

"Hey, Novak." Lance walked in with Darius and both strode to their table. Kevin winced. He needed them here like a hole in the head.

Lance ignored Kevin and nearly lifted Cara out of her seat to give her a bear hug. "My God, you look great! It's good to see you, Cara."

"Same here, Lance."

Darius moved in and gave Cara a hug, too, his low, easy voice greeting her. "You have brightened my day, woman."

"Hi, Darius. How have you been?"

"I've got no complaints."

Cara beamed seeing the two and, without invitation, both Lance and Darius took a seat, cramming Cara and Kevin into the booth. Kevin sat back and listened as Cara and his friends caught up on their lives.

The interruption actually was more beneficial than he'd originally thought, since it had lifted Cara's mood. They'd gotten way off course with the discussion earlier and Kevin fully intended on charming his wife tonight. He'd been thinking about seeing her all day. And if nothing else, he could rely on a sinfully erotic chocolate dessert to get her in a risky frame of mind.

* * *

Cara had indulged herself fully, devouring obscene, hot-fudge cake while enjoying Kevin and his friends. She'd missed their friendship and remembered how much fun they'd all had in college. At the time, Kevin was the only one of the three men in a serious relationship. Now, the opposite was true. Lance had Kate, and Darius had Summer, while she and Kevin teetered on the edge of a divorce.

"They haven't changed much." Cara smiled, feeling melancholy on the drive back to her hotel.

"Those clowns? They'll never change." Kevin grinned.

When he stopped at a red light, he glanced at her, then leaned over to wipe a smudge of hot fudge from her bottom lip. "You're messy."

"Am not."

Kevin licked the hot fudge from his thumb, making Cara squirm a little in her seat. His gaze focused on her mouth, and erotic thoughts entered her head.

"Oh, no?" Kevin's voice went low and deep. "Then why do I have to clean you up?"

Puzzled, Cara squinted. "You don't have to—"

"Yeah, I do." He leaned in farther to cup her head in his hand and slanted his mouth over hers, his tongue doing a thorough swipe over her lips. Cara relished the liberties he took with her, enjoying every second of the kiss. When she began to kiss him back, savoring the moment, the car behind them honked.

"Darn it," Kevin said, moving away. He glanced

in the rearview mirror at the car behind them. "Hold your horses, buddy." Kevin straightened in his seat and drove out of the intersection.

Cara's chuckle had him turning her way.

"What's so funny?"

"You haven't changed your driving habits. Still arguing with everyone on the road."

His eyes twinkled. "Idiots. All of them." When he looked at Cara, a deep, rumbling laugh emerged.

"All of them but you, right?"

"You got that right, babe." His charming grin unnerved her.

Cara settled in her seat, still smoldering from that one red-light kiss and feeling light of heart at the same time. Kevin and chocolate had that effect on her.

Memories flooded her senses of all the silly, lighthearted moments they had shared during their courtship. Kevin had been entertaining and easy to be with. He'd been irresistible, too, and Cara found that tonight, all those traits that made up the man she'd loved had surfaced.

Kevin reached for her hand. "It's early and a beautiful night. Want to take a walk?"

Cara didn't hesitate. She'd enjoyed the evening and didn't want it to end. "I'd like that."

Kevin squeezed her hand and nodded. "I know just the place."

Cara leaned back in her seat, trusting Kevin to entertain her. He'd been doing a good job of it since she'd arrived back in Houston. Though their marriage was over, this short time together would help them heal from wounds inflicted years earlier. Maybe this was the salve they needed to repair their injuries so they could move on with their lives.

Whatever the reason for her carefree mood, Cara wouldn't analyze it too deeply. She was on vacation from life at the moment, a small black hole in time where she and her soon-to-be-ex husband could enjoy each other's company without repercussions.

She'd forget his blackmail for the time being, shoving his motives out of her head. In less than two weeks she'd be back in Dallas, planning her new studio design, doing what she loved doing.

Kevin stopped the car on a dirt road that overlooked Somerset Lake. Brilliant moonlit waters glistened with sapphire illumination. Kevin got out of the car and opened the door for her.

The air felt heavy and warm, typical for a summer Texas night. Crickets chirped on and off and, in the space of quiet, the gentlest rippling of waves could be heard.

Cara swallowed hard as she took in the view. This was the place they'd come with all their friends, to have picnics and bonfires during the summer. This was *their* place, the spot right beyond the picnic tables, where she and Kevin had first admitted their love for one another.

Cara took Kevin's offered hand and followed him down a dusky, bluebonnet-laden path that led to the water. She took each step with care. She hated trampling on the flowers.

"You're not going to hurt them, babe. They look delicate, but they're resilient."

Cara had heard that from Kevin before, in much the same way, but not about bluebonnets. He'd spoken those words about her when they'd had arguments about his workaholic tendencies.

You look delicate, but I know you're resilient.

Apparently, he hadn't thought she could be hurt. Yet even the most durable of flowers had a breaking point.

"Why take the chance?" she said softly. When Kevin glanced at her, she shrugged. "I don't want to destroy them."

Kevin let the comment go and Cara doubted he caught her true meaning.

"Remember this place?" he asked.

"How could I not? We came here almost every weekend in the summer."

"That was some summer, wasn't it?"

She knew he meant the summer when they'd fallen in love. They'd been inseparable. She nodded slowly and held his hand as they walked along the lakeshore.

"Tell me what happened after you left Somerset."

Cara took a long, slow breath. A cricket chirped a few times, before she was able to formulate the words. "I… It was hard, Kevin. The hardest time of my life."

Kevin remained silent. He gazed ahead, refusing to look into her eyes.

"When I decided to start Dancing Lights, my whole world opened up again."

Kevin's mouth twisted, though he tried very hard to conceal his angst.

Cara didn't want to spoil the evening by talking about a sore subject. "I'm sorry, but you asked."

They walked along the little cove and reached a clearing by another group of redwood picnic benches.

"Care to show me a thing or two about dancing? You know I have two left feet."

"Here? There's no music. And you *don't* have two left feet. As I recall, you have some pretty good moves."

Kevin grinned with mischief. He clamped his hands on her waist and pulled her against him. "As *I* recall, you liked all my moves."

Cara gasped, immersed in the gleam of his dark blue eyes.

"But I'm talking about dance moves, babe. I could use a refresher, since I'm inviting you to Lance and Kate's wedding reception at the club. I wouldn't want to embarrass you with my lackluster dance steps."

Cara blinked in surprise. She couldn't go to Lance's reception with Kevin. It was one thing to see him for a few casual dates privately, but being on his arm at a formal affair would give the wrong impression and make her dream things she had no right dreaming. "You won't have to. I can't go."

"How do you know? I haven't told you the date yet."

"Because," Cara said, stepping away from him to look at the calm waters for comfort. Weddings always made her sentimental and she already had enough to deal with. She didn't need a reminder of their utter failure. "It's just that I think—"

"Shh, you think too much," Kevin said softly, searching her eyes. "You're so beautiful in moonlight, Cara." He leaned in and kissed her tenderly on the lips.

Her insides melted at his gentle touch and she reached up on tiptoes to kiss him back, wrapping her arms around his neck. Maybe it was this place and the memories it evoked, or maybe she'd just been too long without any real tenderness in her life, but right now, she needed to be with Kevin, kissing him and feeling like a woman again.

It wasn't long before Kevin's kisses turned her into Silly Putty, except there was nothing silly about the intensity he displayed. He pulled her along, walking backward until he sat upon the edge of a picnic table. He fitted her between his legs and continued to nibble on her mouth until he drew his lips downward to the base of her throat.

Pinpricks of excitement flew up and down her body. She tingled everywhere, breathing in his sexy cologne. The musky scent she recognized from years before drove her further into oblivion.

It was easy for him to untie her rope belt and pull her blouse down. With a groan of appreciation, he murmured her name and her heart rate sped up.

Kevin unfastened her bra with adept fingers and he pulled the garment away from her. "Damn it, sweetheart," he murmured, the curse a soft and beautiful endearment.

Exposed from the waist up, the pushed-down sleeves of her blouse trapping her arms slightly, Cara could only watch as Kevin touched her breasts, caressing, weighing, cupping her with such tenderness, she wanted to cry.

He made eye contact as he flicked his thumbs over her nipples, toying with them and making her moan with pleasure.

"You still like me touching you," he whispered, his torturous fingers breaking her out in a sweat.

She bit her lip and nodded. She *loved* the way Kevin touched her. He'd been the only man who could turn her on so fast, so furiously. But Cara gave as good as she got and she never let Kevin have the last word. "Seems to me," she said, breathless, "you could put that mouth to better use."

Kevin chuckled, then clamped his hands around her trapped arms and brought her closer. Her breast grazed his mouth and he teased her with tiny tongue swipes until her knees nearly buckled.

"Better?" he asked in a whisper and she nodded enthusiastically.

He filled his mouth with her, suckling and blowing hot breath over her breast. Her nipple stood erect and a rush of sizzling heat invaded her body. Everything below her waist throbbed.

Kevin was in no better shape. His body was rigid, the bulge of his desire pressed against her clothes. Crazy thoughts entered her head of making love to Kevin right here, out in the open, beside the lake where they'd first revealed their love for each other.

Kevin's thoughts couldn't have been far behind. He kissed her soundly and stood up, his manhood grazing her between the legs. "I need more, baby."

Cara nodded and helped Kevin unzip her pants. He cosseted her close and slipped his hand inside. With nimble fingers, he pulled her panties aside and cupped her womanhood.

"Ohh." His touch sent her mind reeling. She'd been so long without this, without Kevin bringing her pleasure.

Alone at the lake in the darkness, the night lit only by moonlight, Cara succumbed to Kevin's ministrations. He slid his hand back and forth, his fingertips caressing her most sensitive skin. She rocked and swayed, and he kissed her while she moved over his hand.

"You feel so good, Cara," he whispered over her lips. He slipped one finger inside.

Cara's eyes closed. She surrendered to Kevin's will. Every single part of her body tingled as he stroked her, slipping his finger up and down until she moved in rhythm like the music of a sexy samba. When she arched her back, Kevin followed her, sliding his lips along her throat, creating sensations that burned like a branding iron.

Whimpers of pleasure tumbled from her lips and Cara's face twisted in ecstasy. "Oh, sweet heaven."

Kevin cupped her breast with one hand and stroked her unmercifully with the other. Again and again, until Cara's body rocked out of control.

"It's so good, baby. Remember?"

Cara remembered. Kevin had always been an unselfish lover. But her thoughts stopped there, because she was too far gone to answer him. Her pleasure heightened and heightened, Kevin drawing out every quiver, every earth-shattering morsel of ecstasy, relentless in his pursuit.

Her muscles contracted and squeezed, her body quaked, and Kevin stopped his assault, allowing her to enjoy this moment on her own terms. He knew, oh, yes, how he knew to bring her the utmost pleasure.

Her orgasm came in slow, torturous, drawn-out bursts. Cara relished each mind-blowing second of shuddering release. Then slowly, slowly she came back down to earth.

When she opened her eyes, Kevin was watching her, his gaze smoldering with lust. "That was—"

"Heaven," Cara whispered, not shy about her display.

Kevin shook his head. "The sexiest thing I've ever witnessed."

Cara glanced down at his obvious erection. "Are you…okay?"

"I could make love to you ten times on this picnic table and not be satisfied."

Cara squirmed, tempted by the erotic thought.

Kevin worked her zipper up and handed her back her bra. "But a deal's a deal."

Fully sated and feeling very lighthearted, Cara dressed. "A man of his word."

Kevin inhaled a sharp breath. She knew how much he'd held back, for her pleasure. "Would have been safer to teach me how to dance."

Cara couldn't contain her smile. "Safety is over-rated at times."

Five

"So, you'll come to Lance and Kate's reception with me?"

Cara turned to Kevin before entering her hotel room. He stood close, boxing her in by the door. Her face still glowed from the attention he'd paid to her at the lake, and the taste of her lips still lingered on his mouth.

"Are you trying to manipulate me?" she asked coyly.

Kevin winced and faked a stab wound to the heart. "You're killing me, Cara."

Cara nibbled on her lower lip with indecision. She'd had him at his boiling point. It had been all he could do not to make love to her on that picnic table tonight. Desire and lust combined made for a heavy aphrodisiac.

"Why do you want me to go?"

Kevin tilted his head and spoke in a serious tone. "Regardless of what has happened between us, Lance has always been your friend. I know he'd want you to be there."

"Why do you?" Cara asked, searching his eyes.

"You're awfully suspicious."

"Don't I have a right to be? After all, you're blackmailing me."

"It's not blackmail, Cara. We made a deal. And tonight, I asked you to celebrate the marriage of a good friend. It's as simple as that."

Kevin wanted her on his arm that night and he wanted to spend as much time with her as possible during these two weeks, but it surprised him how much it mattered to him.

Cara finally relented. "Okay. I'll go and share in the celebration. Lance is a good man."

Kevin nodded, glad that she'd changed her mind. "Good night, Cara." He leaned in and pressed his mouth to hers, relishing the soft, subtle nuances of her giving lips and baby-soft skin. "I had a good time tonight."

Cara closed her eyes briefly. An image of her panting out a rocking orgasm flashed in his head.

"Uh, Kevin. Maybe we shouldn't—"

Kevin leaned in and kissed her a second time, stopping her next thought. "I'll call you tomorrow."

She gazed into his eyes and shook her head as if

trying to figure him out before turning to enter her hotel room.

Kevin left her and drove to his penthouse. He stripped out of his clothes immediately and walked into an icy-cold shower. The brisk spray rained down, easing his stubborn lust. But sexy images of Cara stayed with him throughout. It wasn't easy to wash Cara from his system.

He wanted to make her pay for abandoning him. He wanted to charm her and bend her to his will. He'd succeeded somewhat, but Cara had always been bright. She was correct to be suspicious of him. The only trouble was that he, too, paid a price for his little plan.

He wanted her.

After he toweled off, he headed for his bar and poured himself two fingers of bourbon. Leaning against the black-granite counter, he lifted his glass in midair. "Here's to you, Cara. My wife for just a few more days."

After her lake encounter with Kevin, Cara warned herself she was playing with fire and vowed to keep her distance from her husband until Lance and Kate's reception. It was much safer that way. She needed to keep her perspective and remember why she'd come to Houston.

She'd maintained that resolve for exactly twelve hours, until Kevin knocked at her door midmorning, wearing a full Astros baseball getup. She glanced at him, puzzled, noting his red jersey and baseball cap with the Astros' official star logo. He waved box-seat tickets for the afternoon game in front of her and shot her a delicious grin.

When it dawned on her what he had in mind, she could hardly refuse his enticing offer. She was a huge Houston fan, going back to her high-school days. Going to a day game felt sinful and luxurious, and she felt that doubly with Kevin by her side.

Now, she sat in a box seat at Minute Maid Park, just behind home plate, eating a hot dog and slurping down a Diet Coke.

"Want another?" he asked, after inhaling two hot dogs in record time.

"Nope, but toss me that bag of peanuts and I'm good to go."

Kevin smiled and set the bag on her lap. "Have at it, babe."

They munched on peanuts, booed the bad calls, cheered the good ones and jumped from their seats when an Astro player made it on base. Kevin excused himself for a minute and when he returned, he plopped a red cap with a big white star on her head and handed her a jersey that matched his.

"Thank you!" After she put the jersey on over her blouse, she reached over and planted a big kiss on his cheek.

Kevin turned his head toward her and her kiss slid to his lips. He tasted of mustard and soda and sunshine and their kiss lasted far longer than expected. Kevin took her into his arms and, much like two teenagers in love, they lost themselves.

"Hey, get a room!"

The shout came from a few rows back and Kevin smiled as he broke off the kiss. "Not a bad idea."

"Oh!" Cara straightened in her seat, a full flush of heat rising up her neck. She refused to look Kevin's way for a few minutes but she did hear him chuckle several times.

The Astros won the game and, with their spirits buoyed, they strolled the ballpark hand-in-hand until the crowds diminished. Cara stood in the Grand Union lobby, the famous entrance to the ballpark that went back to the early beginnings of Houston. "Remember when they built the stadium?"

"Yeah, traffic was stopped up for months."

Cara glanced at him. "But you thought it was cool that they'd use Union Station as the entrance."

"Still do. It brings a lot of people to the downtown area. From a business standpoint, it was a great idea."

"Speaking of business, how did you manage to get away from the office today?"

When they were living as man and wife, Kevin would have rather cut off his right arm than take a day off from work.

"I'll make up for it tonight. Got a load of paperwork to sift through."

Cara figured as much. He'd never let his work go, not even for a day. There were times he wouldn't come to bed until two, the computer more of an enticement than she was. In the morning, she'd wake up to find him gone.

She remembered those lonely days and nights. Those memories stayed with her and marred the pleasant day she'd just had.

She remained quiet as Kevin took her back to the hotel, deciding it was a good idea not to invite him in. "I had fun today. Thank you for the invitation." Her voice stiff and formal, Cara made up for her lack of grace with a little smile.

Kevin didn't seem to notice the change in her. "Me, too. It's been ages since I went to a game."

"Because you're too busy?"

Kevin weighed her question, studying her. "I know how to delegate work now, Cara," he said, his tone none too gracious. "I haven't gone to a game because…hell, you're gonna make me say it?"

Stunned, Cara blinked. "Say what?"

Kevin shook his head and cursed. "Because it's what *we* did. Me and you."

"Oh." She wasn't sure she understood.

"I went a few times with the guys," he admitted. Then Kevin's voice went deep, and he tapped her baseball cap twice, planting it farther down on her forehead. "But they don't look as cute as you in a baseball cap."

Before she could react, Kevin leaned down and kissed her soundly on the lips, putting to shame the kiss they'd shared at the ballpark. After five minutes of making out hot and heavy at her door, Kevin backed away and caught his breath, his eyes devastatingly blue. "I'd better go. I'll call you tomorrow."

Cara slumped by the door, not knowing if she was glad he'd left or angry that, once again, his work took precedence over her.

What difference did it make, anyway?

Soon she'd be the *ex* Mrs. Kevin Novak, and what he did or didn't do with his time wouldn't matter.

She clung to that thought and took it to bed with her, trying not to wonder when Kevin would call her again.

Cara fumed for the next two days. Kevin didn't call. She knew she should be glad that she'd been given a reprieve from the relentless attention he paid her, yet she thought it all a waste of time. He'd forced her to stay in Houston for two weeks to obtain his signature. She'd put her life on hold for him. She'd made umpteen calls to her dance studio, dealing with problems and making important decisions from her hotel room instead of being where she was most needed.

Cara looked in the mirror and fidgeted with her unruly mop of hair, finger-combing strands back in place while she debated about going out for dinner or calling room service. Anger bubbled inside and she decided to take a brisk walk to cool off. She picked up her purse just as the hotel phone rang.

She stared at it for a long while, debating whether to pick up. Finally, she relented. "Hello?" she said, tapping her foot.

"Hi, Cara."

Cara winced when she heard Kevin on the other end. She wished she'd listened to her first instinct and not answered the phone. His voice sounded odd and distant, as if he were calling from a cave. "Where are you?"

"Home. Do you still make that killer chicken soup?"

"My grandma's recipe? Yes, why do you—" Then it dawned on her. Kevin didn't sound like himself. In fact, she'd never heard him sound so *off*. She put two and two together. "Are you sick?"

"You could say that," he whispered.

"How sick?"

"I've been in bed for two days and nights, going crazy."

Guilt washed over her and Cara was ashamed of how many unpleasant thoughts had entered her mind about Kevin. She had been certain that he'd been playing games and toying with her emotions, telling her he'd call and then deliberately avoiding her.

"Do you have a fever?"

"One hundred and two."

Oh, man. She softened immediately. "Have you eaten?"

Certainly a millionaire living in a penthouse would have someone to cook and clean for him.

"Toast, yesterday. Not much of an appetite. But I'm craving your grandmother's soup."

Cara inhaled sharply. She was hardly Kevin's nursemaid, but she was still his wife. And his pride wouldn't allow him to ask, unless he really needed her help. She remembered that Kevin hated being sick, never took a day off to heal and was the worst patient she'd ever seen. "I'll catch a cab and be right over."

"I sent a car for you. You can stop off and get the things you need. He should be there any minute."

Cara sighed. "Kevin, how'd you know I'd come?"

"I didn't," he said, his voice trailing off. Cara backed away from giving him grief—he really sounded ill. "But a man can hope, right?"

Kevin felt better already just knowing Cara was on her way. He didn't know what had hit him since he rarely got sick, but he'd been knocked for a loop after taking Cara to the Astros game. He'd spent the next two days in bed, hating every minute of it. His fever had spiked and he hadn't had a drop of energy. Today, he'd gotten up and worked from his home office until he couldn't move a muscle. He'd climbed back in bed, cursing, and the only thing he'd thought of besides his rotten luck was Cara.

In truth, since she'd come back to town she'd consumed his thoughts. His plan for payback was working exceptionally well. Maybe too well, because he'd spent the past two days dreaming of her and the dusky, molten look he put on her face every time they came together. Building up to their one night of lovemaking was killing him, but he enjoyed every torturous minute.

Tonight, he decided, he'd call a truce. He couldn't

take advantage when she'd come so willingly to help him recover, but he felt no guilt whatsoever for the little fib he'd told to get her here.

His fever had broken before he'd called her and he was feeling human again. But he hadn't lied about his craving. He wanted to see Cara in his kitchen, cooking her grandmother's hearty chicken soup. It was the best way to get her to his penthouse—he doubted she'd have come otherwise. But why the hell he'd pictured Cara in his kitchen in a little domestic scene instead of sprawled out across his silk sheets was a mystery to him.

Kevin took a shower, hoping to wipe out the last remnants of his fever and bring some color back to his face. He soaped up and the cool spray of water raining down invigorated him. He shampooed hair that he'd let go for two days and, once he'd turned the faucet off, he toweled dry and stepped out of the shower. This was the most activity he'd had in two days. Looking in the mirror, he let out a groan. "Shabby, Novak," he muttered, "and pale."

His beard served well to cover his sallow appearance, so he opted not to shave. After slipping on his briefs and a comfortable pair of jeans, he threw on a black shirt but didn't have the energy to button it. When the doorbell chimed, he walked the distance to the front door on legs that still felt like rubber.

He opened the door and found Cara holding a brown sack of groceries. "Hi, Kevin."

Cara's gaze immediately drifted to his bare chest, where his shirt spread open. His heartbeat sped up watching lust invade her pretty blue eyes. The flash of instant desire scorched him more than the fever he'd just fought. Then she blinked and redirected her gaze to his face, the moment gone. Soon, he'd put that look back on her face. Tonight, though, it was all he could muster to take the grocery bag from her arms. "My salvation. I'm glad you came, Cara."

"I, uh, sure. I'll make the soup and then let you rest. You really should be in bed."

"I've *been* in bed. It's boring. And lonely."

Cara arched her brow. "I'll find my way around. Point me toward the kitchen."

He placed his hand on the delicate curve of her back, wondering what she'd been up to today, dressed in a classy, sleeveless black-lace blouse and white slacks. Had he interrupted her plans tonight? "C'mon. I'll show you where it is."

Cara darted glances back and forth from one room to the other. Kevin liked his penthouse, having decorated it himself, but he imagined Cara didn't. Too much black and granite and hard angles for her liking—there was nothing here that spoke to a woman's feminine side.

"It's a nice place," she said politely. "Big. How many rooms?"

"Seven." He shrugged. "It's home for now."

When they reached the kitchen, Kevin set the bag on the polished-granite countertop. Cara took in the state-of-the-art stainless steel appliances and nodded. "Either you don't cook much, or you have an expert cleaning staff."

Kevin cracked a smile and it actually hurt his face. He hadn't smiled in two days. "Both. I know the place looks sterile. I eat out a lot or bring in food. You know I'm not a cook."

"Yeah, I remember. Boiling an egg is your specialty." She smiled wide. "I thought that might have changed."

He sat down on the counter stool across the island from Cara, content to watch her. "Some things have changed, but not my cooking abilities. I'm still pretty hopeless in the kitchen, but I make up for it in other ways."

She blinked, looking a little flustered, and rubbed her hands down her slacks. "Okay, well, I'll just get started."

She removed the groceries from the bag and started laying things out, opening and closing kitchen drawers until she had all the utensils she needed. "Are you going to sit there and watch me?"

He nodded. "Unless you need help."

God, he hoped she didn't. He'd sat down because his rubber legs needed the break. He'd felt better after his shower but, as the hour wore on, weakness consumed him again.

"Nope, this is a one-woman job." She smiled and went to work efficiently. "Just watch and learn."

Cara scooped up the carrots and potatoes she'd cut into small chunks and tossed them into the big soup pot. The chicken pieces were already cooking and she'd used caution with the spices. Normally, she'd spice up the soup to give it a sharp bite, but she had to stick to more bland ingredients for Kevin's sake.

He watched her intently, making small talk, asking her about the recipe, truly engaged in what she was doing. But each time Cara glanced at him, he appeared to slump lower on the stool. His voice droned in quiet tones and only his stubborn nature kept him in the kitchen instead of the bed, where he really needed to be.

"You're exhausted, sweetheart," she said softly. "The soup's going to need an hour of simmering. Let me get you into bed. I'll come get you when it's ready."

Kevin pursed his lips and stared at her with feigned irritation. Hell would freeze over before Kevin would ever admit defeat, but she knew he was grateful for the reprieve. "Only because you called me sweetheart."

"That was my strategy all along," she said, wiping her hands on a dish towel. She moved to his side of the island. "Can you get to your bedroom okay?"

He lowered his dark blond lashes. "Sure, but it'd be more fun if you helped me."

Cara couldn't tell if he was joking. He really did appear weak and his color had faded since she'd first arrived. She feared he'd overdone it. "Okay, I'll get you there."

Kevin stood and wrapped his arm around her shoulder. She followed his lead to the farthest room down the hallway. Double doors opened to a room that could only be described as a suite in itself. A black-manteled fireplace stood across from the massive bed. An enormous flat-screen television covered one wall and a room-size balcony ventured out from two French doors, overlooking the Houston skyline.

Cara refrained from commenting. Kevin had certainly come up in the world. Everything he owned spoke of great wealth. He had achieved his goals. He was a brilliant success. A part of her wanted to shed tears all over again, for the marriage that he'd sacrificed without realizing it. For the love that had taken the brunt of his success and for the shattering of vows spoken.

There was a moment of awkward silence when they'd reached his beautifully crafted bed. Would this be the place where they'd seal their divorce deal next week?

Cara heaved a sigh and ducked away from Kevin. "There you go," she said brightly. "I'd better go stir the soup. Get some rest, okay?"

Kevin removed his shirt and let it drop slowly. He stood by the bed in jeans and bare feet, his short hair disheveled and his face sporting stubble that made him look dangerous and sexy. Dear heaven. Cara's breath caught tight in her throat. Her husband was gorgeous, ripped with lean muscle and extremely appealing even in his weakened state.

She shook her head and backed out of the room. Images of Kevin opening the door earlier with droplets of water beaded on his fine chest hair invaded her thoughts. She'd wanted to lick each one and then run her hands over him, again and again. "Chase those thoughts from your head, Cara," she whispered as she reentered the kitchen. "And don't you dare fall for Kevin Novak again."

Six

Cara stood over the six-burner Viking range and stirred the soup. Every time she made this soup she thought of the sweet nature of her grandmother, who had taught Cara step-by-step how to prepare it. What set this soup apart from all others was the fresh crushed tomatoes she used and the cup of red wine that she put in during the last twenty minutes of cooking. It was her grandmother's secret ingredient and her signature meal.

She hadn't made this soup once since she and Kevin had broken up. But now, images of standing beside Grandma Flo in her kitchen, helping toss in ingredients, came to mind and lingered in a pleasing way. The aroma of oregano, basil, fresh tomatoes and onion drifted throughout the kitchen and brought her back to a happy time in her childhood.

She had Kevin to thank for that. Not that she wanted to see him sick, but she missed cooking for someone else, deriving great satisfaction in it. "There you go," she said, giving the soup one last stir before allowing it to simmer.

Cara looked about the kitchen, wondering what to do next. She'd already cleaned up the mess she'd made chopping up the ingredients. On impulse, she walked to Kevin's room and peeked inside the double doors that she'd left ajar earlier.

He slept.

That was a good sign. What wasn't a good sign was her unexpected physical attraction to him, seeing him sprawled out on the bed, nearly naked but for the jeans he wore. She had an uncanny urge to both nurture him and make crazy love to him.

Quickly, Cara stepped away and mentally scolded herself. "Don't go there," she whispered. Then curiosity got the better of her and she perused the rooms in the penthouse, looking for signs of…what? Another woman? Something that would clue her in as to what he'd done with the past four years of his life.

Sourly she admitted that Kevin wouldn't have been celibate for four years. She wondered how many relationships he'd had. How many women had he brought up here to admire the view?

She entered his office and noticed a soft, buttery-brown sofa, the only piece of furniture that looked welcoming. His mahogany desk was littered with files and papers. She walked behind the desk to look out at the Houston skyline and pictured Kevin twirling around in his chair to take a breather and look out the window. "Nice."

Cara wandered over to a sturdy wall unit and lifted up a few picture frames sitting on the shelf, noting that every scene depicted Kevin with one or more of his friends—Lance and Kevin on the golf course, and Darius, Mitch, Lance and Kevin on the tennis court. She glanced at a photo of Kevin with Kate and Lance, the happy threesome smiling into the camera.

Cara picked up a picture of Kevin standing beside his parents at his University of Texas graduation. Still in cap and gown, Kevin's face displayed confidence and determination. She saw the resolute gleam in his eyes—nothing would stop him from achieving his goals. Had she been so blindsided by love that she hadn't noticed that quality in him before? Or had she thought she wouldn't fall victim to his dogged persistence and drive? Cara had been at his graduation and at one point had stood beside him and his parents for a photo. But that picture, she presumed, was long gone, tossed out when she'd left, which he considered abandonment and she considered survival.

Regret and nostalgia brought a whisper of a sigh to her lips. She recalled how they'd celebrated his graduation that night.

In bed.

And making plans for their future.

Now, she wondered who'd be making future plans with Kevin once he was single again. Bemused, Cara's curiosity escalated. She entered the other two bedrooms in the penthouse and noticed, with a good deal of relief, there were no pictures of Kevin with a woman. She dared to peek inside the walk-in closets, loathing the nosy-body she'd become but too curious to keep herself from snooping.

Cara walked back into the kitchen and stirred the soup again. Thankfully, it was ready. She closed her eyes and the flavorful aroma hit her anew, but she couldn't shake the feeling that she'd learned far more about herself than Kevin on her little escapade through his house.

The elation she felt seeing no signs of another woman anywhere in his home caused her great concern. She nibbled on her lip and made up her mind to get out as quickly as she could.

"Something smells good in here."

Cara whirled around. Kevin stood at the doorway, barefoot in those same soft jeans. Thankfully, as he made his way into the room, he pulled a T-shirt on over his head, covering the chest she itched to touch.

"The soup's ready. I was just about to come get you."

"What, no dinner in bed?" He wiggled his eyebrows in that charming way he had.

"I see you've got your sense of humor back," she bantered. "How're you feeling?"

He stopped his approach to take assessment. "Rested. The best sleep I've had in two days."

"Must be the powers of the soup," she said, taking out a bowl from the dark maple cabinet.

Kevin scratched his head. "The powers of something."

They stared at each other across the kitchen, his deep-blue gaze penetrating her until she thought she'd bubble over, like the soup she'd just prepared.

Cara made herself really busy, slicing French bread she'd bought at a bakery down the street. She poured Kevin a bowl of soup and set a thick slice of bread on his plate.

"I should go," she said.

Kevin's gaze never left hers. He walked over to the cabinet and took down a second bowl. "Do you have a hot date tonight?"

An unfeminine chuckle erupted from her chest. "Yeah, with my book."

"Then stay. Have a bowl of soup with me. I could use the company."

Dumbfounded, Cara watched Kevin's efficient movements around the kitchen. Before she knew it, he'd duplicated his own meal for her.

He took both of the plates to the living room and set them down on a cocktail table. "You'll never guess what's on TV right now."

Cara groaned. She knew Kevin had her. She followed him into the living room. "James Bond marathon."

Kevin worked the remote and Bond's classic opening music played as an image of 007 filled the screen.

"Oh, man, and I really wanted to finish that book tonight."

Kevin smiled and sat down on the sofa, stiff leather squeaking as he got comfortable.

She was a sucker for Bond. They both were. So when Kevin patted the seat directly next to him, Cara didn't hesitate, the temptation too great. She sat down beside him and together they watched the movie and enjoyed her grandmother's delicious, hot soup.

Somewhere between *Dr. No* and *Never Say Never Again,* Kevin felt the grip of illness dissipate. He'd woken up past midnight on his sofa with a more than healthy erection. The flat screen droned in the background, long since forgotten. Cara was sprawled on top of him, her head on his shoulder, her silky blond hair tickling his chin, her soft breathing giving testimony to her slumber.

Kevin let go a silent groan of pain. Cara's breasts crushed his chest, but it was her softly feminine, erotic scent that had his mind reeling with possibilities. For now, all he could do was stroke her hair, weaving tendrils through his fingers. Her blouse had drifted up her back, exposing skin that dipped below the waistband of her white slacks.

Kevin stretched his fingers out, debating whether

to give in to impulse and run his hand over her back and dip under her waistband. Man, oh, man, how he wanted to, but she'd been a good sport about coming over here and making soup so he couldn't very well wake her now for his own selfish reasons.

Could he?

Kevin asked himself, why not? He'd had a reason and purpose to have her stay in Houston for two weeks. She owed him and he meant to make her pay for leaving him high and dry. Having her lying atop him tempted him beyond belief. She'd only be his wife another week, so why not derive as much pleasure as possible from the situation now?

Kevin stroked her back lightly and she stirred, letting go a little moan.

Kevin's erection stiffened. Yet he couldn't bring himself to disturb her peace. Holding her, he closed his eyes again, enjoying the feel of her in his arms. Wouldn't be too long before he'd lose the legal right to do so.

Less than a minute later Cara moved, and Kevin opened his eyes to find her casting him a sleep-hazy look. "Hi, babe."

She blinked, disoriented, and lifted her body somewhat to stare into his eyes. Kevin noted the exact moment when Cara's eyes widened with dawning knowledge of where she was and how aroused she'd made him. "Oh."

"I've recovered," he said, before lifting the corners of his mouth. "But now I have another problem."

Cara pushed against his chest and made a move to get up. "What time is it?"

Kevin wrapped his arms around her, gently bringing her back down. "After midnight."

She looked around the room, spotting a tuxedo-clad Pierce Brosnan racing for his life on the flat screen. "I fell asleep."

"*We* fell asleep."

She stared into his eyes. "How are you?"

"Except for the obvious," he said, his gaze dropping down to her spectacular cleavage, "I'm feeling great."

She stared at him and silence ensued as she took stock of her position and the strain of his jeans against the apex of her legs. "You're turned on."

"Big-time."

She nibbled on her lower lip, clearly panicked. The pulsing sensation where they joined wasn't one-sided. Heat and pressure built and Cara couldn't deny she was just as turned on. "I should go."

"Stay, Cara." Kevin put his hand behind her neck and pulled her head down. They looked into each other's eyes before Kevin nipped at her lips. Once, twice, then he wrapped his arms around her more tightly and those nibbles became full-fledged, hot, hungry kisses.

Cara whimpered in her throat, eager for more and fully aroused. Kevin dipped his tongue into her mouth and swept through, tasting her with long, openmouthed motions. As the kisses went deeper, she moved on him, rubbing her body over his erection until he thought he'd die of agony.

Kevin lifted her enough to bring his mouth to her breast. He suckled her through the lace of her blouse, moistening her until the material became nearly sheer. Her nipple strained, tight. Kevin flicked the tip with his thumb and simultaneously, they both pulled her blouse up and over her head. Kevin didn't take time to undo her bra, he simply reached inside and released her breasts from their enclosure.

Cara kissed him hard on the lips and allowed him free rein to do whatever he wanted. He took his time, cupping, weighing, adoring each breast, licking the tips and wetting each perfect globe until Cara's breathing became frenzied.

She lifted up partway and pushed his T-shirt off over his head. She dropped her mouth on him immediately, kissing his chest, her hands roaming freely. "Ah, Cara," he murmured, his pleasure heightening.

She circled his flat nipples and nipped at the tips, her fingers weaving into his scattered chest hair. She pulled at him and he smiled at her prowess, while his erection strained even harder against his jeans.

He ran his hands in her hair, enjoying every second Cara made love to him. It was better than he remembered, having her hands caress him, having her mouth drive him crazy.

Revenge can be sweet, he thought, and wondered if his plan was working, or if Cara simply derived sexual pleasure from him. Either way, he wouldn't question it now.

Kevin took Cara's hand and set it on his waistband, directly over the zipper that was ready to combust. "Touch me," he whispered. "Like you used to."

Cara closed her eyes and inhaled sharply. Then, after a second of thought, she slid slightly to the side to unsnap his jeans. Kevin held his breath. He ached for her touch, for Cara to ease his need. The top of his waistband opened and, with two nimble fingers, she moved the zipper down slowly.

Cool air hit him yet his body flamed. Her touch was light and tentative as she stroked him initially. He lifted up, slanting his lips over hers, deepening their mounting desire.

"This is dangerous," she whispered between kisses.

"You've never shied away from danger, babe."

"It's better to be safe."

"Didn't you once say safety is overrated?"

Cara laughed and the sound of her lightheartedness turned the tide. Kevin laughed, too, his body no less hard-pressed for her, but they'd reached a playful plateau that they might have called their trademark, once upon a time.

"We always had fun together," he added.

"I know, but I didn't come here for fun."

"Why did you come?"

"Soup, remember?"

"No, I don't remember. Anything that happened more than ten minutes ago is a complete blur."

Cara punched him lightly on the shoulder and Kevin reacted by taking hold of her arm and tugging her down. He tasted her lips again and again, the playfulness forgotten as heat and passion consumed them again.

Kevin relished every second Cara touched him, her soft hand against his shaft stroking him in her subtle then bold ways, creating sizzling hot tension. He wanted nothing more than to ease his lust inside her. To feel her soft perfect body welcome him. Man, oh, man, he remembered how it was to be with Cara. He'd never forgotten. No woman had ever compared. But he couldn't make love to her tonight. Not yet. Kevin sat up abruptly before he lost all control.

"Are you feeling weak again?" she asked, seriously concerned.

"Just a dose of Cara fever," he said with a quick smile.

Her expression softened and Kevin rose before he gave in to his desire to make love to her.

He reached down to grab her hand. "It's late. I'll drive you home."

They dressed quickly, both silent in their thoughts. But when he escorted Cara to her hotel room, she turned to him, puzzled. "Kevin, I don't understand any of this."

She looked sex tousled and beautifully confused. "That makes two of us."

The trouble was, Kevin knew his plan the way a general knew his battle strategy, but that didn't make it any less confusing to him, either. They stared at each other for a long moment, searching one another for the truth and coming up short.

"Thanks for coming to my rescue tonight," he said finally. "The soup was great." Then he added, "You haven't lost your touch."

Kevin turned from Cara and forced himself to walk away without looking back.

Cara was at her wit's end, wanting Kevin so terribly that the tension caused her a sleepless night. Sensibly, she knew she and Kevin were doomed as a couple, so making love to him could only hurt her. Her rational side understood that. But her heart and her body were a different matter. She wanted to have sex with her husband—was that so wrong? She had asked that of herself last night and then again this morning. She craved Kevin. He knew how to make her skin prickle and how to satisfy her innermost desires. But the sad fact remained that, once she got what she wanted, their marriage would be over.

When her cell phone rang, Cara looked at the number and hesitated before answering. "Hi, Kevin."

"You cured me last night."

"I'm…glad."

"How about letting me make it up to you. Dinner, tomorrow night? I promise to be better company. I'll even shave."

Cara laughed. She rubbed the slight beard-burns on her face where his stubble had bruised her last night. Memories rushed forth. She shook her head and knew she should make up an excuse and refuse him.

It's for the best, Cara.

Cara opened her mouth to say no, and surprised herself. "I'd love to."

She slammed her eyes shut. Why did she find Kevin so irresistible? Had he changed? Could she trust him? None of it mattered, anyway. In less than a week she'd be gone, with her signed divorce papers in hand.

After making arrangements with him, she hung up the phone, at odds with herself. When her cell phone rang a second time, she answered it quickly, happy to receive Alicia's call.

"Hi, Cara. It's Alicia."

"Alicia, I'm so glad you called."

"Are we still on for lunch and shopping this afternoon?"

"I'm looking forward to it." Cara needed a girl's day out to clear her mind.

"I'm in town, so I'll pick you up and we'll head to Somerset. Can you be ready in half an hour?"

"Yes." So ready, she thought. "I'll be waiting for you downstairs."

After she hung up the phone, Cara dressed in brown slacks and a sleeveless crème top. She slipped her feet into comfy, chocolate-brown Jimmy Choos and pulled her curly hair back into a tortoiseshell clip. She grabbed her matching handbag and exited the hotel room.

Alicia drove up just as Cara exited the Four Seasons. The doorman wished her a good day and off she went, ready to put Kevin out of her mind for the next few hours.

Cara took in the sights as the bustling downtown soon gave way to quiet residential roads. Somerset, in the heart of Maverick County, was a small, beautifully constructed town northeast of Houston. Cara had once loved living there in a modest home with Kevin. There were times in Dallas when she would be reminded of their house—she'd see a fabric similar in design to her kitchen curtains or smell fresh mint and recall the stone pathway that led to their front door, laden with the herb. She would sigh, wondering how her life had changed so much. Sentimental feelings would rush in, but Cara had always quickly shooed them away.

Now, as Alicia drove on, Cara looked to a digital sign set atop a tall post just outside the front gates of Maverick High School, announcing in flashing yellow letters the first dance of the new semester. "I hear those Friday-night dances were something wild. Lance and Mitch were always going on and on about them. I bet they stopped just short of telling me how much trouble they'd really gotten into back then."

Alicia shrugged. "I wouldn't know. I didn't go to many dances."

"No?"

With a shake of her head, Alicia replied, "No, I, uh, didn't care to…"

"Dance? Now, Alicia, I bet you can move."

"I like to dance," Alicia said carefully, "but Alex

didn't want me to go to the dances. He, uh, thought people looked down on us." Alicia turned to her, her dark eyes almost apologetic. "Alex has a lot of pride."

Cara remembered how protective Alejandro Montoya was of his little sister, just from bits and pieces she'd heard of Kevin's conversations with his friends. Alicia was timid and Alex had done his best to shield her. Cara still couldn't believe that Alex would have had anything to do with the fire at Brody Oil, though he may have been resentful of the men who had more than he had while growing up. He had come from a different social standing, working at the Texas Cattleman's Club as the groundskeeper, but now he was just as wealthy and powerful as Kevin and his friends. Alex may hate the Brodys, but Cara refused to believe he was a criminal.

"You two are very close."

"Yes, and I have to keep reminding him, I'm all grown up now."

"Sometimes men can't see what's right in front of them," Cara acknowledged.

Alicia beamed with amusement. "So true."

They dined at a little outdoor restaurant on Somerset's main street. Wrought-iron chairs and umbrella-covered mosaic-stone tables gave a Spanish ambiance. After glancing at the menu, Cara noted the fare was mostly Southwestern, which suited her just fine. She was in the mood for hometown spice.

She loved eating outdoors on warm days and

didn't get too much chance to do so in Dallas. Usually, she ate her lunch in the office at the dance studio, going over accounts or viewing video of her students' progress.

"This is really nice," Cara said.

"It's new. I thought you might like it."

They sat in silence for a minute looking at the menu and when the waiter walked up, offering the daily specials, Cara and Alicia both decided on spicy Southwestern chicken salad with chipotle, and strawberry margaritas.

The margaritas arrived first. Cara lifted her glass in a toast. "To friends," she said with a smile.

"To friends," Alicia repeated, and they touched together their full margarita glasses before taking a sip.

Cara told Alicia all about her dance studios, explaining about how her background in gymnastics and dance had given her the idea when she and Kevin had split up. She admitted she'd had to do something with her life. She'd been brokenhearted and depressed. Pouring herself into her work and seeing the progress she'd made in just a few short years had come to mean so much to her.

"And now I'm back for a short time."

Alicia cast her a curious look. Cara had never really explained why she'd come back and Alicia had been too polite to inquire, but she assumed her friend was puzzled. If the roles were reversed, Cara would be, too. "I've been spending some time with Kevin."

She couldn't bring herself to confess that the reason she'd been seeing Kevin was his blackmail. Admitting so wouldn't shed a positive light on either of them. The entire subject brought bitterness to her mouth. She sipped her margarita, sweetening up the sour subject. "We're mending fences, sort of."

"Are you two dating?"

"Well," Cara said, taking a deep breath, "I guess we are. We've gone on a few casual dates."

Alicia observed her carefully and Cara wanted to confide in her friend. She needed someone to talk to. Her mother was out of the question, and none of her friends in Dallas would understand her dating Kevin now when she'd been so adamant about getting on with her life. She added, "Actually, we're going out to dinner tomorrow night. And he's taking me to Lance's wedding reception."

"Sounds very hopeful," Alicia said.

The entrees were delivered to the table, releasing Cara from commenting further. They both dug into the salads. "So, what got you interested in working for the museum?" Cara asked. Alicia had mentioned she was the curator of the Somerset Museum of Natural History.

"I love history." Alicia shrugged with a little smile. "It's a small museum, but I enjoy getting up in the morning and going to work. There's so much history in this area."

Cara noted a gleam in Alicia's dark eyes when she spoke of her work. "It's a fulfilling job."

Alicia nodded. "Yes, I feel fortunate."

Cara felt fortunate, too, at the moment. Alicia's sweet nature reminded her of all the good things in her life.

An image of Kevin popped into her head. They were getting closer each day. Was that one of the good things in her life?

Cara concentrated on shopping the rest of the afternoon. She and Alicia walked the long streets, entering various shops, an antique bookstore, a pottery store filled with hand-painted vases and plates, and an art gallery. As they strolled along sharing anecdotes, Cara remembered why she'd been so fond of Alicia. She was easy to be with and their conversation flowed naturally. Their last stop was Rebecca Huntington's lingerie boutique, Sweet Nothings.

"Wait until you see the gorgeous lingerie in here," Alicia said.

The minute Cara entered Somerset's newest shop she saw for herself what Alicia had meant. Lace, satin and silk lingerie in a variety of pastels was displayed throughout the shop. Cara took all of it in, noting the exquisite fabrics presented on satin hangers. Mirrored wall shelves showcased exotic perfumes. A sitting area with sofa and chairs surrounded a marble table set with delicate coffee cups and teapots for a little respite between shopping sprees. "How lovely," Cara said.

A woman with stunning red hair that was pulled

into a knot at the back of her head approached. With green eyes as warm as her manner, she greeted them. "Hello and welcome to Sweet Nothings." She looked at Alicia with a slight slant of her head. "You're Alejandro Montoya's sister, aren't you?"

"Yes, Alex is my brother. I'm Alicia. I've come into your shop a few times, but wasn't sure you recognized me. You're Rebecca Huntington, aren't you?"

Everyone at the Texas Cattleman's Club knew the Huntington name, of course. Her father, Sebastian Huntington, was one of the oldest members of the club and he was well-known but not well liked, from what Cara recalled.

Rebecca's eyes lost their glow for a second, then she nodded. "Yes. I was sorry to hear about your mother's death. Carmen was a lovely woman."

Emotion flitted through Alicia's gaze and Cara sensed a history between the two women, and not a good one.

"Is there anything I might show you?" Rebecca said, looking from Cara to Alicia. "Or would you like to browse?"

"Browsing, first," Cara said. "You have a lovely shop. I want to see *everything*."

Rebecca cast her a wide smile. "Thank you. Just let me know if you need any help."

Rebecca walked behind the counter to resume her duties, and Cara and Alicia ventured farther into the shop.

"Look at this," Alicia said, strolling to a rounder.

Her attitude warned that she didn't want to discuss her past relationship with Rebecca. She pulled out a hanger holding a skimpy, pink baby-doll two-piece set striped with black lace. She held it up for Cara to see.

"Oh, that would look great on you, with your olive skin."

Alicia let go a chuckle. "And where would I wear this? Or more exactly, for whom?"

"There's no one special in your life, Alicia?" Cara asked, keeping her voice low.

"No," she said. "There are days when I wonder if I'll ever have someone to wear such exquisite things for."

"How about for yourself? Pamper yourself a little."

Alicia glanced at the nightie one last time before quickly setting it back on its rounder. "Someday, maybe." But the longing in her voice belied her fast action. She turned her attention to Cara. "Maybe you should pick up something for your date with Kevin."

Cara smiled and glanced around the store, her gaze stopping on a rack that held one-of-a-kind black-lace nighties. Cara wanted to blow Kevin's mind with a naughty number that would create a lifelong memory for them both. "I intend to, and you're gonna help me find just the right one. Come look at these over here."

Alicia followed her to the rack. Cara held up a garment that appealed to her and ran her hand inside to demonstrate how the fine, delicate, lacy threads would expose more skin than they covered. "What do you think?"

"Makes a statement," Alicia said with twinkling eyes.

Cara grinned. It was perfect. "I think so, too."

Alicia let go a deep sigh. "You're glowing." She looked at Cara with a tilt of her head, her voice filled with yearning. "Must be nice to be so much in love."

Love?

Had Cara fallen back in love with Kevin?

Cara's heart surged. Warmth spread through her body and the realization struck that she *was* in love with Kevin Novak. All over again. Maybe she'd never stopped loving him. And the night she'd wear this lingerie would be her last night with Kevin before they finalized a divorce that had been four years in the making.

Only now, she wasn't certain she wanted it at all.

Seven

Kevin glanced at his watch for the twentieth time today. In just three hours, he'd be picking Cara up for their date. Anticipation coursed through his body, making him impatient and eager.

He peered down at the completed files on his desk. Working like a madman today, he'd managed to get through most everything in record time and hold a team meeting for his latest apartment complex project on the outskirts of Houston. He had a few notes to make about the project before turning them in to legal.

He was just finishing up his last thoughts when Darius and Lance walked in, unannounced. Kevin glanced past them to the opened door and his secretary, Marin, who sat at her desk. "Can't get decent help these days. She lets just anybody walk into my office."

"I heard that," Marin called out. "You're lucky to have me."

"Yeah, you're lucky to have her," Darius said with a wide grin.

"We came to deliver you from all this," Lance said, sweeping his right arm over Kevin's paper-laden desk. "It's happy hour, starting right now."

Kevin twisted his mouth, stood up and walked to the door. "Kidding," he said unnecessarily to his secretary. She'd been advised to never hold Lance or Darius in the outer office unless he was in a meeting. He closed the door and looked at his friends. "Can't. Not tonight."

"Why not?" Darius asked.

"I've got a date in a few hours."

"With Cara?"

Kevin folded his arms over his middle. "That's right."

Darius shook his head. "I know what you're up to. I recognize all the signs. You're trying to get back at Cara for hurting you. But trust me, it's only gonna come back to bite you in the ass."

"It's something I need to do," Kevin said in his own defense. "What makes you such an expert?"

"I did the same thing with Summer. I wanted revenge for what she did to me seven years ago, but I hurt myself in the process by denying my love for her. I almost lost her, Kevin."

"My situation's different."

"If you're that angry and hurt, it's only because you're still in love with her and won't admit it."

Lance agreed with Darius. "I think you should listen to him, Kev. You'll see it more clearly over a good drink."

"Yeah, well, maybe I'm changing my mind about having drinks with you two."

Lance scrubbed his chin.

Both men grabbed him by the elbow, one on each side, and bulldozed him out of his office. "Maybe if we'd have pulled you out of your office more, back in the day, you two would still be together. On your way to making us uncles," Darius added.

Kevin yanked his arms free and regained his composure just before reaching his secretary's desk. "We're closing up early. Go on home and have a good night," he said, ignoring Lance's and Darius's smug smiles.

"Thanks, Mr. Novak."

They rode the elevator down. "Five years ago, I'd have punched both of you out for trying that stunt."

Darius threw his head back and laughed heartily. "You would've tried, Novak. But not succeeded."

"Five years ago," Lance began, "you never would've stopped working, not even for a drink with friends."

"Meaning?"

Lance cocked his head and shrugged his broad shoulders. "Meaning, you're making progress. Though you're a slow learner."

Kevin shook his head. "You guys don't let up."

"C'mon," Lance said, stepping off the elevator. "The bar is calling. We won't make you late for your date with Cara."

"Better not." What Kevin wouldn't tell them was that his plan had already worked. Cara was falling for him again. He saw it in the soft way she looked at him now and in the sweet tone of her voice when they spoke on the phone. "The last thing I want to do is tick her off."

By eight-fifteen, Cara was pacing the floor of her hotel room. At eight-thirty, she glanced at the phone on the nightstand, then pulled out her cell phone and gave it a sour look. Kevin had been due to pick her up half an hour ago. He hadn't called. Cara vacillated about whether to call him or not. But rising anger won out. She slammed her phone shut and tossed it back into her purse.

"He knows how to reach me," she muttered.

Cara's mind rewound to all those days he'd come home later than she'd expected, all those dinners she'd worked on meticulously going untouched. The lonely nights she'd waited up for him. And later, the lonely nights when she'd gone to bed before he'd come home. She'd begun to think it was her. After all, all the other young married women she knew had husbands who came home like clockwork. They ate their dinners together. They spent their weekends doing fun things. She'd found herself longing for Kevin, when it was obvious he hadn't longed for her.

He'd never needed her company, not like that. Not like most newlyweds, who couldn't get enough of each other. She'd begun to feel inadequate as a wife, like she couldn't keep her husband interested. Her feelings had escalated when she'd wanted to have a baby and Kevin had kept putting it off. "There's time for that. We're young yet."

She'd been a sucker then, forgiving him after each excuse, until finally after years of hearing him out, his excuses had fallen on deaf ears. At least she was grateful they hadn't had children. She didn't want to raise a child in a broken home. Because when the pain had gotten too strong, Cara had had no option but to leave, and salvage what was left of her heart.

She wondered what excuse he'd come up with now. And then lightning struck.

"I'm not sticking around to find out."

Cara wasn't the understanding, innocent young wife she once had been. She grabbed her purse and took a quick look at herself in the mirror. Dressed in her little black dress, her blond curls resting on her shoulders, she gave herself an approving nod before walking out the door.

With each step she took, her anger rose. She rode the elevator down to the lobby and headed straight for the concierge desk. She found a middle-aged man with a kind face standing behind the counter.

"I'd like a cab. Where can I find a nice place to listen to music and have a drink?"

The concierge, whose name tag revealed his name was George, smiled. "Well, a cab might not be necessary. The Fairfield Room is available to our guests tonight and the band is scheduled to go on in a few minutes."

"Perfect," Cara said. She could have a drink or two and not worry about finding her way back to the hotel. "Just point me in the right direction."

"I'll do better than that," he said, coming around the counter. "I'll walk you there myself."

Kevin knocked on Cara's door at precisely eight forty-five. He was late picking her up, but it couldn't be helped. After having one drink with Lance and Darius, he'd gotten a call from the night watchman at the apartment complex project. The apartment structure had been vandalized. Teddy Burford had been roughed up a bit and knocked unconscious for a few seconds.

Kevin had given the elderly night-guard the job personally. He was a war veteran who'd been qualified for the job and he had sensed the old guy needed to feel useful in his later years. Kevin stayed with Teddy while he gave the police his story. Nothing was stolen and, from Teddy's description of the culprits, it appeared to have been a teenage prank. Teddy had startled three boys. They'd panicked and one of the boys had shoved him hard. He'd hit his head against the wall and blacked out for a few moments.

Kevin had waited with Teddy until his daughter had picked him up to take him to the emergency room for observation. Then he'd finally glanced at his watch. When he'd realized he'd be late for his date with Cara, he'd called her immediately. She hadn't answered her phone.

Now he stood outside her door, knocking more loudly the second time. "Cara, it's Kevin."

No answer.

He let go a vivid curse and knocked one more time before leaving. He dialed her cell phone number again on his way to the elevator and it went straight to voice mail. She'd turned off her phone.

In the lobby, Kevin spoke with two bellmen, then three women behind the registration desk. One of the employees pointed out the concierge.

Kevin nodded and headed his way. "Excuse me, but I'm looking for my wife, Mrs. Novak. Blond, about so high—" he gestured to her five-foot-eight height "—and beautiful."

George looked him over carefully, then nodded. "I just walked your wife over to the Fairfield Room. It's on the third floor just off the—"

"Thanks." Kevin took off before the concierge finished giving him directions. He'd planned on being with Cara tonight and nothing was going to stop him. Even though he might have to grovel a bit, he'd make her understand why he'd been late.

Kevin followed the sounds of live music, a soft, sultry ballad leading him easily enough to the Fairfield Room. He stood in the double-door entrance to a room with elegant swag draperies, Venetian chandeliers that sparkled like diamonds and a dark wood, parquet dance floor. People huddled around the long bar. Kevin leaned casually against the doorjamb, arms folded, in search of his wife.

When he spotted her, he lifted away slightly to get a better look at Cara in the arms of a stranger, slow-dancing and making conversation.

She looked beautiful in her little black dress and long, glittering earrings, showing enough leg to make a grown man cry.

Kevin tried to temper his frustration, yet the voice in his head wouldn't let it go.

What did you expect?

She's young and beautiful and once you sign those papers, she'll be free to date other men.

Get used to it, buddy.

When the man dancing with Cara brought her up closer, Kevin's frustration transformed into something that made him stride into the room with deliberate steps. His gaze pinned solely on Cara, he walked up to her and set a hand on her arm. She whirled around, her eyes wide.

"Sorry I'm late, babe."

Her mouth dropped open. "Kevin."

She glanced at the man she'd been dancing with and smiled apologetically.

He gave her a quizzical look, then spoke to Kevin. "We're in the middle of a dance."

"I'm aware of that." Kevin couldn't fault the guy for his attempt at chivalry. "But you're dancing with my wife." He cocked the man a smile. "I can take over now."

The man stared at Kevin, then darted a glance at Cara's ringless left finger before dropping his arms from her.

"Soon to be divorced," she added in explanation. The man nodded and lingered. A tic worked at Kevin's jaw.

"Nice meeting you, Cara."

"Same here, Dylan. Sorry about the interruption."

Kevin's patience ebbed. "If you'll excuse us, I need to speak with my wife."

"Sure thing." Dylan eyed Cara once more before walking off the dance floor.

"That wasn't pretty, Kevin." Cara's eyes darkened.

"Maybe not, but it's justified. I'm apologizing for being late."

"Apology declined." Cara marched off the dance floor.

Kevin rolled his eyes and had a good mind not to follow her, but damn it, she'd hear his explanation and then she could decide to be angry or not.

She walked to a table and picked up her purse, tucking it under her arm. "You ruined my evening, Kevin. And you ruined a perfectly nice dance I was enjoying."

"With *that* guy?" Kevin pointed in the direction of the dance floor.

Cara ignored his question. "As I recall, it was you who wanted me to be in town for these weeks, pending our divorce. The least you could do is *show up* when you say you will."

Kevin took a deep breath. "Let's sit down and I'll explain."

"Kevin, don't you see? I don't want your explanations. I heard all of your excuses years ago."

"Okay, if you won't sit down, then dance with me."

"Kevin," she said, exasperated. She ran a hand through her hair and looked away.

He stroked her cheek and she turned to face him. He smiled and said softly, "I'm sorry. I called you as soon as I could."

"I was always second best."

He heard the pain in her voice.

It was important to him that she understood what had happened tonight. She'd always accused him of not putting her first, when that's exactly what he'd done. She'd left him for ill-conceived reasons and he wouldn't let her go to bed tonight thinking she'd been right all those years ago and right tonight as well.

The band played a mellow tune. He took her purse from her and set it down on the chair. "One dance. I'll tell you what happened tonight. I'll tell you about Teddy Burford. Then you can decide what happens next."

Cara's pretty blue eyes gave away her curiosity. "Who's Teddy Burford?"

"Dance with me, and I'll tell you."

"Blackmailing me again?" She whispered the question with a slight tilt of her head and the sweetest curve of her lips.

Kevin's resolve bumped up a notch. He stared at her soft pink lips. "Seems to be the only way with you."

"Not true," she said as she started toward the dance floor. "But I do enjoy dancing."

He watched the sexy twitch of her hips as she moved without him on the dance floor. Without another second of hesitation, he took her into his arms, bringing her up close, her body flush with his. "Ah, Cara. You feel good." He ran his hands up and down her sides, from shoulder to hip.

"Uh-huh." She took his hands and planted them firmly on her hips. She wrapped her arms around his neck and leaned back. "So what happened tonight?"

Kevin explained how he'd first met Teddy Burford when they'd been renovating the Community Senior Center. Teddy had sat among bingo-playing women, looking miserable. He'd lost his wife the year before and was living with his daughter. Though she hadn't complained, Teddy had felt as though he was intruding on her family life.

"I'd meet him for lunch and he'd tell me his war stories. He served two tours of duty in 'Nam. Earned a few medals, too. I kept thinking it was a shame that he wasted his days at the senior center. He'd told me he'd been looking for work, but he wasn't having any luck. You know, he wanted some financial independence. Anyone would want that."

"But he was too old?"

"Only in years. Not in heart. So when the night watchman job came up at the apartment complex, I told him to apply. I didn't want him to think I was giving him the job, but I knew I would. He's a tough old guy with military experience. He knows his stuff."

"Sounds to me, you might have given him the job, regardless," she mused.

"Lucky for me, he was qualified. And he appreciated the work."

"I like him already," Cara said.

"I was having a drink with Lance and Darius tonight when he called. He sounded pretty shaken up."

Kevin went on to explain about the vandals and Teddy's injuries. "Really, Cara, the old guy is my friend. I didn't go there for any other reason but to make sure he was okay. He was distraught, not about having been knocked out, but because he didn't protect the property. He thought he'd failed me and I assured him he did his job and then some. I stayed with him until his daughter picked him up. By that time, I was late calling you. I know I should have called you sooner, but—"

Cara shook her head. "I get it, Kevin. You did the right thing. But even you have to understand why I'd think the worst. You've left me standing alone a hundred times in the past, so why should I have thought any differently tonight?"

Kevin inhaled the fresh citrus scent of her hair and closed his eyes. "You were never second-best, Cara."

Kevin felt the exact moment Cara surrendered. Her shoulders loosened, her body relaxed and she put her head on his shoulder. "Just dance with me, Kevin."

He tightened his hold on her, satisfied that she'd understood and forgiven him. They didn't have much time left together and he wanted to make the most of every minute.

Two hours later, the band called it quits. Cara stood on the dance floor facing Kevin, her body sizzling. They'd had drinks and danced through the night. Cara had a sneaking feeling that Kevin had paid off the band to play only slow, sultry tunes. The music, sweet to her ears, and swaying to each song in Kevin's strong arms was a heady mix she couldn't deny.

Kevin's lips constantly brushed her forehead, his warm breath caressed her throat and his hands roamed to places on her body that were just this side of decent. She moved against him and taught him to seduce the music. And in turn, he'd very nearly seduced her.

She ached for him. Deep down. Not only had she forgiven him but his friendship with a down-and-out, lonely war veteran endeared him to her even more.

"It's getting late." Everyone on the dance floor had dispersed. The band began packing up their gear.

Kevin nodded. "The night didn't turn out as I'd planned. It was even better. Did you have a good time?"

Cara closed her eyes briefly and sighed. "Yes. I love dancing." She loved being with him. They'd talked and laughed, and then got hot and bothered in each other's arms. "Thank you."

"We'd better leave before they kick us out," he said.

A uniformed clean-up crew had entered and were removing the tablecloths from the tables.

"Did you know Pavoratti once sang in this very room?"

Kevin shook his head as they walked to their table. He handed over her purse. "Didn't know that."

"George told me on the way up here."

"Ah, George, the concierge. I think he was smitten with you."

"No, just a nice man."

"Cara, there are no *nice* men. Not when it comes to a beautiful woman. I thought I'd have to fight off that Dylan character just to get a dance with you."

They walked toward the elevator. "You used the wife card, instead."

Kevin let go a chuckle. "Worked like a charm."

"Technically, I'm not your wife. Or I won't be in a few days."

Kevin's tone changed instantly. "Would you rather I'd socked the guy in the jaw?"

Cara laughed. "You wouldn't."

One brow lifted and his eyes narrowed. "I would."

Cara walked on. Kevin wrapped his hand around

hers as they headed to the elevator. "I can make it to my room from here."

"I'll walk you." His jaw firm, his tone determined, she wouldn't argue.

They stepped into the elevator and the second the doors closed Kevin backed her up against the wall. "I've been waiting all night to do this."

One hand flattened against the elevator wall while the other hand wound around to the back of her head, bringing her face close to his. His mouth swooped down and he crushed his lips to hers.

Pent-up tension uncurled in the pit of her stomach. She welcomed the release, craving him with fiery need. His lips sought hers again and again and she matched each kiss with equal ferocity. The sharp taste of hard alcohol mingled with his breath. Her heart pounded and goose bumps rose up her arms.

He dropped his head, bringing his lips to her throat, nibbling, nipping. She curled her fingers in his short, thick hair and allowed him access. He kissed the swells of her breasts, then brought his hands around to caress each one through the material of her dress. His touch made her toes curl. Her nipples stood at full attention. He slid his fingers over the tips, and heat surged through her body.

"Kevin," she cooed, his name slipping from her lips.

The elevator continued to climb and he continued his assault, his kisses frenzied now. Cara huffed out quick breaths, wrapped up in the thrilling moment.

Kevin hiked up the hem of her dress and stroked her along her inner thigh. Rapid-fire sensations shot up her leg, making every cell in her body alert and aware. She moaned from the sheer pleasure, Kevin's hands roaming all over her, his kisses hot and wet and determined.

His erection pulsed against her.

Oh, no, she thought. We can't make love in the elevator. Can we?

The elevator dinged. She froze and looked at the digital display above the doors. She'd reached her floor.

Kevin backed away from her and composed himself.

The doors opened. Luckily, no one was on the other side. Both of them looked disheveled, hair mussed, clothes awry as if…as if they'd had sex in the elevator.

Cara quickly stepped out and looked at Kevin.

His back against the elevator wall, he cast her a crooked smile.

He looked adorable, like a mischievous schoolboy who'd gotten away with ditching class.

"Just four more days, baby."

Heat crawled up her neck. Cara nodded, unable to say a word, but picturing the night they'd finally make love. Kevin hit a button and the doors closed, leaving Cara alone on the hotel floor, hot, bothered and angry with herself for having made this deal with Kevin in the first place.

Four more days before they'd satisfy their desire.

And four more days before Cara was a free woman.

She didn't know which of the two worried her the most.

Eight

"All right, Marissa. I'll see you in a few days." Cara hung up the phone after averting a disaster with two of her most talented dance instructors. Both had threatened to quit and Cara spent the entire morning consoling each one, listening to their complaints about the other and asking them to hold on until she could talk with them in person.

Felicia and Marissa were as temperamental as they come. When Cara was in Dallas, she managed to keep the peace between them. Quite frankly, she was tired of being their intermediary and babysitter. When she returned, she'd lay down the law. If they wanted to continue working at Dancing Lights, they'd have to get along. Period. Cara would hate to lose either one of them, but she'd learned that professionalism was not only admirable but necessary in her employees. She'd learned a good deal about owning a business in the past few years. But she'd always vowed never to allow her business to dominate her personal life.

Her thoughts turned to Kevin. *He* was her personal life right now. For the next four days, anyway. She'd had a great time with him last night. Even though the evening had begun badly, he had managed to turn the night around to become something she would long remember. If there had been any doubt before, being with him last night had convinced her that she'd fallen for him again.

"I love you, Kevin," she whispered in the quiet of her hotel room. She could hardly believe her own revelation. Cara closed her eyes, refusing tears.

Grateful that he was out of town today, Cara could spend the rest of the day trying to sort out her feelings. She'd go online to get some work done, shop for a wedding gift for Lance and Kate, and spend the evening alone with her thoughts.

She needed the time to think things through. She'd get the divorce she'd come to Houston for, but was that what she really wanted? Was she guilty of the same thing she'd accused Kevin of doing, putting business before her personal life? Should she try to work things out with her husband? He hadn't given her any indication of what he wanted for the future. Cara had one day to mull over her situation before

Kevin would knock on her door to take her to Lance and Kate's wedding reception. One day to figure out what she wanted for the rest of her life.

At precisely six-thirty the next evening, Kevin stood at Cara's door wearing a three-piece tuxedo in James Bond fashion. No, she amended—he looked better than 007, and Cara had to purse her lips tight to keep her mouth from dropping open. In black from head to toe, except for the silver-gray tie tucked into his vest, Cara had never seen a more handsome man.

He's my husband.

And I'm standing here drooling.

"I missed you yesterday," were the first words he spoke.

Cara had a hard time keeping her ego from floating off into space.

"I had a contractual meeting in Austin that had been planned months ago or I would have cancelled in a heartbeat."

"I understand." He really had no obligation to see her every day, yet he'd called her three times yesterday when he'd had free time.

"You look beautiful. Red is my favorite color on you." His gaze stayed on her glossy-red lips for a long moment, then drifted down to her off-the-shoulder dress, then farther down to her red heels.

"I bet your toenails are red, too."

Cara kicked off one shoe and wiggled her toes. "You guessed right. Candy-cane red."

"Ah, Cara." He grabbed her hips and brought her close, then bent his head to lay a mind-boggling kiss on her lips. Staying close, his mouth just a breath away, he whispered, "Don't invite me in."

Cara blinked.

"Lance would never forgive me if I showed up late. But he's gonna owe me one, big-time."

Cara chuckled and took his arm. "Then maybe we'd better go."

"Yeah, I was afraid you'd say that."

Twenty minutes later, they pulled up to the Texas Cattleman's Club. A valet opened the door to the Jag and helped Cara out. Kevin handed the valet his keys and was beside her instantly, putting a solid hand on her lower back. He guided her inside and they entered the formal dining room.

Two tall, white columns draped with deep-red rose arrangements stood in invitation at each side of the entrance. White tablecloths and flowered center-pieces in rich earth tones of red, amber and wine decorated each table. Twinkling lights illuminated the arched cathedral window and a dozen round pillar candles lit the carved travertine-stone fireplace mantel. Soft music from a four-piece orchestra played in the background. "Wow, it's stunning."

Kevin glanced around the room, then turned to her. "You make it so."

Her heart did a little flip. "Thank you," she whispered. Kevin had been so complimentary lately and so attentive that she could barely relate him to the man she'd left four years ago, or the man who'd blackmailed her into this two-week charade.

He escorted her farther into the room and she set her gift on a table. "What did you get them?" he asked.

"Personalized wineglasses and a wine tour."

"A wine tour?"

"A bottle of wine delivered each month of their first year of marriage from different regions of France and Italy."

Kevin nodded. "Very original. I'm sure they'll love it."

"Hmm, I hope so. It's hard choosing a gift when you've been out of the loop as long as I have." With a tilt of her head, she looked into Kevin's eyes. "I bet you chose a perfect gift for them."

Kevin shrugged. "I made a sizable donation in their name to their favorite charity."

Cara rocked back on her heels, overwhelmed at Kevin's sensitivity. "That's…very generous."

"I think they'll appreciate it."

A butler served them a glass of merlot and Kevin made a private toast. "To you, Cara. I hope all your dreams come true."

"And to you, Kevin," she said, offering a sentiment of her own. "I hope you find happiness."

They touched glasses gently and looked into each other's eyes as they took a sip.

Kevin remarked, "I'm pretty happy now."

So was she.

Cara's stomach clenched. Blood drained from her

face. Could she give all of this up? Could she divorce Kevin and not wonder if she'd made the worst mistake of her life? Was being with Kevin her real dream? He'd courted her for days now yet he hadn't said one word to lead her to think he wanted to reconcile.

"Anything wrong?" he asked.

"What could be wrong?" Cara answered quickly, pasting a smile on her face.

A tic worked in Kevin's jaw. That same tic that had always come out when they'd argued. He lowered his voice and his tone grew serious. "Yeah, what could be wrong?"

Justin Dupree walked up with a young, leggy blond woman. Cara recognized her immediately as Mila Jankovich, a supermodel she'd seen on a dozen magazines lately. Justin had classic good looks, a handsome profile and dynamic blue eyes, and the two together made an eye-catching couple. Introductions were made and more wine was poured as they conversed.

Mila seemed infatuated with Justin, being years his junior, Cara presumed. And though she'd always thought Justin a nice guy, he had a reputation with women. No father in his right mind would like to see Justin Dupree courting his daughter.

The orchestra quieted and an announcement was made when Kate and Lance entered the room. The small crowd of friends and family applauded.

Kate beamed with joy and Lance had never looked happier. Cara's heart sank even further. She remembered her own wedding and the brightness that had filled her when she and Kevin had spoken their vows. She'd had hopes of a happy future, with a new husband and children someday. None of that had happened for her. Yet, here she was, standing beside Kevin, unsure of their relationship.

Should she tell him she loved him?

Or should she take him at his word, that he wanted to part as friends?

Friends?

She didn't want him as a friend. Not anymore. She wanted more. She'd seen the changes in Kevin and believed that he was a different man than the one who'd hurt her so terribly.

Could she trust in that?

Kevin held Cara in his arms on the dance floor, the orchestra strings creating a romantic mood. He breathed in her exotic scent and threaded his fingers into her blond curls. He had trouble holding on to his bitter need for revenge when he had her in his arms. Soft and feminine and the most beautiful woman in the room, Cara made him forget all the pain she'd caused him. Kevin had never had a woman run out on him before. He'd never been left holding the bag, racked by humiliation, his pride shredded to pieces. He remembered those drunken days after she'd first left, the ache of desolation mixing with anger and frustration. He remembered having to tell his parents and friends the truth. He'd hated their pity and sympathy. He'd felt like a failure in his personal life, when he'd been nothing but successful in his professional life.

Those feelings had stayed with him for four years. His resentment was fueled even more by the reason she'd come back for a divorce—to get a bank loan. He'd seduced her for the past eleven days with one goal in mind, and he wasn't a man to deviate from a plan once it was constructed. But perhaps he'd laid out his plan too well because he was softening to her.

"Are you okay?" she asked, her blond brows furrowing.

"I'm fine." He gave her a reassuring smile.

Darius tapped him on the shoulder. "Mind if I cut in?"

Yeah, he minded, but Cara had already released him. "Darius, I'd love to dance with you."

Kevin relented, turning Cara over to Darius. He took up his glass of wine and found it lacking in alcohol content. He headed to the bar in search of a stronger drink, needing a moment to get a grip, to back off from feelings he wanted no part of. Lance came up beside him and leaned one arm against the bar, facing him.

"Whiskey, straight up," Kevin told the bartender. "And bring the groom one, too."

Lance laughed. "Cara's getting to you, isn't she?"

"Nice party, Lance." Kevin refused to take the bait.

"Glad you're enjoying yourself. Cara seems to be, too."

"She's having a nice enough time."

"You haven't let her out of your sight for two hours."

Kevin scratched the back of his neck. "Are you keeping track?"

The bartender slid two drinks their way. Lance smirked before he took a sip of his drink. "Hell, I saw the look you shot Darius when he interrupted your dance. If looks could kill…"

"She's only here a few more days."

"Are you still working on your brilliant plan to get back at her?"

Kevin winced. He lifted his glass to his lips. "Maybe."

"Man, don't be stupid."

"Shut up, Lance."

"Am I hitting too close to home? Are you having doubts? If you are, then I'd say you're making progress."

"You have no idea what you're talking about."

"I know you were hurt, Kev. I know you thought she abandoned you. But did you ever consider her side? Maybe both of you were right and both of you were wrong."

Kevin sucked in oxygen. "I'm so glad I came to your wedding reception. Does Kate know what a nosy-body she married?"

"She knows I love my friends."

"Two more whiskeys," Kevin said to the bartender, then turned to Lance. "Do me a favor, don't love me so much."

"Funny, Kev. You're a real comedian."

Kevin nodded. "Whether you think so or not, I know what I'm doing."

Lance sipped his second whiskey and put a hand on Kevin's shoulder. "That, my friend, remains to be seen."

When Kevin returned to the table, Darius and Summer approached, along with Justin, Mila and Mitch Brody. They all sat down, and Summer and Cara struck up a conversation.

"What gave you the idea to develop a chain of dance studios?" Summer asked Cara.

Cara's eyes sparkled. "Well, I'd always loved to dance. I studied several forms of dance as a young girl. Ballet, of course, but swing, too, and some ballroom and I...well, I—" She glanced at Kevin, then shrugged and sipped her drink.

"With all the dance competitions on television now, I imagine it's very sought after in the real world," Summer said.

Cara nodded, her smile wide. "There's a good-size market out there now. People want to feel good about themselves. There's nothing more freeing to me than moving with the music."

"You do it well," Darius added. He looked to Summer. "She gave me some pointers when we danced."

Cara chuckled. "Oh, no. I'm not taking credit for that. Darius has enough rhythm for a three-piece jazz band. He could very well be on my staff as an instructor."

"Right," Darius said with a shake of his head. "I'd probably scare off your clients."

Summer laid a hand on his arm. "Darius is a man of many talents."

"You keep saying that," Justin chimed in with a twinkle in his blue eyes, "but no one else sees it."

Darius feigned an angry look. "Careful, pretty boy."

Kevin listened as his friends bantered back and forth, for the most part keeping quiet. Cara shot him curious looks from time to time while she engaged in conversation. He noted the strong, confident woman she'd become. She'd always been intelligent and clever, but Cara had grown in other ways and, more and more, he liked what he saw in her. And as she spoke with Summer about her social work and the Texas Cattleman's Club shelter, Helping Hands, the two discussed how to best serve the community. It was clear Cara had made a new friend.

But Cara wouldn't have time to develop that friendship. It would all end soon. After they consummated their deal, he'd sign the divorce papers and let her go, his revenge complete.

And by letting her go, he'd be free, too.

To move on with his life.

Yet Lance's words kept reverberating in his head.

Don't be stupid, Kevin.

Am I hitting too close to home?

Are you having doubts?

Damn it, yes. He had doubts. He had feelings for

Cara that he couldn't deny. The more he tried to push them out of his mind, the stronger they'd become.

Thankfully, Mitch Brody interrupted his train of thought. "How about a game of tennis tomorrow after work?"

"Yeah, sure." He'd make the time. Maybe knocking a ball around would knock some sense into his head.

Twenty minutes later, Cara slipped away from the party to use the ladies' room. She needed a breather from Kevin and the thoughts of reconciliation that kept entering her head. Being on his arm tonight, meeting up with old friends, more and more she felt like she could slide right into the role as wife to Kevin. He'd changed from the type-A personality businessman he'd been, driven to succeed no matter the cost to his personal life. He'd made his millions and, with nothing more to prove, he seemed to have figured out how to keep an equal balance between business and pleasure.

It felt right being here with him and feeling a part of the Somerset community again. A swirl of excitement coursed through her system. Caught up in the festivities and the romance of Kate and Lance's wedding reception, Cara felt like she belonged.

She entered the ladies' room lobby. "Cara!"

Cara faced Alicia Montoya in the large, gilded vanity mirror. Alicia swirled around with lipstick in midair to face her directly.

"Alicia, hi! It's good to see you."

Alicia set her tube of lipstick down and they embraced. "What a nice surprise."

"I'm here with Kevin. Remember I told you about Lance and Kate's wedding reception?"

"Yes, I know. Alex and I were having dinner in the café and we could hear you all having a great time."

"We are." Then Cara lowered her voice. "Especially me. It's been a really wonderful night."

Alicia leaned in. "Wonderful enough to use your new Sweet Nothing purchase?"

Cara chuckled. "Who knows what the night might bring?" She wouldn't explain that she'd wear her new lingerie the night she and Kevin made love, in a few days. Not before. She really wanted to knock his socks off and make a lasting memory.

Alicia bubbled with excitement. "I may have to make a trip back to that store soon. I just met the most dreamy man here at TCC and he asked me out."

"Oh, Alicia. That's great. Who is he?"

Alicia's face took on a glow and her dark brows lifted. "His name is Rick Jones. We had a brief conversation outside while I was waiting for Alex. I would have remembered if I'd seen him before. He's not a man a woman could forget. Not with those amazing blue eyes."

"Well, you'll have to spill all the details after your date. I'm dying to hear how it all works out."

"No more than me, Cara. I haven't had a date in a while. And, well, Rick is charming and handsome. He's attending the wedding reception."

"Oh, really?" Cara tried to figure out which of the partygoers could be Rick Jones, but she came up short. Though the reception was relatively small, Cara didn't know all of Kate and Lance's friends.

"I've been floating all night, driving Alex crazy with my good mood."

Cara took her hand and couldn't stop the grin that pulled at her mouth. "Good for you. For being happy, that is, not for driving Alex crazy."

Cara couldn't blame a man for being attracted to Alicia's sweet demeanor and beautiful looks. Cara had always admired her light olive skin tone and dazzling brown eyes. Tonight, she looked stunning in a simple, brown, off-the-shoulder sweater and pencil skirt, her dark hair swept back in curls. "Whoever this Rick Jones is, he's a lucky guy."

Alicia hugged her again. "Thanks, Cara. I'd better go before Alex thinks I deserted him."

"Okay. Enjoy the rest of your evening. We'll talk soon."

"Yes, we will. Have a good time tonight with Kevin." Alicia wiggled her fingers in a farewell wave and dashed out of the ladies' room.

Cara returned to the reception minutes later, surprised to find the orchestra had ceased playing, replaced by piped-in rock music. Alcohol flowed in abundance, the dance floor was in full swing and the small crowd filled the room with laughter and shouts to the bride and groom. She found Kevin swinging the young supermodel around on the dance floor, the lanky blonde laughing heartily and sipping her drink.

Cara's heart sank seeing Kevin with another woman, seeming to enjoy the attention she bestowed him. Cara searched the reception for Justin Dupree but couldn't find him anywhere.

When the music ended, Kevin headed her way. "Hey, I thought you'd never come back."

Cara granted him a quick smile, concealing the jealousy she felt seeing Kevin with Mila. He was by Cara's side again now, giving her his full attention. "I ran into a friend in the ladies' room. What happened to the orchestra?"

Kevin grinned. "Lance made a deal with Kate. A few hours of sedate orchestra music, then we let our hair down."

"Wow. Now it looks like a party."

"Yeah, an open bar and heavy rock can do that to a perfectly good wedding reception." Kevin glanced at Mitch Brody. "I think they're ready for the toasts. C'mon," he said, taking her arm. "I want you next to me when I roast Lance."

"Over a fire pit?"

A wicked smirk crossed his features and Kevin's eyes gleamed. "Yeah, something like that."

But after Mitch's toast to his brother, amid whistles and hoots from the boisterous crowd, a stern-looking man entered the room and spoke directly to Lance.

Cara watched Lance argue with the man, shaking

his head until Kate put her hand on Lance's arm. Lance spoke briefly with Kate and then rose to speak with their guests. "Apparently, we're having too much fun in here for someone at the club. Complaints have been lodged from the room next door about the noise level and we've been asked to leave."

The entire room groaned in unison.

"I know, I know," Lance said, holding his apparent anger in check.

Kate rose and spoke to her guests. "This has been an amazing party, and Lance and I want to thank all of you for coming. I can't tell you how much it means to both of us to have our dearest friends here to celebrate our marriage."

"Yes," Lance said. "Thank you all for coming, but Kate and I don't want the party to end. We're inviting all of you back to our place. And I promise you, we can make all the noise we want there!"

The crowd in the room applauded.

Cara turned to Kevin. "Can they do that? Break up the party because of noise?"

Kevin shrugged. "TCC has rigid rules and apparently whoever complained made a big stink about it. Lance is furious, but he's keeping his cool for Kate's sake. So, what do you say? Want to go to the after party with me?"

"I wouldn't miss it," Cara said, grinning.

The party guests followed Kate and Lance out the front entrance of the club. Kevin noticed Sebastian Huntington speaking with Cornelius Gentry under a streetlamp. Gentry, a wiry little man known to be Huntington's foreman, glanced over to the group. Both men wore smug expressions on their faces.

Immediately, Kevin's suspicions were aroused. Huntington, a snob in the worst way, hated the "new money" millionaires at the club. He didn't think they were good enough to rub noses with the elite of Houston and he never failed to make his feelings well known.

Kevin tightened his hold on Cara, squeezing her hand gently as they walked with the group toward the valet station to wait for his car.

Cara glanced up at him and smiled sweetly. Her smile made him forget his suspicions and he concentrated on how beautiful she looked tonight. He bent his head and kissed her lightly on the lips.

"What was that for?" she whispered.

A swell of possessiveness filled his heart. He looked into her soft blue eyes and couldn't come up with a witty reply. He opened his mouth to say something, but emotions overwhelmed him and sensations swept through his system as he realized his time with Cara was coming to an end.

"You son of a bitch!"

Kevin whirled around to find Lance marching toward Alex Montoya just outside the doors of the TCC. With each determined step he took, his eyes filled with more rage.

"You did this! You broke up my wedding reception!"

Alicia stood beside her brother, her eyes wide, her expression terrified.

Montoya stiffened and stared at Lance with hard eyes and tight lips. "What the hell are you talking about, Brody?" Alex took note of the guests standing behind Lance. Immediately, he shielded his sister by taking a step in front of her. Patience and understanding were not virtues in either man when they faced each other. It was bad enough that Lance believed Montoya had set fire to his refinery, but now Lance was accusing him of shutting down his wedding reception.

"You complained about the noise at my reception and had us all booted out of there!"

Alex's face flamed with indignation. "Now, why would I do that? I don't give a damn about your pathetic little wedding reception."

They stood nose-to-nose now, each man refusing to back off.

Kate watched the scene unfold, fear entering her eyes. "Oh, no."

"This is low, even for you." Lance glared at Alex.

"Watch it, Brody." Alex kept tight control of his temper. "Don't go making accusations you can't prove."

Alex turned around to take Alicia's arm. "Let's get out of here."

"Not so fast, Montoya. I'm not through with you!"

Slowly, Alex turned back around, his expression grim. He released his sister's arm. "You're not *through* with me?"

The situation had gone from bad to worse. Cara bit her lip and Kate appeared panicked. Lance and Alex were heading for trouble.

Kevin strode purposefully toward the two men. He faced them like a referee breaking up two line-backers ready to brawl. "Come on, Lance. Kate's upset. Let's not add to it."

Lance darted a glance at him. "Stay out of it, Kevin."

"Yeah, stay out of it, Novak." Montoya eyed him with disdain. "If the groom's got a bone to pick, I'm ready."

Lance gritted his teeth. "Damn right, I have a bone to pick."

Kevin scratched his head, wondering if he should let them have it out once and for all. They'd been rivals since high school and this would be the cul-mination of years of hatred and resentment. But one glance at Cara with those hope-filled blue eyes and Kevin knew what he had to do.

He stepped between them, facing Lance. "C'mon, man. Let's get out of here. Kate's waiting for you."

Lance inhaled sharply and peered around Kevin to cast Montoya a hard look. He took a long second to stare. Kevin held his breath. Finally, Lance relented. "This isn't over."

"Don't ever toss accusations at me again, Brody," Montoya warned with stern indignation. "But for the record, I had nothing to do with breaking up your party."

With that, he grabbed Alicia's arm and guided her back into the club.

"Bastard," Lance muttered.

Kate ran over to him. "Lance, are you crazy?"

Lance took one look at Kate's concerned face and threw his head back and laughed, finding humor in the situation. He reached for her, wrapped his arms around her waist and pulled her close. "Yeah, I'm crazy. About you. You deserve a beautiful wedding reception."

"And I got one. Tonight was wonderful. I enjoyed every single minute of it. Now, let's be good hosts. Our friends are waiting."

Lance glanced at the group who had witnessed his outburst. "The party's still on. At our house."

Satisfied, Kate kissed him lightly, then turned to Kevin. She mouthed a silent thank-you to him and he nodded.

Cara strode over and slipped her hand under his arm. "My hero."

Kevin glanced into her pretty eyes.

"You averted a disaster," she said.

"Heroes do that." He grinned, making light of the situation, yet couldn't shake his gut feeling that there was more to all this than met the eye.

Nine

The after party continued into the wee hours of the night. Cara and Kevin found a cozy corner of the living room and stayed cuddled together, kissing like two high-school teenagers who couldn't get enough of each other. When the party wound down, just the four of them remained. "I think we should give the newlyweds some privacy now."

Kevin glanced around, just noticing that they were the last of the guests. "Yeah, I bet they want to get to bed." He shot Cara a sizzling look, lowering his voice and leaning in. "I want to get you to bed, too."

His hot kiss erupted tingles on her arms. It had been like that all night—steamy kisses and smoldering glances and enough innuendo to bring her fantasies to life.

Fantasies of loving Kevin wholly and completely.

It had been nearly two weeks of torture. Two weeks of wondering, of being tempted beyond belief and two weeks of needing to quench the thirst she had for her husband.

Lance walked up with a crystal whiskey decanter in hand. "Ready for another?" he asked Kevin.

Kevin rose and took Cara's hand. "No, thanks. I think we're going to let you two get to bed."

Lance laughed, swaying a little. He grabbed Kate and kissed her smack on the lips. "Good idea."

"I think he's partied a little too hard tonight," Kate said, patting his arm lovingly.

Lance swayed a bit more and Kate wrapped her arms around his waist to steady him.

"Just…happy," Lance said, slurring his words slightly and casting Kate a crooked, silly smile.

"I can get him to the bedroom for you, Kate. It'll be like old times back at UT," Kevin offered.

"Nah," Lance said. "Don't need your services tonight, Kev. My wife knows how to take care of me." He wiggled his brows in villainous style.

Kate chuckled. "Well, I'm learning."

"You're a lucky man." Kevin slapped Lance on the back. Lance disengaged from Kate and smiled at him. "Kate, will you walk Kevin to the door?" Lance turned to Cara and offered his arm. "Cara?"

She slipped her arm through his and he tottered a

bit before straightening up. He waited until Kate and Kevin were steps ahead of them, then looked at Cara through lowered lashes. "Kevin's a good guy," he leaned in to whisper, his words running together. "Damn hardheaded though…I warned him to be careful…not to hurt you."

"How will he hurt me?" Cara asked, confused and wondering if she should pay attention to anything he said while intoxicated.

"I think he already has." Lance mumbled a curse, then shook his head as if shaking off cobwebs. "Never mind. Forget I said anything." He placed her hand in his and smiled warmly, then walked her to the front door.

That night, the last thing Cara could do was forget Lance's comments. She replayed his parting words over and over in her head, trying to make sense of them. He may have had too much to drink, but Lance wasn't so intoxicated that he didn't know what he was saying. She heard his true concern in the sobering way he whispered in her ear. What bothered her the most wasn't that she stood to get hurt by Kevin, but that Lance had knowledge of it. What was going on? What had Kevin said to Lance to make him believe she'd get hurt?

Or had Lance simply been way off in his assessment of the situation? Cara tossed on those thoughts before falling asleep that night.

In the morning, with sunshine pouring into her window and all things looking bright, she rose early, worked out to a Pilates exercise program on the flat screen and felt too happy to worry about anything. She'd spend the afternoon with Kevin today. They'd made those arrangements during the reception and, after a spellbinding good-night kiss, he'd reminded her that they'd have a day of fun in the sun. "We're going to play all day," he'd said to her.

A thrill ran up her spine. Kevin was proving to her again and again that he wasn't the same man she'd set out to divorce. He'd learned how to delegate. He'd learned how to have fun. He'd learned that there was more to life than work. Cara smiled as she showered and pulled on a breezy, flowered sundress.

When Alicia Montoya called, Cara couldn't refuse to meet her for coffee. Clearly upset, Alicia needed a friend. Half an hour later, they sat on tufted sofa chairs drinking espresso at a local coffee shop near Cara's hotel.

"Thanks for meeting me on such short notice," Alicia said, her pretty face forlorn. Dressed in black, as if in mourning, she wore her hair pulled tightly back, held by a clasp. Light pink lipstick brought color to her olive skin tones.

Alicia played with the rim of her coffee mug, searching for the right words. "This is…hard."

"I know," Cara said, compassion filling her heart. Alicia wanted so much to be accepted. It couldn't be easy being Alejandro Montoya's sister. Alicia had been on cloud nine last night when they'd last spoken. She'd been so happy that she'd met Rick Jones and he'd asked her out. Cara still didn't know who Rick was, but judging by the look on Alicia's face last night, he'd made her very happy. Then there had been the blowup outside of the club and poor Alicia had looked panic stricken. "I'm glad you called me."

"Are you? I think I'm putting you in the middle."

Cara reached for her arm. "No, I'm not in the middle of anything. You're my friend."

Alicia lowered her stiff shoulders and let go a sigh. "Oh, Cara. I can't tell you what that means to me."

"It means a lot to me, too."

"It's just that everyone thinks the worst of my brother."

"I can't pretend I don't know that. Alex and Lance go way back and none of it is pretty."

"Your husband doesn't like him either."

"Kevin thinks Alex blocked one of his projects. It's business more than a personal thing."

Alicia nodded her understanding, her expression somber. "Alex didn't break up the reception last night. He wouldn't do that."

"Are you certain?"

"Yes. I'm sure. I was with him all night, except for the time I met you in the ladies' room. He never complained about the reception. In fact, he didn't know about it until I mentioned it to him."

"But you said you'd heard the music playing."

"Alex barely noticed it and it certainly didn't

bother us. He may think Lance a rival, but he's not that petty. I just know in my heart Alex would never do something like that."

No, Cara thought. If only Alicia knew what bigger crimes the Brody brothers accused him of perpetrating, she'd be devastated. "Alicia, I believe you. But Lance and Alex are going to have to find a way to work out their differences on their own."

"My brother isn't perfect. He's stubborn and prideful, but he's a good man. It hurt to see him being accused last night in front of so many people. It's a good thing Kevin intervened."

"Yes, I agree. Lance looked ready for a fight."

"And Alex never backs down from one."

Cara smiled at her friend with sadness in her heart. "Not a good combination, I'm afraid." She didn't have any answers but she knew Alicia didn't expect any. She only needed a friend to talk to.

"I'm glad we spoke."

"Me, too. I hope it helped a little."

"It did." Alicia sipped her espresso, which up until this point had gone untouched. "Oh, this is good."

Cara sipped her decaf. "So what are you doing the rest of the day?"

A smile broke out on her face. "Well, I think they're having a sale at Sweet Nothings today."

"You're going back for that pink baby-doll lingerie!"

"I think so. Just in case, mind you. It's nice to know there's hope of wearing it one day."

Cara's laugh displayed her great delight. "That a girl."

"What about you? Do you have plans for the rest of the day?"

Cara nodded with thoughts of Kevin's deep-blue eyes on her as he'd bid her good-night. "I have plans with Kevin later today."

Alicia took her hand and gazed directly into her eyes. "I hope it works out for you and Kevin, Cara. You deserve to be happy."

Cara couldn't agree more. She wanted to be happy again. "Thank you. And remember, I'm here if you need me."

At precisely 1:00 p.m., Kevin picked Cara up in front of her hotel. He opened the car door for her, took her tote bag and tossed it into the trunk. "What's in the bag?"

"Everything necessary for fun in the sun," she quipped. "Bathing suit, sunscreen, oils and lotions."

Kevin shot her a heated glance from the driver's seat. He looked simply edible in tan trousers and a black polo shirt sitting behind the wheel of his powerful sports car. "Sounds perfect."

He gunned the car and they took off toward Somerset. "Are we going to the club?" she asked.

"No way. I have something better in mind." He swiveled his head to gaze at her once again. "You look beautiful, Cara."

So do you, she didn't add. Her heart sang. "Thanks."

Kevin reached over to take her hand as he drove on, his fingers wrapping around hers with gentle possession. Cara closed her eyes briefly. Electricity flowed between them. She felt it and knew that what they had was more than simple physical attraction.

Kevin pulled up in front of a large, lovely cottage-like home on the outskirts of Somerset. Cobblestone and a white picket fence marked the entry, the garden robust with colorful pansies in full bloom and sculpted greenery.

Cara stared at the home, then questioned Kevin with a curious look.

"It's a rental I own. Vacant at the moment and ours for the day."

"How convenient," she teased.

"Isn't it though?"

Kevin opened the car door for her and lifted her tote bag from the trunk easily, laying it onto her shoulder. With a hand to her back, he guided her down the cobblestone path to the front door. Fidgeting with a set of keys, he finally came up with the one that fit in the lock. "Here it is."

"Good, because breaking and entering won't look good on my record."

Kevin kissed her smack on the lips. "Sassy today."

"Always."

"That's what I love about you."

The minute the words were out, she knew Kevin wished he hadn't spoken them. He turned away from her quickly and fumbled with the key. After a few seconds, he managed to get the door open. "Sticky lock," he explained with a little hitch in his throat.

Cara remained silent.

He guided her into the house, which had a country feel to it. From what she could see, the entry hall led to a massive living space, complete with a ceiling-to-floor stone fireplace, wood beams above and large windows on either side of an oak-framed set of French doors.

"Very nice. How long has it been empty?"

"A month. The previous tenants moved to Europe. The new tenants move in next week. It's been cleaned and polished to a shine."

"I can see that." Cara stared at the shiny wood floors beneath her feet and imagined dancing on them. "The rooms are big, but it still feels cozy to me."

"Looks even better with furniture."

Kevin tugged on the tote bag hanging from her shoulder. "C'mon. I want to show you the grounds."

Kevin opened the French doors wide and led her out to a large stone patio. Three sets of love seats wrapped around an in-ground fire pit. Kevin took her hand and led her down a small staircase to the private garden below, infused with bright color.

"Beautiful," Cara murmured.

A swimming pool the size of a small lake came into view beyond a low outcropping of dark green hedges.

Kevin gestured to a mini-replica of the cottage serving as the pool house. "Two pitchers of margaritas are waiting for us in there, one strawberry."

Cara peered into his eyes. "You thought of everything."

Kevin grinned. "That remains to be seen."

Cara walked along the path to the black-bottom pool. Kicking her sandals off, she dipped her toes in. "You did think of everything. It's the perfect temperature for me."

"Well, then, let's take a dip."

"But where's your stuff?" she asked, noting that he hadn't brought a beach bag for himself.

"Don't need anything." He sat down in the center of a slatted lounge chair and took off his shoes.

He didn't need anything?

Cara's heart raced.

Next, he stood and removed his shirt, pulling the polo over his head in one fluid move. Texas sunshine streamed down on his bare chest. Ripped with muscle and bronzed as a golden statue, Kevin took her breath away. When he unzipped his trousers, she took a deep gulp of oxygen, unable to avert her gaze. "Kevin?"

He pulled down his trousers and stepped out of them, his swim trunks appearing underneath.

"What's taking you so long?" He gestured with a nod of his head. "The pool house has a dressing area."

"R-right," she said, taking hold of her senses. "I'll be back in a sec." Just before she entered the dressing room, she heard a splash from Kevin's dive into the pool.

After donning her two-piece, strawberry-red bathing suit, she grabbed two plush white towels and hugged them to her chest. Feeling foolishly self-conscious at the amount of skin showing, Cara glanced in the mirror and wondered what had possessed her to buy this skimpy suit.

She'd never worn it in public before. And granted, being poolside with her husband wasn't exactly like being on the sands of Waikiki in the middle of summer, yet she still felt terribly exposed.

"Cara, you coming?" Kevin's boyish tone brought a smile to her lips. "I'm getting lonely out here."

She glanced at the refrigerator in the small kitchenette on the way out. "You want a margarita?" she called.

"Later, babe."

Cara nibbled on her lip and exited the pool house just as Kevin glided out of the water, his head lifting and his gaze zeroing in on her. Water sloshed off his shoulders as he rose to stand in the pool. He swiped back his short hair and smiled, reaching for her. "Drop the towels, Cara."

She let them fall from her hands near the edge of the pool. "Don't pull me in."

He secured her hand in his. "I won't. Take your time, babe. I could stand here all day and look at you."

Heat crawled up her neck from the soft tone of his voice and the captivating way his gaze stayed on her. Slowly, she lowered her body down to sit on the edge of the pool. Putting her feet in, she wiggled her toes. "Feels good."

Kevin ran his hands along her thighs, moistening her legs with pool water. "Yeah, it does."

"I don't just jump into things anymore," she explained.

"You used to." Kevin's deliberate touch along her thighs made her bones melt.

"I've changed." She was more mature, more thoughtful about things. She'd learned a valuable lesson being married to Kevin. She hadn't really known him when they'd married. His drive and ambition had caught her off guard. She vowed not to let her emotions dictate her future anymore. Every single decision she'd made since leaving Somerset had been done with great thought and deliberation.

"I have, too."

Cara stared at Kevin. He had changed. He'd proven that over the past two weeks. But she didn't know if she could trust in that. Or in him anymore.

But she did love him.

That fact couldn't be denied.

Kevin parted her legs and grabbed her around the waist. "Whenever you're ready."

She nodded. She was ready to take a chance. She wrapped her legs around his waist and her arms around his neck. He lowered her gently into the water, swirling her around and around, slowly, their eyes never parting.

Buoyant and floating, Cara felt a wave of peace and happiness she hadn't experienced in a long time. She reached out to touch his face, the stubble of his day-old beard grazing her fingers. Then she leaned in and kissed him softly on the mouth.

Kevin stopped and cast her a long, penetrating look, his eyes searching hers intently. Tingles ran up and down her body. Her throat dry, powerful emotions swept over her.

"Cara?"

Cara pressed her fingers to his lips. "Shh, don't say anything, sweetheart."

She couldn't bear to hear what he had to say. She didn't want the mood to turn serious or change in any way. It had been so long since she'd felt such serenity. She wanted to live in the moment and not analyze every word Kevin spoke or scrutinize every gesture he made. "Fun in the sun, remember?" She kissed him again.

Pleased, he groaned deep and waded through the water with her in his arms until they reached the wall of the pool. Resting his back on the tile, he tugged her closer, her breasts rising above the water to press against his chest.

Kevin kissed her fiercely, his mouth traveling over her face, her chin, her throat and shoulders, nipping at her skin and creating impossible tingles that spun her mind in ten different directions.

"Did I tell you how much I like your bathing suit?"

Cara kissed his shoulder. "You neglected to say that earlier."

He cupped her rear end, his fingers spread over her cheeks. "I do. I like it a lot. What there is of it."

"Oh, yeah?" She wiggled out of his arms and dived into the water, swimming a few laps from width to width. Things were heating up too fast between her and Kevin. As much as she wanted him, she had an impending need to protect herself.

When she came up out of the water after her swim, she faced Kevin from across the shallow end of the pool. "I'm ready for a margarita."

"I'll get them," he said without hesitation and she watched him lift himself out of the water and head to the pool house.

Kevin poured Cara a strawberry margarita, then rimmed his glass with salt and poured himself one from the other pitcher. Putting the pitchers back in the refrigerator, he lifted out two covered plates—lunch. He'd had a chef from his favorite restaurant prepare gourmet sandwiches and salad, and had them delivered here, refusing the chef's offer to serve the meal. Kevin wanted to be completely alone with Cara today.

They had two days left together.

He winced, thinking his days were numbered in regard to her. Soon, he'd be a free man, his plan accomplished and revenge complete.

He hadn't expected to regret his decision, though. He'd become accustomed to having Cara by his side again. Yet it was her decision to come to Somerset for a divorce. She hadn't wanted reconciliation and if he hadn't blackmailed her into seeing him these past two weeks, she would have been long gone, signed divorce papers in hand. He couldn't get over that. She'd rejected him not once but twice in his life.

His ego had taken a pounding and his pride was at stake. On many levels, he wished he hadn't come up with his brilliant scheme for payback. Because he, too, had suffered the consequences of spending time with Cara and wanting her with a need so great, he'd had trouble keeping to his plan, again and again.

Kevin set the dishes on a tray along with the margaritas and hesitated before bringing them outside.

Why not give in to his needs now? Why not seduce her today and be done with it? They'd been leading up to this point since the moment she'd agreed to his plan. Why wait? Why extend the torturous need they had for each other?

Kevin debated that notion as he picked up the tray and carried it outside. He found Cara in a chaise lounge, sliding sunscreen oil onto her legs. He stopped to take in the scene, watching her finish coating her legs with the golden liquid. Once she was done with her legs, she spread the oil onto her torso, working it in and then farther up, onto her chest. She grazed over the swells of her breasts with the oil and slid her fingers slightly underneath her swimsuit top, making sure to cover every inch of exposed skin.

"You should have let me do that," Kevin said, making light of the extremely sexy scene he'd just witnessed.

"You were taking too long, buster. A girl's got to protect herself, you know?"

Kevin set the tray down on a glass table between her lounge and his. He gazed at her very appealing chest for a few lingering seconds. "Hungry?"

"Famished," she said. "Swimming gives me an appetite."

He liked that about Cara. She wasn't one to not eat when hungry. Usually, she scarfed up her food with enthusiasm.

He handed her the margarita. "To…us."

She gazed at him, puzzled. He picked up his glass and touched it to hers. "To us," she finally replied with a small smile.

They conversed while eating lunch and sipping margaritas in the sunshine. Cara told stories of her dance students, some of whom had gone on to real careers in dance and other lonely souls who'd pay the fee just to have some one-on-one attention from a pretty dance instructor. Kevin enjoyed listening to her—the animation in her voice and her broad gestures spoke of her love and commitment to her business. When she'd first arrived, he'd resented hearing of her success, but now he felt proud of what she'd accomplished.

"You know," she said in a thoughtful tone, "I think Somerset might need a dance studio."

Kevin stopped chewing for a second. He gazed into Cara's bright eyes. Finally swallowing, he asked, "Here?"

"Why not? I like it here. I could expand my horizons in this direction as well as any."

Kevin didn't reply. It was one thing being divorced from Cara while she was miles away, but having her come back here as a single woman? He didn't know if he was ready for that. Visions of bumping into her while she was on a date with another man, or seeing her with his friends, didn't sit well with him. A dozen emotions swirled in his gut. He felt sick to his stomach at the prospect.

When his silence became obvious, Cara asked, "Kevin, would you have a problem with that?"

Hell, yeah. "No, not at all," he lied, hoping the idea was just a passing fancy.

Cara watched him carefully, then lowered her lashes. "It's just a thought." She sipped her margarita and shrugged. He couldn't help but feel he'd disappointed her somehow, though.

Shoving the notion from his head, he was determined to enjoy the day with Cara without worry. They went on to more amiable topics of discussion as they finished their lunch.

Cara sighed and leaned back in her chaise lounge, lifting her face to the sun. "This is really nice, Kevin. I'm glad you invited me here."

"Don't get too comfortable, baby. You still have to do me."

Cara lifted partly up from the lounge and peered at him. "What?"

He pointed to the sunscreen oil. Then grinned.

Cara shook her head, a wide smile erupting on her face. "Funny, Kevin."

"Well?"

"Okay, lie back." Kevin obeyed without hesitation. Cara poured oil onto her hands and straddled his legs.

He looked up into her pretty sky-blue eyes, barely able to contain his lust. When she touched him, her hands splaying across his chest, he groaned inwardly. She massaged the oil in, her fingertips light, gliding over his skin. He watched her as she leaned forward, intent on her task, her beautiful cleavage in full view and practically begging for his touch. It took every ounce of his willpower not to pull her down on top of him and show her what she did to him.

Once she'd massaged his arms and shoulders, he took the bottle out of her hand. "I think you've done enough."

"You don't sound grateful," she said, her teasing tone too much to take.

"Oh, I'm very grateful," he said, wrapping his arms around her neck and pulling her close. "You know, it's very private here. No one can see what we're doing."

Her eyes went wide with surprise. With that, he pulled her closer and crushed his lips to hers, absorbing every inch of her. But it wasn't nearly enough. He parted her lips and drove his tongue into her mouth, tasting the sweetness of strawberries and her unabashed passion.

In just a few seconds, Kevin had Cara sprawled atop him, his erection straining the confines of his swim trunks. She fit him perfectly and made him crazy with want. He untied her top easily, one little slice of material keeping him from heaven. Her breasts spilled out and Kevin caressed them, holding their weight in his hands, flicking his thumb over both tips until they pebbled into beautiful erect buds.

His gaze trained on hers, he took one perfect globe into his mouth. Cara's eyes slowly closed and a beautiful expression flowed over her features.

He suckled her until both buds were moistened and glowed in the warming sunshine.

Kevin wrapped his hands around her bottom and positioned her onto his erection until she felt the full force of his desire. "I can't wait to have you."

Cara moaned and kissed him fiercely, her breasts crushing his chest. In another second, they'd both be beyond reason. But Kevin held back. This wasn't in his plan. He wanted a full night with Cara, under his own terms. He had it all set in his mind.

Yet he wouldn't deny them both this moment of pleasure. He dipped his hand under her swimsuit and touched her sweetly sensitive spot. "Feel good?" he whispered.

Beyond words, Cara nodded, her lids half-closed. Kevin stroked her carefully with deliberate movements, laying his fingers along the soft folds of her sex.

Wrapping his other hand around her curly blond locks, he pulled her head down to his and kissed her over and over again, her body rocking back and forth, finding a sensual rhythm.

"Oh, Kevin," Cara whimpered, as he continued to glide his fingers over her folds. Kevin watched as tension built quickly, her body rocking forcefully, an expression of sheer lust crossing her beautiful face.

His heart ached witnessing her sheer abandon as her breathing escalated and her body tightened. He stroked her harder, deeper and longer. She arched up and her release came in powerful short bursts of exquisite movements. Watching her orgasm stole his breath.

And made him rethink his plan.

Once spent, a satisfied sigh escaped her throat and she laid her head on his chest. He massaged her lower back, holding her loosely in his arms. "Damn."

"Yeah, damn," she repeated.

Thoughts of making love to Cara on the lounge chair entered his head. Hell, he was ready and Cara wasn't denying him. But once they made love, he'd have to make good on his deal to deliver signed divorce papers.

She wants out of our marriage.

This is the price she's willing to pay.

And I'm paying for it, too, a little annoying voice inside his head reminded him.

"You know what we both need?"

Cara chuckled, the sound emanating from deep in her throat. "Oh, yeah. I know."

Kevin laid one last kiss onto her lips. "Good, then come with me."

Kevin lifted her up and in one sweeping movement, he jumped into the pool, taking Cara with him.

Ten

Cara lay in bed the next morning with thoughts of Kevin intruding on her sleep. Visions of their day together raced through her mind.

Fun in the sun.

Yes, Kevin had seen to that. And much more. Her body still sated from the incredible climax he'd provided her, Cara relived every exquisite moment of his unselfish sexual advance. She was completely, one hundred percent in love with him and had come close to telling him ten times yesterday by the pool.

But Kevin had never spoken of the future to her. He'd never once let on that he wanted reconciliation. He'd held back his own desire yesterday in order to keep his blackmail deal with her.

Why?

Had nothing changed between them over these past two weeks?

Lance's comments about Kevin hurting her were never far from her mind. What had he meant? She couldn't help but think Lance, even in his intoxicated state—or maybe because of it—had set out to warn her about Kevin.

And then at the pool, when she had mentioned her plan to open a dance studio in Somerset, Kevin's nonreaction had stung her pride. He hadn't said much about it, until she had pressed him for an answer. He'd given her a halfhearted reply. It had been clear that Kevin didn't like the idea.

In fact, for a few seconds, his whole demeanor had changed. She hadn't dwelled on his reaction yesterday—they'd been too wrapped up in each other for her to have entertained clear thoughts. But now, in the clarity of morning, she faced facts.

"He doesn't want me in Somerset," Cara muttered, her heart hurting with that realization.

Cara mustered her courage. Instead of deliberating about it all day, driving herself crazy, she made up her mind to find out the truth.

Or at least find out what Lance's comments had meant.

With that notion in mind, Cara rose from bed and showered. She dried her hair and put on a bright canary-yellow sundress, slipped her feet into sandals, then grabbed her cell phone from her purse and dialed Lance's number.

An hour later, she faced Lance Brody in his high-rise executive office at Brody Oil and Gas. "Thanks for seeing me on short notice," Cara said, taking one of two seats facing his desk.

"My pleasure," he said, sitting casually on the edge of his desk, just a few feet from her. "Would you like a cup of coffee, breakfast, anything?" Lance leaned over his desk, with a finger on the intercom button, ready to accommodate her.

"No thanks, Lance."

He straightened and smiled. "Okay." His dark eyes searching, he wore an earnest expression. "I was a little surprised that you asked to see me. What's up?"

Cara straightened the folds of her dress, then looked deep into his eyes. "It's about Kevin."

"O-kay," Lance said slowly, looking a little confused.

"The other night at your house, you said something to me that I didn't understand."

Lance tossed his head back with self-deprecating laughter. "I probably said a lot of things that didn't make sense that night."

"You made a point of taking me aside and warning me about Kevin. You said he was hard-headed. That he would hurt me."

Lance averted his gaze. He found the floor interesting, then the wall. "Did I?"

"Do you remember saying that to me?"

Lance shot her a direct look. "No, I don't remember saying that."

"But you do know what that means, don't you?"

Lance rose, walked behind his desk, then faced her again.

"Cara," he said, taking a deep breath. He rubbed the back of his neck. "If I said something to upset you that night, I apologize."

Cara shook her head and stood. "The only thing that's upsetting me is not knowing what you meant. You know what's going on with Kevin. Now, are you going to tell me the truth?"

Lance stared at her for a few long seconds. She could almost see the debate going on in his head. He *knew* something. She pinned him with a penetrating gaze, refusing to back down—even if it meant hearing something about Kevin that she didn't want to hear.

"He's one of my best friends," Lance said.

Cara stood her ground, patiently. She wouldn't let Lance off the hook. She continued to stare.

"Okay," he said with reluctance. "Have a seat. It's probably better this way. You two need to talk this through. I'll tell you what I know."

Cara glanced at the clock radio on the hotel's night table. Kevin would be here any second. It would be their last night together and she planned on making it memorable.

She'd had to pull the words out of Lance's mouth earlier today. Poor man. He'd tried hard not to hurt her, but it hadn't taken too many words to make Cara see the whole picture. She'd always been great with putting puzzle pieces together, making them fit. And once she'd gotten the corners of Lance's knowledge assembled, she'd put the entire puzzle together very quickly.

She knew Kevin's plan and was through playing his game. It was high time she took control of the situation. Tonight, she'd play her own game and sadly, no one would come out the winner.

Furious with her soon-to-be ex, Cara hadn't had time to feel the tremendous hurt she knew would follow. Right now, fury fueled her to give Kevin a dose of his own medicine.

"You deserve it, *sweetheart*."

When the knock sounded on her hotel door, Cara assumed the guise both mentally and physically. She tossed her arms into her silk robe and walked over to the door.

Taking a deep breath first, steadying her nerves, she opened the door.

Kevin stood in the doorway, wearing a very expensive dark Italian suit. Groomed to perfection, there was no denying his sexual appeal and charisma. Cara's heart lurched, but she ignored the pangs.

His expression dropped, seeing her in her robe. "Hi. Am I early?"

Cara shook her head. "No, you're right on time."

Kevin's brows furrowed, puzzled. "I'll tell the limo driver to wait. Dinner's not until eight. I have a great night planned—"

Cara dropped the robe, letting it puddle at her feet. She took great satisfaction seeing Kevin's deep-blue eyes widen with appreciation. She allowed him a few seconds of shock, seeing her dressed in the one-piece formfitting black-lace unitard. Strategically placed lace was meant to tease and tempt, exposed skin in erogenous zones that would make Catwoman blush.

Cara grabbed Kevin by his sleek silk tie and yanked him inside the room. Extending her leg past him in a fluid lift, she kicked the door shut and pinned him against it. "No date, no dinner. It's time, Kevin. For us."

Cara wrapped her arms around his neck and crushed her mouth to his, leaving the taste of wild cherry on his lips.

She backed away and stared at him. Thoroughly confused, Kevin glanced around the hotel room. Two dozen pillar candles lit the room and flavored the air with a sweet vanilla scent. Rose petals decorated her king-size bed, the sheets turned down provocatively. Chocolate-covered strawberries and a champagne bottle chilling in a silver bucket stood on a tray by the window table.

Kevin leaned back, thumping his head against the wall. "Cara, what is all this?"

She smiled. "You talk too much, baby." She loosened his tie and lifted it over his head. "The time for talking is over. Make love to me. It's what we both want."

Kevin blinked, then stared into her eyes. Cara

kept the ruse up—she wouldn't deny herself this night. As long as she was in control, she'd be fine. She unbuttoned his shirt and ran her hands along his hard, perfect chest. "C'mon, babe. I thought you'd be as hot for this as I am."

Cara nipped at his lower lip, then rimmed his mouth with her tongue. Kevin groaned and slipped his tongue into her mouth, taking her on a wild erotic ride with just that one frenzied kiss.

"Mmm, Kevin," she said, licking her lips, pulling away from him just a bit. "I can't wait for you to be inside me."

Kevin groaned deeper and pulled her close, so that every juncture of their bodies touched. Exquisite tingles ran up and down her length, his manhood already evident. "Damn it, Cara. Keep talking that way, and we won't make it over to that bed."

She tossed her head back, a throaty laugh escaping. "Since when did we *ever* need a bed?"

Cara nipped at his lips again. Kevin heaved a breath and pulled off his shirt. Immediately, Cara touched him again, running her palms over his skin, pressing her tongue to his erect nipples.

Kevin lifted her easily and started for the bed. "I'm older now. I like creature comforts."

Cara shook her head, gazing into his eyes. "Oh, that's a shame. I wanted to dance for you."

Kevin stopped in midstride. He peered down at her with inquisitive eyes, his voice filled with keen interest. "Dance for me?"

She nodded innocently.

"What do you want me to do?"

"Just lie down on the bed and watch."

Kevin sucked oxygen into his chest. "Okay."

He set her down. Cara put her iPod in the dock on the nightstand and hit Play, selecting a specific song. When she turned around, Kevin was bathed in candlelight, lying on his back on the bed, his head propped up on her pillow.

"You are a beautiful woman, Cara Novak," Kevin said in a humble tone.

Cara closed her eyes and felt the music fill her. Then she began to move, swaying her body, her hips gyrating sensually. Everything she had inside, everything she felt for Kevin, the love she'd never declared, came out in the dance.

She gave Kevin this gift, this exposing of her innermost being, so that he would never forget her. So that he would look upon this time with her and know that no other woman could provide what she had given to him.

She danced, flowing to the music, lost in her own movements, giving to Kevin what she'd never given another man.

Cara didn't have a vengeful bone in her body, yet this she felt compelled to do. For her own sense of justice. He'd hurt her beyond belief and she hoped this gift would be his undoing. She danced and danced, her eyes half-lidded, her body in seamless motion with the music and her spirit free.

When the song ended, Cara opened her eyes fully, facing Kevin. The awed expression on his face nearly caved her resolve. "Cara," he said, opening his mouth to speak. He couldn't find the words and Cara knew at that moment what Kevin felt was genuine and true.

She smiled and for a few seconds she forgot his deceit.

"I'm not through."

She chose a different song. It was smooth and sensual, filled with lyrics about suspicions. She moved slowly, erotically, peeling herself out of her lacy one-piece. She stepped out of the garment and stood before Kevin, naked. "Touch me, Kevin. I want to remember your hands on me."

"Cara," Kevin said, his voice little more than a croak. He came to her on his knees and helped her onto the bed. On her knees, too, they faced each other. Kevin kissed her, then touched his fingers to her lips. He moved his hand down her throat and kissed her there, then lower. He cupped her breasts in his hands, circling them and making Cara's nerves go absolutely raw.

She closed her eyes and hung on to him, relishing the feel of his hands caressing her. He skimmed his hands down her torso, teasing, tempting, then cupped her womanhood gently, his fingers lingering just enough to make her head swim.

Next, he touched her thighs as far as he could

reach and wound his hands around her legs to the back. Her skin prickled in anticipation and when he touched the rounds of her buttocks, she let go a pleasured moan.

Kevin took hold of her head then, his restraint nearly spent. He crushed his lips to hers, again and again. "You're killing me slowly, babe."

Tension wound in her belly. She needed Kevin. She needed to make this memory, before she bid him goodbye for good. Taking the reins, she shoved at his chest, pushing him down on the bed. He went willingly with a big smile on his face.

She undid his belt and pulled it free of the loops. Next she took off his shoes and socks, tossing them aside before removing his slacks. He lay naked before her now, his thick erection a temptation all in itself. Cara cupped him, wrapping her hand around his silken shaft. She stroked him several times, eliciting curses from deep in his throat. "Babe?"

"I know what I'm doing, Kevin."

"Ah…uh, no doubt, but—"

Cara replaced her hand with her mouth, taking Kevin inside and silencing any complaints he may have had. He lay back quietly while she made love to him that way.

Tension built quickly from there. Their breathing heaved hard and they moved with a need that could only be satisfied one way. Scalding heat and sticky moisture fused their bodies. Cara wanted this. She'd dreamed of this. And she wouldn't be denied.

She rose atop Kevin, straddling his legs, and peered deep into his eyes. He seemed to understand her need. He reached for her hips and she lowered down on him, taking him inside her. Sensations ripped through her system, pleasure and desire, need and want, fulfillment and appreciation. Cara cried out. Kevin groaned as if in pain. She looked into his eyes, joined with him now, complete. Vivid memories of earth-shattering sex and dire love crossed between them.

"Oh, yes, Cara."

"I know, babe."

She moved down farther and he let go a grunt of satisfaction. She rose up and then took him in even deeper. Her skin prickled. Her body tightened around him. Her nipples budded to round peaks.

They peered at each other amid candlelight and rose petals. But none of that mattered anymore. Their sheer joining was enough to warrant erotic images and romantic atmosphere. It was all that either of them needed.

With Kevin's guidance, Cara moved on him, riding him up and down, each time taking him deeper, fuller, faster until Cara's body grew tight with climactic tension. Hot currents shocked her nerve endings and she rose up.

"Let go, baby," Kevin whispered, his voice strained.

She slammed down on him, as small rockets of sensation whipped through her. She moved back and forth, her body tight, her nerves sensitized. Her release exploded hard and fast and shook her to her core.

She reveled in the sensation a moment, before Kevin reached for her, bringing her down onto his hot body. "That was amazing," he said, between kisses.

"Now it's your turn," Cara said, kissing him fiercely.

"Oh, yeah."

Kevin rolled her onto her back and placed little kisses along her face, jaw, chin and throat. He cupped her breast and paid a good deal of attention to the erect bud with his tongue.

His thick erection still unfulfilled, Cara squirmed under him. "Hurry, baby. I need you inside me again."

"Just making sure you're ready."

"I'm always ready."

Kevin kissed her one last time, before spreading her legs and entering her, driving deep in one thrust. "I love that about you."

Cara felt as if she'd come home. Being with Kevin, making love, sharing intimacies, all seemed so right. There were so many things Kevin said he loved about her…yet he didn't love her at all. Sadness filled her heart again, knowing that this was all a vengeful little game. Only tonight, she'd made up the rules.

Soon, it would all be over.

Cara pushed those thoughts away and focused on the pleasure Kevin brought her. She vowed to make him remember this night and nothing would stop her.

Kevin sustained slow, fulfilling thrusts long enough to arouse Cara to the peak of orgasm again. He moved on her as if committing her to memory, every powerful drive of his body deliberate and controlled. "Cara, I've missed you."

Cara blocked that from her mind. She refused to believe him and passed it off as ramblings from a sexually aroused lover. Instead she focused on the wonderful little explosions occurring in her body.

When Kevin arched, his face given to release, Cara rose up, those tiny explosions waiting, building. Kevin called out her name, driving one last force into her body and Cara let go. The orgasm rocked them both, each lifting, releasing, the complete, agonizing pleasure of their bodies aligning and bursting as one.

Kevin came down on Cara gently, taking her in his arms. He kissed her passionately, murmuring, "I knew it would be like this."

Cara smiled sadly. The truth was the truth. "Me, too."

Cara woke up to an empty bed. The room bathed in candlelight, she squinted and focused her eyes as she sat straight up in bed. Kevin stood across the room, his slacks on, his feet bare, pouring two flutes of champagne. "Nice nap?" he asked, turning to her.

"Mmm." They'd exhausted each other, making love again, christening several corners of the room both in standing and sitting positions. After, they'd both fallen into a deep, if short, slumber.

"It's time for champagne, babe."

Cara looked at the digital clock on the nightstand, then rose and pulled on her robe. She tightened the belt with a tug and approached him. "To toast our divorce?"

Kevin visibly winced.

Cara gathered her fury. "Or maybe you'd like to extract another ten or twenty minutes out of my soul?"

"Cara, what's wrong?" He attempted to hand the flute to her, but she wouldn't take it. She refused to take anything from Kevin, ever again.

Cara walked over to the nightstand and opened the drawer. "I think I've met all the terms of your blackmail, Kevin." She pulled out the divorce papers. "Now it's time for you to sign on the dotted line."

A tic worked in Kevin's jaw. He eyed her carefully and set down the champagne flutes.

"It's almost midnight. My two weeks are over." Cara rolled her eyes dramatically. "Thank God."

Kevin's face flushed with color. He strode over to her and grabbed both of her arms. "What's gotten into you?"

"Besides you?"

Kevin flinched as though he'd been slapped.

"I want my divorce, Kevin. I've earned it." Cara's voice wobbled as she mustered her courage. She refused to cry, to let Kevin see his victory.

He'd wanted to hurt her and he had. She'd taken the bait, hook, line and sinker. She'd fallen in love with him, but she wouldn't give him the satisfaction of knowing that he'd won his little game.

"I don't believe you."

Oh, how she hated him.

"Why? Why don't you believe me? Because I played along and let you manipulate me the entire time I was here? Did you think I'd fall head over heels in love with you again?"

Cara walked away from him, picked up a glass of champagne and downed it in one giant gulp. She turned her back on him. "Sign them and leave, Kevin."

"You're angry, Cara. Damn it, so was I. When you left me. I couldn't believe you walked out on our marriage. Was it so easy for you? You just picked up and started a new life in Dallas."

She whirled around. "That's not what this is about, Kevin. Not at all. I thought you'd changed, but you've proven that you haven't. You're still out for blood, to win at all costs, no matter who gets hurt. You had to have your revenge, didn't you? You had to break me. You had to—"

"Who told you that?" Kevin approached her, his gaze piercing. "Where did you hear that?"

"Don't deny it. I know it's true."

Kevin sucked oxygen in and shook his head. "Damn it, Cara. Damn it all."

Cara downed the second glass of champagne, then turned her back on him once and for all. Her heart ached just looking at him, thinking of the passion they'd just shared. Not once had he apologized. Not once had he offered any sign of hope. Not once had he confessed to wanting reconciliation. The ache went deep, slicing through her gut. Her body shook painfully and tears welled in her eyes. "Sign the papers, Kevin. Then get out."

"Fine," he said. She didn't dare look at him. She didn't dare turn around. She waited, with her back to him, listening as he picked up his clothes and slammed the door shut behind him.

Then Cara fell apart. Tears streamed down her face and she sobbed in painful shudders. She felt as if she'd been broken in half. Her head ached and her heart plummeted to deep depths of despair.

Her marriage was over. She made her way to the bed and lowered down, shaking and seeking the bed frame for support. Braving a glance at the nightstand to see the signed evidence of her broken vows, she blinked. "What?"

Catching her breath, she got up and gave the nightstand a better look. With a quick tug, she opened the drawer and myriad thoughts flooded her head.

The divorce papers were gone.

Kevin slammed his penthouse door and tossed his jacket aside. Ten bouquets set about the room scented the air with sweetness. Candles stood at the ready in every corner of the penthouse, waiting to be lit. Decadent finger desserts arranged on the dining-room table added to the ambience, as champagne chilled in the wine closet. The seduction scene he'd planned mocked him with sickening clarity.

Cara had beaten him in his own game. She'd been cunning and clever and sexier than any woman he'd ever known. She'd fooled him and he hadn't seen it coming.

Yet he'd accomplished his goals and hated himself for it. Everything they'd built upon during the past two weeks had been wiped out in just a few minutes tonight. Kevin had thought he knew what he wanted. Apparently, he'd been wrong. Unmindful of the time, he picked up his cell phone and dialed Darius, waking him.

"Hey, man, do you know what time it is?"

"Yeah, sorry. Listen, I need to know if you spoke with Cara today."

"No, I didn't speak with Cara. Aren't your two weeks up yet?"

"As of about an hour ago, yeah. My time's up. Gotta run."

Next, he dialed Lance's number. "Did you see Cara today?"

Lance hesitated before answering. "Yeah, Cara came to see me today. She knew something was up with you and she asked me for honesty."

"What did you tell her?"

"I didn't have to tell her too much. She's an intelligent woman. She figured out what you were doing. You should have seen the look on her face."

"Mad as hell, I assume?"

"No, that would have been easier to take. More like complete devastation. She looked defeated and hurt. She's in love with you."

Kevin squeezed his eyes shut. He'd seen the devastation on her face tonight, heard it in her quivering voice. He'd wanted to go to her and tell her truths he'd only just realized, but she'd been too angry and too hurt. She wouldn't have listened to him. She wouldn't have believed him. He'd needed to regroup and figure some things out. "I blew it with her. And don't tell me, 'I told you so.'"

Lance sighed into the receiver. "Did you sign the divorce papers?"

"No. It's the first time I've ever reneged on a deal. But I couldn't sign them. I took them with me."

"Do you love her, Kev?"

"Yeah, I just realized it tonight. I've never stopped loving her. But telling her wouldn't have meant anything to her. Not after the hell I put her through."

"Now what?"

"Now I'm going to have to blackmail her one more time, to get her to listen to me."

"Oh, man. Good luck."

The divorce papers are signed. You just have to come pick them up.

Cara fumed as she drove her rental car to the address Kevin had given her. He'd called this morning, offering a limo service to take her to the destination. But Cara had refused. She didn't want anything to do with Kevin Novak, his limo or his life. From now on, she could only count on herself.

"Why is everything with you so difficult, Kevin?" she muttered as she drove into Somerset. "Couldn't you have just signed the papers last night? No, you have to do everything on your own terms. You always have to be in control."

Cara cursed as she sped along, looking at the address Kevin had given her. She had just enough time to pick up her divorce papers and get to the airport. Her flight left in two hours.

She pulled into a newly built mini-mall in an upscale location of Somerset and double-checked the address. She was in the right place. She parked the car and took a deep breath, then got out and strode into a building still under construction.

She found herself standing in the center of a large, empty shell of a space, sawdust on the floor and windows yet to be installed. Kevin came out of the shadows to face her. For what it was worth, he looked as awful as she felt, his eyes red, his face troubled. Wearing the same clothes he'd worn last night, he appeared rumpled.

"Hello, Cara."

Cara drew a steadying breath. "Did you bring the papers?"

He nodded and gestured toward a workbench in the corner of the room. She glanced over and recognized the pages sitting atop the wooden slats.

"They're signed."

"Thank you," she said stiffly, then headed over to retrieve them.

"Wait," Kevin said abruptly and she stopped.

He approached her, his gaze never leaving her face. Cara backed up a few steps. "There's nothing more to say, Kevin."

He pierced her with a sincere look. "How about, I love you. I've never stopped loving you, Cara. But I didn't realize it until last night. I've been a fool and I apologize a hundred times over for how much I've hurt you."

Cara shook her head, unwilling to forgive and forget so easily. "How can I believe you? How can I possibly trust you? You deliberately set out to hurt me. And you succeeded."

Kevin took a few steps closer, his gaze intense. "I'm not going to justify my actions. They were wrong, both then and now. I'd been fooling myself all these years. I let my pride and ego get in the way. We should have talked this out, years ago."

"I'll admit, I probably shouldn't have run away like I did. I was distraught. I didn't know how to get through to you," Cara confessed, finally owning up to her part in their breakup. "And when you didn't come after me, I thought you didn't care anymore."

"Cara, I should have come after you. God knows, I loved you very much. Everything I did was for you. I had something to prove and now I know, I made mistakes along the way. But you have to believe me when I say I'm crazy about you."

Cara let a smile slip out and Kevin smiled, too. "I love you, Cara. And I'll spend the rest of my life proving it to you."

"We're officially divorced now. Unless you lied to me and you didn't sign those papers over there."

"I signed them, to prove how much I love you. If you really want to leave me and Somerset, you can take them and go. But…if there's a chance for us, I want to offer it to you." He made a sweeping gesture with his arm. "This place can be your dance studio, Cara. You can open up Dancing Lights right here in Somerset. I'll build you a house and we'll fill it with children. I want all of that with you. And I'll prove to you every day and night how much you mean to me."

Cara's heart lurched. She could picture a new dance studio here. The place was perfect. More important, she could picture making a home with Kevin…a fresh start. And *children*. Oh, God, he was offering her the sun, the moon and the stars. She wanted to trust him, to believe him.

"I love you, Cara. Do you love me?"

Cara peered into his hopeful, gorgeous blue eyes. "Yes, of course I love you," she said softly. "I've never stopped loving you."

Kevin took her hand in his and squeezed it gently. "Give us a second chance, sweetheart."

Cara smiled. She found the truth in his eyes, the faith

she had in him restored. She walked over to the work-bench and peered down at the signed divorce papers.

"It's up to you, Cara."

Kevin had given her an out. He'd given up control and let the decision rest solely in her hands. He'd let her go if that was what she wanted. But he *loved* her. And she loved him right back.

She picked up the divorce papers. "I don't really have a choice." She ripped them in two, letting the pieces fall to the ground. "I love you too much."

Kevin strode over to her and wrapped her into his arms. His strength and love enveloped her and she knew she'd made the right decision.

They began to sway together.

"Hmm, I hear music," Cara said with a satisfied smile as sweet, joyous music played in her head.

"I hear it every time I hold you." Kevin tightened his arms around her as they rocked gently back and forth. "I can feel the love, sweetheart."

Reminded of their wedding night and the Elton John song that had become their signature, Cara kissed him softly on the lips. "Me, too."

"Promise me one thing, Cara."

"Anything."

"You'll dance for me every night."

"I promise."

And they continued to move to the rhythm of love that played solely in their hearts.

* * * * *

Meet The Sullivans...

Over 1 million books sold worldwide!

Stay tuned for more from The Sullivans in 201

Available from:

www.millsandboon.co.uk

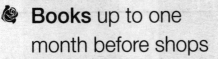

The World of Mills & Boon®

There's a Mills & Boon® series that's perfect for you. We publish ten series and, with new titles every month, you never have to wait long for your favourite to come along.

Blaze.
Scorching hot, sexy reads
4 new stories every month

By Request
Relive the romance with the best of the best
9 new stories every month

Cherish™
Romance to melt the heart every time
12 new stories every month

Desire™
Passionate and dramatic love stories
8 new stories every month

Visit us Online

Try something new with our Book Club offer
www.millsandboon.co.uk/freebookoffer

What will you treat yourself to next?

*Ignite your imagination,
step into the past…*
6 new stories every month

 NTRIGUE…

Breathtaking romantic suspense
Up to 8 new stories every month

Medical Romance

*Captivating medical drama –
with heart*
6 new stories every month

MODERN™

*International affairs,
seduction & passion guaranteed*
9 new stories every month

nocturne™

*Deliciously wicked
paranormal romance*
Up to 4 new stories every month

 MODERN
tempted™

*Fresh, contemporary
romances to tempt all
lovers of great stories*
4 new stories every month